With a degree in English and American Literature, Julie Haworth worked as an English teacher for a number of years, specializing in working with learners with literacy difficulties, before launching her own freelance copywriting business. She has recently become a member of the Romantic Novelists' Association, and *Always By Your Side* is her debut novel, which she wrote while recovering from Covid in 2020.

# Always By Your Side

## JULIE HAWORTH

SIMON &
SCHUSTER

London · New York · Sydney · Toronto · New Delhi

First published in Great Britain by Simon & Schuster UK Ltd, 2022

3 5 7 9 10 8 6 4 2

Simon & Schuster UK Ltd
1st Floor
222 Gray's Inn Road
London WC1X 8HB

Simon & Schuster Australia, Sydney
Simon & Schuster India, New Delhi

www.simonandschuster.co.uk
www.simonandschuster.com.au
www.simonandschuster.co.in

A CIP catalogue record for this book
is available from the British Library

Paperback ISBN: 978-1-3985-1783-7
Audio ISBN: 978-1-3985-2430-9
eBook ISBN: 978-1-3985-1543-7

Typeset in the UK by M Rules
Printed and Bound in the UK using 100% Renewable
Electricity at CPI Group (UK) Ltd

To Great Aunt Jean
19/06/1927 – 01/01/2022
This one's for you. xx

# Chapter 1

Rose hesitated before knocking loudly on the new head-teacher's door.

A booming voice answered. 'Come in!'

Rose took a deep breath and tried to quash her nerves. She knew she wasn't one of Mr Dawson's favourite teachers in the school, but she'd just taught an excellent lesson on fractions and she was sure her lesson observation feedback would be fine. True, Dawson had been looking at her a little sternly during his observation, but that didn't mean anything sinister, did it?

'Oh, Miss Hargreaves. Do come in and take a seat,' he said. Rose looked around the room and managed to perch herself on the edge of a chair covered in piles of notebooks. Dawson's office really wasn't the tidiest place in the school.

'Thank you for allowing me to sit in and observe your lesson this morning as part of your performance management review. How do *you* feel the lesson went?' As Dawson spoke, Rose saw the glimmer of a smirk appearing on his top lip. It was just visible under the grey hair of his moustache, which Rose also noticed still contained the traces of the digestive biscuit he had clearly been enjoying before she'd entered the room. She shuddered internally.

'Oh … erm … I think it went well. The children were engaged with their learning and they all met their objectives by the end of the session.'

Dawson broke out into a beaming grin and Rose felt herself relax a little. She'd done it. She'd made it through the dreaded lesson observation, despite the warnings from her colleagues that the new headteacher was out to get her.

Dawson's grin deepened, but there was something about his smile that didn't look quite right to Rose …

'Unfortunately, Miss Hargreaves, I couldn't disagree with you more. I'm afraid to tell you that I've graded your lesson "unsatisfactory". I'll be placing you on capability procedures with immediate effect and informing the governors of my decision at our meeting this evening. I'm sure you're aware that your temporary contract here at Trinity Grove Primary School is up for renewal? Unfortunately, your poor performance today has left me no choice but to recommend that your contract isn't renewed. If I were you, I'd start looking for teaching positions elsewhere.'

Her jaw dropped and she found her hands trembling. She wanted to argue back, to tell Dawson that this couldn't possibly be right. There was no way her lesson had been 'unsatisfactory'. Since she'd qualified as a teacher three years ago, Rose had always received outstanding feedback on her lessons from all her tutors and the previous headteachers she'd worked for. Mrs Barton, the school's former headteacher, had even asked Rose to act as a mentor for the trainee teacher the school currently had on placement.

But when Rose tried to tell Dawson all of this, she faltered and couldn't find her voice. Her mouth was dry, and a lump had formed in her throat.

'Well, if that's all, then, Miss Hargreaves, I've got another appointment waiting. Be sure to close the door on your way out.'

Rose found herself silently leaving Dawson's office and walking as fast as she could towards the staff toilets. She could feel tears burning the back of her eyes and she didn't want any of the parents, who were already lining up at the school office to collect their children, to see her cry.

Maya, Trinity Grove's Year 6 teacher, and Rose's best friend at the school, called after her from the staffroom.

'Hey, Rose, how'd it go? Rose? Rose, where are you off to?' Maya shouted.

Rose didn't slow down at the sound of Maya's voice. If anything, her walk was now turning into a slow run. She made it to the staff toilets, went into the ladies, found a cubicle and bolted the door firmly. As she flipped the toilet lid down to act as a seat, the tears flowed and she could taste salt at the back of her throat. *Unsatisfactory?* Her contract with the school to be terminated? *How? How could this be happening?* All she'd ever wanted was to be a teacher. And she was good at it. Really good.

Within seconds, Rose heard Maya banging on the cubicle door.

'Rose? Are you in there? How'd it go with Dawson? I'm dying to know.'

Rose didn't answer.

'Rose? Come on, I know it's you! I saw you as you ran in. Don't tell me it went badly? It couldn't have. Even Dawson's bright enough to realize you're one of the best teachers we have. Come on, talk to me.'

Rose got up slowly, wiped her tears away with the back of her hands and gingerly opened the door a crack.

'What on earth's happened? Are you crying?' Maya enveloped her friend in a big hug, and Rose felt more warm tears flowing.

'It's Dawson,' she said, 'he's graded my lesson as unsatisfactory.'

'What? I've seen you teach enough times to know that, even on your worst day, you'd never teach an unsatisfactory lesson. The man's clearly insane. Mind you, last time he taught a class, dinosaurs were probably roaming the earth, so I don't imagine he has much of a clue as to what makes a good lesson. Don't let his ignorance get you down, hun.'

'It's worse than that though. You know how I was only brought in on a temporary contract for a year?'

'Yeah . . .' said Maya, her voice faltering slightly.

'It's up for renewal at the end of term and Dawson's not going to keep me on. He's recommending to the governors that my contract's terminated at the end of term, so I'll be gone after Easter.'

'What? He can't do that!' Maya yelled, the outrage clear on

her face. 'The other teachers won't stand for it. The parents will be horrified. The kids in that class have come on in leaps and bounds since you arrived. And you know I'm not saying that just because I'm your best friend.'

To see the indignation Maya was showing on her behalf brought a weak smile to Rose's face. Her friend was right. Rose was a great teacher, and she wouldn't let Dawson or his twisted agenda make her doubt that.

'You do realize, don't you,' Maya continued, 'the only reason he's singling *you* out is because you've spoken up against the dreadful changes he's brought in. All he cares about is league tables and results. He treats this place like an exam factory where all we do is teach to the test. He's not bothered about the individual needs of the kids at all. You know we all think it, Rose, but you're the only one who has dared to stand up to him.'

'I know,' Rose whispered, 'but that doesn't make it any easier. I've still lost my job. Maybe I should have just kept quiet . . .'

'Ah, but then you wouldn't be the Rose that we all know and love, now, would you? Anyway, we can fight this. Get the union involved. I'm sure what he's trying to do would breach employment guidelines?'

'I doubt it,' Rose sighed. 'I'm on a temporary contract so I'm pretty sure he can do what he likes. Anyway, I don't want to fight it. As if I'd want to stay here working for that awful man any longer. And maybe I just don't have what it takes to be a teacher anyway . . .'

'What do you mean? You're the most passionate teacher I know! You really care about the kids and making a difference and, let's face it, teaching in London can be pretty tough. Don't give it all up just because of Dawson.'

'It's not just him though, is it? Our funding's always being cut, the focus is always on getting the kids through some stupid test. It's our job to help them become well-rounded adults and not just worry about performance management targets. When I decided to be a teacher, I wanted to make a difference – a *real* difference – and I'm not sure that's part of this school's priorities any more.'

'Listen, don't make any rash decisions while you're feeling so upset.' Maya wiped Rose's tears away with a paper towel she'd grabbed from the dispenser on the wall. 'Just head home, relax and chat things over with Ollie tonight.'

'Oh God. Ollie!' Rose groaned.

'What? Is he going to be annoyed about you getting the push?'

'Annoyed? Are you joking? He'll be over the moon. I don't think he sees being a teacher as a "proper" job. I swear he thinks all we do is play rounders and do arts and crafts all day. According to him, we're practically part-timers 'cos we finish at three and it's always the school holidays.' Maya rolled her eyes.

'As if being an investment banker counts as a "proper" job! They spend most of their time wining and dining clients and going on jollies. Can you remember the last time we spent the afternoon drinking Prosecco on expenses?' Rose shook her head and stifled a giggle. 'My point exactly. Right, let's get you ready to face the world again, Miss Hargreaves.'

As Maya wiped the remainder of Rose's tears away, the door to the staff toilets banged open and Sandra, the school secretary, came rushing in.

'Rose, I've just heard the news. I can't believe it. I'm absolutely fuming with that dreadful man.'

'Argh, I can't believe it's out already. I've only been in the bathroom for five minutes,' said Rose, resting her head in her hands.

'Oh, don't worry, it's only me who knows. Dawson just had me add to the agenda for the governors' meeting. I can't believe he's not renewing your contract. I nearly choked on my coffee when I read what he'd written. You've been an absolute godsend the year you've been with us. You're going to be a huge loss to the school and the man's a fool if he can't see that.'

'Thanks, Sandra, that means a lot.'

As Rose walked the short distance from the Tube station to the flat she shared with Ollie, she could feel the butterflies rising. Ollie and Rose had been together for almost five years now and had been engaged for six months. They had met while in their final year of university at Durham and had become firm friends quickly. There was a definite spark of attraction, but as they were both seeing other people, nothing had happened between them until they found themselves living in London and newly single at the same time. Things had been great between them in those first couple of years together. Rose had been finishing off her teacher training and Ollie had bagged himself a high-flying job in the City with an investment banking firm. It was exciting times for them both; they were dazzled by the bright lights of London and looking forward to their future together.

In the last year, though, Rose had to admit to herself that things had been slightly different between them. For one thing, they didn't see as much of each other as they used to. Ollie was often out in the evenings wining and dining clients and Rose was usually too shattered from a full day's teaching to join him at functions. When the weekends finally arrived, Rose was to be found marking and lesson planning to get herself prepared for the forthcoming week at school. This had been the source of quite a few arguments recently, as Ollie was becoming increasingly resentful of the time Rose devoted to her teaching workload. Their argument from the previous Sunday afternoon stuck particularly in Rose's mind. Ollie had wanted her to join him and his friends for a pub lunch and to watch the rugby, but Rose had had to bow out early as she had so much work.

'Oh, come on, Rose, it's not even like they pay you enough in that job to be putting all these hours in. They just don't value your hard work. I hardly ever get to see you these days.'

'Well, it's not really about you though, is it? At least I'm doing something *meaningful* and actually helping others rather than spending my days schmoozing clients at some City bar.'

'Look,' Ollie softened, 'all I'm saying is that you work too hard. You need to relax and have some fun. Just stay for the rugby and you can get your work finished off tonight.'

'I'm sorry, Ollie, I just can't. I've got too much to do to have everything finished in a couple of hours tonight. I need to be prepared for Monday. I've got an assembly to prep, a week's worth of literacy planning and it's World Book Day this week.'

'Fine,' Ollie hissed back between gritted teeth, his eyes narrowed. 'Do what you like. But don't say I don't try and make an effort, Rose.' He downed the rest of his pint and headed back to the table where his group of friends were sitting in prime position waiting for the rugby to start.

As Rose turned her key in the front door, she could hear the TV on, so she knew Ollie was home.

'Hey, babe,' he shouted, 'I'm in the bedroom. I've just got to grab a change of clothes for this client dinner tonight.'

Rose headed straight up the stairs and sat on the bed.

'How was your day?' he said, planting a kiss on her cheek.

'Eventful,' she answered quietly. 'I've got some news actually.'

'Oh?'

'Well, I'm not going to be staying on at Trinity Grove when my contract finishes at the end of term,' Rose replied.

Ollie broke into a huge grin and crossed the room to give her an unexpected hug.

'Wow, that's brilliant news, darling. You certainly kept

that quiet, didn't you? I know I've been saying for ages that you deserve to be paid more for what you do but I wasn't sure you were really listening. I'm so pleased you've finally come to your senses! This calls for a celebration. Let me grab some champers from the fridge.'

Rose's heart sank. She had known he was going to react like this. She didn't know what to say next. Should she confess that she wasn't leaving through choice and that Dawson had branded her as an 'unsatisfactory' teacher and was ousting her against her will? Before Rose had a chance to formulate her response, Ollie had reappeared in the doorway with two glasses of champagne in hand.

'To new possibilities,' he said, after handing a glass to Rose. He clinked his flute against hers and took a sip. Rose managed to let her own glass slip straight through her fingers and it smashed on the wooden bedroom floor. 'Honestly, darling, you really can be a klutz at times, but it's just one of the many things I love about you,' he said, bending down to pick up the largest shards of glass.

'I know, I know. Look, leave that for now,' she said, nodding towards the broken glass on the floor. 'Listen, I'm not sure that I'm leaving teaching *forever*. I just need a bit of time to think about what I want to do next and where my priorities lie. I'm just not sure that Trinity Grove was the right fit for me.'

'Of course it wasn't the right fit for you, darling. I mean, we were never going to be able to afford the deposit on a house in Surrey with what they were paying you.' Before

Rose could protest, he continued. 'Listen, I'll have a word with Marcus tonight. We've always got openings at the firm and they might be looking for some more recruits in the project management department. That would be a *perfect* fit for you.'

Before Rose could argue, Ollie's phone rang and he was deep in conversation about some mundane work matter. Before she knew it he was putting his shoes on and waving at her as he left to go out for the evening. Rose exhaled deeply and slumped back on the bed. Why hadn't she spoken up for herself and told Ollie the real reason she was leaving Trinity Grove? That was the second time today she'd found her voice had deserted her when she needed it the most. Why hadn't she protested when he suggested talking to Marcus at the firm? There was no way she was giving up teaching to work at an investment banking firm. Even though her teaching career seemed to be lying in tatters around her and she had no idea what the future held for her, Rose did know one thing: it certainly wasn't an investment banking firm in the City. That wasn't what she wanted at all.

Rose's final two weeks at Trinity Grove passed rapidly. Thankfully, the end of term was always busy with activities and her class had been making Easter cards and decorating eggs alongside their usual lessons. She'd been in too much of a rush most days to exchange more than a passing nod at Dawson, which had made things more bearable. Dawson himself had made an announcement in the school newsletter to let the parents and pupils know about Miss Hargreaves' departure. Dawson being Dawson, though, he had cleverly spun things to make it look as if Rose was leaving of her own accord by saying she was departing to 'further her career' and thanking her for the huge difference she had made during her time at the school.

Dawson had a far tougher job on his hands when the rest of the teaching staff heard about what had happened. They all knew the real story behind Rose's departure and were suitably outraged. Most of them pleaded with Rose to get the union involved and fight the decision, but they understood when she explained the reason she had decided not to.

At Rose's leaving drinks on the final day of the spring term, most of the teaching staff joined her at the pub across the road from the school, The White Horse. Dawson was not invited. It was a bittersweet moment for Rose, as not only did she not want to be leaving, but she had absolutely no idea what she was going to do next.

'Why don't you sign up for some supply agencies?' Maya suggested helpfully. 'They'll absolutely bite your hand off, I'm sure. You know good supply teachers are worth their weight in gold.'

'I guess so. I have been thinking about it, but I'm just not sure.'

'Why not? It would be a great way to try out some local schools and see which ones you like and which ones have a head like Dawson that you'll want to avoid like the plague.'

Rose chuckled.

'Maybe you're right. I suppose I've got nothing to lose. I'll think about it and give some agencies a call during the holidays to test the waters.'

'That sounds sensible. I guarantee by the end of next term you'll have your perfect teaching job lined up ready for September.'

'I really hope you're right,' Rose said as she took a rather large swig from her glass of Merlot. Still, she couldn't quite shake the feeling that, if her perfect teaching job really was just around the corner, that would just be yet another hurdle for her to overcome with Ollie.

# Chapter 2

Rose woke early the next morning. Her throat felt dry and parched and she was aware of a terrible thumping growing in her head. She stretched an arm out from under the duvet, feeling around for the glass of water that she usually kept on the bedside table. Locating it, she lifted the corner of her eye mask, sat up and took a large gulp. *Exactly how much had she had to drink last night?* The events of the previous evening still felt a little fuzzy, but Rose had been touched by just how many of her colleagues had come out to see her off and told her how sad they'd be to see her go. The Trinity Grove chapter of her life may have come to an end, but who knew what would be next for her?

Feeling suddenly buoyed by the possibilities that the future might offer, Rose grabbed her mobile phone from the bed-side table and crept out of the bedroom, being careful not to wake Ollie, who was still snoring deeply under the duvet. She made her way to the kitchen, opened the blinds and the room filled with glorious sunlight. The kitchen of the flat she shared with Ollie was modern and stylish, the décor perfectly co-ordinated and minimalistic, and yet, somehow, she had never felt quite at home there. Rose knew she was fortunate to live in such an exclusive development – it was something she could never have dreamt of on her teaching salary alone – but she always felt as though she didn't quite 'fit'. The only piece of furniture she'd brought with her on moving day was an antique oak chair that had belonged to her parents, but Ollie had been quick to cover it with an expensive angora throw as soon as the removal men had left. Rose made a point of removing it every time she sat down.

The first day of the Easter holidays looked as though it was going to be a beautiful spring day. Rose grabbed her favourite mug from the kitchen cupboard; it was pale pink and had the slogan 'World's Best Teacher' embossed across it in gold lettering. She made her morning coffee and switched on her mobile phone. It beeped furiously to let her know she had missed calls and messages.

*Honestly,* she thought, *my phone's only been off for a few hours. What on earth could be so desperate?*

Rose had nine missed calls. Most of them appeared to be from her dad, whilst the rest were from a number she didn't recognize. Rose felt a sense of panic rising in her chest. Her dad was currently on a world cruise and wasn't due back for weeks. He was supposed to be in the middle of the Caribbean Sea. He'd only be calling if it was a real emergency. Rose dialled her voicemail to hear the first message.

'Rose, it's Dad. Listen, don't panic, sweetheart, but I've just had a call from the hospital in Sussex. It's Great Aunt Jean. She's had a fall and it sounds like a bad one. They've taken her in with a fractured hip. I don't have all the details but she's been there a couple of days. They couldn't get hold of me, so I've given them your number. We're the only family she's got, and I know you're busy with school, but I was hoping you might be able to head down to Sussex and find out what's happening? I'm looking at flights to get home and our ship's in port tomorrow, sweetheart, so I'll call you again then as I should have a phone signal. Love you.'

Rose skipped ahead to the next message. An unfamiliar voice with a curt, hurried tone rang in her ear.

'This is a message for Rose Hargreaves. I believe you are the next of kin for Jean Hargreaves. Jean's had a nasty fall and we've admitted her to Nightingale Ward here at Conquest Hospital. Please call us on the following number and ask for extension 284 so we can update you on her condition.'

Rose's brain whirred as she noted down the hospital's phone number. *Great Aunt Jean. A fall? In hospital? All alone?* Rose had always been close to her Aunt Jean, and their bond had become even stronger after her mum had passed away. Rose had spent most of her school holidays with her in East Sussex. Rose berated herself for not checking her messages when she'd got in from the pub last night. Think of all those valuable hours she'd lost. *What to do first? Pack a bag? Call the hospital? Get in the car? Get on a train?*

*Rose Hargreaves, you stop panicking this instant*, she said sternly to herself. *Panicking will get you nowhere. Stop, take a deep breath and think.*

Rose's first instinct was to wake Ollie and let him know

what was going on. He had met Aunt Jean several times and she valued his advice in a crisis. She was sure he'd know what to do.

'Ollie? Ollie!' she said with gradually increasing volume. He continued to snore. 'OLLIE!'

'Rose, what on earth? I was fast asleep.'

'Listen, I need your help. There's been a family emergency. It's Great Aunt Jean. She's had a—'

'Great Aunt who?'

'Great Aunt Jean. Look, just listen, will you? I've picked up a voicemail from Dad. He's been trying to get hold of me all night. Aunt Jean's had a fall and she's in hospital. I don't know how bad things are, but Dad's asked me to head down to Sussex and make sure she's okay.'

Ollie sat bolt upright.

'What do you mean "head to Sussex"? You can't go to Sussex today!'

It took Rose a few seconds to process the callous nature of Ollie's words. *Not go to Sussex? He surely couldn't be serious? Could he?*

'I'm not sure you've grasped what I'm saying. Aunt Jean's hurt – badly enough to have ended up in *hospital*.'

'But, Rose, you *can't*,' Ollie howled. 'We've got tickets to watch England at Twickenham this afternoon. This is too last minute; you can't let me down. What will everyone think?'

'Let *you* down?' Rose hissed. 'Are you serious? There's an eighty-two-year-old woman lying in a hospital bed, with no family to count on apart from me. Watching a load of oversized men with inflated egos chase each other around a rugby pitch isn't something that I'm particularly concerned about right now.'

Turning her back on Ollie, Rose flung open her wardrobe, grabbed her overnight bag from the top shelf and threw in a random assortment of underwear and clothes. She needed to pack enough to get her through a few days at least. Anything she'd forgotten – well, she could sort that out once she'd got to Sussex. Ollie threw back the duvet, got up from the bed and grabbed her arm.

'Come on, darling. Your aunt's not going to expect you to drop everything to rush to her bedside, is she? It doesn't even sound as though it's anything life-threatening. It'll be a wasted journey.'

Rose shrugged his arm away.

'I really can't be any clearer about this, Ollie. I'm going to Sussex, and I'm going *now*. The matter isn't up for debate.' She turned to face him. 'Do you know what? I actually thought you'd be able to help me with this. I assumed you'd have my back and offer to come with me for moral support. Looks like I couldn't have been more wrong. Just let me finish packing and then I'm on the first train out of London.'

'Well, how long do you think you'll be gone for?'

'Seeing as I don't know what the situation is yet, I've no idea. At least a few days, but maybe longer if things are bad.'

At that revelation, Ollie flapped his arms in outrage.

'A few days?! But I've arranged that meeting for you with

Marcus in HR about the project management vacancy for first thing on Monday morning.'

'I never asked you to do that, Ollie. I'm not even remotely interested in a career as a project manager. Anyway, I'm sure that Marcus will understand, given the circumstances.'

'*Understand, given the circumstances*,' Ollie parroted back. 'Oh, well, that's all okay, then. Don't worry if it reflects badly on me.'

'I hardly think me dropping everything to dash off and help a relative reflects badly on you, does it? Ollie, you know how important Aunt Jean is to me. I spent practically every summer with her in Sussex after Mum died.' Ollie shifted his gaze uncomfortably. 'I know I don't always get back to visit as often as I like, but she needs me now.'

Ollie took her hand. 'Look, I'm sorry, Rose, I know Jean means a lot to you. If you need to go, I understand. Just hurry back, won't you?'

Rose zipped up her overnight bag, pulled on the pair of Converse trainers she kept by the front door and left the house, closing the front door behind her. As she walked down the steps leading from their apartment building, Rose tried to ignore her sense of unease about Ollie's reaction to Aunt Jean's fall and concentrate instead on getting to East Sussex as quickly as possible. She didn't want to waste time getting the Tube to St Pancras Station, so instead hailed the first black cab she saw.

Once she was on her way, a quick Google search on her

phone revealed that the trains to Rye ran regularly from London on a Saturday, but she'd have to change at Ashford International. If everything went smoothly, she might even be at the hospital by midday. Rose tried her dad's number but it went straight to voicemail. She reminded herself that there wasn't great network coverage in the middle of the Caribbean Sea and wifi on board was expensive – he wouldn't be able to connect until he docked. She'd have to try later.

Once Rose was on the train, she found herself a seat at an unoccupied table, threw her overnight bag into the overhead luggage compartment and began setting up her laptop. Her first job was to call the hospital and find out exactly how bad her aunt's injuries were. She reached the ward on her first attempt. The ward sister only confirmed what her dad had already told her and Rose explained that she was on her way from London and would be with her aunt soon.

A fractured hip wasn't ideal, but it could have been so much worse, Rose thought. At least it was nothing life-threatening. She inhaled deeply. This was positive news, wasn't it? Rose tried to call her dad but, once again, she was unable to get through. She decided to send him a text instead. At least that way if he did manage to pick up a phone signal, he'd have an update.

*I'm on a train now and should be arriving at the hospital in a couple of hours. Don't worry, I've got this xx*

As she was popping her phone back into her pink leather handbag, she heard it buzz and made a sudden grab for it, assuming it was her dad. Her heart sank a little as she realized it was a message from Maya.

*Hey lovely, was such a great leaving do last night. Let me know how you get on with the supply agencies next week. Onwards and upwards. Maya xx*

Rose smiled. Maya was always looking out for her and supporting her decisions. *Why couldn't Ollie be more like that?* Surely it wasn't too much to ask that her fiancé would be able to see things from her point of view and take her side, if only once in a while?

Things hadn't always been like this between them. She remembered how sweet Ollie had been when they'd first got together. On the night he'd officially asked her to move in with him, he'd arranged a beautiful candlelit supper on the rooftop terrace of his London office – a space usually reserved for entertaining clients. He'd set up an elaborate treasure hunt leading Rose to an envelope taped beneath her chair, which contained the estate agent's listing for the flat he'd just rented for them – their first proper *home* together. It had been the most romantic evening of her life and she still had the envelope safely stashed away in her memory box among her other most treasured possessions.

Rose shook her head. She had more pressing concerns to focus on right now. The first of them being getting to the hospital to find out how Aunt Jean was.

As soon as the train driver announced their arrival at Rye, Rose gathered her belongings and hurried towards the doors as the train pulled into the platform. She knew her way around the station well, having been down to visit Aunt Jean more times that she cared to count.

She'd always loved coming to Sussex, ever since she was a child, and she had so many happy memories of staying at Jasmine Cottage. When she was young, she had thought the place was an adventurer's paradise. As an adult it had always been a safe haven – somewhere to retreat to when she needed some peace and quiet or to recharge her batteries and escape from the stress of daily life. Since qualifying as a teacher, Rose had always made sure she visited Aunt Jean for a few weeks every August, and she always returned to London feeling refreshed and reinvigorated.

Some of the happiest times in her childhood were spent with her aunt in the village of Blossom Heath. She would always take her exploring, and they'd pack a picnic and go out for the day to see what new adventures they could find. She remembered one particular summer, her aunt had pitched a tent in the garden of Jasmine Cottage and they'd had hours of fun building a fire, toasting marshmallows, telling ghost stories and looking at the stars before they fell asleep. She couldn't help but smile when she thought about those days.

After a short taxi ride from the station, Rose soon found herself passing through a set of cream double doors with the words 'Nightingale Ward' clearly marked above them. She located the nurse's station and went over to introduce herself.

'Hello, I'm Rose Hargreaves,' she said to the blonde-haired

nurse sitting behind the desk. 'I rang ahead earlier? I'm here to see Jean Hargreaves.'

'Ah yes, it was me you spoke to. I'm Sister Clarke.'

'How is she? Can I see her?' Rose asked quickly.

'I'm afraid Jean's fracture was a complicated one, and she's had to have surgery to insert some pins to keep the injury stable. She's doing well physically, although it's going to be a long road to recovery for her. It's actually her mental state we're more concerned about. She's very down, and her confidence has taken a real knock. I believe she lives alone?'

'Yes, that's right.'

'Well, that may be an issue going forward,' said Sister Clarke. 'She may not be able to live independently after a fall like this. It could be a risk to her safety.'

'Oh, I see,' said Rose, her face falling. 'Yes, I can see how that might be difficult for her,' she agreed. 'She's fiercely independent though and I'm honestly not sure how she'd cope if she thought she couldn't go home again.'

'Well, let's not jump the gun just yet,' replied Sister Clarke. 'Best not mention anything to her and let's see if your visit can lift her spirits. Let me take you to see her.'

She led Rose into the ward and motioned to one of the rooms along the corridor. 'She's just up here, third bed from the left,' she said.

Rose spotted her aunt immediately, although she looked much paler, and somehow smaller and more fragile than she remembered. She had lost weight, too, and her face seemed drawn. If Rose was honest, she looked like a shadow of the cheerful, rosy-cheeked auntie that Rose remembered from her visit just last summer.

'Jean, you've got a visitor,' Sister Clarke said as she approached the bed. 'She's travelled all the way from London to see you. Isn't that something?'

Aunt Jean looked up and Rose saw a glimmer of interest in her eyes.

'Aunt Jean, it's me, Rose,' she said as she approached the bed. 'What kind of trouble have you been getting yourself into, eh?'

'Rose, is that really you? How did you even know I was in here? I told them not to bother anyone. You've not really come all the way from London, have you?'

'I'll leave you to it,' Sister Clarke said as she walked back towards the nurse's station.

'Of course it's me and of course it's no bother.' Rose pulled up a seat next to Aunt Jean's bed. 'I was worried about you. So is Dad. I came as soon as I heard.'

'Ah okay, love. I'm glad you're here, really I am. I don't mean to sound ungrateful. I just hate the thought of you leaving behind your busy life to check in on me. It's not as if I live down the road now, is it?' she said, wringing her hands.

'Well, it's the school holidays for one thing, so I've got plenty of time on my hands, and it'll be nice for me to have some time away from London. I've left it too long to visit and I want to help and make sure you're okay. You're my number-one priority right now, so you're stuck with me for a while.'

'It's lovely to see you, dear, really it is,' Aunt Jean said, clasping Rose's hand in her own.

'How are you feeling? Are they treating you well? Is there anything I can get you?'

'I'm not too bad. I just feel so foolish, taking a tumble like that. Causing all this fuss just because I wasn't watching where I was going. I'm a silly old fool, that's what I am.'

'Now listen, I'll have none of that,' Rose said in her best schoolteacher's voice, wiping a tear from her aunt's cheek. 'Accidents happen. That's just the way life goes. I'm just as likely as you to take a tumble. You know how clumsy I am!'

Aunt Jean chuckled.

'"Clumsy" – now that's one word for it. More like a walking disaster zone,' she laughed, throwing her head back. 'If I had a pound for every time your mum and dad had to take you to A&E as a child with some mishap or other. It's a wonder you didn't end up on social services' radar.'

'Alright, alright,' Rose giggled. 'It's good to see a smile on your face, even if it is at my expense. It really is good to see you, Auntie. I'm sorry it's been ages. I'm not sure how long I'll be here for but I wondered if I could stay at the cottage for a few nights?'

'Of course, dear, I didn't expect you to be going back to London tonight. A word of warning though, I'm not as house proud as I used to be. To tell you the truth the housework has been getting a bit too much for me these days. You might need to run the hoover around when you arrive.'

'As if that will bother me,' Rose rolled her eyes. 'You know how much I love Jasmine Cottage. It'll be like a holiday, and if I can help you out with some housework while I'm here, well, that's just a bonus.'

Aunt Jean fumbled around in her nightstand to find the keys to Jasmine Cottage and handed them to Rose. The keychain was a circular, silver piece of metal with a picture of a Border Collie on it.

'Hey, this looks just like Jack.' Jack was Jean's black and white Border Collie that Rose remembered from her childhood. He had been devoted to her aunt, and his death ten years ago had hit her hard. She'd said she could never get another dog, as she couldn't stand the pain of losing them.

'It does look like Jack, doesn't it? That's why I chose it. I spotted it one day in the village gift shop and it reminded me of him so much that I had to buy it. He was a dog in a million, that one. I miss him every day,' she said wistfully. Rose yawned and stretched her arms out in front of her. 'Right, young lady, you get yourself off to the cottage, settle in and I'll see you tomorrow. There's a fish and chip van in the village tonight so you can get yourself some supper and have a relaxing evening.'

'Sorry, I had a late one last night with some friends and I think it's catching up with me. Are you sure you don't want me to stay for a bit longer?'

'You've done more than enough for one day. Do as you're told for once, will you? Go and get settled and you can come back and see me tomorrow. The key for the car is on that fob too, so make sure you use it to get around in. There's no point in you taking taxis everywhere, is there?'

'Okay,' Rose agreed, realizing that it would be futile to argue. She gathered up her bags, planted a kiss firmly on her aunt's cheek and made her way to Jasmine Cottage.

# Chapter 3

Jasmine Cottage was just outside the village of Blossom Heath, down a winding road which was separated from the rolling Sussex hills by dense hedgerows on either side. As her taxi got nearer to the cottage, the road became narrower, until there was barely enough room for one car to pass. Jasmine Cottage was the last house at the very end of the lane, with no immediate neighbours. Rose got out of the car and looked around. How she loved this place.

After paying for the taxi, she picked up her luggage and headed for the cottage door, inhaling the smell of the roses as she turned the key to let herself in. The scent reminded her of how she'd begged her aunt to let her use the precious petals to make rose perfume as a child. She'd even set up a stall in the cottage's front garden to sell her bottled concoctions to the villagers for fifty pence a piece, and Aunt Jean had made sure all her friends from the WI stopped by. She smiled at the memory.

As she stepped into the cottage's hallway, however, her smile turned into a grimace as a very different kind of smell filled her nostrils: the overwhelming odour of mildew and mustiness. She wrinkled her nose in response. The cottage's curtains were closed and it was so dark she could barely see where she was going. She flung her bags down, opened as many curtains and windows as she could, and took a good look at her surroundings.

Her aunt always kept the house in beautiful condition. Vases of fresh flowers would adorn every room and pretty cushions and brightly coloured throws made the place look cheery and inviting. Things couldn't be more different now. There was clutter everywhere, stacks of plates and mugs around the living room and kitchen, and a huge pile of unopened post in the hallway.

Rose climbed the staircase to see if things were any better upstairs. She saw from the condition of the white porcelain bathroom suite and the build-up of mould and mildew that they weren't. She set herself up in Aunt Jean's spare bedroom, which was where she always slept when she visited, and was relieved to see that this room at least seemed relatively untouched. The bedding was crisp and clean and, apart from some piles of laundry that needed sorting and putting away, all she'd need to do in here would be to run a duster around and open up the window to let some fresh air in.

Rose sat on the bed and looked around the room. *How could things have changed so drastically for Aunt Jean in such a short time?* She felt dreadful that she'd had no indication of just how bad things had become. It wasn't only the state of the cottage that concerned her; she thought about how much her aunt herself had changed, how she had noticeably lost weight and seemed so much smaller and more fragile than Rose remembered.

She pulled her mobile out of her pocket – no new messages. She texted Ollie to let him know she'd arrived and then tried her dad's number again just in case he'd found some phone signal, but it went straight to voicemail. Rose needed a plan. Even if her aunt's hip healed, she obviously couldn't manage living alone, and that was going to have implications for her and for the future of Jasmine Cottage.

Faced with that daunting prospect, Rose tried to focus on what she could do to help in the short term. There was no denying it – Jasmine Cottage needed a facelift, and Rose decided to make it her mission to return it to its former glory. She headed back down to the kitchen, grabbed a notepad and pen, and began looking through the cupboards to see what cleaning products she could find. Perhaps unsurprisingly, given the state of the place, there were hardly any, and those that were there had long since dried up or discoloured. As well as some old tumble dryer sheets for a machine her aunt had got rid of years ago, she even found a bottle of cleaning fluid with faded packaging and a price sticker from Gateways, a shop in the village which hadn't been open for the past fifteen years or so. It was the same story with everything else in the cupboards. After deciding to simply throw everything in a bin bag, Rose resolved to buy replacements at the village shop when she went out in search of food. Once the cottage was equipped with the best that modern-day cleaning products had to offer, it would make light work of getting the place shipshape again. She just needed to channel her inner Mary Poppins, she told herself.

After a couple of hours spent tidying, Rose was alerted to the time by the growls her stomach was making. When she looked at her watch, she was shocked to see that it was already nearly 6pm. She took a quick look in the fridge to see what she'd need to stock up on and her heart sank as she realized that it was practically empty. There was a pack of unopened ham that had already turned a pasty shade of grey, half a tin of tomatoes that had a layer of fur on top, a block of cheese, and some yoghurts with an expiration date of over a month ago. Rose scooped everything up and threw it all into another bin bag. After taking both bags outside, she picked up her handbag and headed for the village shop.

Located on the outskirts of Rye, the village of Blossom Heath was everything you might expect a quintessentially English village in East Sussex to be. It had winding country lanes, thatched cottages, a village green (complete with duck pond) and a quaint little pub, as well as a village store and a handful of other businesses. The shops around the village green were at the heart of life in Blossom Heath, where the villagers came together to chat and catch up on all the local gossip. If there was one thing you could always rely on in Blossom Heath, it was that everyone knew everyone else's business, and secrets didn't stay secret for very long.

The village shop, Harrisons, as the name suggested,

was run by Maggie and Ted Harrison, a friendly couple in their late fifties who had grown up in the village. Ted and Maggie knew all the local goings-on, and if you managed to find some news that the couple didn't already know about, then it probably wasn't worth knowing. Rose remembered that a visit to Harrisons at the weekend used to be the highlight of her week when she was staying in the village as a child. Her aunt would always let her fill up a bag of penny sweets until it was overflowing, and Maggie would sneak some extra chocolate mice into the bag as she knew they were Rose's favourite. She could almost smell the sweet sickly scent of the confectionery jars if she thought about them hard enough. The bell on the shop door chimed as Rose entered.

'Rose? Is that you? What on earth are you doing here?' Maggie said. 'I thought you'd be up to your eyes with work in London. We weren't expecting to see you back in the village until the summer holidays.'

'Hi, Maggie, good to see you. I wasn't expecting to be back so soon either, but I suppose you've heard about Aunt Jean's fall?'

'Ah yes, of course. How's she doing? Is there any news?'

'She's not doing too badly, all things considered, but they reckon it'll be a while before she can go home. It's going to take time for her to heal, and then there's the question of how steady she's going to be on her feet.'

'You know Jean – she won't let something like a fractured hip slow her down. She's a fighter, that one.'

'I really hope you're right. I don't know how she'll cope if going home to the cottage isn't an option.'

'It won't come to that, I'm sure,' Maggie said. 'Think positive. That's half the battle sometimes. How long are you down for, love? Are you back to school after the Easter holidays?'

Rose hesitated before answering.

'Well, I'm taking a bit of a break from teaching, so I can stay for as long as I'm needed. I've just popped in to grab some cleaning supplies for the cottage,' she said quickly, eager to change the subject. 'I thought I may as well make myself useful and give the place a good spruce up whilst I'm here, get everything ready for Aunt Jean's return.'

'That's the spirit. You give me that list and I'll see what I can help you with.'

Rose and Maggie walked around the store together filling Rose's basket with everything she needed to give Jasmine Cottage a spring clean, and Rose also threw in some bread, cheese, milk and a couple of bottles of wine for good measure. While Maggie was ringing everything up on the till, Rose had an idea. 'While I think of it, Aunt Jean mentioned there's a fish and chip van in the village tonight. I'd kill for a hot meal that I don't have to cook myself.'

'Ah, Murphy's? They park just behind the village green at the back of the church. I go for a large cod and chips every Saturday night. You won't go far wrong with that,' Maggie said.

'Thanks, Mags, I'll head over there now and grab

something. Then it'll be a hot bath and an early night for me. It's been a long day,' she said, stifling a yawn.

'You take it easy tonight, my love, and give my best to your aunt. Tell her the whole village is thinking of her and we can't wait to have her back and causing havoc. Throw this box of chocolates in from me and Ted,' she said, placing the largest box of Milk Tray in the store into Rose's shopper.

'Thanks, Mags, I'll tell her. I'll back in a few days for more supplies, so I'll give you an update.'

When Rose arrived back at Jasmine Cottage, she put the fish and chips in the oven to keep warm, whilst she set to work cleaning the sitting room. The freshly cleaned room was now dust-free and smelt of furniture polish and beeswax. Rose had even cleaned the windows, which now glinted in the sunlight as the setting sun shone through the clear glass. She rearranged the cushions, grabbed the fish and chips from the oven and settled herself on the sofa with a bottle of wine. Maggie hadn't been wrong about ordering the cod and chips. They were delicious and just what Rose had needed. She scoured the TV channels for some light-hearted Saturday night entertainment and plumped for a game show she'd always wanted to watch but knew that Ollie loathed, hosted by someone she vaguely recognized from reality TV. Rose checked her phone and found a message from Ollie.

*I'm sorry about the way I reacted this morning, darling. I hope you made it to Rye safe and sound and your aunt is OK. Call me when you can, love you xx*

Her heart lifted a little, but she found herself clutching her phone tightly as she thought about his initial attitude towards her aunt's accident. At least he had acknowledged that he'd been in the wrong, she reassured herself. That was more like the Ollie she knew and loved. With that in mind, she typed out her reply:

*Thanks for saying sorry. Speak tomorrow, love you too xx*

Rose was woken the next morning by the sound of birdsong outside. She pulled the duvet over her head, groaned and rolled over. She wasn't ready to be awake yet. It was no use though – she had too much on her mind to allow herself to fall back into a peaceful slumber. Thoughts of Aunt Jean, of Ollie and of her dad were all whirring inside her head.

Rose sat up, pulled off her eye mask and reached for the glass of water at her bedside table. She took a long drink and got up to open the floral curtains. The view really was stunning. All she could see for miles beyond the lane were fields of rolling green hills, with sheep dotted among them in the distance, like tiny balls of cotton wool on the horizon. She'd forgotten how beautiful it was here. How peaceful. It was so different to being in London with all the sounds and smells of city life. Rose opened the window and took in a deep breath of country air. Memories of her childhood came flooding back. There was something about being in Blossom Heath that reminded her of how she had felt as a young girl, the sense of anything being possible ...

Downstairs, Rose put on some coffee and toast and

checked her messages. Still nothing. As soon as she put her phone down, it started to ring and Rose could see from the caller ID that it was her dad.

'Dad! Can you hear me?'

'Yes, loud and clear, sweetheart. We've docked in Antigua and I've finally got a signal. I did try you earlier but it must have been the middle of the night there.'

'I guess. I decided to give myself an early night to recover from the journey and I was out like a light by ten.'

'So, how's your aunt? Have you been in to see her?'

'Yep, the nurse said her fracture's a bad one but that the surgery went well. I think they're a bit concerned about her state of mind though, Dad. She's very down and they're worried about whether she's going to be able to come home when she recovers. The cottage stairs here are so steep and I'm not sure what we could do to make it any easier for her.' There was a long pause on the line and then Rose heard her dad let out a long, heavy sigh.

'That's something I've been worried about for a while if truth be told. I've not said anything as I didn't want to worry you, sweetheart, but it's been playing on my mind. Jean's not getting any younger and her mobility hasn't been great for the last couple of years. Let's not jump to any conclusions just yet though. We need to focus on getting her well again and see where we go from there.'

'Oh, I didn't realize how bad things were,' said Rose, her voice cracking a little. 'I feel terrible that I've not been down to visit since last summer.'

'It can't be helped, sweetheart. Don't feel bad. Your aunt knows what a busy life you lead. She wouldn't expect you to drop everything to come and check on her. Knowing Jean, she'd have guessed something was up if you did and she'd have sent you back to London with your tail between your legs,' he chuckled.

He was right of course. Rose wondered if now would be a good time to tell him that she didn't actually have a teaching job to return to. She hesitated and the moment was lost.

'I've been looking at flights back to London and there's one into Heathrow tomorrow morning that I've . . .'

'Don't you dare think about coming home! This is a *world* cruise and you've only just set off! You're not due back for weeks!'

'But, Rose—'

'No, Dad! It's the holiday of a lifetime, please don't ruin it over this. There's nothing you can do here. I've got everything under control. Just focus on enjoying yourself and *forget* about coming home. It's the school holidays, so I've got nothing else on,' she said, attempting to reassure him.

'I've got all the confidence in the world in you, sweetheart, but if you need me, just say the word and I'll hop on a plane and be back in Sussex in a flash.'

'Honestly, Dad, it's really not necessary. Just leave everything here in my capable hands and if I run into any problems, I'll let you know. But I *promise* you that isn't going to happen. Enjoy your holiday and catch up on some sun while you can.'

Feeling suitably reassured that her dad wasn't about to abandon his holiday and head home, Rose ended the call, finished off her breakfast of cold toast and coffee, jumped in the shower and rooted around in her travel bag to find a clean change of clothes. Settling on a pair of light blue jeans with a crisp, pale pink shirt, she threw on her Converse trainers, scooped her long dark hair back into a ponytail, grabbed her jacket and handbag and headed out to the car.

Aunt Jean's car was an old automatic Ford Focus. Her aunt had given up driving a manual a few years ago after an unfortunate incident that involved reversing into the wall of the village church while attempting to change gear. Aunt Jean had spent time in Italy, teaching English at the embassy school in Milan, and she had most definitely picked up some very Italian driving habits. She thought nothing of accelerating and overtaking at the most inopportune moments. As a child, Rose had thought this exciting and invigorating, but as she had got older it had seemed slightly more risky and definitely less thrilling. With that on her mind, she put her seatbelt on, started the ignition and set off for the hospital.

When she arrived on Nightingale Ward, Rose could see the nurses' station was vacant. She spotted Aunt Jean sitting up in bed, tucking into a cup of tea and a couple of digestive biscuits.

'Rose!' her aunt beamed when she saw her. 'I didn't expect you to be here so early, my dear. Come and sit down and tell me how you got on at the cottage. Did you find everything you needed?'

Rose planted a kiss on her aunt's cheek and pulled a chair up next to her bed.

'Of course! Thanks for the tip about the fish and chip van. I ate enough to feed an army but it was delicious, so totally worth the calories,' she said, patting her stomach. Her aunt chuckled. 'How are you feeling today?' Rose asked.

'Oh, not so bad. The nurses are lovely, but I can't wait to get up and about and start thinking about going home. It's no fun being stuck in this bed and having to press a button every time I need something. I feel like a real nuisance.'

'Don't be silly,' Rose said affectionately. 'That's what the nurses are here for. You're not a nuisance to anyone.'

'Now, what's all this I'm hearing about someone being a nuisance?' Sister Clarke asked, appearing from behind Rose.

'That would be my aunt insisting that you've all got better things to do than run around after her,' Rose answered, rolling her eyes in mock exasperation.

'That's hardly true now, is it? You're here so that we can help get you back on your feet, and I wouldn't call that being a nuisance, would you?'

Aunt Jean gave her a sheepish look. 'Well, no, I suppose not.'

'Good, so that's that settled,' Sister Clarke said firmly. 'Your appetite has perked up a bit today hasn't it, Jean?' She pointed at the tea and biscuits in Jean's hands. 'You've just missed the consultant, Rose, but he said everything is healing nicely. I want to prepare both of you though: it looks like you're going to be with us for a couple more weeks, Jean, before we can think about getting you home.'

'Weeks!' Rose and Aunt Jean both chorused at the same time, looking bewildered.

'Yes, I'm afraid so,' Sister Clarke continued. 'Your fracture was a serious one and we can't risk you taking another tumble. You need to stay with us until the doctor's happy, I'm afraid. I'll leave you two to catch up, but you know where I am if you've got any questions.'

'Weeks,' Aunt Jean repeated once Sister Clarke had left. 'I thought I'd be home again in a few days.'

It broke Rose's heart to see the disappointment evident on her aunt's face.

'Well, I know that wasn't what you wanted to hear, but this really is the best place to be while you're getting your strength back. It's not ideal, but why don't you look at it as having a mini holiday?' Rose suggested. 'You've got a buzzer with waiter service, your own TV, and I can bring you in some bits from home to make things more comfortable. Oh, that reminds me,' she said, bending down for her bag, 'these chocolates are from Maggie and Ted with their best wishes. They said to tell you that the village is missing you and they can't wait to have you back soon.' She handed the chocolates across to her aunt, who had a tear in her eye.

'That's very sweet of them. They didn't need to do that. You tell them thanks and that I can't wait to get back home, if these damn doctors ever agree to let me out.'

'Look, the time will pass quickly enough. I'll bring you some magazines and books to keep you entertained, and how about if I bring your knitting in too?'

Jean's face brightened.

'Oh, Rose, would you? I've got a project on the go and I've been itching to finish it off since I've been stuck in here. Everything I need is in my craft bag – down the side of the sofa in the lounge.'

'Consider it done,' Rose said, beaming. 'I'll pop in with it tomorrow and I'll bring anything else you might need. Nighties, underwear, toiletries . . . you name it.'

'I must have been very good in a former life to deserve a great niece like you,' said Aunt Jean with a teary look in her eye.

'Oh, don't be silly. It's an absolute pleasure. What else are great nieces for?'

# Chapter 4

Before returning to Blossom Heath, Rose decided to stop at the big supermarket on the outskirts of Rye. Now she knew she was going to be in Blossom Heath for the next few weeks at least, she may as well do a proper shop and stock up on everything she needed. While she was there, she picked up a couple of new nighties for her aunt, as well as toiletries, magazines and a few little foodie treats, including some salted caramel dark chocolate – Aunt Jean's favourite. She hoped it would help to lift her aunt's spirits while she was stuck on the ward. After all, what problem couldn't be solved by chocolate?

As Rose made her way back to the village, her thoughts turned to Ollie. He was going to be furious when he found out that she was planning to stay on. She felt her grip on the car's steering wheel tighten. *Well*, she thought, *I'm out of a job anyway, so it's not as if I have any other commitments to be worrying about right now.* Surely he would understand that? And if he didn't, well, that was just tough. This was where she was needed and this was where she was going to stay.

As Rose got closer to the village, the roads became

narrower and more rural. The country lanes twisted and turned sharply in ways that meant only the locals were daring enough to navigate them confidently. Rose took things slow and steady, feeling herself wincing slightly every time she rounded one of the tight, hairpin bends. As she increased her speed a little on a slightly wider, straighter stretch of the lane, something up ahead caught her eye. There was something in the road, just up ahead on the left-hand side. *What was it?* Rose pumped the brake gently to slow the car down. *Was it an animal of some kind?* Whatever it was, it was moving, so she put her hazards on, slowed right down and pulled up just in front of what now appeared to be a mass of black fur. As she got closer, Rose could see that it was a dog – a black and white Border Collie to be exact. Rose could tell that it was injured. *Had it been hit by a car?* she wondered. Spurred on by a wave of adrenaline, Rose put the car's handbrake on, unclipped her seat belt and very slowly made her way over to the injured dog. She crouched down, so as not to spook the poor creature, and held her hands out gently towards it.

'Hey, you. It's okay, I'm not going to hurt you. Have you got yourself into some trouble, little one? What's been going on?' She knelt down beside the dog and touched her on the top of her head. She let out a quiet whimper. Rose noticed that there was blood around one of the dog's front legs. Rose gingerly tried to get a better look, but as soon as she did the little dog whined and tried to scrabble away from her.

'Okay, okay, don't panic,' Rose said, resisting any further attempt to inspect her injuries. The last thing she wanted to do was cause the dog to panic and try to run away from her. Rose made herself comfortable next to the dog and began stroking her ears gently. She relaxed and let her head drop into Rose's lap.

Taking a minute to figure out the best course of action, Rose found the telephone number for the local vets on her phone but quickly realized she had no reception. She stood on her tiptoes and tried waving her mobile in the air, but there was still no signal. She decided the only thing to do was to get the dog into her car and head to the vet surgery in Blossom Heath as soon as she could.

'How do you feel about me picking you up, little one? Would that be okay?' She got up slowly and walked towards the car to open the back door. Fearing she was about to be left again, the dog tried to get up and follow her but yelped out in pain. 'No, no, no, don't try and move. I'm not going to leave you behind – honest,' Rose said, rushing back towards the dog.

She scooped the Border Collie up in her jacket and carried her towards the car. She was surprised at how light the dog was. Whoever her owners were, they clearly hadn't done a good job in taking care of her. Very carefully, Rose placed the injured dog on the backseat of the car and hopped into the driver's seat.

'It's okay now. You're safe with me, sweetheart. We're going to find a vet who can make you feel better.' Rose felt a bit like she was talking to one of the children at school. She was used to dealing with scraped knees and bumped heads on a daily basis, but an injured and bleeding Border Collie was slightly out of her comfort zone.

When Rose arrived at Brook House, the village's veterinary practice, she found the surgery doors were locked, but the number for the on-call vet was pinned to the door. Thankfully, the vet answered Rose's call on the first ring and was keen to help. Within five minutes, a dark green 4x4 pulled into the car park and its female driver hopped out.

'You must be Rose?' she called through the passenger's window as Rose parked up in the practice's car park.

'Yep, that's me.'

'I'm Grace Ashworth. And I'm guessing this one is our patient?' she asked, looking through to the backseat.

Rose nodded. Grace opened up the back door of the car and quickly had the Border Collie scooped up safely in her arms. Once they'd got into the surgery, Rose followed her into a consulting room.

'You found her on Pound Lane?' Grace asked, placing the dog on the examination table. Rose nodded. 'And there was no sign of an owner anywhere?'

'No one that I could see. Although I didn't think of checking her collar for her a tag?'

'Don't worry, she's not even wearing a collar by the looks of things. Right, young lady,' Grace said, addressing the dog directly. 'Let's see what's been happening, shall we?' Grace turned her attention to Rose. 'It's her leg you said was injured?'

'Yes, her left one, but she wouldn't let me take a closer look. I've no idea what's happened but I spotted the blood straight away,' Rose said, bending down to stroke the little dog's head. 'She really does seem to be the sweetest thing, despite everything she's been through.'

'I'm sure animals always know when someone's trying to help them,' Grace said with a smile. 'Ah, there's the problem. It looks as though she's got herself in a bit of a tangle with some barbed wire. It's wrapped tightly around that left leg. The more she's tried to struggle the deeper it's become embedded.'

'Oh no! That's gotta hurt,' Rose said, wincing and giving the dog a gentle tickle behind the ear. 'At least she's not been hit by a car,' she continued. 'That would have been a lot worse.'

'I'll make sure there aren't any other hidden injuries, but if it's just the barbed wire, we'll sedate her, give the wound a clean and then she should be good to go with some anti-biotics and pain relief. She's not in great condition though. She feels very skinny and her coat isn't in good shape either,' Grace said with a frown.

'I thought so too. Whoever owns her can't have been looking after her properly for a while.'

'My guess is that she's a stray. We sometimes get them turn up around here. Some are farm dogs that have been turfed out, or people get a dog and don't realize the work involved. Suddenly their cute puppy has turned into a crazy adolescent who is destroying the house.'

'Wow. Do people really do that?' Rose said, shocked.

'Afraid so. All we can do is be here to pick up the pieces. And luckily for this one, you happened to be passing by just when she needed help.'

'Well, anyone would have done the same.'

'You'd be surprised how many people would have driven by without a second thought – not their problem,' she shrugged. 'I have heard of a couple of local dogs going missing recently, but this girl doesn't fit either of their descriptions. One was a French bulldog and the other a cock-apoo, I think. Let's just make sure she's not microchipped.'

Grace reached for a handheld scanning device and ran it carefully around the back of the dog's neck.

'No, just as I thought, she doesn't have a chip. It's going to be a case of getting her fixed up and calling the dog warden to take her to the pound. We'll put posters up in the surgery and around the village, but I think the chances of anyone coming forward are pretty slim.'

'But she can't go to the pound!' Rose yelled, surprising herself a little at the strength of her reaction. 'She's been through enough already today, surely? A cold, scary kennel won't be good for her. Isn't there another option?'

'Unless you're offering to foster her until she's ready for a new home, there really isn't anything else I can suggest.'

'I'll do it,' Rose said without thinking. 'She can come home with me.'

'Okay . . .' Grace said, her eyes widening. 'Well, I probably need to know a bit more about you first. Do you even live in the village?'

'Oh, well, yes, sort of,' Rose tried to explain. 'Do you know Jean Hargreaves? Well, I'm her niece. I'm living at her cottage while she's in hospital so I'm going to be here for a few weeks at least, until she's well enough to come home,' Rose explained.

'Ah yes, I was sorry to hear about Jean's accident. Are you sure you're up for this though, Rose? It's a big commitment. And this dog doesn't need any more upheaval if you change your mind in a few days' time,' Grace said, giving the dog a tickle under the chin.

'Definitely. We always had Border Collies growing up and I know they're not for the faint-hearted. I'm more than capable of nursing her and I promise I won't let her down. She's had more than enough of that recently.'

Grace eyed Rose up and down slowly, as though she was trying to work out if she was going to make a suitable canine carer, before apparently deciding she would do. 'Alright, you've got me convinced,' she said, unfolding her arms. 'I'll just have to give the dog warden a call and square it with her. She's definitely taken a shine to you, I can see that, and it will be better if she can be fostered in a home environment rather than going to the pound. But remember, Rose,' she said more seriously, 'if her owners come forward in the next seven days, legally she'll have to go back to them.'

'I understand,' Rose nodded.

'It looks like you've got yourself a new canine housemate then,' Grace said, smiling. 'Just give me a couple of hours to get her cleaned up. I'll have to sedate her while we remove the barbed wire, so she might be a bit woozy this evening. If you head back here for . . .' – she looked down at her watch – ' . . . let's say 4 o'clock, she should be ready to leave with you.'

'Perfect,' Rose said, beaming. 'That gives me plenty of time to buy her all the bits she's going to need from Harrisons and get the house ready for her.'

'Great,' said Grace, 'we'll see you later, then. You've fallen on your paws here, missy,' she said to the dog, 'Oh and, Rose, you realize that you can't keeping saying "her"? This little lady deserves a proper name. What's it going to be?'

'Scout,' Rose said instinctively. 'She's called Scout.'

# Chapter 5

By the time 4pm came round, Rose had been to Harrisons and racked up quite a bill in the pet aisle, considering she was currently jobless. What with the dry dog food, treats, dog bed, a pretty pink patterned collar and lead, food and water bowls, soft toys, chew toys and tennis balls, Scout was going to be one spoiled pooch, that was for sure. Well, Rose thought, she certainly deserved it after the ordeal she'd been through.

While she was getting Jasmine Cottage set up for Scout's imminent arrival, Rose heard her mobile phone ringing from the depths of her handbag. Her stomach did a little flip when she saw it was Ollie. *What was she going to say to him?* She'd have to tell him that she was going to be staying in Blossom Heath for longer than planned, and how on earth was she going to explain Scout? He wouldn't approve of a canine addition. Rose perched on the edge of the sofa and answered the call.

'Hi,' she said.

'I've not heard from you, darling, so I thought I'd find out how you're settling in.'

'I thought it would be best to let you cool off for a bit. I hardly left you in the best of moods, did I?'

'Well, you did rather spring things on me, and I'd only just woken up, so you can't really blame me for flying off the handle. Anyway, how are things going?'

'They've done surgery on Aunt Jean's hip but she's not going to be allowed home for a while. She's got a lot of convalescing to do. The cottage is in a bad way too. It's obviously been too much for her to keep on top of things,' she said with a sigh.

'Well, you have to expect this sort of thing when people get to her age. I mean she's hardly a spring chicken, is she?' Rose felt herself bristle in response. 'Anyway, the good news is that I've managed to switch your interview with Marcus from Monday to Thursday, so that gives you plenty of time to sort things out and get back to London.'

'Ollie, I'm not going to be back by Thursday! My aunt is going to take *weeks* to recover and there's no way I'm leaving her on her own. There's so much work to be done on the cottage too ... It makes sense for me to stay for a few weeks and start getting things sorted out.'

'*A few weeks?*' Ollie replied, the horror evident in his voice. 'Rose, you can't stay for a few weeks. What about the interview with Marcus? What about ... well, what about *me*?'

'What about *you*?' Rose said through gritted teeth. 'The last time I checked you were perfectly capable of looking after yourself, and it's not as if you can't come down here to visit. As for that interview with Marcus, I'm sorry, Ollie, but I couldn't give two hoots. I don't *want* a job at your firm. How many times do I have to keep saying it?'

'I just wish that you wouldn't keep making decisions without consulting me, darling,' he said, his tone softening. 'I mean, they involve me too, you know. Did you ever stop to think that I might be missing you and just want you home?'

'Look, I've had a long day. I'm tired, I've got a lot to deal with and the last thing I need is an argument.' Rose glanced at her watch, conscious of the fact that it was nearly time for her to go and collect Scout. 'I need to head out to the shop and get something for dinner before they close,' she lied. 'I'll give you a call back later in the week.'

'Okay. Just *promise* you won't make any other big decisions without keeping me in the loop. I miss you, darling,' said Ollie, and with that he rang off.

Rose slumped back into the sofa and sighed. She knew Ollie was just missing her, but she couldn't help feeling he should be a *little* more supportive about her staying here to look after her aunt. And why did she feel so relieved not to be going back to London? She remembered how excited she'd been to move there with Ollie after they'd graduated. On the evening she'd bagged her first teaching job, he'd arrived at the flat with a bright red leather satchel from the Cambridge Satchel Company that she'd been mooning over for months but couldn't afford. He'd expertly wrapped it in gold tissue paper and had it embossed with her initials and a heart. She still remembered the crinkling sound of the tissue paper as she'd ripped it away and that brand-new leather smell filling her nostrils. Although it scared Rose a little to admit it, it seemed like a lifetime ago since she had felt that kind of excitement.

As Rose walked the short distance to the vets with Scout's new lead and collar ready in her handbag, she felt a pang of guilt that she'd not mentioned anything about Scout to Ollie. But then again, what was there really to tell? She was only fostering Scout, and if she wanted to take in a stray dog for a while, then who was he to question her? Anyway, the last thing she'd wanted was to add more stress to their phone call, and the mention of the arrival of her soon-to-be foster dog would definitely have accomplished that.

When she arrived at the vet practice, Grace was behind the reception desk ready to greet her.

'Hi, Rose, glad to see you back. You've not changed your mind, then?'

'No, definitely not. I've just spent a small fortune kitting Scout out with everything she's going to need, so there's no backing out now,' Rose laughed.

Grace beamed at her. 'I'm pleased to hear it. I've spoken to the dog warden and she's cleared you as a foster home. I just need you to fill out this form with your details and sign at the bottom.' Rose grabbed a pen from the reception desk and begin filling it in. 'I can see that you've got a collar and lead for her, but I'm guessing you've not been able to get an ID tag?'

'Oh no! I didn't even think of that!'

'No problem. I've got one here with the surgery's details

on as a temporary fix. If Scout does decide to do a disappearing act, anyone who finds her can contact us here. I've microchipped her with our details, too, and her new owners can transfer those over in the future.'

'Wow, seems like you've thought of everything.'

'We try to. Scout's doing really well. I've put a few stitches in her wound and given it a good clean. She's had an antibiotic injection and she's come around from the sedation. Judging from her teeth, I'd say she's around eighteen months old and she's weighing in at 9.8kg, which is definitely too skinny for a Border Collie. I've written down some instructions on how much food to give her, but aim for four small meals a day. We need to build her up slowly, as if she wolfs down too much in one go, she's likely to vomit. She'll need to take it easy for the next forty-eight hours, lots of rest. After that, keep her walks short for the first few days, just twenty minutes on the lead, and we can review things when we see her next week.'

'Thanks, Grace. I really appreciate everything you've done.'

'It's what I'm here for. I'm just glad that you stopped to help and she's not spending another night out on her own. I'll just grab her from the kennels and then you can get her home and settled.'

Grace disappeared through the door behind reception and it wasn't long before she reappeared with Scout leading the way in her new collar and lead, her shiny silver ID tag glistening in the light. When she spotted Rose, Scout's whole body wiggled. Rose dropped to her knees to greet the little dog and Scout flipped straight onto her belly, waiting for a tummy rub.

Rose and Grace chuckled.

'Well, it looks like you've made a firm friend there,' Grace said, smiling. 'She's clearly pleased to see you and I'm sure you're going to be dishing out lots more of those tummy rubs this evening.'

'I'm more than happy to oblige,' said Rose, rising from her knees and taking Scout's lead from Grace. Following Rose's example, Scout hopped to her feet too. 'Right then, Scout, are you ready to come and see your new pad for the next few weeks?' Scout tilted her head to one side as if she was carefully considering Rose's offer. She let out a short, high-pitched bark.

'We'll take that as a yes, then, shall we?' Grace laughed. 'If you have any questions just give me a call. Seeing as you're new to the village, why don't we grab a drink at the pub in the next few days? As a thank you for stopping to save this one?' she nodded towards Scout.

'That would be lovely. I don't really know that many people here,' Rose said, smiling. 'And thanks again for all your help today.'

Rose opened the door of the practice and, after a final wave to Grace, made her way down the road towards Jasmine Cottage with Scout obediently walking along beside her.

'Okay, Scout, it's just you and me now,' Rose whispered to the little dog. 'We've got this.'

Scout spent the first hour in her new temporary home, exploring every inch of the cottage. She spent an age carefully sniffing every room downstairs and, when Rose opened the kitchen door to let her into the garden, Scout stepped outside very gingerly.

'It's okay, Scout,' Rose said quietly. 'Out you go and explore. This is your garden now.'

Sensing her hesitation, Rose stepped out onto the patio to join her and then went and sat in the middle of the lawn. Slowly but surely, Scout took her time exploring the patio, sniffing Aunt Jean's garden pots and gradually making her way over to Rose. After she'd had a quick cuddle with her, Rose could sense Scout's confidence gradually building as she ventured further into the garden. She walked around the borders, sniffing the shrubs and bushes carefully, and then finally stopped to relieve herself in the middle of the lawn.

'Well done, Scout, good girl,' Rose said, stroking her on the head. 'Hopefully that means you're house-trained?' Scout tilted her head to one side again, looking at Rose quizzically. 'That's one less job for me,' she said, smiling.

As Rose made her way back inside, Scout trotted along beside her like a little shadow. In the kitchen, Rose took out Scout's new food bowl and weighed out the correct amount of kibble, as instructed by Grace. Scout got very excited when she saw there was food in the offing and whined excitedly.

'Alright, alright, I'm being as quick as I can. Patience, young lady,' Rose chuckled. 'Now, let's see if you've had any training.' Rose held the food bowl slightly above Scout's head and in a clear but firm voice she gave the command, 'Sit.'

Scout's bottom hit the floor and she presented Rose with the perfect doggie sit.

'Excellent,' said Rose, placing the bowl of kibble in front of Scout, who was licking the bowl clean within ten seconds. She looked up at Rose again expectantly, letting out a small whine. 'Wow, you were hungry, weren't you? There's no more tonight I'm afraid – Grace's orders. We can't have you making yourself sick, can we?'

After Rose had heated up a vegetable lasagne and eaten it nearly as quickly as Scout had demolished her bowl of kibble, she settled down on the sofa to watch TV and Scout hopped up to join her. She nestled herself into Rose's side, lay her head down on her lap, and within a few minutes Scout was snoring away contentedly, the effects of her sedation obviously not quite out of her system. Rose stroked Scout's head gently and found herself wondering how Scout had managed to find herself straying on the outskirts of Blossom Heath. She had clearly been neglected – she was so underweight, and her coat was in such poor condition – and yet she had such a beautiful, gentle nature that Rose found it hard to imagine how she could be unwanted. She seemed to be house-trained, too, and the fact that she walked well on the lead and knew some basic commands led her to believe that she'd had a home at some point. *Was there a family out there somewhere looking for her?* Rose wasn't sure. The one thing she *was* sure of was that, for now at least, Scout had found a safe haven at Jasmine Cottage.

# Chapter 6

When Rose awoke on Monday morning, she was pleasantly surprised to find Scout curled up at her feet at the bottom of the bed. Rose had planned to have Scout sleep in the bedroom with her on her first night to help settle her in, but nothing she could try would encourage her upstairs. It was almost as if Scout had never seen stairs before. Perhaps she had been wrong, and she hadn't ever lived in a house. Giving up, Rose had made Scout's bed up in the kitchen, but she must have found her courage during the night to make it upstairs to join Rose. She reached out a hand to give her a tickle behind the ears.

'Morning, you,' she said, sitting herself upright. As soon as Rose moved, Scout wiggled herself up the bed for a cuddle. 'This is certainly a nice way to be greeted in the morning,' Rose said, tickling the top of Scout's head. 'We can't be lazing around up here all day though. We've got things to do today, Scout,' she said, throwing back the bedsheets. 'First on the list is I need coffee and you need breakfast.'

Rose pulled on her slipper boots and headed downstairs.

When she looked round, however, Scout was standing at the top of the stairs and started to whine.

'Don't tell me you don't know how to come down the stairs?' Rose said with a chuckle. 'Stay there.' She went to the kitchen to grab some dog treats, thinking they might help to entice her down. Scout was having none of it though, and stayed stuck on the landing, whining away and hopping from paw to paw. She clearly wanted to come downstairs but had no idea how to. Deciding to try a different tack, Rose went up the stairs on all fours and placed a dog treat one step down from where Scout was standing. It was just out of reach, and Scout would have to put her front paws on the top stair to reach it. Scout looked at the treat, looked back to Rose, and whined again.

'Come on, Scout, you can do this,' Rose whispered. Encouraged by the sound of Rose's voice, Scout put her paws on the first step down and snaffled the treat. 'Good girl,' Rose said, beaming. 'Come on, let's try again,' and together they repeated the process, step by step, until Scout had reached the bottom of the stairs.

'See, I told you you could do it!' Rose said, bending down and throwing her arms around Scout's neck. 'You are a clever dog, aren't you? Now you've conquered the stairs, I think it's about time we had some breakfast, don't you?' Scout barked in agreement.

After a quick breakfast and a shower, Rose was ready to face the day. Scout had found her confidence with the stairs and was now running up and down them with ease. *If only all of life's problems were that easy to solve*, she thought.

'Right, Scout, it's time for me to go and visit Aunt Jean, and you can't come with me, I'm afraid. I'm trusting you to be a good girl and look after the house while I'm gone. No chewing the furniture and no inviting your doggie friends over for a party, got it?'

Rose gathered up everything that she would need in her handbag and took the biggest dog chew that Harrisons had to offer out of the kitchen cupboard. Scout dropped obediently into the sit position.

'Clever girl,' said Rose. 'Hopefully this should keep you busy and you won't even notice I'm gone.'

Aunt Jean looked a bit brighter today, Rose was pleased to see, and she chatted to Rose animatedly about all the comings and goings on the ward. In true Aunt Jean style, she seemed to know everything about her fellow patients already. Rose was quick to share the story about her rescue of Scout and how she was settling into the cottage, when it struck her.

'I didn't think to ask you if you'd mind me fostering a dog?' Rose said. 'It is your cottage after all. If you don't want her there, I can always sign her over to the dog warden and she can move to kennels?'

'Sign her over to the dog warden? Rose, have you lost your marbles? Of course she can stay at Jasmine Cottage. I won't hear of you returning her. Kennels is no place for a Border Collie – they're far too sensitive. It sounds like the poor little mite needs a bit of TLC, and I think you're just the person to give it,' Aunt Jean said with a wink.

'Thanks, Auntie, I thought that's what you'd say. Scout and I are both very grateful.' Rose took her aunt's hand. 'I've got some pictures of her on my phone if you'd like to see?'

'She's a little heartbreaker, that's for sure,' Aunt Jean agreed after she'd ooohed and ahhhhed over all the pictures Rose had taken of her the previous evening. 'Promise me you won't go getting yourself too attached though? Remember she's a foster dog; her family might be looking for her.'

'I know, I know. I won't. Even if no one claims her, there's no way she'd be able to come back to London and live in a flat while I'm out at work all day. It wouldn't be fair. I promise I won't get too attached. Honest.'

Secretly, however, Rose feared that this would be a promise she was destined to break.

When Rose arrived back at Jasmine Cottage, Scout was waiting to meet her in the hallway, and she greeted her with her trademark body wiggle, which made Rose laugh out loud as she bent down to stroke her on the head. She was pleased to find that Scout had been the model canine house guest, too, and nothing looked out of place. Rose fired off a quick text to her dad:

*Just been to see Aunt Jean, she's doing fine and she's in good spirits. Don't worry about us and enjoy your holiday x*

Hopefully that would go some way towards reassuring him that she had things under control and there was no need for him to cut short his cruise.

After a quick lunch, Rose decided to pay a visit to the

hardware store at a new retail park that had sprung up on the outskirts of the village recently. She wanted to make a start on fixing up Jasmine Cottage ready for her aunt's return, and Harrisons just wasn't big enough to stock everything that she needed.

'Are you ready for a road trip, Scout?' Rose asked as she clipped the dog's lead to her collar. 'I'm not leaving you stuck home alone more than once in a day, so this time you can tag along with me. What do you reckon?' Scout tilted her head to one side again as if she was listening to Rose's suggestion and thinking it over carefully. Rose laughed. 'Come on, girl, let's get going,' she said, patting her thigh to encourage Scout to follow.

Scout hopped eagerly into the car and settled herself down on the back seat. Rose switched the radio on as she pulled out of the cottage's driveway and began singing along to 'Parachutes' by Coldplay at the top of her lungs. Scout did not look impressed, Rose noted, when she checked on her in the car's rear-view mirror. If dogs could speak, Rose was sure that Scout would be telling her to stop her out-of-tune wailing.

When Rose arrived at the DIY store, she left Scout in the car with the passenger side window open slightly and began scanning the aisles for everything she'd need. She quickly found the mop, bucket and carpet cleaner she was after, but other items were proving more tricky, and she was conscious that she didn't want to leave Scout on her own for too long. The store was much larger than Rose had anticipated and it was going to be easier to locate everything she needed if she asked a member of staff to help. She looked around her. Spotting someone at the end of the aisle, Rose grabbed her chance. 'Excuse me, I'm trying to find the bath plugs and light pulls. Could you point me in the right direction, please? Only this place is a bit of a maze.'

As the man in front of her turned around, Rose felt her cheeks burn – and not just because the stranger in front of her was incredibly handsome.

'Ah, if I actually worked here, that might be something I could help with,' he said with a grin.

Rose felt her cheeks burn more deeply.

'Oh God, I'm sorry,' she said with a groan. 'I saw you were dressed in black and thought you must work here. Don't worry, I'm sure I can find someone to help.'

Rose glanced around the store and it suddenly appeared to be deserted – well, except for her and the handsome stranger of course.

'Ah, every member of staff appears to have vanished just when you need them . . . isn't that always the way?' the man said with a laugh. 'Listen, I know this store pretty well, so I can probably help you find what you need.'

'Oh, well, only if you're sure? I don't want to be a bother,' Rose said, the heat in her cheeks gradually starting to cool.

'I'm sure,' the man said warmly. 'Bath plugs and light switches, wasn't it?' Rose nodded. 'Follow me, madam,' he continued, gesturing in front of him with his left arm.

As Rose followed him towards the bathroom aisle, she

couldn't help noticing his tall and muscular build, and how his dark brown hair flopped slightly to one side. When he turned around to face her, she marvelled at his brilliant blue eyes. He wasn't completely clean-shaven; he had a couple of days' worth of stubble around his jaw line, but, if anything, this just added to his charm. It struck Rose how different he was to Ollie, and she instinctively reached for her engagement ring.

'May I present our range of bath plugs,' the stranger said with a mischievous glint in his eyes and a wave of his arm.

'Wow, who knew there were so many different kinds,' Rose said in amazement. As she reached up to take a plug from the nearest box, she overstretched and sent the whole box crashing to the ground, scattering the contents around her feet. She groaned as she knelt down to clear up the mess. The man bent down to help and smiled.

'Thanks,' she said once they had returned everything to its rightful place. 'I'd have been wandering the aisles forever trying to find these. If you're ever out of a job, I'm sure this place would hire you in an instant.'

He laughed. 'Well, I'll certainly bear that in mind. My job's one for life though, hopefully.'

'Oh, right. Lucky you. What do you do, if you don't mind me asking?' Rose was aware that she should let him get on with his shopping, but she found herself enjoying his company so much she didn't want the conversation to end.

'I run a farm in Blossom Heath.'

'You're from Blossom Heath?' Rose said eagerly. 'Me

# Always By Your Side

too – sort of. I'm from London really, but my aunt lives in the village. I'm just staying there while she's in hospital and I thought—'

'Ah, so you must be Jean's niece? I'd heard you were staying in the village. I'm Jake, by the way.'

'Rose Hargreaves,' she replied, laughing. 'Wow. News really does travel fast round here.'

'Nothing stays a secret in Blossom Heath for longer than thirty seconds,' he chuckled.

'I'm beginning to realize that,' Rose said. 'Anyway, her cottage is looking a bit ... neglected, so I thought I'd try to get things sorted before she's sent home – hence finding myself wandering the aisles of a DIY store.'

'That makes sense,' Jake agreed. 'And if you need any help, well, I like to think of myself as a bit of a handyman, so feel free to rope me in. I'm sure that would go for everyone in Blossom Heath too. Your aunt is a bit of a local treasure, you know.'

'Thanks, Jake, I'll keep that in mind,' Rose replied, 'and thanks again for your help today.' As he walked away, Rose's gaze lingered on him slightly longer than it needed to.

After finding the last few bits and pieces that she needed, no sooner had Rose made it through the checkout than she found herself bumping into Jake again in the car park, as his 4x4 was parked in the space next to hers. As she approached, Scout made herself visible at the window. She was clearly delighted to see Rose and let out a small bark. It was then

65

that Rose saw the heads of two Border Collies, a tri colour and a blue merle, pop up at Jake's car window.

'You clearly have excellent taste in dogs,' said Jake as he opened the boot of the 4x4 to let his two hop out to greet her. 'Let me introduce you to Finn,' he said, pointing to the blue merle collie, 'and Tagg,' gesturing towards the tricolour dog.

'Aw, it's lovely to meet you both,' said Rose, leaning down to stroke the two dogs. 'And this is Scout,' she said, pointing at the little dog pressing her nose up against the glass.

'Scout? As in *To Kill a Mockingbird*?' said Jake. 'I do love that book.'

'Yes!' Rose said in delight. 'She's one of my favourite characters, but not many people get the reference. And technically she's not actually my dog . . . I'm fostering her until we can track down her owners or find her a new home.'

'Well, either way, it sounds like she's got a pretty good set-up with you,' Jake said with a smile. As he got into his jeep and drove away, Rose couldn't help thinking that Jake's skill as a handyman wasn't the only reason she hoped to see him again.

# Chapter 7

Before Rose knew it, Scout had been with her for nearly a week. The time had flown by. Between visits to the hospital to see her aunt, cleaning and tidying at the cottage and taking Scout on some lovely walks to explore the local area, Rose had well and truly settled into the pace of village life. She really hadn't missed London at all, which had come as a surprise given how much she loved the buzz of being in the city, and she felt a sense of guilt creep up on her when she realized that she hadn't missed Ollie either. In fact, she had tried not to think about him since their decidedly frosty phone conversation last Sunday evening.

With a shake of her head, Rose decided to put all thoughts of Ollie out of her mind for this evening. It was Sunday night, and she had arranged to meet Grace at the village's one and only pub, the Apple Tree, at 7pm. Grace had told Rose that the pub was dog-friendly so Scout, much to Rose's delight, was welcome to join them. Rose struggled to decide on her outfit for the evening, but in the end opted to play it safe with a pair of light blue jeans and a sparkly pink top. She applied her make-up carefully and stopped for a moment to study her reflection as she combed her long dark brown hair. That would have to do, it was already nearly time to meet Grace.

As Rose made her way down the lane leading to the centre of the village, she could already hear the gentle hum of voices coming from the pub's beer garden. It was nearly dark, being early April, but it was a surprisingly warm spring evening and people were making the most of the opportunity to be outdoors. Rose wandered slowly along the lane, allowing Scout the opportunity to sniff along the grass verges at the side of the road. At one point Rose spotted a missing dog poster plastered to one of the lampposts. An apricot-coloured cockapoo by the look of it. This must be one of the missing dogs that Grace had mentioned when they first met. *How awful*, she thought. Rose bent down and stroked Scout gently behind the ears just to reassure herself that she was still there. Scout was still only allowed short bursts of exercise while her leg was recovering, but she was clearly enjoying the opportunity to explore the sights and smells of the outdoor world.

'Come on, Scout, you can't possibly sniff every blade of grass on the way to the pub or we'll be late to meet Grace,' Rose said gently. Scout looked up from the patch of grass that she was busy sniffing and, with a short tug on the lead, trotted along obediently by Rose's side.

'That's better,' Rose said. 'Who taught you to walk on the lead so perfectly?' Someone had obviously taken the time to train her, and the thought made Rose wonder again how she had ended up stranded at the roadside. Perhaps they'd never know. She frowned at the thought.

Rose walked through the gardens at the front of the Apple Tree and smiled when she saw the huge fruit tree from which the pub took its name. The Golden Pippin tree was full of beautiful pink blossoms and it framed the entrance to the pub perfectly. As she walked through the main doors, she could see straight away that it was a packed Sunday night. Pete, the pub's landlord, spotted her straight away. 'Rose!' he shouted from across the bar. 'How lovely to see you! Beth, look who it is!' he called to his wife. 'We've not seen you back in the village since last summer, have we, Rose?'

'No, not since last August. I can't tell you how much my summers in Blossom Heath help me to survive winter in London,' she laughed.

'Ah, Rose. Maggie mentioned that you'd been in, so I thought we'd be seeing you in here soon enough. How's Jean?' Beth asked.

'She's not doing too badly. Eager to get home though.'

'I bet she is! I was saying to Maggie this morning, they'll not be able to keep Jean Hargreaves confined to a hospital bed for long. The doctor will have met his match with that one,' she said.

Rose laughed. 'She seems to be doing as she's told so far, but I'm sure she'll be back in the village soon.'

'I'll always remember Jean bringing you into the pub as a nipper, Rose. Do you remember the bonfire parties we had? We'd all head down to Rye, watch the pageant and come back here for cider and hot jacket spuds,' Maggie said.

'Oh, I'd forgotten all about that! No one does a bonfire

party quite like they do in Sussex. And I used to love the parade. Do you remember that huge fire-breathing dragon? Scorcher, was it? He had real flames coming out of his nose!'

'Ah, yes, that one always sticks in my mind too,' Pete agreed. 'What are you drinking, love? It's on the house.'

'Are you sure?'

'No arguments,' said Pete. Rose ordered a large glass of red wine and scanned the bar looking for Grace. She spotted a few faces that she recognized from her trips around the village with Aunt Jean and a couple of the locals gave her a nod of acknowledgement. As she took a sip of wine, she felt a tap on her shoulder.

'Rose, hi! It's me . . . Jess.' Rose turned to see a tall, slender girl with long red hair and expertly applied black eyeliner dressed in ripped jeans and a Metallica T-shirt. 'You know, Maggie's daughter . . . from the village shop?'

'Oh, wow, Jess! I never would have recognized you,' said Rose, giving Jess a hug. 'Boy, you have grown up since the last time I saw you!'

'Well, it's been a few years, so I'll let you off the hook,' she said, taking a sip of her beer.

'So, what have you been up to?'

'I've not long finished uni. I was doing art at York.'

'Wow, impressive.'

'I'm just helping Mum and Dad out at the shop while I figure out what's next. I can't wait to get away to be honest. It's a *nightmare* being back home. You know what Mum's like – *nothing* gets past her. They seem to have forgotten that

I'm not ten years old anymore,' she said, rolling her eyes. 'I'm applying for a Masters at Cardiff, so I'm hoping that pans out.'

'Sounds like a good plan. I still can't believe how grown up you look. I reckon the last time I saw you I'd have been around eighteen, which would have made you—'

'Twelve, I think.'

'Practically a lifetime ago.'

'It's great to see you back, Rose. Sorry I can't stop, but I'm off to a gig in Brighton.'

'Wow, get you. Who're you seeing?'

'The Red Admirals. Ever heard of them?'

'Afraid not, but I'm an old nearly married hermit nowadays,' said Rose, flashing her engagement ring.

'Yikes! Rather you than me,' Jess replied as she downed the rest of her beer and waved Rose goodbye.

Rose looked around the bar again and this time spotted Grace waving at her from a corner booth.

'Rose, over here!' Grace called, waving her arms. 'I didn't know what you'd be drinking, so I took a punt and got you a glass of red in.'

'Great minds think alike,' said Rose, holding up her glass of red. 'It's packed at the bar already, so you've bagged a great spot.'

'Ah, you know us locals – we know the best ways to secure the perfect table at the village pub,' Grace chuckled. She bent down to give Scout a scratch under the chin. 'How's she doing?'

'Remarkably well, all things considered,' Rose said with

a smile as she took a seat opposite Grace and settled Scout underneath the table, loosely securing her lead to one of the table legs. 'She's actually been the model house guest. She's house-trained, she's been fine when I've left her, and she even knows a few commands. It seems crazy to think how she ended up at the side of the road. She's such a lovely girl.'

'It is a mystery, but you'd be surprised at the number of dogs who are abandoned that have lived for years as someone's pet. Sometimes priorities change and they suddenly find themselves out on the street.'

'I take it no one has come forward to claim her?'

'Nothing yet. If no one comes forward by Monday, she'll have served her seven days as a stray and can legally go up for rehoming.'

Rose was surprised to find that her heart sank a little at Grace's words. What if someone did come forward to adopt Scout in the next few weeks? She was amazed at how attached she'd become to her in just six short days. How would she feel at having to give her up? There was no point in trying to deny it. She'd be heartbroken. So much for her promise to Aunt Jean that she wouldn't get attached.

Grace and Rose chatted away happily over the course of the evening, and Rose was surprised by how much they had in common. Grace came from a family of teachers, and she'd bucked the trend when deciding to go to veterinary college. She was, however, interested to hear all about Rose's teaching career in London and how she found herself between posts right now. Grace's father was a headteacher in Surrey

72

and she insisted that she'd put Rose in touch with some of his London colleagues who might know of a suitable teaching vacancy for her. Rose warmed to Grace quickly and, to her surprise, she found herself confiding in the village vet about her situation with Ollie.

'I have to admit, Ollie's less than thrilled with me being here,' she explained.

'Why's that?'

'Oh, I don't know,' Rose shrugged, 'I think he'd much rather me go and work at his firm than stick with teaching.'

'Really?'

'We're supposed to be saving for the deposit on a house and that's not quite as easy as it sounds on a teacher's salary.' Rose paused. 'It's not just that, though ... I've not even told him about Scout. I know that I should have,' she added hurriedly, 'but I'm just not sure he'd understand.'

'Well, you're not going to be able to keep that a secret indefinitely,' said Grace, reaching down to tickle Scout on the top of the head. 'I'm sure she'll be able to work her magic on him. I mean, just look at that face! How could he resist?'

Rose wasn't usually so quick to share such personal information, but there was something about Grace that she felt drawn to, and she proved to be exactly the kind of sympathetic but impartial ear that Rose needed.

'I know you didn't choose to have your aunt in hospital, but a change of scene might be exactly what you need.'

'I can't tell you what a relief it's been to be away from

London and just have a bit of alone time. For one, I don't have to worry about explaining myself to anyone, which is absolute bliss. How did you end up in Blossom Heath anyway? Sorry, I don't mean to keep going on about me. What about you? I'm no expert but I *definitely* don't have you down as a local.'

'You're spot on there. I'm a Surrey girl. Mum and Dad are in Dorking and my two brothers are in Richmond.'

'And you never thought about going into teaching yourself?'

'No way! I'd rather deal with a raucous heifer than a class of kids – no offence!'

'None taken.'

'I worked in Richmond when I was straight out of uni but small animal practice really isn't for me. I love getting called out to the farms and working with larger animals. I'm never happier than when I'm up to my ears in cow dung, and there's not much call for that kind of work in Surrey.'

'No, I suppose there isn't,' Rose snorted, 'and it *is* lovely here, so I totally get why you'd want to stay. And is there a love interest in the picture?' she asked Grace with a grin.

'Nope, I'm most definitely single for now. To be honest I'm working all hours so there's not much time for anything else. I've not had a serious boyfriend since vet school and that was years ago. I think it's safe to say that I'm married to the job and, anyway, Blossom Heath doesn't *exactly* have a wide selection of eligible bachelors to choose from.'

At that precise moment, the door to the bar banged open

and in walked Jake, the farmer Rose had met at the DIY store last week. His Border Collies, Finn and Tagg, were trotting obediently at his heels. At the sight of the dogs, Scout suddenly decided to make a break for freedom from under the table and she shot off eagerly to greet them. Rose's reactions were too slow to grab Scout's lead in time and, before she knew it, Scout had rushed up to the two dogs and was greeting them enthusiastically.

'Scout,' Rose called as she ran after her. 'I'm so sorry, Jake, I thought I'd tied her lead to the table leg but ... obviously not tightly enough,' she said. Why was she always making a complete idiot of herself whenever she bumped into this man?

'No worries,' said Jake, smiling at her, 'Finn and Tagg seem quite taken with her.' Scout wiggled at Jake's feet and quickly rolled over to demand an obligatory belly rub.

'Well, they're not the only ones,' Rose laughed. 'I'm pretty taken with her myself if truth be told.'

'You're going to struggle to give her up I reckon,' Jake said with a smirk. Rose sighed.

'I've *promised* myself not to fall for her. London isn't the place for a Border Collie, so needs must unfortunately,' she said.

'Right, well I'd best let you get on with your evening,' said Jake, directing a wave over at Grace in the corner booth. 'I'm meeting some friends in the beer garden, so I should go and track them down.'

'Yes, I'd better be getting back, but enjoy your evening,' Rose said, smiling.

'You too. It was nice to bump into you again, Rose,' Jake said with a smile that made Rose's stomach flip and her pulse quicken. She really needed to get a grip on herself; she was an engaged woman for God's sake.

'Speaking of eligible bachelors,' Grace smirked when Rose had secured Scout back at the table. 'I see you've already managed to meet the most eligible of the bunch.'

'Oh, well ... er, yes, I guess so,' Rose stammered. 'We met the other day at the DIY store. I'm not in the market for eligible bachelors though,' said Rose, tapping her engagement ring.

'Tell yourself whatever you like, but I could spot the sparks between you two a mile off.'

'What? No. Not at all,' Rose stammered, her voice cracking slightly. 'Anyway, *you're* the single one ... Are you not tempted? He's a farmer, you're a vet – surely that's a match made in heaven?'

'Me and Jake? No way!' Grace laughed. 'We are *definitely* just friends. He's not my type, either – far too rugged, dark and brooding for my tastes. I'm more of an Aussie surfer type of girl. Blonde and tattooed is my vibe,' Grace said wistfully.

'Well, good luck with that in Blossom Heath,' Rose chuckled. 'I think you'll be in for a long wait.'

'Me too,' said Grace, nodding. 'Me too.'

# Chapter 8

Rose was woken early on Monday morning by the sound of someone hammering on the front door of Jasmine Cottage. Scout leapt from her spot on the bed, barked and ran down the stairs to investigate.

'Quiet, Scout,' Rose murmured as she reached out to grab her phone from the bedside table and check the time: 7.20am. *Who on earth could that be at this time in the morning?* She didn't even really know anyone in the village, and surely it was too early for visitors? Rose got up, padded across the bedroom and hurriedly pulled on her dressing gown. The hammering on the door continued and Scout's barking persisted.

'I'll be there in a sec,' she shouted. For one moment Rose considered the possibility that her surprise visitor could be Ollie, but when she thought about it, she realized it was a weekday, and there was no way her fiancé would miss work. She sped down the stairs and grabbed Scout by the collar to stop her running out of the front door when it was opened. As Rose fumbled around taking off the security chain and unlocking the door's bolts, she struggled to keep hold of Scout, who was bouncing around with excitement at the prospect of an early morning visitor. Once Rose finally managed to open the front door, she was met by a short, rather rotund woman who looked to be in her early sixties, with curly blonde hair and a beaming smile.

'Hello, I'm sorry to disturb you so early in the morning, but are you Rose Hargreaves?'

'Erm, yes ... that's right, I'm Rose.'

'I'm Eileen Connolly, headteacher of Blossom Heath Primary. Would you mind if I came in for a moment? There's an urgent matter that I'd like to discuss with you.'

'Of course,' said Rose, although she couldn't think what the headteacher of the local school could possibly want with her.

Mrs Connolly stepped over the threshold of Jasmine Cottage and, as Rose closed the front door, Scout made a beeline for the headteacher, wiggling her whole body and jumping up excitedly.

'Oh, what a gorgeous dog!' Mrs Connolly cooed. 'This must be Scout, the stray you're fostering? I've heard all about her from Maggie.'

*News in this village really did travel fast*, Rose thought again.

'Yes, that's right, this is Scout. She certainly seems to like you,' Rose smiled.

'I'm a great dog lover,' Mrs Connolly explained as she bent down to give Scout a belly rub. 'I've got a chocolate Labrador called Bertie at home. Now, Rose, let me explain the reason for my visit,' Mrs Connolly continued, straightening herself up. 'Am I right in thinking that you're a teacher?'

'Yes, I am,' said Rose, fastening the tie on her dressing gown more tightly.

'Ah, good, good,' Mrs Connolly interrupted. 'Maggie told me as much, and not much gets past her, as I'm sure you know.'

'I'm beginning to realize that, yes.'

'I'm in a spot of bother and I'm hoping you can help. Our Year 2 teacher has been taken ill this morning. I've tried our usual supply agencies, but they've come up short and don't have anyone they can send me. I was wondering if you'd consider helping us out? We'd pay you the daily rate of course, and I'd be hugely grateful.'

Rose didn't know how to respond. Questions buzzed through her head.

'Teach? Today?'

'Yes, today. I realize it's incredibly short notice, but I can't tell you how relieved I was when I remembered Maggie mentioning we had another teacher residing in the village. It suddenly hit me that you could be the solution to our staffing problem.'

Rose struggled to formulate a response. She pulled at the left sleeve of her dressing gown. What if Dawson had been *right* about her not being a good enough teacher? She was sure that Mrs Connolly wouldn't be quite so eager to have her teach for the day if she knew her last lesson observation had been graded 'unsatisfactory'. Perhaps she wasn't cut out for teaching at all.

'I'm not sure what to say, Mrs Connolly. I have Scout to

think of, for one. I can't leave her on her own all day – it wouldn't be fair. And then there's my Aunt Jean. I was going to visit her later in the hospital.'

'I thought you might say that, which is why I took the liberty of calling Jane, Bertie's dog-sitter. Jane looks after Bertie for me occasionally. Bertie's the school dog, you see, so he's usually with me, but on the odd occasion he can't come into school, he goes to Jane. She's happy to have Scout today and I can cover the costs if it means you can come in and teach.'

'You have a school dog?' Rose said in surprise.

'Yes, Bertie's been such an asset to the school. The children absolutely adore him and I can't tell you what a positive impact he's had on some of our more vulnerable pupils.'

'Wow, I've never heard of that before. It sounds like a fabulous idea.'

'And as for your aunt, I'm sure she'd love to hear that you've pitched in to help the school. Could you perhaps visit her this evening instead?'

Rose mulled this over. She could visit Aunt Jean this evening she supposed, and she was sure that Scout would be fine with a dog-sitter for the day. She had to admit she was missing her class in London and Mrs Connolly was right, she would be helping the village by saying yes. She really shouldn't let Dawson's comments on her teaching skills get in her head.

'Okay, I'll do it,' she said quickly before she had time to change her mind.

Mrs Connolly let out a small 'whoop' of delight. Rose

got the distinct impression that Mrs Connolly was a very difficult person to say no to once she had set her mind on something.

'Oh, Rose, thank you *so* much. You really are helping us out in our hour of need. I won't forget this,' Mrs Connolly said with smile. 'It's half past seven now, so if you can get to school by half past eight? That will give me time to go through the lesson plans and get you up to speed. Do you know where we are?'

'Heathview Lane?'

'That's right. If you give me Jean's spare key, I'll pop that to Jane and she'll come and collect Scout in around an hour.'

'Okay, great,' said Rose as she walked to the kitchen to grab the spare key. 'I'll get myself ready and see you at school in a bit.'

As soon as Mrs Connolly had left, Rose fed Scout, let her out into the garden and grabbed herself a quick bowl of cereal. She jumped into the shower and changed in record time. It took her longer than she'd planned to find a suitable outfit as most of the clothes she had brought with her to Sussex were on the casual side. Eventually she decided on a pair of dark blue, cropped trousers and her white blouse with tiny blue hearts embroidered into the fabric. It wasn't ideal, but she was sure that Mrs Connolly wouldn't mind, given the circumstances. Rose said a swift goodbye to Scout and left her with a chew toy to keep her occupied while she was waiting for Jane to collect her. As she walked in the direction of Blossom Heath Primary School, Rose felt a buzz of excitement in her chest. It may just be for today, but she was a teacher again, and it felt good.

Rose arrived at the school on the dot of half past eight and Mrs Connolly was at reception waiting to greet her.

'Rose, thank you so much for this. Let me introduce you to Sally, my PA and the office manager. I'd be lost without her. If there's anything you need today, come and ask her. If she doesn't know the answer, she'll be able to find it for you.'

'Pleased to meet you, Rose,' said Sally, shaking Rose's hand firmly. 'I've sorted out your DBS check, so that's all organized.'

'Thanks,' said Rose, 'that's a huge help.'

'What did I tell you, Rose?' Mrs Connolly said, laughing, 'Sally makes sure everything behind the scenes runs smoothly at Blossom Heath Primary. Now let me take you along to our Year 2 classroom,' she continued, leading Rose out of the office. 'You've got twenty-six pupils in Butterfly Class and they really are a lovely bunch. They're a job-share class, and you're covering for Mrs Jackson, who teaches them Monday to Wednesday. Here we are then.' She opened the classroom door and showed Rose in.

'Wow, what a fantastic classroom,' Rose said, looking around, her eyes widening as she took everything in. The teaching space was very different to the Victorian school building with its small, cramped classrooms and tiny windows that she was used to in London. It was a large and airy room with floor-to-ceiling windows overlooking the playground, which flooded the school room with light. 'I love your displays,' Rose said, gesturing towards a particularly colourful one detailing the events of the Great Fire of London.

'Oh, we're very lucky here,' Mrs Connolly said. 'All our classrooms are very spacious and your teaching assistant, Cheryl Morse, has a fabulous artistic streak, so all our displays really benefit. I'll introduce you to Cheryl as soon as she's in. I've printed out of all the lesson plans for today and taken the liberty of putting the timetable up on the whiteboard. We've got assembly first thing and then you've got literacy and numeracy this morning and guided reading and topic work this afternoon.'

'Perfect,' said Rose, 'that all sounds great.'

'In terms of the children, as I say, they're a great class, but there's a couple to watch out for. Billy Jenkins will try and push his luck when he realizes that Mrs Jackson's not in, and we've got a new lad, Mason Rowe, who has been quite reluctant to come to school in the mornings, so he may need a bit of coaxing. Mrs Morse knows all the children inside out, so if you're unsure of anything she can fill you in. Ah – speak of the devil . . .' Mrs Connolly said, gesturing towards the classroom door.

A tall, dark-haired woman who looked to be in her midforties walked into the classroom, smiling enthusiastically at both Rose and Mrs Connolly.

'Ah, Cheryl, perfect timing as always. Let me introduce you to Rose Hargreaves. Rose is covering for Mrs Jackson today.'

Cheryl stepped towards Rose and gave her a wave.

'Great to meet you, Rose. It's a relief to know we've got some cover today. I know we were struggling to find someone.'

'Ah, it's not a problem,' said Rose with a smile. 'I'm in the village for a few weeks so I'm happy to lend a hand.'

'Right, I'm going to leave you both to it,' Mrs Connolly said briskly. 'Rose, do you want to pop over to my office at lunchtime and let me know how you're getting on?'

'That would be great,' Rose said. 'I'll see you then.'

'Good luck,' said Mrs Connolly, 'and thank you again for agreeing to help out at such short notice.'

After Mrs Connolly had left, Cheryl spent some time chatting to Rose and taking her through all the basics of life in Butterfly Class. Before Rose knew it, several tiny faces were pressed up against the classroom window, all peering inside.

'Looks like we've got company,' Cheryl chuckled. 'Word must have spread that Mrs Jackson is out for the day. I'll give it a couple more minutes and then I'll start letting the children in.'

'Perfect,' said Rose. 'I'm just going to write my name up on the whiteboard so they know who I am.'

As Rose was busying herself making her final few preparations before the school day began, Cheryl opened the classroom's external door to allow the children to filter into the cloakroom. As they busied themselves hanging up their coats and lunchboxes, Rose could hear them chatting and murmuring excitedly.

'Who's that lady, Mrs Morse?' a girl with curly blonde pigtails asked Cheryl.

'Yeah, where's Mrs Jackson?' a tall boy with dark hair and a Pokémon lunchbox asked.

'Just put your things away for now, Year 2, and come and sit down on the carpet,' Rose instructed. She felt herself pulling her shoulders back and standing up straight, taking a deep breath in as the children busied themselves getting ready.

A small girl with a big red bow in her blonde hair ran straight over to Rose and sat down cross-legged on the floor in front of her.

'Are you our new teacher?' she asked, her big wide eyes staring up at Rose in awe.

'Just for today,' Rose answered, with a smile. 'What's your name?'

'Poppy,' the little girl replied, 'and this is my best friend, Tiffany.' She pointed at a girl with red hair and square glasses. 'Did you know, Miss, that Tiffany has just got a puppy?'

'I did not know that, Poppy. How exciting, Tiffany. What's your puppy's name?'

'Buttercup,' the little red-haired girl answered in a whisper that was barely audible.

'What a lovely name.'

Tiffany beamed at her.

Gradually more and more of the class took up their spaces on the carpet and sat cross-legged in front of Rose, looking up at her expectantly. Rose noticed that Cheryl was chatting quietly to a little boy and his mum at the doorway.

He seemed reluctant to come into the classroom, and Rose guessed that this must be Mason, the new boy that Mrs Connolly had mentioned. Cheryl had the situation under control, however, and she managed to persuade Mason into the cloakroom, where he hung up his coat and bag through stifled sobs before joining the rest of the class on the carpet.

'Good morning, Butterfly Class,' Rose said in a bright and cheerful voice. 'My name is Miss Hargreaves and I'm going to be your teacher for the day as Mrs Jackson can't be with us. Mrs Connolly has already told me what a fabulous class you are and I'm really looking forward to spending the day with you. We're going to get the register done first and then we're off to assembly. If you can put your hand up for me when you answer your name that will help me get to know you all.'

Rose went through the class register and all the children obediently put their hands up as instructed when their name was called.

'Well done, Year 2, that was excellent,' Rose said with a beaming smile. 'Now, shall we see if you can all line up sensibly by the door ready for assembly? I think if we're quick we could be the first class into the hall. Now wouldn't that impress Mrs Connolly?'

The children all nodded eagerly, the looks on their faces indicating that impressing Mrs Connolly was at the top of their list of priorities for the day. They promptly lined up at the door with minimal pushing and shoving, clearly hoping to show their new teacher that Butterfly Class could live up to its reputation of being a fabulous class.

'Now, let's see how sensibly and quietly we can walk through the school,' said Rose as she led the line of children through the classroom door and towards the school hall.

Butterfly Class were indeed the first to arrive for assembly and they filed into the hall and sat down cross-legged on the floor in front of Mrs Connolly, who was beaming at them.

'Well done, well done, Butterfly Class,' Mrs Connolly said enthusiastically. 'What a fantastic example you are setting to your new teacher. I'm sure Miss Hargreaves was impressed to see that you could all file into the hall so beautifully, and in complete silence too. What an excellent impression of our school you must be making on our visitor.'

The children all turned to look at Rose expectantly and she smiled back at them. Mrs Connolly gave Rose a nod and a wave, indicating that she was free to return to her classroom to spend some time familiarizing herself with the lesson plans for the day, while the children were occupied with assembly.

Back in the classroom, Rose could see that Cheryl was already busy setting out the resources for the literacy lesson, which was due to start as soon as the children were back. Rose skimmed over the lesson plan and could see that she'd be teaching a session on fairy tales, which was something she'd done dozens of times before.

'All set?' Cheryl asked Rose.

'I think so. I love the fairy tale unit. The kids always enjoy it, so hopefully we should be off to a smooth start.'

'It looks to me like you've already made a great first impression.'

'I hope so. Year 2 can be a tough crowd,' Rose said, reaching for her water bottle to quench her dry mouth. 'Was that Mason I could see coming in last this morning? He looked upset?'

'Ah yes. Did Mrs Connolly tell you about him?'

'Only that he was new and having some issues settling in,' Rose said, nodding.

'It's a bit of a sad story to be honest. His mum has just moved back to the village to be near family again. His dad recently passed away, so he's had a lot of change to deal with. But he's gradually making progress.'

'Wow, that is a lot for a seven-year-old to process. Poor Mason.'

'My heart really goes out to him, poor lad.'

Rose could hear the murmur of voices winding their way down the corridor towards the classroom.

'Uh oh, looks like assembly's out.' Rose got up from her chair ready to greet the class as they came back in. 'Right, Year 2, can you come and sit down on the carpet for me as quickly and quietly as you can? That's it. Well done, Poppy. Well done, Tiffany and Mason. Today we're going to be finding out all about fairy tales. Can anyone tell me the names of any fairy tales they already know?' Rose asked.

An array of hands shot up into the air. Billy Jenkins quickly shouted out, 'Hansel and Gretel.'

'Hand up please, Billy. We don't shout out answers in Year 2, do we?' Rose took another swig of water from the bottle on her table. *Why was her mouth suddenly so dry?*

Billy shook his head in agreement and shot his hand up into the air, straining until it looked as though his chest would burst.

'Yes, Billy.'

'Hansel and Gretel.'

'Excellent choice,' said Rose, 'and well done for putting your hand up that time.' He beamed up at Rose. Cheryl gave Rose a quick thumbs-up from the back of the classroom.

Before Rose knew it, the rest of the morning had whizzed by and it was time to get the children ready for lunchtime. Her literacy and numeracy lessons had gone by without a hitch and she'd thoroughly enjoyed being back in the role of teacher again. As the children filtered out into the play-ground, Rose sat back down in her chair and breathed a sigh of relief. Cheryl laughed.

'Well done this morning, you did a great job. The children loved every minute of that literacy lesson. Why don't you go and grab yourself some lunch, I'll tidy up here and then are you off to see Mrs Connolly?'

'Lunch!' Rose said with a gasp. 'I've completely forgotten to bring anything!'

'Don't worry,' Cheryl said with a smile, 'go and see Hilary in the canteen and she'll sort you out. Mrs Connolly always offers supply teachers a hot lunch. I think you'll find it's jacket potatoes today.'

'Perfect,' said Rose, 'that bowl of soggy cereal I had this morning feels like hours ago.'

With her stomach full of a lunch consisting of jacket

potato, cheese and baked beans, followed by a bowl of fruit salad, Rose made her way to Mrs Connolly's office and knocked loudly on the headteacher's door.

'Come in,' Mrs Connolly called.

As Rose let herself in, she was greeted by a rather chunky chocolate Labrador, who she guessed must be Bertie. He was wearing a maroon jacket and gave Rose an obligatory sniff before returning to his bed in the corner of the office.

'This must be Bertie?' Rose said with a smile. 'He's a rather handsome chap.'

'Isn't he?' said Mrs Connolly, beaming. 'He's getting on a bit now though. He'll be twelve this August,' she said with a sigh. 'How's your morning with us been, Rose?'

'Really good so far,' Rose said with a smile. 'You were right, they're a lovely class. I've only been out of my last job for a fortnight, but I was already missing being in the classroom, so it's been great.'

'What made you leave your last post if you don't mind me asking?'

'I was on a temporary contract,' Rose explained, swinging her necklace from side to side and feeling that familiar dry sensation return to her mouth. 'It was never meant to be a long-term role. I suppose it's worked out well as, what with Aunt Jean's fall, it's meant I've got no ties back in London so I can take my time while she recuperates and be around for her.'

'Ah I see. Sometimes things are just meant to work themselves out, aren't they? I've always been a big believer in fate,'

Mrs Connolly said. 'Speaking of fate, I've had a bit of news about Mrs Jackson ... She's been admitted to hospital with suspected appendicitis, so she could be out of action for a few weeks.'

'Oh no! I hope she's okay.'

'I was wondering if you'd be willing to help us out in the longer term? Cheryl said you've been doing a sterling job today and I was hoping you'd consider teaching here Monday to Wednesday for ... say ... the next six weeks? Until Mrs Jackson is fully recovered?'

'Wow, I don't know what to say,' Rose said, her face flushing red. 'That's an incredible offer, but I'm not sure how much longer I'll be in the village. It all depends on what's happening with my aunt, and then I've got Scout to think of.'

'I've checked with Jane, and she said Scout's been an absolute pleasure this morning and she's happy to have her Mondays to Wednesdays, so hopefully that gives you one less thing to worry about?'

Rose took a deep breath in, a mountain of possibilities whirring through her head. Could she really stay in Blossom Heath for six weeks? What would Ollie say for starters? Rose knew that she'd have to work hard to get him onside with any decision that meant she'd be away from London for an extended period. There was Aunt Jean to think about too. If Rose committed to the school, she wouldn't be able to go and visit every day as she'd originally planned. And then there was the biggest question of all. Did she even *want* to jump straight into another teaching commitment after everything that had happened with Dawson? As much as she hated to admit it, she couldn't quite shake the doubts that Dawson had planted in her mind about her teaching ability. Maybe she just wasn't a good teacher?

Mrs Connolly fixed Rose with a stare.

'I can see you're mulling everything over and I know there's a lot for you to consider logistically speaking. I don't want to put you under any pressure, so how about if you take the rest of the day to think things over and let me know later this evening? Here's my mobile number.' Mrs Connolly passed Rose a Post-it note with her contact details.

'We'd be very lucky to have you, Rose, and I can't help but think it's fate that you ended up in the village just when we needed you.'

'Thank you. I really do appreciate the offer and I'll definitely think it over. I'll talk to my aunt this evening and make sure she's happy for me to stay on at the cottage, and there's also my fiancé in London to consider.'

'I completely understand. Whatever you decide, could you let me know by 8pm? It's just that, if it's a no, I'll need to contact the supply agencies so they can organize someone for us,' Mrs Connolly said, rising from her chair.

'Of course. I'll let you know as soon as I can.'

The rest of the school day passed by in a whirlwind, and when 3.15pm came around Rose led the children down to meet their parents at the school gates. They were all eager to tell the waiting mums and dads about the day they'd had and introduce them to their new teacher, Miss Hargreaves, which brought a smile to Rose's face.

Rose didn't stay at school for long after the children had all been collected as she was keen to pick up Scout, take her for a quick walk and then pop over to the hospital to check in on her aunt. Rose was pleased to hear that Scout had been a model house guest for Jane and the little dog was thrilled to see Rose when she arrived to collect her.

'You didn't think I'd abandoned you, did you?' she asked Scout as she took her for a quick walk around the village. 'How do you feel about spending another day with Jane tomorrow?' She bent down to give her a tickle behind the ears. Scout looked up at Rose with her head tilted to one side and gave out a short sharp woof. 'I swear you can understand every word I say,' Rose said, laughing. 'I'll take that as a yes, then, shall I?'

After dropping Scout back at the cottage, Rose set off for the hospital. She couldn't wait to tell her aunt all about her day spent teaching at the local primary school. It certainly wasn't what she was expecting when she woke up this morning, that was for sure, but it felt good to get back into the classroom. Blossom Heath Primary seemed like such a lovely place to work, and Mrs Connolly was worlds apart from the awful Mr Dawson. Even though her confidence had taken a knock after what he'd said, she'd had such a good time teaching Butterfly Class. If she did decide to accept Mrs Connolly's offer, she'd only be committing herself to teaching at the school for six weeks. It wasn't like it was going to be forever … Before she got ahead of herself, she resolved to talk everything through with her aunt when she went in to visit. Aunt Jean always had a knack of making everything seem much clearer.

Her aunt beamed when she spotted Rose walking into the ward at the hospital.

'Rose, it's lovely to see you,' Aunt Jean said with a smile. 'Come and give your old aunt a hug, would you?' She reached out her arms. 'You look like you've had a good day, my dear. That's a very contented look on your face,' she said. Rose's aunt had always been able to read her mood, just from a quick glance, ever since Rose had been a young child.

'Am I that transparent?' Rose said, laughing. 'I've had a lovely day, so you're in luck.'

'Well, sit down and tell me all about it.'

Rose went on to tell her all about the day she'd had, starting with the unexpected house call from Mrs Connolly first thing this morning, right up until the offer the headteacher had made her to stay on at the school for longer.

'It sounds like you've had quite the adventure,' Jean chuckled, 'and now you've got a decision to make. I've always liked Eileen Connolly. There's nothing she wouldn't do for those kids and that school. What's holding you back from saying yes?'

'Well, there's you for a start. I wasn't sure how you'd feel about me not coming in to visit every day, and whether I could even stay on at the cottage for longer? We don't know when you're being discharged, and I don't want to outstay my welcome.'

'I'm not a complete invalid, Rose! I don't need you checking up on me daily. I'm happy keeping myself entertained on the ward. I've got Agatha for company now and she's an absolute hoot,' Jean said, waving across at the white-haired lady in the bed opposite. 'As far as I'm concerned, you can stay at the cottage for as long as you like, and whether that's weeks or months – well, that's up to you, dear.'

'Thanks, Auntie, that means a lot,' Rose said, reaching out to give her aunt's hand a squeeze. 'There's also Ollie to consider. I don't think he'll be happy to find out that I'm not going back to London for the foreseeable, especially as he doesn't think that teaching is even the right career choice for me, what with us trying to save up for a house . . .'

'Now you listen here, Rose. You do what makes you happy, not what you think *should* make you happy. If that's staying in the village for longer and teaching at the school, then fine. If it's going back to London, that's fine too. All I'll say is you're a natural with the kids and you light up when you talk about your work.'

Rose swallowed hard, blinking back tears. She didn't think her aunt had ever been as honest with her as she had just now. What did she really and truly want to do? She knew in her heart that it was to take up Mrs Connolly's offer of covering at the school and staying in Blossom Heath for as long as she was needed. She knew that Ollie wasn't going to be happy about her decision but, right now at least, she realized she didn't care.

When Rose returned to Jasmine Cottage, the first thing she did was send a text message to Mrs Connolly.

*I'd like to accept your offer of employment at Blossom Heath Primary School for the next six weeks. Many thanks, Rose Hargreaves.*

Within seconds, Rose's phone buzzed to alert her to Mrs Connolly's reply.

*Fantastic news, Rose. I'll see you bright and early tomorrow morning.*

All that was left for Rose to do now was explain her decision to Ollie. She automatically glanced down at the solitaire diamond ring on her engagement finger and began twirling it around absent-mindedly, a habit she had developed whenever she felt nervous.

She remembered the night Ollie had given her this ring; it was the most beautiful thing she had ever seen. They had been on holiday in the Maldives when he proposed. He'd gone to the trouble of having the ring hidden underwater inside a shell, which he had miraculously 'found' and presented her with while they were scuba diving. It had been such a grand romantic gesture. She'd jumped at the chance to say yes to him; there wasn't a doubt in her mind that she wanted them to spend the rest of their lives together. There had been so much certainty and passion in their relationship in those days. Why did things feel so different now? What was it about being in Blossom Heath that just felt so right? She couldn't explain it. She'd always thought that she was clear about what she wanted in life; she had a plan. A future with Ollie, a house with a mortgage and a family of their own one day. What had changed? As she picked up the phone to call her fiancé, something told her that his reaction to her latest piece of news was likely to be *very* different to Mrs Connolly's.

# Chapter 9

Rose was woken by her alarm at 7am the next morning. She hadn't been able to get hold of Ollie on the phone last night and, as much as she hated to admit it, she was feeling more than a little relieved about that. She had a left him a voicemail to say that everything was going well in Blossom Heath and that she would try calling him again this evening. Rose hadn't mentioned anything about her temporary new job at the school, or about Scout. These were not topics that she wanted to cover for the first time in an answerphone message. She needed to speak to Ollie himself, so she could explain things to him properly and gauge his reaction.

Pushing all thoughts of Ollie out of her mind, Rose got herself ready for the working day ahead. When she switched on her phone, she had a voicemail message from her dad.

'Hi, darling, I know it's the middle of the night there but I wanted to check in and see how things are with Jean. Can you message me in the morning with an update? I've been looking at flights and there are plenty of options for me to get back if you need me. I don't want you feeling like you have to deal with this alone. Love you.'

Hearing from her dad always brought a smile to Rose's face, but there was no way she was going to let him cut his holiday short. She quickly typed out a reply:

*Everything's fine here. Jean is healing well and should be home in a few weeks. I've got everything under control. Just make sure you enjoy your holiday and stop worrying!! I'll call you soon. Love you xx*

Rose finished getting ready and dropped Scout off with Jane as arranged. Jane was also looking after a Westie called Hamish for the day, much to Scout's delight, and she had gone running off to play with her new best friend in Jane's garden without so much as a backwards glance.

Rose arrived at school by 8am so she would have plenty of time to go over the lesson plans for the day before the children arrived. When she got to her classroom, Mrs Connolly was just leaving.

'Oh, Rose, good morning, I've just printed out the lesson plans for today and left them on your desk. I'm so pleased you've agreed to stay on. I can't tell you what a weight off my mind that is. It's so much better for the class if we can have some consistency rather than different supply teachers coming and going.'

'I'm happy to help,' Rose said, grinning. 'They really are a lovely class.'

'I'm glad you think so. The plans for today should be self-explanatory, but if you've got any questions just shout. I'll introduce you to Heather Phillips tomorrow. She teaches Year 2 on Thursdays and Fridays and always comes in on Wednesday afternoons to do a handover.'

'Okay, great,' Rose said eagerly. 'It would be a real help to go through the plans for next week with her.'

'Exactly,' said Mrs Connolly. 'I can release you from class for an hour on Wednesday afternoon so you can spend some time with her.'

'That sounds great,' said Rose.

'Right, I'll leave you to it. And if you need anything else, just drop by my office.'

Rose spent another enjoyable day at Blossom Heath Primary. She had learnt practically all the children's names now and they had been overjoyed when she had told them that she was going to be teaching them until Mrs Jackson recovered. Rose sent them all home at the end of the day with a letter from Mrs Connolly in their book bags, informing parents of the temporary arrangements. By the time Rose had tidied the classroom and got everything set up in preparation for the following morning, it was time for her to rush off and collect Scout in readiness for her final vet appointment.

When Rose arrived at Brook House vets with Scout trotting at her side, the spring light was already beginning to fade. She was greeted at reception by a smiling, blonde receptionist.

'Hello there. You must be Scout?' she said, leaning over her desk to give Scout a stroke. 'I'm Tara. I've heard all about this little one. Well done you for saving her,' she said to Rose.

'Anyone would have done the same.'

'I don't know about that, but I'm betting Scout was pretty

pleased you did. Aren't you pleased that Rose stopped to help you, Scout?'

To Rose's surprise, Scout gave a succession of short, high-pitched barks.

'See, I told you,' Tara said triumphantly. 'Scout clearly agrees with me.'

At the sound of the barking, Grace poked her head out from behind the consulting room door.

'Ah, I'd know that bark anywhere. Do you want to bring her straight through?'

Rose took Scout through to the consulting room and lifted her up onto the examination table.

'Wow, she's certainly heavier than she looks,' Rose said, chuckling.

'That's a good thing, compared to how skinny she was a week ago. You needed a bit of fattening up, didn't you, Scout?' Grace said, stroking her on the top of the head. 'How's she been doing?'

'Good, as far as I can tell. I'm no vet of course, but the wound looks like it's healed and she seems to be walking fine on it.'

'Let's take a look,' Grace said, taking Scout's paw so she could get a closer look at the injury. 'That's healed up perfectly. Good job, Scout. I reckon those pesky stitches can come out tonight. Can you just hold her head?'

Gently and carefully, Grace removed the stitches from Scout's leg and the Border Collie remained perfectly still and calm while she worked.

'What a model patient,' Grace said. 'I think that deserves a treat, don't you?' She lifted Scout down from the examination table and took the lid off the jar of dog treats that she kept in the consulting room. As soon as Grace produced a treat, Scout automatically went into a perfect 'Sit'.

'Someone's been training you well. I'm impressed,' Grace said.

'I can't take the credit,' Rose said, chuckling. 'She could do that from day one. Someone has clearly taken the time to do some training with her.'

'Seems like it,' Grace said, frowning. 'What a mystery you are, Scout. Now, do you think you can do that for me again, but this time on the scales?'

Grace led Scout towards the set of scales located on the back wall of the consulting room and once again Scout sat down perfectly.

'10.5kg. That's great, Rose. She's put on nearly a kilo in ten days. Just goes to show that any weight loss was due to a lack of food and not an underlying medical issue.'

'That's reassuring,' Rose said, giving Scout a tickle behind the ears. 'How're things going on the rehoming front? Has anyone expressed an interest in her?' she asked hesitantly.

'Nothing yet, I'm afraid. We've got her details on the practice website and the dog warden knows that she's up for rehoming, so she'll pass any enquiries at the kennels on to us.'

'I'm happy to have her for as long as it takes,' Rose said, perhaps a bit too quickly.

'And you're sure there's no chance that she might

have worked her magic on you and found her forever home already?'

Rose felt a pang in her chest.

'I've got to go back to London at some point and I don't think it would be fair on her being cooped up in a flat all day. It's no life for a Border Collie. I wouldn't be the right match for her long term,' she said with a sigh.

'The word on the street is that you've got a job at Blossom Heath Primary if I'm not mistaken?' Grace said, raising her eyebrows.

'Let me guess ... Maggie.'

'The one and only.'

'Honestly, is *nothing* a secret in this village?' Rose laughed.

'Not for longer than thirty seconds. I've learnt to embrace that now as part of village life. Secrets are definitely for city dwellers,' Grace said while opening the consulting room door. 'You're all done for now, Scout. We don't need to see you again. Unless there's anything you're concerned about, Rose?'

'No, I think we're good. Thanks, Grace.'

As Rose made her way back into the main waiting room, she spotted Jake with Finn and Tagg. Scout made a dash to greet the two dogs, pulling Rose across the waiting room in the process.

'Scout, honestly, I am still *attached* to the end of the lead!' she said, slightly out of breath with the exertion.

Finn and Tagg leapt up from underneath Jake's chair to greet Scout and, before Rose knew it, Scout's lead was in a tangled mess, along with Finn and Tagg's. As she reached down to untangle the leads, her hand touched Jake's for the briefest of moments and her stomach flipped.

'Sorry,' she said, 'we seem to be in a bit of a tangle.'

'Not to worry,' he laughed. 'How's she doing?'

'All good, she's just had her stitches out and Grace has given her a clean bill of health.' Rose reached down and tickled Scout under the chin. 'How are your two? I hope nothing's wrong?'

'Oh, they're fine. We're just in for their booster vaccinations, so just routine stuff,' he said with a shrug. 'Hey, I heard you're teaching at the primary school. Is that right?'

'Wow, that news really has spread around the village in record time,' Rose laughed. 'I am, but just for a few weeks while the regular teacher's out of action. I'm only there Monday to Wednesday, but it does mean I haven't started on any of the jobs I was planning to get done at the cottage yet.'

'I've got some spare time on Thursday. I'd be happy to give you a hand if you like? If you need a bit of extra muscle power, that is ...' he flexed his arms and smiled. 'I could bring the dogs and we could walk them when we've finished?'

'Oh God, I wasn't hinting, honestly,' Rose said, her face flushing hot.

'It's fine,' said Jake, 'I know you weren't. I offered the other day and I meant it. Jean's done enough for me since I've been in the village – I'd like to return the favour.'

'That would be great, but only if you're sure?'

'I'm sure,' he nodded. 'I'll be over around two, if that works?'

'Two would be perfect,' Rose said, clearing her throat. 'Right, I'd better get this one home. Good luck with your appointment,' she said, waving as she left.

When Rose got back to Jasmine Cottage, she knew she'd have to face up to things and give Ollie another call. She couldn't put it off any longer. There had been so many changes in her life already this week and she hadn't kept him in the loop about any of them.

'Oh, Scout, are you sure you don't want to ring Ollie for me and get me off the hook?' she asked with a sigh. Steeling herself, Rose sat down at the kitchen table and looked at her mobile phone. 'Here goes nothing ...'

Ollie answered on the first ring. Rose's mouth went dry.

'Hi, darling. I'm sorry I missed you last night. I had that finance dinner with Marcus and Hugo and I couldn't duck out,' Ollie explained. 'How's things? When are you getting back to London?'

Rose took a deep breath to steady herself before answering.

'Well, it's been a bit of a whirlwind here. Quite a lot's happened in the last few days—'

'Such as?'

'I've got some good news actually. I'm doing some supply work at the local primary school. One of the teachers has appendicitis and the head asked me to help out. It's a lovely school and it's only a short-term thing for the next six weeks,' she added quickly. 'Seeing as I could do with the cash, I thought I'd give it a go ...' There was silence at the end of the phone. 'Ollie, did you hear? I said I'm going to give it a go, so it looks as though I'm going to be in Blossom Heath for slightly longer than planned.'

The stony silence continued for what seemed like an age before Ollie finally broke it. 'I thought we'd agreed you were *done* with teaching,' he said, exhaling. 'We've already discussed this. That's why I've taken so much time and trouble to set you up with that interview at my firm. You know we've been saving up for the deposit on a house and that's never going to happen on a teaching salary.'

'You mean *you* decided, Ollie. I've never once said I was done with teaching for good. This is a *really* good opportunity; it would have been foolish to turn it down.'

'Well, I suppose the extra cash will come in handy,' Ollie continued coolly.

Rose forced herself to keep breathing,

'Listen, I really need you to support me on this. I know you don't think teaching is a good career choice, and that I should do something that earns more money, but it's *my* decision. I don't want to give up on a career that I love and I think working here will help me get my confidence back so that I can find a new school when I'm back in London,' she explained calmly.

'If it's that important to you, I can see I'm wasting my breath trying to talk you out of it. But please don't write off the job at my firm. At least agree to go for the interview when you're back and then you can make a final decision?' Ollie's voice softened as he added, 'I'm just looking forward to after we're married, Rose. We'll need a big house with a garden.'

Rose hesitated; she really didn't want to go for an interview for a job she had no intention of ever taking, but Ollie had made concessions, so perhaps she ought to?

'Okay fine, but I'm not promising I'll take the job. I need to make sure we're clear on that.'

'All I'm saying is just hear them out, see what they've got to offer. Don't dismiss the job before you've heard about all the benefits. I just want you to be *happy,* Rose, and I'm not sure that teaching is the answer. You work far too hard for what they pay you, Rose, you really do.'

'Okay, I'll hear them out, as long as you understand that agreeing to an interview doesn't mean I'll definitely take the job,' she repeated with a steely tone to her voice.

At that precise moment, Scout decided to let out a loud bark to alert Rose to the fact that she wanted to go out into the back garden.

'What was that?' Ollie asked. 'It sounded like a *dog*. Have you got a dog there, Rose?'

'Oh, erm, yes. Well, I mean ... sort of. I was going to explain that to you next ...' Rose faltered.

'Sounds like you better explain now. What else haven't you been telling me?'

'It was all a bit of an adventure actually. Last weekend I found an injured dog and she turned out to be a stray. I'm fostering her until the local vet can find her a new home.'

'This happened *last weekend* and you're only mentioning it to me now? Rose, you *promised* you'd keep me in the loop on things!' He let out a long, deep sigh. 'Is "fostering" a dog even really a thing? Aren't foster homes meant for children? Not animals?'

'Yes, foster homes for animals are a thing,' Rose replied flatly. 'I couldn't send her off to boarding kennels after what she'd been through. She's a gorgeous girl. Her name's Scout and she's a Border Collie,' she said, smiling down at her.

'Well, as long as you understand that she's not coming back to London with you. I mean, a dog in this flat? Can you *imagine*? There would be hair all over the sofa and the carpets are cream for God's sake!'

'Of course I realize she can't come back to London. I'd never leave a dog cooped up in a flat all day while we're out at work. It just wouldn't be fair.'

'At least that's something we agree on. No dogs in London,' Ollie said with a sense of finality that made Rose's heart sink.

'No dogs in London,' Rose echoed and, with that, she said her goodbyes and ended the call. 'Did you hear that, Scout?' Rose bent down to give her a tickle behind the ears. 'No dogs in London.'

Had Ollie always been so concerned with things like pristine carpets and sofas that were free of dog hair? Maybe he had been, but she had never noticed? She shook her head. She couldn't imagine the Ollie from her student days caring if a mud-encrusted St Bernard had rampaged through his student house. Rose felt as though the more successful Ollie had become in his career, the more his focus had shifted to the importance of money and material possessions. The house in Surrey, the obligatory 4x4 and holidays in the Maldives. She didn't care about any of that stuff. Why couldn't he see that? She wanted to be happy in her job, to feel like she was making a difference, to be part of something that mattered – that's what was really important to her. What had happened to the man who had waited for Rose at the school gates with a bottle of champagne to celebrate her first official week as a teacher?

# Chapter 10

Rose couldn't believe how quickly Thursday afternoon had come around. She'd spent the morning running errands and popping over to the hospital to visit her aunt, who, much to Rose's relief, was in good spirits. On the way back to Blossom Heath, Rose stopped at the retail park on the outskirts of town to buy herself some new clothes. The contents of her overnight bag weren't going to last for six weeks, particularly given the fact that she was now teaching three days a week. She'd also stocked up on some essential food supplies at the large out-of-town supermarket, since there was only so much you could get from the local shop.

When Rose returned to the cottage, she was greeted by Scout, who wagged her tail eagerly and did a little dance around Rose's feet as she was packing the shopping away.

'There's nothing in here for you, I'm afraid. This is all very much human food – nothing for nosey doggies,' she said, closing the fridge door. Rose checked her watch. It was nearly 2pm – Jake would be here any minute. She made sure that Scout's water bowl was full so there would be plenty of refreshments to go around for Finn and Tagg, and she opened the back door so the dogs could run straight outside and play. Just then, Rose heard a knock on the front door, which sent Scout into a barking frenzy.

'Alright, alright, it's only Jake,' Rose said to Scout reassuringly as she followed Rose to the front door. 'Hi, Jake,' she said, opening the door and bending down to greet Finn and Tagg, 'and hello to you two,' she said with a smile. 'Come on in.'

'Thanks,' said Jake. 'I'll show these two straight to the garden if that's okay with you. That way the three of them can play without getting under our feet.'

'Sounds like a plan,' Rose agreed as they all walked through to the kitchen. The three dogs shot out of the back door and Scout was eager to engage her two new friends in a game of doggie chase. She play-bowed in front of Tagg and, much to her delight, he began chasing her in circles around the garden.

'Well, they certainly seem to be getting on like a house on fire,' she said with a smile.

'I thought they would,' Jake said. 'It'll be good for Scout to socialise with other dogs – help build her confidence up after everything she's been through.'

'Definitely. I've already noticed her relaxing a lot more in the last few days, so we're moving in the right direction,' Rose said with a smile. 'Can I make you a cuppa?'

'We should probably get some work done first!' Jake laughed. 'Where do you want to get started?'

'Well, I've given the house a really good clean-up this week.

Hoovering, dusting, washing, and I've thrown a lot of things away that were just cluttering up the place. Nothing that's sentimental for Jean, of course,' she quickly added, 'just things like expired medication and old cleaning bits. But there are definitely some DIY tasks that are a bit beyond me, I'm afraid.'

'No problem. I've got my tool kit, so I should have whatever we need to get started.'

'Er, I've actually made a list if that's okay . . . I thought that might help make things easier? And who doesn't *love* ticking things off a list?' she laughed.

'Wow, you certainly are organized!' Jake said, taking the piece of paper from Rose.

'I guess so . . . I think it's the teacher in me,' she laughed. 'I do love a bit of organizing.'

'Alright, as long as I'm not going to be in for a detention at the end of the afternoon, I think we're good to make a start.'

Rose and Jake worked happily alongside each other for the rest of the afternoon. They chatted about Jake's farm, Rose's teaching career, life in Blossom Heath. Rose found the farmer incredibly easy to talk to – there was something about him that just made her feel naturally at ease. His DIY skills around the cottage certainly put Ollie's to shame, and she felt the heat rise in her face at such a disloyal thought. The dogs entertained themselves playing happily in the garden, every so often appearing in the house to check in on Rose and Jake before disappearing back to their games.

The afternoon flew by and, before she knew it, Rose realized it was nearly 5pm. Jake insisted on making them both a cup of tea and Rose opened a packet of chocolate digestives. She watched Jake as he moved around the kitchen and, no matter how hard she tried, she couldn't stop herself from noticing just how attractive he was. They had made good progress on Rose's list of jobs and while they had their tea she sat at the kitchen table crossing off all the completed tasks with great satisfaction. They had fixed a broken shelf in the bedroom, put up a curtain pole in Rose's room, mended most of the kitchen cupboards and drawers that needed attention, installed door stops on all the internal doors, fixed the dripping bathroom tap and reinstated the sign saying 'Jasmine Cottage' outside the front door.

'Wow, would you look at your face, checking off that list. I've never seen anyone look so happy,' Jake teased. 'You weren't joking when you said you love a list, were you?'

'But look at how much we've done! Don't tell me you're not impressed?' Rose laughed, taking another sip of her tea.

'Alright, we've definitely got through more than I thought we would, but there's still a lot of work that needs doing,' Jake said seriously, pulling his chair closer to hers. 'You could do with a new shower for starters – that one up in the bathroom is ancient. Most of the light fittings and switches need updating, and it's probably worth getting someone in to give the boiler a once-over.'

'I'm already on it,' Rose said gleefully. 'See, I've just added all of that to my list while you were talking,' she said, pointing to her notepad.

'Looks like you're one step ahead of me, then,' Jake

chuckled. 'I know a good electrician and plumber who will be able to help you out. They're mates of mine from school and they both know Jean, so it wouldn't surprise me if they gave you a hefty discount. Now, how about we take the dogs out for a walk? I could do with some fresh air.'

'Great,' said Rose, clearing the mugs away from the kitchen table. She gave a little shriek as one of them slipped through her fingers and smashed on the floor. She groaned. 'Honestly, I'm the clumsiest person on the planet!'

Jake threw his head back and laughed. 'Let me clean this up while you go and get ready,' he said, grabbing a kitchen towel from the worktop.

'Are you sure? You've done enough for me today.'

'Then one more job won't make any difference.'

'Thanks, Jake. Just let me go and grab my trainers. Where were you thinking of going?'

'I thought we could all pile into the truck and head up to the farm. There's acres of land up there and I could show you around,' Jake said, as he finished cleaning up the broken cup on the floor.

'Perfect, I'd really like to see the place. I'll go and get ready and leave you to round up the dogs,' she shouted, already halfway up the stairs to get her things.

Soon all three dogs were piled happily into the back of Jake's truck. Scout was definitely one of the pack now. Tagg, in particular, was totally smitten with her. The farm was only a five-minute drive from Jasmine Cottage but it was a road out of the village that Rose wasn't familiar with.

'In all my years of visiting, I don't think I've ever taken this lane out of town. I didn't even know it existed,' she said, her eyes wide as she took in the rolling landscape leading up to the farm.

'Ah, that would be because it doesn't really go anywhere. Well, only up to the farm, and we don't get that many visitors.'

As they drove closer to Harper Farm, the lane began to narrow and Rose felt the bumps as Jake's jeep navigated the sizeable potholes.

'Wow, they're certainly not big on resurfacing the roads around here,' she gasped as the jeep hit one of the larger holes with an almighty thud.

'Nope, it doesn't do much for your suspension but thankfully this jeep is built more like a tank. Aren't you, girl?' He patted the steering wheel affectionately.

As the truck pulled into the farm's main yard, Finn and Tagg began barking in anticipation.

'Sounds like someone knows we're home,' Jake laughed, and Scout joined in with the canine chorus as Jake hopped out of the driver's seat to let the dogs out of the back.

The stone-built farmhouse was gorgeous. It looked warm and inviting and had a trail of pale pink rose bushes forming an archway around the front door. It really was picture-perfect.

Scout explored the yard excitedly, her nose firmly planted to the floor as she began sniffing out all the farmyard smells at breakneck speed, not sure which scent trail to follow first.

'Should I put her on a lead? She's never been off lead with me before and the last thing I want to do is lose her!'

'She'll be fine,' Jake said reassuringly, 'she'll stick to Finn and Tagg like glue. Here, watch this.' Jake pulled a whistle out of his jeans pocket and gave it a short, sharp toot. The response from Finn and Tagg was instantaneous. They both stopped what they were doing, looked straight at Jake and then ran towards him, sitting obediently at his feet. To Rose's astonishment, Scout followed suit and did the same. Jake pulled a handful of treats from his pocket and gave one to each dog.

'What on earth?' she said, her eyes wide. 'How did you get her to do that?'

'I can't take all the credit,' Jake laughed. 'It's all down to these guys,' he said, pointing at Finn and Tagg. 'Scout's following their lead now. She should stick with them pretty closely, so this is the best time to let her off and practise some recall training. Here ... take some of these,' he said, passing a handful of dog treats to Rose. 'Shove them in your pocket for now and we'll use them later to do a bit of training.'

'Right, thanks,' Rose said, sniffing the handful of treats and wrinkling her nose in disgust. 'Eurgh, what are they? They absolutely reek!'

'That would be the finest dried liver that Harrisons has to offer,' Jake said, laughing. 'You'd better get over the smell – there's far worse to come now you're a fully fledged dog owner.'

'Worse than this?' Rose said in horror. 'You've got to be joking?'

'If only I was,' Jake said, his eyes lighting up mischievously. 'You wait until Scout decides to have her first roll in fox poo. That smell will assault your nostrils in a way you never thought possible. Take my word for it – I've had first-hand experience.'

'Oh God,' she groaned, pinching her nostrils together in mock outrage. 'Grace definitely forgot to mention that particular perk of being a dog fosterer,' she laughed. 'I'll be having stern words with her the next time I see her. Let's just hope we get through today's walk without encountering any.'

'Right, well I guess I'm leading the way,' Jake said, straightening up, 'this being my land and all. I've got a circular walk in mind that takes us right around the farm, so you should be able to get a good sense of the place. We might have to pop Scout on a lead when we get near to the Romneys, but other than that she can roam free the whole way round.'

'The Romneys?'

'The sheep. Romney is their breed name. They originated on Romney Marsh, just up the road.'

'Right, well, I've got Scout's lead in my pocket, so just give me the word when I need to put it on,' she said, giving Jake a salute and grinning widely.

'Let's get this show on the road then,' he said with a grin, whistling to call the dogs to follow him, which they obediently did.

Rose took some time during the walk to appreciate the beauty of the Sussex landscape. There was nothing but rolling green hills as far the eye could see and the cool, clear water of Rye Harbour was visible in the distance.

'So, have you lived here all your life?' she asked as they walked side by side, the dogs setting the pace in front of them.

'Pretty much, yeah. Obviously Mum and Dad ran the place when we were younger, but they died just after I graduated from agricultural college, so I've been the one running things since. My sister, Kate, helps out when she can, but she's got two kids of her own so her life's pretty hectic. We've got a good staff here though, so they help me keep things running. Michael's been here since I was a kid and he knows the farm inside out. I really couldn't have kept things going without his experience if I'm honest.'

'Wow, that's tough about your parents. And what a lot of responsibility for you at such a young age,' she said, her brow furrowing. 'Do you mind me asking what happened to them?'

'Car accident,' Jake replied, his voice catching a little.

'Oh, Jake, I'm so sorry.' Rose reached out to touch his arm instinctively. 'That really is tough.'

'Life goes on and all that,' he said, forcing a smile. 'Things are good now, but it definitely took me a while to get everything back on track. Anyway, what about you?' he asked, apparently keen to change the subject. 'What brought you to Blossom Heath, other than your aunt, that is?'

'Well, Jean's my dad's aunt. They've always been really close. Dad grew up in Rye and moved to London when he married Mum, so I've always been a city girl really. Jean bought Jasmine Cottage when I was a kid. We always spent summer holidays down here and I've got great memories of those days. They really were idyllic,' Rose sighed, her green eyes filling with tears. 'We lost Mum to cancer when I was twelve and I think that's why I've always been so close to Aunt Jean. Dad would send me to stay with her every summer while he had to work, and she became like a second mum to me really.'

'Sorry to hear about your mum, Rose. That must have been rough when you were just a kid yourself,' he said, placing a hand on her shoulder.

'Like you said, life goes on. It all seems so long ago now. I think those summers spent in Blossom Heath are why I've always returned as an adult. I love it here, and it's nice to get away from London.'

'I bet. I don't know how people manage to live there. I think I'd go *mad*. All the people for a start. I just couldn't cope with feeling boxed in, without any green spaces,' he said, indicating the landscape around them with sweeping arms.

'It can be tricky. Mind you, I'm usually so busy with work I don't have time to notice my surroundings,' she said flatly.

'Oh, come on, Rose. Don't teachers get six months' holiday a year and finish at three?' he said, his facial expression letting Rose know that he was joking.

'Oi! You are *so* lucky that I know you're joking, Mr Harper,' she said in her sternest teacher voice, punching Jake playfully on the shoulder, 'otherwise you really would be

Julie Haworth

for it.' She was unable to keep her laughter under control any longer.

'You know, I'm surprised we've never run into each other before, what with you spending all your summers up here as a kid.'

'Ah ... I didn't want to say anything ... but I think I might have met your parents ...'

'Seriously? When?'

'Erm ... it's actually a bit of an embarrassing story,' she said, biting her lower lip.

'Now you'll *definitely* have to tell me,' Jake replied.

'Did your parents ever judge the dog show at the village fete?'

'Yes ...'

'Well, I entered one year with Aunt Jean's Border Collie and we made it to the "Best in Show" class ...'

'Oh my god, I *remember* now.' His eyes lit up. 'Were you that girl with the dog who cocked his leg up my dad's trousers?'

Rose hung her head and groaned. 'Please tell me you weren't there to witness that.'

'I had a front-row seat ... it was *hilarious*,' he said, taking short, sharp breaths to break up his laughter.

'Nooo! It was *so* embarrassing. I remember wanting the ground to open up and swallow me. Your dad was lovely, though. He just shrugged it off and told me that's what happens when you work with animals – you never know what they'll do next.'

'He still gave you the "Best in Show" rosette, didn't he?'

'He did. He seemed like a lovely man.'

Jake smiled, nodded and then turned away abruptly as if to change the subject. 'This is the perfect spot to practise a bit of recall training with Scout, if you're up for it?' Jake said, a serious tone returning to his voice. 'Grab those treats I gave you earlier. I'm going to get the dogs to follow me and then I want you to yell "Scout, come" as loud as you can. She should head straight for you.'

'Fingers crossed,' said Rose, glancing over her shoulder.

Jake walked determinedly away from Rose, calling the dogs to follow at his heels. When he got a few hundred yards away from her, he bent down to grab Finn and Tagg's collars and gave Rose a thumbs-up signal.'

'Scout, come!' Rose shouted at the top of her lungs and, to her amazement, Scout turned her attention away from Jake and the other two dogs and began running at lightning speed towards her. She stretched her arms out wide and squatted down to welcome Scout in towards her and, as soon as she was in touching distance, she gave Scout the treat.

'Good girl, well done,' Rose said, patting her on the head and tickling her behind the ears. 'Who knew you were so clever?'

Jake ran towards them both, followed closely by Finn and Tagg.

'See! I told you she was going to be the model student. I wouldn't be surprised if she's had some training before, you know. Either that or she's just an incredibly fast learner.'

'Or maybe I'm just a great teacher?' Rose said, standing up to hug him and then, thinking better of it, awkwardly pulling herself away. 'Grace and I both thought that someone had put some work into training her, which makes it even more strange that she ended up straying. Oh, Scout, if only you could talk and tell us what happened,' she continued, reaching down to give her a pat on her flank.

'I guess we'll never know for sure, but she's certainly doing well with her training, and Border Collies are incredibly fast learners. There's not much that you can't teach them. They're the Albert Einsteins of the dog world.'

'Did you hear that, Scout? Apparently you are one smart cookie,' Rose said, rubbing Scout on the end of her nose, which was already trying to snuffle into Rose's pocket in search of more liver treats.

'We'd best be making a move back towards the truck if I'm going to get you back home before the light starts to fade,' Jake said, checking his watch.

As Rose nodded her head in agreement, she was surprised at the feeling of disappointment she experienced at hearing those words. She *really* didn't want this walk to end.

# Chapter 11

The next day at Blossom Heath Primary had been a frantic one for Rose. A nasty stomach bug was working its way through the school population, which meant that almost half of the teaching and support staff were out sick. Unable to draft in enough supply cover for all the classes, Mrs Connolly had been forced to step into the breach and teach Year 6 for the day. Rose had spent the morning running around trying to arrange lesson plans for the two supply teachers who were covering, as well as getting her own lessons sorted. By the time the bell rang for lunch, she was utterly exhausted. To top things off, she was also scheduled to be on playground duty at lunchtime, as there weren't enough midday assistants to cover.

As soon as she reached the playground, the children in her class swarmed around her.

'Miss Hargreaves, Miss Hargreaves, what are you doing out here?' Poppy asked her eagerly.

'Yeah, you're not a dinner lady,' Tiffany added, reaching out to grab Poppy's hand.

'I know, girls, but we've got loads of people out sick with

that awful stomach bug today so I'm helping out.' Rose took a huge bite of the cheese and ham baguette she'd grabbed from the dining hall on her way. She honestly hadn't realized how hungry she was until she started eating.

'And that's what we do at Blossom Heath, isn't it, Miss?' Poppy replied happily. 'We help each other out.'

'We do indeed, Poppy. We always help each other out, whenever we can,' Rose said with a smile.

'Hey, Miss, what's in your sandwich?' yelled Billy as he made a beeline for her across the playground.

'It's ham and cheese, Billy, and it's delicious,' she laughed, giving her stomach a rub.

'How come you're allowed to eat your lunch out here anyway?' Billy asked, sounding slightly disgruntled. 'We have to wait until the dinner ladies ring the bell for us to go into the hall.'

'Ah well, that is one of the many benefits of being a teacher,' Rose explained with a grin. 'It won't be too long until they're calling you in for lunch, Billy, and I'm sure you can find plenty of things to occupy yourself with until then. Why don't you all go off and play? You don't want to spend your lunchtime chatting to me.'

At those words, Billy ran off and rejoined the game of football that he had been playing on the field with some older boys. Tiffany and Poppy stayed put.

'We don't mind keeping you company, Miss,' Tiffany said with a shy smile. 'I can tell you more about my puppy, Buttercup.'

'Aw, how's she getting on? She's been with you a few weeks now, hasn't she?' Rose asked.

'We've had her for two whole weeks. She plays games with me when I get home from school and she jumps around my ankles all excited,' said Tiffany, hopping up and down on the spot by way of illustration. Rose realized this was the most confidently she had heard Tiffany talk in the last couple of weeks – she was usually such a quiet child in class.

'That sounds lovely, Tiffany. I bet you two have lots of fun together,' Rose said warmly, and Tiffany smiled and nodded.

Just then, Rose noticed a group of children huddled together at the far side of the school playing field. They seemed to be looking at something on the ground, and then she heard one of the Year 6 girls let out a high-pitched scream. She spotted Billy and Mason from her class running across the playground towards her, waving their arms frantically and shouting, 'Miss, Miss!' at the top of their lungs. Their faces looked white and stricken with panic. Rose knew in her gut that this wasn't kids messing around. Something was wrong. Seriously wrong.

Reacting instinctively, Rose dropped her baguette and began running towards Billy and Mason, yelling back to Tiffany and Poppy to find one of the other dinner ladies and send them over. As Rose got closer to the boys, she could hear Mason shouting.

'Miss, Miss, it's Hayden! Something's wrong with him! He can't breathe!'

Rose didn't slow her pace; she kept running full pelt

towards the children gathered at the edge of the playing field and waved her arms to indicate that Billy and Mason should follow her. As she approached, the group quickly moved aside to let her through.

'Hayden, Hayden, it's Miss Hargreaves. Everything's going to be just fine,' she said, dropping to her knees and taking Hayden's hand to reassure him. She looked up at the children gathered around her, who all looked white with shock. Hayden appeared to be completely unconscious. A couple of the girls were crying and hugging each other. 'Does anyone know what's happened to him?' Rose asked the group, looking up at them frantically.

'I don't know, Miss,' one of the Year 6 girls replied, 'one minute he was fine and the next ... he couldn't speak properly and ... he just fell down,' the girl continued, her face streaked with tears.

Rose knew from the information she'd been given about the class that Hayden had a nut allergy, and she was quickly able to identify that he was showing all the symptoms of anaphylaxis. He was clammy to the touch and his breathing was fast and shallow. What worried her most though was that he seemed completely unresponsive. Rose knew that anaphylaxis could become very dangerous very quickly and that she needed to act fast, but at the same time she was sure that Hayden was sensible about his allergies. He'd never knowingly eat something that had nuts in it.

Just at that moment Mrs Simms, one of the dinner ladies on duty, arrived at Rose's side looking red in the face with exertion. Rose sent her straight off to find Mrs Connolly and she asked two of the Year 6 girls, who she knew competed in the county athletics team, to run straight to the school office and ask for someone to bring her an EpiPen for Hayden Mackenzie right away and to call an ambulance. Rose was very aware that every second counted.

'Has he eaten anything?' Rose asked the group of children. They looked back at her with an uncomfortable silence. Rose noticed that one of the Year 6 boys, Seamus, looked straight at the floor. Trying to think through the panic, Rose asked Seamus directly, 'Seamus, has Hayden eaten anything? You're not in any trouble but it's really important that you tell me the *truth*.' She looked Seamus straight in the eyes.

'I gave him some of my chocolate, Miss. But nothing with nuts in it though,' he added quickly. 'Hayden knows he can't have nuts,' Seamus blurted out, tears welling up in the corners of his blue eyes.

'Do you still have the wrapper, Seamus?'

'Yes, Miss.' Seamus fumbled around in his trouser pockets and pulled out the packaging from a chocolate bar. Rose grabbed it quickly and scanned the list of ingredients. Her heart sank when she read the phrase '*May contain traces of nuts.*' There was no doubt about it. Hayden was having an anaphylactic reaction.

'Where is that EpiPen?' Rose groaned. She knew that the quicker she could give Hayden that shot of adrenaline the better.

'Is he going to die, Miss?' Seamus asked in a small, quiet

voice. He looked distraught. Before Rose could answer, a small but determined voice said, 'Of course not. He's going to be fine. Miss knows what she's doing, don't you, Miss?' Rose was shocked to see that it was Mason, the new boy in her class, who had spoken.

Mason knelt down on the floor next to Hayden and took his other hand. 'You're going to be fine, Hayden. Miss Hargreaves is here. I'm here and all your friends are here. We're not going to let anything happen to you.' Was this really the same timid child who was so reluctant to come into class in the mornings? The boy who had recently lost his own father and was having trouble fitting in at his new school?

'That's right, Hayden,' Billy said, nodding at Mason, 'none of us are going to let anything happen to you, are we?' he continued, looking around at the group of assembled children. There were murmurs of agreement from the group and Rose could hear muffled voices saying, 'Mason's right. You've got this, Hayden.'

Rose felt a lump in her throat at this outpouring of strength the children were showing for their friend. They were putting their own fears aside to be there for Hayden, and Rose felt her heart swell with pride.

Seconds felt like hours while Rose waited for any sign of someone bringing her Hayden's EpiPen. Suddenly, she spotted a group of adults running towards her across the playing fields in what seemed like slow motion. From thereon in, everything happened very quickly. Mr Barker, the Year 5 teacher, was first to reach Rose, and he was holding the

EpiPen in his outstretched hand, like a baton in a relay race. Rose grabbed it and acted quickly. Thankfully, she had recently had her EpiPen refresher training at Trinity Grove Primary. But having the training and actually delivering the injection in an emergency situation felt very different. Could she really do it? What if she made a mistake? She was all too aware that she only had one shot at this.

Cheryl had moved the group of onlooking children away from Hayden now and was herding them back towards the main school building. Rose was conscious that Mrs Connolly had now arrived on the scene and she knelt down alongside Rose, laying a steadying hand on her left shoulder.

'Rose, are you happy to deliver the injection?' Mrs Connolly asked seriously, grabbing Rose's arm, her eyes wide with concern.

'It's okay,' Rose replied, forcing herself to keep her breathing slow and steady. 'I'll do it,' she continued in a steely and determined voice.

Mrs Connolly and Mr Barker held Hayden's body steady and, before Rose really had time to think about it, she had taken the EpiPen out of its case, grabbed it in a firm fist-grip, removed the cap, and identified the large muscle in Hayden's thigh where she would deliver the life-saving shot. With a deep breath she repeated the words from her EpiPen training: 'Press, click and hold. Press, click and hold.' Rose pressed the orange part of the EpiPen firmly against Hayden's thigh muscle until she heard the 'click' and then held the pen in place for another ten seconds.

Releasing the pen, Rose looked anxiously at Mrs Connolly and Mr Barker. All three teachers held their breath and stared down at Hayden hoping to see some sign of recovery. *Maybe it wasn't anaphylaxis after all?*

'Hayden, come on ... Hayden, can you hear me?' Rose whispered in his ear. She could feel her breath sticking in her throat as she waited for a response. 'Hayden, Hayden, it's Miss Hargreaves.' With every fibre of her being, Rose willed there to be some sign that Hayden was responding. Within a few seconds he began to murmur and stir. He was regaining consciousness.

Mr Barker reached over and patted Rose on the back. Mrs Connolly gasped and clapped her hands to her mouth. As Rose sank bank onto the grass, she could see the glistening of tears forming at the corner of the headteacher's eyes.

'Oh, well done, Rose, well done,' Mrs Connolly whispered, barely able to speak.

To Rose's relief she could hear the sound of a siren getting closer and closer, until it sounded as though it was right upon them. In the distance she spotted the school's caretaker, Mr Jarvis, opening up the emergency access gates to the school field to let the ambulance through. Hayden was starting to come around and Mrs Connolly was busy talking to him and reassuring him that everything was going to be fine. Within seconds, the paramedics were with them and Rose was able to explain exactly what she thought had happened as she handed them the EpiPen to let them know what she had administered. The paramedics had Hayden sitting up quickly after giving him a thorough check-over.

'Well, it looks like your teacher has done our job for us already, Hayden,' the male paramedic joked. 'Did you know that she was also a trained superhero in disguise?' he continued, and Hayden mustered a weak laugh. 'Seriously, though,' he said to Rose, pulling her to one side, 'great call with the EpiPen. Acting fast can be the difference between life and death. Well done.'

'Thanks,' Rose said, her hands still shaking. 'I'm just glad it worked and he's doing okay.'

'Right, young man, let's get you loaded up into the ambulance and we'll get you checked over at the hospital, just to be safe,' the paramedic continued. 'Is Mrs Connolly coming along with us?' he asked the headteacher.

'Of course,' Mrs Connolly replied, but Hayden interrupted her.

'Please can Miss Hargreaves come with me instead?' he said quietly. Rose felt her cheeks burn.

'Of course, Hayden. Whatever the patient wants is fine with me,' Mrs Connolly replied, patting Hayden gently on the arm.

'But what about my class this afternoon?' Rose asked.

'Don't you worry about that,' Mrs Connolly replied. 'We'll all pitch in and sort something out. These are exceptional circumstances after all.'

'I think your teacher might need a cup of strong sweet tea when we get to the hospital, don't you, Hayden? She's looking a bit peaky to me,' the paramedic joked.

'I don't think Hayden's the only one who's had a shot of

adrenaline this afternoon,' Mr Barker said with a smile. 'I think we're all feeling the effects.'

As the paramedic crew loaded Hayden into the back of the ambulance, promising him that they'd have the blue lights going all the way to the hospital, Rose climbed in to follow. Just as they were about to close the doors, Cheryl ran over to catch them. She gave Rose her handbag and told her that Hayden's mum would meet them at the hospital.

'Don't worry, Hayden,' Cheryl said. 'I bet your mum will beat the ambulance to the hospital and be there waiting for you. You've only got to put up with Miss Hargreaves for company for a bit longer,' she said with a cheeky wink, which made Hayden laugh. As the ambulance doors closed and they drove away from the school grounds, Rose slumped in her seat with a deep sigh. She had never felt so relieved in her whole life.

# Chapter 12

By the time the ambulance arrived at the hospital, Cheryl had been proved right and Hayden's mum was already waiting in the ambulance bay to greet them.

'Hayden!' she called, running towards the open doors of the ambulance and kissing her son on the top of the head as the paramedics lifted Hayden's stretcher out.

'Mum!' Hayden cried in relief. 'Mum, it's okay, I'm alright. Miss Hargreaves looked after me. I feel fine now. Honest,' he said with a grin.

'I can't thank you enough, Miss Hargreaves,' Hayden's mum said between sobs. 'I always tell Hayden to be so careful about his allergies. I can't imagine how this has happened. If you hadn't acted so quickly ... well, I just dread to think what could have happened.'

'Let's not think about that for now. Hayden's doing fine and that's the main thing,' Rose replied with a smile.

'We'll get this little lad checked in at reception, and then we'll be on our way,' the female paramedic said cheerfully. 'You were a very brave boy today, Hayden, and I wouldn't be surprised if your mum finds you a treat in the gift shop later,' she said with a wink.

'As long as it's not a chocolate bar,' said Rose.

'I think we might be safe with a cuddly toy,' Hayden's mum said, ruffling her son's hair affectionately.

'A cuddly toy sounds perfect,' Rose agreed, smiling at Hayden. 'I tell you what, why don't I go and check out the gift shop and you and your mum can go with the ambulance crew? If I'm not mistaken, they might even have some Lego. That should keep you out of mischief while you're waiting for the doctor.'

'That would be great. Thanks so much, Miss Hargreaves,' Hayden's mum said, reaching for her purse. Rose stretched her hand out to stop her.

'This is my treat,' Rose insisted. 'You just worry about Hayden and I'll sort out the gift shop. Oh, and call me Rose. I think we've been through enough today to be on first-name terms,' she laughed.

'I agree,' Mrs Mackenzie said with a smile. 'Call me Zoe.'

Rose spent some time scanning the aisles of the gift shop and ended up with a cuddly dinosaur for Hayden, as well as a set of Lego blocks and some comics to take back to A&E. As she passed the snack section, Rose realized that she was starving. It seemed like forever since she'd thrown her baguette down in the middle of the school playground. She snuck a large Wispa and some bottles of water into her basket and then, after paying, realizing that she couldn't return to see Hayden with a bar of chocolate in her hand, scoffed down the Wispa in two swift gulps, wiping her mouth guiltily as she walked up to the reception desk at A&E.

'How can I help?' the young blonde woman at the desk asked eagerly.

'I just came in the ambulance with Hayden Mackenzie. I'm his teacher, Miss Hargreaves. Do you know where they've taken him?'

'Oh yes. One moment, just let me double check,' the receptionist said as she tapped furiously at her keyboard. 'Hayden Mackenzie. He's been moved to cubicle 8, so if you go through the double doors, it's the fourth on the left.'

'Thanks,' Rose said as she set off to find Hayden and his mum.

'Hayden? Are you in here?' she asked gingerly as she reached what she thought was the right cubicle, before tentatively pulling the curtain back around the bed.

'Yes, Miss,' a voice called back, and Rose saw that she was definitely in the right place. Hayden's face lit up when he saw the dinosaur tucked under her arm and Rose emptied the contents of the gift shop carrier bag onto his bed.

'I got you some Lego and comics and there's some water for all of us,' Rose said, pointing to the contents of the bag.

'Thanks, Miss, these look great,' Hayden said, making a grab for the box of Lego and tearing it open.

'Thanks, Rose,' Zoe said as she opened one of the bottles of water and took a swig. 'And thanks for everything you've done today. It's good to know Hayden's got such a fabulous teacher, even though you've only been at the school for a few weeks.'

'Well, they're a great bunch of kids, so I can't take all the credit,' Rose said with a nod in Hayden's direction. 'Would you like me to stay with you until the doctor arrives and Hayden's had the all-clear?'

'Oh no, you get off home,' Zoe insisted. 'I've already called Hayden's dad and he's just parking up the car, so he'll be with us any minute. You've honestly done more than enough to help today.'

'Well, as long as you're sure. My aunt's actually up on Nightingale Ward, so I think I'll pop up and visit her and then head home,' Rose replied, taking a swig of her bottled water.

'Oh of course. You're Jean Hargreaves' niece, aren't you?' Rose nodded. 'I was so sorry to hear about her accident. How's she doing?'

'She's on the road to recovery, thanks,' Rose replied as she screwed the top onto her water bottle. 'Now, Hayden, don't give your mum any more scares today and hopefully I'll see you back in class tomorrow, all being well.'

Hayden looked up from his Lego just long enough to say, 'Yes, Miss, I'll see you tomorrow,' before turning his attention back to his construction.

'Erm, Hayden, what else do you have to say to Miss Hargreaves before she leaves?' Zoe asked pointedly, rolling her eyes.

'Thanks for saving my life today, Miss,' Hayden said in a matter-of-fact tone.

'You're very welcome, Hayden,' Rose said, smiling at him.

*

Rose spotted Aunt Jean at the far end of Nightingale Ward and gave her a wave.

'Rose!' Aunt Jean exclaimed, beaming. 'What on earth are you doing here in the middle of the day? Shouldn't you be at school?'

'Well, I have a very good excuse. I've just been in A&E with one of my pupils who has a nut allergy.' Rose sank into the chair next to her aunt's bedside and recounted the dramatic events of the afternoon. Aunt Jean gasped theatrically in all the right places.

'Well, thank goodness the poor boy is alright,' Aunt Jean said with relief. 'Honestly, Rose, what a quick thinker you are. If you hadn't pieced it all together and given him that shot so quickly, who knows what could have happened? It honestly doesn't bear thinking about,' she said with a shudder.

Just at that moment, Rose became aware of her phone vibrating in her handbag.

'Sorry, Auntie, do you mind if I just grab this?' Aunt Jean nodded.

Rose could see from the caller ID that it was Jake.

'Hi, Jake, is everything okay?' Rose asked, wondering why he'd be calling her in the middle of the school day.

'That's funny, I was just about to ask you the same question,' he said, the concern clear in his voice. 'I heard about what happened at school with Hayden and I wanted to see how you were holding up.'

'Wow, I know I shouldn't be surprised anymore, but word

137

really does travel fast in Blossom Heath, doesn't it?' Rose replied, rolling her eyes.

'Are you kidding? Word of your heroism has already spread around *Sussex*. I wouldn't be surprised if they knew about your exploits in Kent by now.'

'I don't know how I could expect anything less,' Rose said, throwing her head back with a laugh. 'Well, you can tell the rest of the village that Hayden's fine, his mum and dad are with him and hopefully he should be back in school tomorrow.'

'And how are you?' Jake asked, his voice becoming serious.

'I'm good. It's just such a relief to know that Hayden's okay,' Rose said with genuine gratitude. She knew the situation could have ended very differently. 'I'm just visiting my aunt and then I'll grab a cab and head home.'

'Don't worry about a cab. I'll come and pick you up. Tell me what time you want me there and I'll hop in the truck.'

'Honestly, Jake, you don't have to do that. I don't mind getting a taxi. There's a rank right outside the hospital.'

At that moment Aunt Jean lurched across the bed and grabbed the phone right out of Rose's hand. Before she knew what had happened, her aunt was talking to Jake.

'Jake, it's Jean here,' her aunt said in a steely voice. 'Oh I'm fine, love, thanks for asking. How are the dogs? Good, good. Listen, thank you for offering Rose a ride home. She'll meet you in fifteen minutes in the pick-up bay by the main entrance. Perfect. Thanks, love.' With that, Aunt Jean ended the call and handed the phone back to Rose. 'Oh, don't look at me like that, Rose. If a handsome young man offers you a lift, you take it. End of story.' Aunt Jean crossed her arms defiantly.

'But—'

'No buts! Jake's a lovely young man, and for what it's worth I think you'd make the perfect couple.'

'In case you've forgotten, Auntie, I'm engaged to Ollie!' Rose laughed, shaking her head in exasperation.

'Oh, engaged isn't married. And there's no harm in exploring your options, is there? Anyway, I saw the sparkle in your eyes when you were talking to Jake on the phone.' Rose raised her hands as if to protest, but her aunt continued, 'A nice country boy is just what you need. Not one of those big city types.'

'Honestly, Auntie, you are incorrigible,' Rose said, trying, and failing, to hide a smile.

'Don't argue with your elders,' Aunt Jean said with a smirk. 'Now get yourself down to the main entrance. And it wouldn't hurt you to run a brush through your hair before Jake picks you up either,' she said with a devilish glint in her eye.

'Honestly, Auntie, I just can't win, can I?'

'I'm glad you realize that, dear,' Aunt Jean replied with a smile. Rose bent down to kiss her aunt on the cheek, said her goodbyes and got into the elevator to take her down to the hospital's ground floor. Whilst inside, she couldn't resist a quick glance in the mirror. She fished her hairbrush out of her bag and ran it quickly through her long, brown hair. She told herself this was nothing to do what her aunt had said, but she couldn't help wondering if Jean was right? Did her eyes really sparkle when she spoke to Jake? Was she starting to think of him as more than just a friend?

# Chapter 13

Rose spotted Jake's red truck turning into the hospital car park from a distance and reached it just as he pulled up to the kerb.

'Hi, Jake. Thanks for this, I really do appreciate it,' Rose said as she opened the door and slid into the passenger seat. As Rose went to put on her seatbelt, she was greeted by the snouts of two Border Collies as they squeezed themselves into the gap next to her headrest to lick her on the ear. 'Well, hello, you two,' she said with a chuckle as she twisted round in her seat to give Finn and Tagg a scratch on their heads.

'No problem. You've had a hell of an afternoon from the sounds of things. Are you sure you're alright?' Jake asked, the concern clear in his voice. 'I'm not gonna lie, that boy gave me a pretty good scare this afternoon,' she said, exhaling deeply. As she did so, she realized that her hands were still shaking and she was starting to shiver.

'You're white as a sheet, and look, even your hands are shaking.' He dropped his left hand from the steering wheel to place over hers, which were resting on her lap.

'I'm fine, honestly. I think it's just the after-effects of all the adrenaline. I'm just a bit exhausted. And hungry. In fact, I'm absolutely bloody starving,' she said, laughing. Jake smiled at her and released her hands to grab the steering wheel again.

'I've got just the thing for that. Why don't we make a pit stop after we've picked up Scout and drop in at the pub for some food? I think you could do with a stiff whisky while we're there too. You've earned it.'

'That sounds perfect, actually,' she said gratefully. 'It's on me though, think of it as a thank you for the lift?'

'Something tells me you won't be paying for any-thing tonight.'

'Why not?'

'You do realize you're the talk of the village again?'

'Oh no,' Rose said with a groan. 'Isn't there someone else the village would like to focus their attentions on for a while?'

'You've got no such luck, I'm afraid. You're our own local hero now. I can see your exploits becoming part of Blossom Heath legend,' he said. 'Future generations will be told about the legendary Miss Hargreaves, who single-handedly saved the life of one of the school's pupils.'

'Well, it was hardly single-handed for one thing,' Rose said with a weak smile. 'It was most definitely a team effort. And if we hadn't had the EpiPen to hand and the ambulance wasn't so fast to arrive . . .'

'Look, don't think about that now. Like you said, Hayden

is fine and the story has a happy ending thanks to you. Don't even think about the alternative.'

Rose took a deep breath and nodded in agreement.

As soon as Rose and Jake walked into the Apple Tree, they were met with a standing ovation. Rose didn't know how to react and she found herself close to tears, moved by the outpouring of gratitude from the villagers. The locals in the pub whooped, cheered and clapped Rose on the back as she made her way over to the bar. She was met with so many offers to buy her a drink that she didn't know which way to turn first, and Beth, the fifty-something peroxide blonde owner of the pub, wouldn't hear of Rose and Jake paying for their dinner or any of their drinks all evening.

'It's the least we can do, love, after what you've done today. Who knows what would have happened if you hadn't acted so quickly?' Beth said with a shudder. 'You've bagged yourself a goodun' here, Jake,' she said with a wink and a playful punch aimed at his shoulder. 'She's a keeper, I reckon.'

'Oh no, but we're not ...' Rose tried, and failed, to explain. She caught Jake's eye and the pair of them quickly averted their gaze from each other.

A large steak and ale pie with chips, followed by the biggest portion of sticky toffee pudding and custard that Rose had ever seen, turned out to be exactly what she needed to fortify herself. The double shot of whisky that Jake had prescribed had also gone some way to help banish the shock that she had felt on the way home from the hospital and soon sleepiness began to set in. Jake insisted on seeing Rose and Scout safely home and, despite the fact that it was barely nine o'clock, Rose felt ready for bed. She was absolutely exhausted. As she took herself off up the stairs, she found herself thinking not about Ollie, but about Jake, and just how perfect he had been today.

As Jake drove back to the farm from Jasmine Cottage, his thoughts were solely on Rose and what Beth had said back at the pub. *You've bagged yourself a goodun' here, Jake. She's a keeper, I reckon.* Although he tried to deny it, he had to admit there was something about her . . . a feeling she gave him that he couldn't quite shake. *What was it exactly?* She was clearly a beautiful woman, there was no denying that, and he was certainly attracted to her, there was no doubt about it. She was kind too. Just look at how she had taken in Scout and cared for her, and how she had helped Hayden today.

It was more than that though. He hadn't felt anything like this since . . . well, since Sarah. He shuddered. *Sarah.* Almost a year had passed and it still hurt to think of her. She'd been the love of his life. Or, at least, he'd thought she was. He couldn't deny her betrayal had hurt him deeply. He felt his hands clench more tightly around the steering wheel, then found them loosening as his thoughts turned back to Rose.

*Hope.* That was it. There was something about Rose that gave him hope. Hope for the future, hope that he could start to feel something again. *No*, he thought, shaking his head firmly as he pulled into the yard of Harper Farm. He wasn't going to put himself out there. He wasn't going to risk getting hurt again. He'd promised himself that when he broke things off with Sarah. And anyway, what did it even matter? Rose was engaged. She'd made a promise and he wasn't going to get in the way of that. That would make him no better than Sarah. No, being single was the way to go, he reminded himself. Things were far less complicated that way.

As he put down his keys on the kitchen table, he noticed the light flashing on the answering machine. He hit play and smiled when he heard his sister's voice.

'Hi Jake, it's Kate. Where have you been off gallivanting this evening? I didn't know you had such a hectic social life. Anyway, listen, I just wanted to give you a heads up. I bumped into Sophie today – you know, from school? She told me that Sarah's broken up with Miles. I don't have any of the details but I didn't want it being sprung on you. I know it'll be a bit of a shock, but I'm here if you need to talk. Love you.'

Jake sat down at the kitchen table. He felt his throat constrict and a tightness rise in his chest. Sarah? Single? He exhaled deeply and let out a hollow laugh. He didn't know what he was supposed to feel. Upset? Angry? Smug? It shouldn't matter to him, should it? Sarah was no longer part of his life. What she did had nothing to do with him. But if that was the case, why did he feel so relieved?

# Chapter 14

When Rose was woken the following morning by Scout nudging her hand gently with her cold, wet nose, she was relieved to remember that it was Thursday, which meant she wasn't teaching today. There was no need to leap out of bed and hurry off to school. She could take her time to get ready at a leisurely pace and recover from the shock of the previous day. As she rose from bed and made her way to the kitchen, Rose could see from the window that it was a beautiful May morning. There wasn't a cloud to be seen in the sky and the birds were already in full song. She decided that she'd take Scout on a walk somewhere new today and spend some time exploring. Rose had been so busy since she'd arrived in the village that she hadn't really had a chance to rediscover the local area.

'How does that sound, Scout?' Rose asked her. 'Shall we go on an adventure today? Somewhere new and exciting?' Scout looked up at her and let out a short, sharp bark in agreement.

When she checked her phone, she saw she had a text message from her dad.

*Can you call me, sweetheart, and let me know how Jean is doing?*

Rose dialled her dad's number and he picked up just before the answerphone kicked in.

'Rose, great to hear from you, sweetheart. How's Jean?'

'She's good, Dad, honestly you need to stop worrying, everything's fine here. If I didn't know better, I think that you didn't trust me to handle this.'

'It's not that, sweetheart, I just hate the thought that I've left you to deal with everything while I'm swanning around the Caribbean.'

'Well, I hope you *are* enjoying yourself and not spending your time worrying about me and Aunt Jean?' Rose asked.

'I'd be lying if I said you weren't both on my mind. You're *sure* Jean's recovering well? Do they know when she'll be coming home?'

'She's doing *really* well, Dad, she should be home in a couple of weeks and I'm sprucing up the cottage so it's ready for her. There's honestly no need to worry, just relax and *enjoy* yourself.'

'Okay, sweetheart, I'll do my best. You know where I am if you need me though?'

'Yes, Dad, you're in the middle of the Caribbean Sea,' she laughed.

As she had breakfast, she considered where she and Scout could go.

'I know, we can drive over to that castle near Rye! What's it called ... Fairbright? Fairylight?' No, that wasn't it. She picked up her phone and did a quick Google search to jog her memory. 'Fornbury Castle!' She hadn't visited the castle since she was a child, but a quick look at the map told her it was only a short drive away, no more than twenty minutes or so. 'It really is the prettiest place. You'll love it, Scout, I guarantee it,' she said, reaching down to give the dog a tickle under the chin.

When Rose pulled up at the visitors' car park with Scout in tow, it was completely empty, which Rose found surprising, given that it was such a beautiful day. Nevertheless, she was pleased that she and Scout would have the whole place to themselves and decided to use this opportunity to practise some training with Scout.

She opened up the boot of the car and gave Scout a firm 'wait' command. The little dog waited patiently for Rose to say, 'Let's go', and then hopped out of the car obediently.

'Good girl, Scout, good wait,' Rose said as she bent down to rub Scout's ears. 'Let's go and explore then, shall we?' Scout looked up at her with her head cocked quizzically to one side, which made Rose chuckle. 'I know I've said it before, but I swear that you can understand every word I say, can't you?' Scout barked in agreement and Rose laughed again.

Rose followed the footpath that led from the car park up to the castle, with Scout trotting along beside her, and as she rounded the corner and the tumbled-down stone walls of Fornbury Castle came into view, Rose let out a gasp of delight.

The castle dated back to medieval times, and she had visited it often with her aunt when she was a child. She had delighted in playing hide and seek among the many nooks and crannies that the ancient ruin had to offer. She used to imagine she was a warrior defending the impenetrable fortress, jumping out on her aunt unexpectedly from the castle's battlements with her invisible sword. Aunt Jean had played along and made out that Rose was the fiercest warrior to have ever defended the abandoned castle.

As she headed towards the ruins with Scout, she unclipped the lead from her collar. Rose was much more confident about letting Scout off the lead now since her training with Jake up at the farm, and she loved nothing more than to see her running around and enjoying her freedom.

The pair spent a good hour or so exploring the castle ruins and grounds. Scout was keen to investigate everywhere with her nose and she found particular delight in hopping over the dip in the ground that was once the castle's moat, although any water to be found there was long since gone.

Rose made her way up the hill and sat down gratefully on the bench that was located there before taking some time to admire the view. You could see for miles.

As Rose took in the view, she could see the spire of the church in Blossom Heath clearly in the distance. She sighed and stroked Scout gently behind the ears. She knew she was going to miss her country life when she returned to London. You certainly didn't get views like this in the city. It wasn't just the scenery that she was going to miss though. She knew was going to miss Scout. The little dog looked up at her and placed her head in Rose's lap. Rose wiped away the tear that had formed in her left eye. 'Seriously though, Scout, how I am going to give you up? I know I said I could, but I'm honestly not sure I can anymore. We make a great team, don't we?' Rose hoped there might be a way to make room for Scout in her London life but she knew that getting Ollie to see things from her point of view would be a major hurdle. She shook head. That was enough overthinking for one day. 'Come on, you,' she said to Scout, 'let's head back to the car.' Scout barked in agreement.

As Rose and Scout began making their way along the flat ground that led back to the car park, Rose became aware of two voices shouting above the noise of what sounded like a loud motorbike engine. Scout flattened her ears backwards and her tail went between her legs. She whimpered softly, looking up at Rose for reassurance.

'It's okay, sweetheart, there's no need to panic,' Rose said in a soft voice as she crouched down to grab Scout by the collar, just in case she decided to bolt. Before Rose could get a firm hold, two off-road motorbikes came haring into view and whizzed past them. Scout wriggled free of Rose's grip and pelted off after them, barking madly as they went around the corner. Scout's chase instinct had clearly kicked in. Rose felt a wave of nausea wash over her and her chest tightened. If Scout made one wrong move and got herself tangled up with one of those bikes, she could be seriously injured – or worse, killed. What were motorbikes even doing up here anyway? It was downright dangerous.

Rose quickly made an about-turn and ran off in pursuit of Scout. When she came into view, Rose was horrified to see that the lads on the bikes were purposely weaving in and out around the dog as if to torment her. Scout was barking at them furiously, but just one wrong move and she was in danger of being run over. Rose didn't think as she ran at the bikes, waving her arms and shouting at the top of her voice for them to stop.

When they saw Rose, the bikers looked at each other, grinned and revved up their bikes. Instead of continuing to torment Scout, however, this time they were heading straight for her. Rose tried to run, tried to move, but found her legs were rooted to the spot. She closed her eyes and covered her face with her hands, waiting for the impact. It didn't come. Instead she felt the wind on her face as the bikes passed her by. Slowly she began to remove her hands from her face. She looked down and saw that Scout was at her feet, giving her an opportunity to grab her and reattach the lead. Her hands were trembling. Scout was panting furiously and shaking all over.

The boys dismounted their motorbikes and walked towards Rose. She could sense an air of menace about them and she took two steps backwards. The boy on the left, the largest of the two, looked at her with a sneer and as he got closer, Rose could see that he had a shaved head, was wearing a rather grubby cream tracksuit and had an ugly tattoo of a serpent on his neck.

'Oi, your dog's a bloody menace,' the larger boy, who

looked to be around seventeen or eighteen years old, shouted at her.

'Yeah, it could've 'ad us off our bikes,' the skinnier lad chipped in.

'You need to keep that animal under control,' the first boy sneered. 'Maybe we should take the law into our own hands and teach it some manners.' He clenched his fists. 'What do you think, Tommy?'

'Yeah,' said Tommy. Rose noticed that both of his front teeth appeared to be missing. 'Teach it some bloody manners.'

'I think you'll find that if anyone needs to be taught manners, it's you,' Rose said, finding some courage at last. 'It's illegal to ride motorbikes on public land. Imagine if there'd been a child around one of those corners. You would have killed them. And that's just what I'll be telling the police,' she said as she fumbled around in her pocket to grab her mobile phone.

'I'll be 'aving *that*,' Trevor said coolly as he lurched towards Rose and grabbed the phone right out of her hand before she had time to react. 'I could do with an upgrade anyway,' he said, holding the phone just out of her reach and laughing.

Scout's hackles went up, and she barked at the boys in a way Rose had never heard before. The dog put herself in front of Rose and began snapping and snarling at the boy's ankles.

'Hang on a minute, Trev,' Tommy said, grabbing his

companion by the shoulder. 'Isn't that one of your Uncle Rick's dogs? You know, the one that escaped from the lock-up a few weeks back?'

The boy Rose now knew was called Trevor gave Tommy a look that clearly told him to stop talking. He took a step back and looked at Scout more intently.

'Do you know what, I think it might be,' Trevor said, his face widening into a menacing grin. 'Well, well, well. Lecturing us about breaking the law and *you're* a dog thief? If this is one of my uncle's dogs, I'll be 'aving her back,' he said, making a grab towards Scout's lead.

'There's no way I'm giving you my dog,' Rose bellowed at him, taking another step backwards. She may have sounded confident and assertive, but inside she was terrified. She was struggling to keep her breath even and her voice audible. *Please just let someone walk around the corner,* she thought. *Where were all the other dog walkers and tourists when you needed them?*

As Trevor and Tommy launched towards Rose again, Scout couldn't hold back any longer. She lunged towards Trevor, teeth bared and ready to bite. Before she had the chance to, however, Tommy stepped forward and kicked her hard in the stomach. The Border Collie let out a cry of pain and was flung through the air, landing with a thud on the ground. Rose screamed and, to her relief, a pair of ramblers rounded the corner. 'Hey, you, what's going on? Get away from that girl!' one of them shouted.

With that, Trevor threw Rose's mobile phone into the bushes and yelled, 'My uncle will want that mangey mutt back.' The lads mounted their bikes and sped off into the distance.

Rose wasted no time and ran over to the spot where Scout was lying on the ground. The ramblers jogged towards her.

'Are you okay? What's happened?' the man asked.

'Those idiot lads scared us half to death on their motor-bikes, threatened me and tried to take my dog.'

'We saw them kick her,' the lady rambler said. 'Is she okay?'

'I think so,' Rose said quietly. 'It's okay, Scout, they've gone now.' She stroked Scout's head gently. Scout managed to get up with some encouragement and she licked Rose's hand. 'I think she's just been winded,' Rose said, relieved, 'but I'll get her checked over by the vet just in case.'

'I'm Dave and this is Bella,' the man said, helping Rose to her feet. 'Do you need a lift anywhere?'

'No, I'm fine, my car is up in the car park and Scout seems pretty steady on her feet so we should be okay. Thanks, though.'

'Let me give you my mobile number just in case you need a witness or something,' Dave said with concern. 'You never know if you may have to get the police involved further down the line.'

'Thanks. Actually, I've still got to find my phone – they threw it in the bushes over there somewhere.'

'Don't worry, I'll look for it,' said Bella, rushing over to the foliage to begin searching. 'You just make sure your dog is okay.'

'Thanks,' Rose said with relief. 'I honestly don't know

what would have happened if you two hadn't turned up when you did.'

'Found it!' Bella passed the phone across to Rose, who gave it straight to Dave to input his details into her contacts.

'We're just glad we could help,' Bella said with a smile, 'and don't think twice about calling us if you need us to be witnesses.'

'Thanks, I may well take you up on that. I'd best get to the vets and get this one checked out,' said Rose as she waved goodbye to the couple. Shakily she made her way to the car park.

# Chapter 15

When Rose arrived at the vets, she was grateful to see that the surgery waiting room was empty. Morning surgery must have just come to a close and Tara, Brook House's receptionist, greeted Rose with a smile.

'Hi, Rose. And hello there, Scout,' Tara said, reaching down from the reception desk to give Scout a stroke. 'You don't have an appointment scheduled for today, do you?'

'No, but we've had a bit of an unfortunate incident this morning and I was wondering if Grace could give Scout a once-over?' Rose went on to explain to Tara everything that had happened in their encounter with the motorbikes.

'That must have been terrifying!' Tara said, once Rose had finished. 'Poor you and poor Scout. I'm sure Grace will be able to see you straight away. Just grab a seat for a moment.' Tara disappeared through a door to the consulting rooms and within a couple of minutes she had reappeared with a concerned-looking Grace at her side.

'Rose,' Grace said, crossing the waiting room to engulf her in a hug, 'are you okay? Tara's just filled me in on what happened. Come straight through, and, Tara, will give you PC Palmer a call? I think he needs to hear about this.'

Rose followed Grace through to the consulting room and lifted Scout up onto the examination table. As Grace examined Scout, Rose spoke in more detail about the events that had unfolded that morning.

'That sounds like the Fallon family to me,' Grace explained. 'They're notorious for being troublemakers. The whole family lives up on the Raven Estate at the outskirts of town and they're not a nice bunch. Trevor and Tommy are cousins and Trevor's dad is Rick. He's a nasty piece of work by all accounts. If Scout did belong to Rick, she's had a lucky escape.'

'But could they try to get her back?' Rose asked, all the blood draining from her face. 'Doesn't Scout belong to them by law? What if they try and claim her?'

'They wouldn't have a leg to stand on. Scout wasn't microchipped when you brought her in, and she's already served her seven days before going up for rehoming. I'd very much doubt that a family like the Fallons would have any kind of paper trail or receipts to show they'd purchased her.'

'I hope you're right, Grace,' Rose said, unconvinced. 'If I thought there was any chance they could take her back I think I'd have to make a run for it. There's no way I'd let those lads anywhere near her again.'

Grace smiled. 'Scout really has worked her magic on you, hasn't she? I knew you'd never be able to part with her. Good girl, Scout, I think you may have convinced your foster mum that you're here to stay. What do you think, Rose, are you still claiming that she's just a foster dog?'

Rose couldn't help but let a smile escape her. 'Is it that obvious?' she said. 'I may as well make if official. Scout's going nowhere. Wherever I go, she goes. Whether that's back to London or staying right here in Blossom Heath ... who knows? But she's staying with me.'

Grace beamed. 'Well, that certainly is something to celebrate. I just want to X-ray her to be on the safe side and then we can sort out the paperwork. She's feeling a little tender around the ribs, so let's make sure nothing is broken.'

'Of course. I guess I need to sort out some pet insurance now I'm officially Scout's owner?'

'Well, let's say today's treatment is on the house. Call it an adoption present if you like? Hopefully this will be the last time Scout needs to pay us a visit for a while in any case, all being well.'

At that moment, Tara popped her head round the consulting room door. 'PC Palmer is here and wondered if he could have a chat with Rose?'

'Perfect timing. I'll get this X-ray done and you can take Rose back through to reception. Oh, and grab Rose a cup of tea with a few sugars in it, will you? I think she needs it after the morning she's had.'

Rose sat with PC Palmer and went over everything that had happened that morning up at Fornbury Castle. He agreed with Grace that it was unlikely the Fallons could make a claim on Scout, and even if they did, after the show of violence made towards the dog by Tommy Fallon, they wouldn't be successful. Rose passed on the contact details of the ramblers who had witnessed the assault and PC Palmer was also going to share the details with the RSPCA, who he thought would be keen to prosecute Tommy under the Animal Welfare Act.

'If you think of anything else, Rose, just give me a call at the station,' PC Palmer said, passing her his card. 'We've been after the Fallons for a while and they always seem to manage to wriggle off the hook one way or another.' Just as PC Palmer rose to leave, Grace emerged from the treatment room with Scout.

'Her X-rays are clear, so she's good to go home,' Grace said, beaming.

'That's a relief.' Scout rushed over to greet Rose and she couldn't resist saying hello to PC Palmer by sitting and offering him a paw. He chuckled. 'Hello there, Scout. I hear you've had quite the morning,' PC Palmer said, grinning. 'She's a sweetheart, isn't she?' he said admiringly as he bent down to tickle her under the chin.

'She certainly is. She's actually found her forever home today too, as Rose is officially adopting her!' Grace said with a smile.

'I am indeed,' Rose said, reaching down to tickle Scout on the head. 'I couldn't resist her charms,' she said proudly, pushing all thoughts of Ollie and London from her mind.

'I can't say I blame you,' PC Palmer said. 'I think you'll be the perfect home for her. Mind you, anywhere would be better than living with that Fallon crew.'

'You're not wrong,' said Grace.

'Right, I'd better be heading back to the station to file a report. I'll be in touch once I know what's happening.'

'If I do think of anything else, I'll let you know,' said Rose.

'I'll sort out those adoption papers and drop them in to you this evening, Rose, if that's okay?' Grace asked.

'Of course,' Rose replied, 'and I'll make sure there's a bottle of wine in the fridge, to say thank you for today.'

'I'll hold you to that,' Grace said with a wink.

On her way home from the vets, Rose decided to treat herself and make a detour to visit Blossom Heath's only tearoom, the Cosy Cup. She could do with a sweet treat after her run-in with the Fallons. The café was owned by Joyce, who had lived in the village for as long as Rose could remember. Rose had been great friends with Joyce's daughter, Tori, as a child. They were of a similar age and had struck up an instant friendship, which had been strengthened by their shared love of ponies. Rose always looked forward to her visits to the stables with Tori, where they would muck out Tori's pony, Flash, and Tori would give Rose a riding lesson in the paddocks as a thank you for all her hard work. When they got back to the tearoom, Joyce would always make Rose the biggest cup of hot chocolate she had ever seen, complete with cream and marshmallows, and the girls would sit for hours eating cake and chatting happily together. She hadn't seen much of Tori since she'd grown up, since she was usually off on a travelling adventure whenever Rose had returned to the village. Despite this, Rose knew the next time she saw Tori again it would feel as though not a day had passed.

As Rose walked into the tearoom, she spotted Joyce behind the counter brewing up one of her delicious tea blends. She'd left Scout in the car – she wasn't clear on the rules when it came to dogs in tearooms and she was fairly certain that the Border Collie was likely to wreak havoc if there was food involved.

'Rose!' Joyce called out, unable to contain her delight at seeing her daughter's friend again. Joyce wiped her hands on her apron, stepped out from behind the counter and engulfed Rose in a hug. 'Oh, it's so good to see you. How's Jean?'

'Well, she's not exactly the model patient, but she's definitely on the mend.'

'That's good news, love, really it is,' she said, straightening up. 'You know, I *should* be furious with you. You've been back in the village a while and this is the first time you've made it in for a cuppa.'

'I know, I'm sorry,' said Rose, hanging her head slightly. 'It's been a bit of a crazy time since I got back.'

'Oh, I'm only messing. I know how much you've got on your plate right now. Listen, grab a seat,' she nodded towards the table in the window. 'What can I get you? Let me guess, a mocha?'

'You know me too well, Joyce,' Rose said, laughing.

'Well, I've known you since you were a little girl, love, and you always did have a sweet tooth, just like your aunt.'

'That's an understatement,' Rose agreed.

Joyce busied herself at the coffee machine while Rose got

settled at her table, which had a pretty pink and pale green patterned tablecloth and a small bud vase full of colourful wild flowers in the centre. While she waited for her coffee, Rose looked around and reflected fondly on all the hours she'd spent in here as a child. It really had been one of her happy places, and her friendship with Tori had helped her so much in those dark days after her mum had passed away. Before long she was snapped out of her daydreams by Joyce, who placed her coffee, as well as a huge slice of lemon drizzle cake, on the table in front of her before pulling up a chair.

'Wow! Don't even tell me how many calories are in this,' said Rose, covering her eyes.

'You deserve it, love, and you're looking far too skinny if you ask me.'

'I'm *really* not, but thanks for saying that,' Rose chuckled. She broke off a piece of cake with her fork and tasted a mouthful. 'Wow! Delicious as always! Honestly, how do you get your cakes to taste *so* good? I can't get anything like this in London.'

'Ah, it's a secret family recipe of course,' said Joyce, tapping her nose.

'Well, if you ever decide to open up a London branch, you'll be giving Starbucks a run for their money.'

Joyce laughed. Rose went on to fill Joyce in on everything that had been happening with her aunt, her life in London, the job at the school and her rescue of Scout. She decided to leave out the incident with the Fallons. She knew it would only worry Joyce, and she could see no sense in that.

'You certainly have been busy, love. Tori's going to be sorry she missed you. It's been a few years since you've seen each other, hasn't it?'

'About five, I think.'

'Honestly, where does the time go? It seems like only yesterday you were both kids, sat here reading your pony magazines and talking about boys.'

'I know, right? It's crazy.'

'Well, Tori should be back in September if you're still around. I know she'd love to see you.'

'Me too,' Rose agreed. 'I think I saw on Facebook that she's in Thailand?'

'That's right, love. She's doing some volunteer work out there, but I'm hoping the next time she comes back she'll be here to stay. Running this place on my own is getting a bit much. I'll be sixty-two next month and I want to start thinking about slowing down.'

'That's fair enough,' said Rose. 'Let's hope I'm still here when she gets home – I'd love to see her again.'

'Tell you what, I'll let her know you popped in next time she rings,' said Joyce.

'Perfect, tell her I'd love to take the horses out again one day,' Rose said, finishing her last sip of coffee. 'Right, I'd best get going and try and walk off some of these calories,' she said, patting her stomach.

'Pop in anytime, love. There'll always be a mocha and slice of cake with your name on it here.'

# Chapter 16

Rose spent the rest of the afternoon relaxing at Jasmine Cottage and mulling over the events of the past couple of days. Who would have believed all the drama that had unfolded in the last twenty-four hours alone? She'd been whisked off in an ambulance, threatened by local thugs and officially adopted a Border Collie. You might expect it when you lived in a city like London, but wasn't life in the countryside supposed to be all cream teas and jam-making? Blossom Heath wasn't quite providing Rose with the slower pace of life that she had expected. But, then again, perhaps that wasn't necessarily a bad thing?

She'd made good friends in Grace and Jake and she loved working at the village school. She really had just slotted into life in Blossom Heath perfectly. If anything, her life in London felt like a distant memory. But it wasn't just a memory, was it? It was her reality, her 'real' life, and she needed to remember that. Her stay in Blossom Heath was only supposed to be temporary, wasn't it? Although maybe it didn't have to be? she thought to herself. She was an adult after all, and she could make her own decisions. What was there to say that she had to live the life mapped out for her in London? She could speak to Ollie and explain how she felt. If only she could get him to come and visit for the weekend, she was positive that he'd see the charm of Blossom Heath. If he met Scout, surely he would see how much joy she could bring to their lives. If . . .

Rose was woken abruptly from her daydream by the sound of a text message alert on her mobile phone. It was from Ollie.

*Miss you darling. Have managed to wangle an early finish from the office tomorrow to come and visit. Arrive in Rye on the 15.45 train. Can't wait to see you.*

It was as if Ollie had read her mind. He was coming to visit this weekend! Seeing it as a sign, Rose decided that this was her opportunity to persuade him that Blossom Heath was the perfect place for them to spend their lives together.

Fuelled by her determination to win Ollie over to life in Blossom Heath, Rose spent most of Friday getting Jasmine Cottage ready for his arrival, scrubbing and cleaning the house to within an inch of its life, humming contentedly as she worked. She couldn't wait to show him around the area and let him discover the charm of the place himself. She just knew he'd love the quaint village pub – and Scout would definitely win him over given half the chance. Maybe *he'd* even suggest they adopt her? If time allowed, she thought, they might make it into Rye and spend some time wandering arm in arm around the cobbled streets and cute antique shops. She'd been to the village store and stocked up on all of Ollie's favourite treats: smoked salmon and bagels, Belgian chocolates, red wine – and she planned on making a Friday night trip to the village fish and chip van that evening for their supper. Scout had been bathed and groomed and Rose had practised Scout's 'high five' and 'paw' commands so that she was certain to make a good first impression.

'How can anyone resist that face?' Rose said as she reached for her car keys ready to leave the house. She had decided to leave Scout at home, so as not to give Ollie too much of a shock when she picked him up from the station.

Rose spotted Ollie from across the platform as he disembarked the train. He looked like the perfect country gent in his navy-blue Barbour jacket and matching cap, pulling his grey Valentino suitcase along behind him. As he walked towards her, she twisted her engagement ring round and round on her left hand nervously. His face lit up as soon as he spotted Rose and he engulfed her in a hug. It felt strange seeing him again after a few weeks apart. Rose knew that she should have felt excited, but suddenly she felt nervous and slightly apprehensive about their weekend together.

'I can't tell you how good it is to see you, darling,' Ollie said after pecking her on the cheek. 'A bit of country air and some R&R is just what the doctor ordered.'

'I'm so glad you could get away,' Rose said as they made their way towards the car park. 'I was actually going to call and invite you down when you messaged. I can't wait to spend some quality time together, away from London. Don't you think?' Her voice increased in pitch slightly.

'Oh yes,' he said, taking her hand. 'London can get a bit much at times, can't it? Having a country retreat to unwind in sounds perfect. Did I mention that Monty from work has got a pad just outside of Rye?' Rose shook her head. 'Having a second home in the country is *very* on trend with the City crowd, so things couldn't have worked out better.'

Rose's smile faltered a little. *Was this trip to see her all about boosting Ollie's status with the boys at work?* She banished the thought quickly, before she had time to dwell on it.

Rose spent the drive back to Jasmine Cottage updating Ollie on all her news from the last couple of weeks. She told him about the incident with Hayden and the nut allergy at school, about Aunt Jean's progress in the hospital and how much she had settled into life in the village. She spoke about Grace and Jake, and even Mrs Connolly got a mention. Rose decided not to bring up the fact that she had adopted Scout on a permanent basis – she could explain that once Ollie had settled in. And she thought it best not to bring up the incident with the Fallon boys either – there was no sense worrying Ollie and giving him a negative impression of the village before he'd even arrived there.

Ollie nodded along while she talked, simultaneously scrolling through messages on his iPhone. Rose got the sense that he wasn't really listening to her and was more interested in checking his Instagram. Rose bit her tongue; she really didn't want to start this weekend off on an argument.

As she pulled into the driveway at Jasmine Cottage, Ollie's face broke into a smile.

'Oh, Rose, this is lovely. It's very . . . what's the word? Ah yes, "rustic".' Rose mentally bristled at his use of the word.

'I can't wait for you to meet Scout. She's so cute and I'm sure you two are going to be the best of friends,' Rose said, taking his hand and leading him to the front door.

'You mean you're still looking after that stray dog? I thought that was only a temporary thing,' he said sharply.

'Well, yes, it is,' Rose lied, trying to sound innocent, 'but she's great company for me and we've really bonded.'

'Ah well, as long as it's temporary, I suppose that's fine,' Ollie grumbled as Scout came running out of the front door as soon as Rose opened it. 'Off, off,' he shouted when Scout rushed over to greet him. 'Honestly, Rose, I don't want my jacket covered in dog hairs. Do you know how much this thing cost me?'

'No, but I can guess,' Rose mumbled. She called Scout over to her and stroked her gently behind the ears. 'Anyway, let's get you in and unpacked and I'll give you the tour. It really is a lovely cottage; it's got so much history to it and the garden is gorgeous.'

Rose took Ollie around the cottage room by room, making sure to point out all the original features. As she talked about the history of the building and all the wonderful summers she had spent there as a child, she found herself twisting her engagement ring around her finger over and over as the nerves fizzed in her stomach. She realized now how this house had become part of her, woven into the fabric of her story from when she was a young girl, and for that reason alone she wanted Ollie to love this place just as much as she did.

'It's definitely got potential. The whole place would need gutting of course and it would cost a few thousand to get a new kitchen and bathroom put in, but the potential is there. I imagine this would rent out really well as a holiday cottage with the London crowd,' Ollie said, his eyes lighting up at the prospect.

'*Gutting?* Are you serious? This is Aunt Jean's home and she'll be back in a few weeks.'

'Oh, I didn't mean *now*, darling! I meant in the future. You're bound to inherit this place one day, aren't you? I'm just planning ahead and thinking how we could utilise it, that's all. It would make a great pension pot for us.'

'Wow. The thought hadn't even crossed my mind, to be honest. Aunt Jean's still got a good few years left, in any case.'

Ollie seemed to realize that he had said the wrong thing and began to backtrack.

'Oh, I'm sorry, Rose. Don't think I'm being insensitive,' he said, putting his arm around her shoulders. 'Of course your aunt has got *years* left. I'm just trying to be practical, that's all. We need to think about our own financial futures, and there's no harm in being prepared, is there? I'm only talking hypothetically.'

Rose softened slightly. 'Let's just forget it for now. I want this to be a lovely weekend for us.' She could feel Scout's wet nose press against her hand. 'Plus, I need you and Scout to get to know each other,' she said, laughing, as Scout held up her paw for Ollie to shake. 'See, she wants to make friends,' Rose chuckled, and Ollie begrudgingly took hold of Scout's paw. 'I thought we could go for a drink at the pub tonight, and there's a fish and chip van in the village, so we could bring some food home and curl up in front of a movie later.'

'Oh, didn't I say? I've booked us in at Rye's top restaurant tonight. Le Maison du Blanc. Have you heard of it? It's supposed to be top notch. It's up in the Citadel – that's where all the most exclusive places are apparently. I've been reading up on it and it has fantastic reviews. Daniel's down at his country pad this weekend, so he and Fenella are meeting us there at half past seven,' he said excitedly.

'Oh,' Rose said, feeling annoyed. 'No, you *didn't* say. I thought you were here this weekend to spend time with *me*, not hang out with your cronies from work. Or have I got that wrong?'

'Oh, don't be like that, darling. We won't be talking shop, and I planned this as a special treat for you. I thought you could use a bit of pampering and fine dining. Don't tell me I'm in trouble for trying to do something nice for you?' He took her hand and looked up at her expectantly.

Rose groaned inwardly. Ollie did have a point, she supposed. A lovely meal out would make a change from her microwave meals from Harrisons. Then she was struck by a sudden thought.

'But I've got nothing to wear! I've only got work clothes and jeans here. They won't be suitable for Le Maison du Blanc,' she said, in a mock French accent.

'I'm one step ahead of you. I packed a couple of your evening dresses from home so that'd you'd have a choice. I've got the black dress you wore for your birthday or a new green one I picked up at Selfridges as a surprise.'

'Oh, well done. I'll definitely wear the green one, seeing as you chose it,' Rose said, her eyes lighting up.

'Listen, Rose, I know I'm not always great at saying it, but I really do love you. I hope you know,' he said, giving her hand a gentle squeeze. 'I realize that things haven't been great between us recently and I want you to know that *you* are the most important thing in my life. I don't want my work or friends to come between us. I'll do whatever it takes to make you happy.'

'Thanks for saying that. It means a lot. I love you too.' Rose leaned in towards him and kissed him gently on the lips. She felt butterflies rise in her stomach. 'I'll just go and have a bath and get myself ready,' she said, feeling genuinely excited at the prospect of getting herself glammed up for a change. She leant in towards him and gave him a lingering kiss on the lips. Placing his hand on the small of her back, Ollie pulled Rose in towards him for a deeper, more passionate kiss, and she responded eagerly.

'I have missed you,' Ollie said as she caressed the side of his face. He began kissing her seductively on the nape of her neck in response and Rose groaned in pleasure. 'I do hate it when we quarrel, darling,' he murmured, his voice throaty with desire.

'Well, perhaps we could take a detour via the bedroom before I go for my bath. I mean, it's practically on the way,' Rose said.

Ollie responded by grabbing her hand and leading her up the stairs to the bedroom.

'Now that, Rose Hargreaves, is the best idea you've had all day.'

As the taxi arrived to take them into Rye, Rose had such a good feeling about this weekend. Spending time with Ollie was just what the pair of them needed. What with the pressures of their jobs in London and the hectic pace of life in the city, they were starting to drift apart, she could see that now. Ollie's declaration earlier had been something that she had needed to hear. Knowing that he was willing to put the work into their relationship and make her his number-one priority had made all the difference to her. All they needed was some time to reconnect – and they'd certainly made a good start on that front in the bedroom earlier. Rose couldn't remember the last time things had got so heated between them. Maybe it was the time apart or the change of scene, but she'd certainly felt a passionate connection rise to the surface in a way that she hadn't experienced for a long time.

The taxi dropped them a few streets away from the restaurant so that they could enjoy the walk up to the Citadel through the town's winding cobbled streets. Rye really did have a beautiful charm to it, even if Rose did have to keep stopping every time her heels got caught in the cobbles. She made a mental note to visit again in the daytime when the town's quirky antique shops and art galleries would be open and she could spend some well-deserved time pottering around.

The dress he had chosen for her fitted like a glove. The emerald green complemented her own colouring perfectly and the silk fabric felt so luxurious against her skin. It was such a thoughtful gift. When they were first together, Ollie would regularly surprise her with little presents and trinkets. She sighed happily. This really was going to be the perfect weekend, and she felt a jolt of excitement at being reunited with her fiancé. When they arrived at the restaurant, the couple were greeted eagerly by the maître d'.

'Good evening, Monsieur, Mademoiselle, and welcome to Le Maison du Blanc. Do you have a reservation?' the slightly balding gentleman asked them.

'Yes, under the name of Johns, Daniel Johns,' Ollie said smoothly.

'Ah yes, Mr Johns is one of our most esteemed patrons,' the maître d' said eagerly, snapping his fingers to attract the nearest waiter. 'Please, let us take your coats and we will show you to Mr John's party.'

'Party?' Rose said, confused. 'I thought we were just meeting Daniel and Fenella?' she asked Ollie directly. His gaze shifted awkwardly and he begun adjusting his tie.

'Oh, well there might be one or two of the work crowd

down for the weekend. You know how it is, Rose. Anyway,
this is Daniel's gig, not mine – how am I supposed to
know how many people he's invited to dinner?' he said
with a shrug.

As the maître d' led the couple to Daniel's table, Rose
could see that there were already eight people sitting there.
The arrival of Rose and Ollie took the number up to ten.
Rose's heart sank as she spotted Hugo and Marcus along
with their wives, Sophia and Camille, as well as a couple
she had never met before. The men in the group rose from
their chairs to greet Ollie and Rose, and Daniel introduced
her to Nathaniel, who had recently joined the firm, and his
girlfriend, Olivia.

'Nathaniel's just joined our project management team,'
Ollie said eagerly. 'He's got a bright future ahead of him,
this one,' he continued, giving Nathaniel a boorish slap on
the back. *Why did Ollie always seem to act so differently when his
colleagues were around? It was so frustrating!*

'Lovely to meet you,' Rose said, holding out her hand.

'And it's great to meet you too,' Nathaniel replied, shaking
her outstretched hand vigorously. 'I've heard so much about
you already from Ollie. And you're joining the team soon
yourself, aren't you?' Rose saw Ollie throw Nathaniel a look
as if to tell him to stop talking. 'Oh, I'm awfully sorry if I've
spoken out of turn?' Nathaniel said, blushing.

'Oh, Rose just has an interview lined up with us, that's
all,' Ollie replied dismissively.

'Of course, we'd love her to join the team,' Daniel chipped

in, 'but she's a bright spark is Rose. She's got plenty of options to look at, I'm sure.'

'Thanks, Daniel,' Rose replied politely. 'I'm teaching at the moment but, like you said, I've been considering my options recently.' Ollie beamed at her encouragingly and placed his hand on her knee beneath the table. Rose batted it away. She was still too annoyed that their romantic dinner seemed to have turned into a work jolly with his London cronies.

'Well, as soon as you're back in the city, Rose, let's get a date fixed in the diary for us to have a chat,' Daniel continued. 'She's been a tricky one to pin down, has Rose. She's not making it easy for us to sign her up,' Daniel said, throwing his head back with a throaty laugh and wagging his finger at Rose directly.

'Yes, I'll do that,' Rose replied, taking a large swig from her glass of red wine, wishing that someone would change the subject to anything other than her career prospects. 'What do you do, Olivia?' she asked, turning her head towards her.

'Oh, I'm in hedge funds,' Olivia replied, sounding bored. 'It's incredibly dull work but it least it pays well and keeps me in Jimmy Choos – until *this* one proposes, that is,' she continued with a high-pitched laugh that sounded like a cat being strangled. 'I plan on hanging up my work shoes as soon as we're hitched and leaving all that career stuff to Nathaniel,' she said, tussling Nathaniel's hair playfully and dazzling him with her best pout.

At that moment the waiters came around with menus and

there was much discussion among the group about what to order, what vegetables were in season and the best wines to pair with fish or red meat. Eventually the starters arrived, and they all eased into a more relaxed form of conversation as the wine began to flow. It didn't take long for the talk to turn to work, however, and Rose made her excuses to head to the ladies' room. As she left the table, Camille raced after her.

'Rose, hold on, I'll come along with you. Us girls have to stick together after all,' she said with a cackle. Rose's heart sank. Of all the wives and girlfriends at Ollie's firm, Camille was Rose's least favourite. She was the worst gossip of the bunch and was often malicious with it. Camille was a stunningly beautiful woman in her mid-thirties, with long blonde hair (which Rose suspected was a very expensive dye job) and piercing blue eyes. She was always wearing the latest designer brands and tonight was dressed in an exceptionally clingy, dangerously low-cut red dress, which Rose had to admit showed her figure off beautifully – not to mention her generously sized breasts. Camille spotted Rose's quick glance at her bust.

'They're spectacular, aren't they?' Camille said, looking down at her cleavage. She had obviously spotted Rose's apparently not-so-surreptitious glance at her bust. 'Well, Marcus says they are, which is a plus, seeing as he paid for them. Mind you, my new personal trainer is also a fan ...' Rose looked at Camille wide-eyed. 'What, darling? You seem surprised? Doesn't everyone have affairs these days? I need to have the odd dalliance. I'd die of boredom if I left it to Marcus to satisfy my needs,' she said with a sly wink. 'He's strictly a missionary-only man, and let's just say I have slightly more adventurous tastes.' Camille licked her lips in delight.

'It's none of my business, Camille,' Rose said coolly.

'Oh, I've shocked you, haven't I, darling?' Camille said with a wicked grin as she looped her arm through Rose's as they entered the ladies. 'But I know my secret is safe with you, isn't it? And anyway, it's not like Sophia isn't screwing the tennis pro at her club too. Everyone's at it, darling. I'm sure you will be too once you and Ollie tie the knot. There's nothing like marriage to kill the passion in a relationship. That's if you haven't already found a strapping young farmer to see to your needs since you've been in the country?' Rose thought of Jake and looked away. 'Oh, I'm onto something there, aren't I, darling?' Camille said with a squeal, clapping her hands together.

'Don't be silly,' Rose said, feeling flushed. She felt a stab of guilt course through her. If she was completely honest with herself, she knew that she was attracted to Jake. He was thoughtful, kind, considerate, not to mention extremely attractive, and what with all the physical work he put in on the farm, his body was . . .

Rose snapped her mind back to Camille. 'No, you've got it wrong, Camille. I'm strictly a one-woman man, and that man is Ollie.' Camille looked disappointed not to uncover any juicy secrets and changed tac.

'If that's the case, darling, you need to lock that down and get a date set before someone else snaps him up. There's a new hire in the office who is making a beeline for him apparently. She's a pretty young thing too by all accounts, although I've not seen her personally. Emily, I think her name is. She's got all the boys at the office hot under the collar, so I'd watch out if I were you. If Ollie is anything like Marcus, he'll be straight in there as soon as he realizes she's interested. Did you know that Marcus has slept with every secretary he's ever had?' Camille fixed her eyes on Rose in anticipation. She was attempting to wind Rose up for her own entertainment and Rose was determined not to rise to it.

'I think I know my fiancé well enough by now to know that I can trust him,' Rose said. 'But thanks for your advice.'

'Oh, darling,' Camille replied, blotting her lipstick carefully with a piece of tissue and leaning in to give Rose a kiss on the cheek. 'I'm only trying to look out for you, but you really are so beautifully naïve.' And with that, she turned and left.

Rose's conversation with Camille set her on edge for the rest of the evening. She knew deep down that Camille was only trying to unsettle her and plant seeds of doubt in her mind by questioning Ollie's fidelity and mentioning this girl Emily, the attractive new hire at the office. Well, Rose wasn't going to play into her hands, and she did her best to dismiss the whole encounter. She reminded herself that Camille was so unhappy in her own personal life that this was how she entertained herself – by making malicious sport of meddling in everyone else's business.

The rest of the evening passed without incident and conversation centred, as Rose had predicted, around work and life in London. Just as they were finishing coffee and awaiting the arrival of the bill, Rose heard Marcus say, 'So what time are we kicking things off tomorrow then, Daniel?'

'Oh, around eleven,' he replied. 'Let's give everyone a chance to sleep off their hangovers first. There's no need to get up with the lark – those grouse aren't going anywhere,' he chortled.

'Rose, will be you be joining us tomorrow? We'd love to see you on the estate for a spot of shooting and lunch,' Daniel asked.

Rose threw a confused look at Ollie and he turned his attention to folding the napkin he had in front of him. 'Sorry, Daniel, this is the first I've heard of plans for tomorrow. Are you all meeting up?'

'Oh, honestly, Ollie, don't tell me you forgot to mention the shoot to the poor girl. It is the whole reason we're down here after all,' Daniel said to him in mock indignation. 'We're having a bit of a party up at the old family pile tomorrow, Rose. A spot of shooting in the morning and then a luncheon that will probably turn into a bit of a drinking session, if I know this lot.' The group chortled in agreement.

'No, Ollie hadn't mentioned that,' Rose said quietly through gritted teeth. 'I'm afraid I'm otherwise engaged tomorrow, Daniel, so I won't be able to make it, but thanks for the invite.'

'Ollie tells us that you two have got a holiday cottage in

the area now, so hopefully we'll see you next time. You're busy renovating it, aren't you?' Daniel asked.

'Not exactly,' Rose said, now really seething with Ollie. *What on earth had he been telling them all?* 'It's a bit of a long story,' she continued. 'I won't bore you all with it.'

'Oh, don't be like that, Rose, you have to come along,' Ollie said, giving her knee a squeeze under the table. 'It won't be half as much fun if you're not there, darling.' Rose could tell that he'd had far too much champagne and red wine and was oblivious to how angry she was with him. As she reached for her coffee cup, she managed to knock the small white ceramic milk jug across the table with her hand, the contents spilling all over Ollie's trousers. He mopped himself down with a napkin. 'Do try to be more careful, Rose, darling.'

'Honestly, Rose, throwing the milk around won't stop you from telling me what on earth you have planned that could be more fun than spending the day with us?' Marcus goaded in mock outrage.

'Oh, didn't you know?' Camille added, giving her husband a mischievous grin. 'Rose's bagged herself a strapping young farmer since she's been hiding out in the countryside. Isn't that right, Rose? What did you say his name was again?' she said with a vindictive wink. Honestly, Rose thought, that woman was an absolute harpy. She lived for creating trouble.

'Don't be ridiculous, Camille,' Rose said, turning towards Ollie. 'It's all in Camille's imagination,' she told him. Thankfully, Ollie had indulged in too much wine to rise to her bait.

But then Camille couldn't resist stirring the pot a little further. 'I saw you blush when I mentioned him to you in the ladies, Rose,' she added. 'That's not the look of an innocent woman . . .'

As Rose walked out of the restaurant, she felt Daniel tap her on the shoulder.

'Well, well, well, Rose. They do say it's always the quiet ones.' His hot breath whispered in her ear and he pressed his business card into her left hand. 'Give me a call when you're back in London. We'll set up that interview.'

# Chapter 17

When Rose awoke the next morning, there was no sign of Ollie. She could hear someone banging around in the kitchen below her, however, so she rose from the bed, grabbed her cream dressing gown and padded down the stairs. Ollie was cooking breakfast: smoked salmon, eggs and bagels.

'Peace offering?' he said, offering her a coffee.

Rose sat down at the breakfast table and Ollie placed the coffee and a plate of food in front of her. She was not going to be won over by a few smoked salmon bagels. She was furious with the way Ollie had behaved last night. After he'd fallen asleep in the taxi on the way home from the restaurant, she'd lain awake in bed for hours – and it wasn't just Ollie's incessant snoring that had left her unable to sleep. Her mind kept going over and over the events of the evening. *Why did Ollie always turn into such a different person when he was surrounded by his work cronies?* She felt foolish when she thought of how excited she'd been as they walked through the cobbled streets yesterday on the way to the restaurant, how quickly the sense of anticipation and excitement she had felt had turned to disappointment and confusion.

'What's wrong?' he asked, finally sensing her mood.

'I thought you wanted to spend time with me, Ollie, but it's blatantly obvious the whole reason you're visiting this weekend is to go to Daniel's God-awful shoot.'

'Don't be silly, darling,' he laughed. 'It's just a happy coincidence, that's all. I wish you would come with us today. You could even bring the dog along if you'd like? I bet she'd love it.'

'Absolutely not. Even if I didn't feel as though you've deceived me this weekend, I absolutely hate hunting. A bunch of grown men killing defenceless animals? What's to enjoy about that? I think it's *disgusting*,' she said, pushing the plate of food away from her and taking a sip of her coffee. 'I don't know what it is when you're surrounded by Daniel and his crowd, but I *hate* the way you behave around them.'

'Well,' he said, choosing to ignore her last comment, 'you don't have to actually hunt anything, do you, darling? You can just hang out with the girls and drink Prosecco. You and Camille were getting on like a house on fire last night, weren't you?'

'That shows how much you know. Are you really that oblivious? Camille's an absolute viper. Did you know that she's having an affair with her personal trainer and gloating about it to anyone who'll listen?'

Ollie at least had the decency to look visibly shocked. 'Is she really? That is a turn up for the books. Oh well, I suppose what Marcus doesn't know won't hurt him. And it isn't as though he isn't already having an affair with his secretary, so I guess that does sort of make them even.'

'Oh, well, if they're both being unfaithful, I guess that makes it all okay then,' Rose said.

'Exactly,' Ollie said, failing to pick up on the sarcastic tone in her voice. 'What is it they say? "All's fair in love and war"?'

'Do you know what, I'm suddenly not feeling very hungry. Why don't you finish up my plate? I'm going for a long, hot bath. I'll see you when you get back. Come on, Scout,' she said, tapping her thigh. Scout obediently got up from under the table and followed her.

'Righty ho, darling. I'll see you this evening,' Ollie replied, before picking up her plate and scraping her leftover breakfast onto his.

Jake walked into Harrisons and dug around in his coat pockets to find his shopping list. It wasn't there.

'Damn,' he muttered, reaching his fingers into the back pocket of his jeans and locating it straight away. He bent down to collect a basket from the stack at the front of the store and waved a silent hello to Maggie, who nodded back, before heading straight to the pet food section and throwing a selection of dog treats into his basket. As he rounded the corner of the aisle, he looked up and saw Sarah directly in front of him. Their eyes locked. Jake felt his chest constrict and his mouth go dry. His grip on the shopping basket tightened and he instinctively took a step backwards.

'Jake!' his ex's cheeks flushed. She looked almost as shocked as he felt. 'Jake, I'm so glad I've bumped into you. I was just about to head up to the farm but I wanted to get some treats for the dogs first. I see you've already beaten me to it though.' She nodded towards his basket and let out a short, high-pitched laugh.

Jake had to cough to find his voice. 'To see me? Why on earth would you want to do that? We've got nothing to say to each other, Sarah. I thought you lived in Hastings now anyway?'

'Well, yes, I do, but I wanted to come and see you, Jake. I was hoping we could ... talk?'

Jake stood there silently staring back at her. He took in her long blonde hair and tightly fitting blue jeans, tucked into knee-high riding boots. This was the woman who, up until a year ago, he had planned to spend the rest of his life with. The woman who he had been madly in love with for the past five years. The woman who had broken his heart.

'Talk about what, Sarah? I think we did all the talking we needed to do when you left me for Miles,' he said, his words firm and clear.

'Well, that's what I wanted to talk to you about ...' Sarah's voice faltered. 'I know I've hurt you badly, Jake, and there's no excuse, really there isn't it, but I've ended things with Miles. I've realized over the last year that I made a ... mistake. Things were never right with him, not in the way they were with me and you ...' She reached out to place a hand on Jake's arm.

He automatically pulled away from her, 'This is hardly a conversation for the pet food aisle of Harrisons,' he said curtly, aware that Maggie was watching the pair of them intently. 'You know what Maggie's like for gossip. Come to the farm.' Sarah beamed at him.

'Of course,' she nodded. 'I can follow you there in the car.'

'No, not now. I'm . . . I'm on my way to meet a supplier.'

'Okay, just name the time and I'll be there.'

'Around seven.'

'Perfect. I'll see you then.' She reached towards him and placed a kiss on his cheek. Jake stiffened at the contact.

He watched her walk out of the shop, her long blonde hair bouncing around her shoulders with every step. The familiar scent of her lingered in the air as she walked away. She looked so familiar and yet at the same time she seemed like someone he barely knew. A walking shadow from his past. Did she mean what she had said? Could she really have ended things with Miles because she wanted to be with him? If that *was* true, could he find it in himself to forgive her? He had spent a year trying to get over her, trying to move on and yet, seeing her here in front of him today, he found his feelings for her stirring in spite of himself. He needed to hear her out. Listen to what she had to say. If there could be a chance of reconciliation, he owed it to himself to at least find out.

After she'd taken Scout for a good, long walk, Rose made herself comfortable on the sofa with the dog for company, cracked open the box of Belgian chocolates that she'd bought for Ollie's visit and put on a movie. She couldn't concentrate on it at all, and instead pulled at the tassels on the cushions with her fingers while mentally going over the events of the weekend.

To say it had been a disaster would be an understatement. Rose had such high hopes that things would go well, that it would be a proper chance for the pair of them to spend time together, away from the city, and to really reconnect. She'd thought Ollie was being *thoughtful* when he had told her about the dinner that he'd arranged with Daniel. She'd wanted to try Le Maison du Blanc for years, and he'd even been considerate enough to buy her a beautiful new dress. The sex they'd had yesterday had been amazing too – the best they'd had in, well, months. She'd truly believed him when he'd told her that she was his number-one priority. How had it all gone so wrong? If anything, this weekend had confirmed the doubts that she'd already been having about Ollie and whether he really was the man she wanted to marry. *Had they just drifted too far apart?*

At around six o'clock that evening, Rose's mobile rang. As she fished it out from under the sofa cushions, she could see that it was Ollie calling.

'Hello, darling. Listen, I just wanted to give you a call to say that I'm going to stay the night at Daniel's and grab a lift back to London with him in the morning. We've all had far too much champagne and no one's in a fit state to drive me back to yours.' Rose could hear drunken voices in the background, Camille's cackle of a laugh audible above everyone else.

'You mean you're not coming back here at all this weekend?' Rose said, astonished.

'Of course I'd love to, darling, but it just doesn't make practical sense. Monty's driving back to London first thing in the Range Rover so I may as well just hop in. The trains back to London are an absolute *nightmare* from Rye. I'll come back soon though and make it up to you properly. We could even go to that village pub you mentioned. What was it again? The Nags Head?'

'Why don't you just do whatever you like, Ollie. You usually do.' And with that, Rose hung up and flung her phone across the sofa. Within seconds it was ringing again and she stretched out her arm to retrieve it. 'I've got nothing else to say to you, Ollie—'

'Excuse me, is that Miss Hargreaves?' a female voice interrupted.

'Oh, yes, sorry – I thought you were someone else,' Rose said apologetically.

'I'm the duty nurse on Nightingale Ward at Conquest Hospital. It's about Jean Hargreaves.'

'Yes,' said Rose, sitting bolt upright on the sofa. 'What's happened? Is she alright?'

'I'm afraid she's developed an infection and we've had to take her back into surgery this afternoon.'

'Okay, what does that mean exactly? Is she in any danger?'

'Infections can happen after surgery, I'm afraid. It's a fairly common complication. In Jean's case the surgeon has removed all the metal plates and pins at the original fracture site and washed out the area. She's on an antibiotic drip and we'll be monitoring her closely.' Rose swallowed hard.

'Well, thank you for calling. When can I come in to see her?'

'I'd wait until after the weekend if I were you. She's going to be pretty woozy from the anaesthetic for at least the next twenty-four hours.'

'You will let me know if anything changes? If she deteriorates?'

'Of course. She really is in the best hands though. Try not to worry, Miss Hargreaves.'

*Try not to worry?* If only it was that easy. Five minutes ago her life couldn't have got much worse after Ollie's behaviour, but, as it turned out, that paled into insignificance after the call from the hospital. She wondered if she should ring her dad, to let him know what had happened. No, she thought, she didn't want to worry him if it wasn't essential. She knew her dad too well and he'd be on the first plane home if she told him about his aunt's additional surgery. That was something she would keep to herself, for now at least.

Jake looked up at the kitchen clock on the wall. It was nearly seven o'clock. Sarah would be arriving any minute. He sat down at the kitchen table and found himself rearranging the unopened post that lay in front of him. He became aware that he was tapping his left foot and put his hand on his left knee to steady himself. Finn whimpered quietly from his basket by the Aga. The dogs seemed to know that he was feeling uneasy. Tagg nuzzled his master's knee and Jake reached down to stroke him under the chin. He flinched as he heard a car pulling up onto the gravel in the yard outside.

'It's alright, boys. It's only Sarah.'

Jake had opened the door before Sarah had the chance to knock. She was dressed in a yellow cotton dress embroidered with small white flowers, and Jake noticed that it showed her figure off perfectly. Her skin was tanned a light golden brown and Jake saw that her blonde hair was an even lighter shade than usual. She had clearly been spending time in the sun. Her make-up was flawless and understated. Jake had forgotten just how beautiful she was.

She flashed her perfect white smile at him and crouched down to greet the dogs enthusiastically. Finn jumped up to lick her face eagerly and Tagg chased his tail in delight, yipping in excitement.

'Traitors,' Jake muttered under his breath.

'Sorry?' replied Sarah, straightening up again.

'Oh, nothing.' He stifled a cough.

'Well, it seems as though these two have been missing me at least.' Sarah moved towards the kitchen table and took a seat opposite Jake. She placed her handbag down in front of her and fiddled with the tassel on the handle. 'Thanks for inviting me, Jake. I know you didn't have to and I appreciate you giving us the opportunity to talk.' Jake took a long, deep breath but he didn't speak. 'I know the last time we saw each other things ended just ... horribly.' Sarah looked down at her hands.

'Well, that was hardly my fault, was it?' He felt his chest tightening, his jaw clenching.

'I know, I know, and I regret that terribly, Jake, I really do. If you only knew just how much—'

Jake couldn't help himself. 'You hardly looked as though you regretted anything when I walked in on you and Miles together—' he interrupted.

'It was a terrible lapse in judgement, Jake, I know that now. A terrible, terrible mistake. If you knew just how *ashamed* I am of how I behaved. You didn't deserve to be cheated on and there's not a day goes by that I haven't regretted what I did.' Sarah wiped a single tear from her cheek. Jake felt himself soften a little.

'Then why did you do it, Sarah?'

'I know it sounds like a cliché, but I think I was just scared. Everything was going so perfectly, with us, with the wedding planning, and I . . . I think I just started to feel trapped. I panicked and made a stupid, stupid mistake.'

'Why didn't you tell me that at the time? You had to know that you could always talk to me about anything?'

'Once you'd found out about Miles, about the affair, and walked in on us like that, I just couldn't look you in the eye. I was too ashamed.' She hung her head. 'It seemed easier to try and make a go of things with Miles than to try and get you to understand . . . to take me back.' Jake exhaled deeply and tried to take in the implications of Sarah's explanation. She may have explained why she had cheated, why she had betrayed him like that, but did the reason really matter? Did it make any difference?

'I appreciate you coming here today and trying to explain, but I just don't know how we can go forward from here. Too much has happened, the trust has been broken . . .' Sarah reached across the table and grabbed Jake's hand. This time he didn't pull away from her.

'I still love you, Jake. Miles was a mistake; you *have* to believe that. I want us to try again, to make things work. I'm prepared to do *whatever* it takes.' He studied Sarah's face closely. Her blue eyes were misty with tears and her breathing was fast and shallow.

'It's incredibly hard to try and stop loving someone but I've tried to stop loving you, Sarah. No one has ever hurt me like that before. I appreciate what you've said today but I have to think about what's best for *me*. Where do I draw the line? For my own sanity?' A silence filled the air.

'I'm not asking for you to make any promises today,' Sarah said softly. 'If you'll just *think* about what I've said. If there's the slightest chance for us, Jake, please promise me that you'll consider it?' He didn't reply. Sarah clutched his hands even more tightly.

'I'll consider it,' he relented. 'That's all I can promise right now.'

Sarah wiped the tears away from her eyes, stood up and smiled at him.

'That's all I'm asking,' she said as she pulled him into a tight embrace and whispered, 'I love you, Jake.'

As he watched Sarah drive away from the farmhouse, Jake felt as though his stomach had dropped through the floor. He didn't yet know how to process what she had told him. Could he believe that she still truly loved him? Would he ever be able to forgive her affair? He shook his head and switched the kettle on. One question that he couldn't quite shake was: if he was still in love with Sarah, why did he keep thinking about Rose Hargreaves?

# Chapter 18

As Rose was giving Scout her breakfast and getting herself ready for the day, she felt her mind drifting back to Ollie and their disastrous weekend together. She'd had such high hopes for some real quality time together, and now she just couldn't shake the feeling that, somehow, things weren't right between them. She knew she'd need to sit down properly with him and get to the root of these feelings she was having, but that was a conversation they'd have to have in person. As she took the first swig of her morning coffee, there was a knock at the door. Scout let out a series of short sharp barks and, as Rose rushed to the door to open it, she could see through the window that it was PC Palmer. A knot formed in her stomach as her hands fumbled with the door lock. Did he have news about the Fallons?

'Morning, Rose,' he said once she'd managed to open the door, 'can I come in? I've got an update for you.'

'Yes, of course. I hope everything's okay?'

'Why don't we have a seat in the kitchen?' PC Palmer suggested, and Rose led the way.

"Can I get you a cup of tea?' she asked.

'Please. Mine's milk and two sugars, and if you've got a biscuit or two going spare, I wouldn't say no,' PC Palmer replied as he took a seat at the kitchen table.

'I'm sure I can dig something out,' Rose smiled, before rummaging in the kitchen cupboards. 'Rich tea or hobnob?' she asked triumphantly, waving two packets of biscuits in the air.

'Hobnob, please.'

After she'd got PC Palmer's tea, Rose took a seat and placed her hands in her lap, interlocking her fingers.

'Now, it's good and bad news, Rose. The good news is that the Fallons don't have a leg to stand on when it comes to making a claim on Scout. There's no record of her being registered to them and they can't produce any documentation to support their claim, so you're clear on that front. I spoke with the ramblers who witnessed the assault and they've given me their statements. The RSPCA think they've got enough to move forward with a prosecution against Tommy Fallon for animal cruelty, so that's something.'

'Well, that sounds pretty promising. So, what's the bad news?'

'Ah well, that's where things get a bit more complicated,' PC Palmer continued, taking a sip of his tea. 'The Fallons aren't ones for following the rules I'm afraid, Rose. When I spoke to Rick, I got the impression that he may just try and take matters into his own hands if the law doesn't lay in his favour. I wouldn't put it past him to try and snatch Scout back, so make sure you stay vigilant over the next few days.'

'Do you really think he'd try and do that? Snatch her, I mean?' She reached down to place her hand on Scout's head.

'Like I said, I wouldn't put anything past Rick Fallon, which is why I wanted to talk to you myself. I'll have a check around the cottage while I'm here, if that's okay with you, and make sure everything is secure. If you've got any locks that need updating, I can let you know.'

As PC Palmer paused to take a bite of his biscuit, there was another knock on the front door and Scout leapt up and rushed towards it, barking. Rose answered the door to a concerned-looking Jake.

'I've just heard what happened the other day with the Fallon boys. Are you okay?' He bent down to give Scout some fuss, Tagg and Finn hot on his heels and ready to say hello.

'Thanks, Jake, that's really thoughtful of you.' Rose smiled at him warmly. She could really use a friend right now after the warning from PC Palmer. As Jake stood framed in the doorway, Rose couldn't help noticing the firmness of his abs underneath his T-shirt and a sudden jolt of desire pulsed through her. Perhaps Camille's suspicions hadn't been so far off the mark after all? Rose steeled herself and cast all thoughts of romance from her mind when PC Palmer appeared from the kitchen.

'Hello there, Jake. I've just been having a look at your back door, Rose, and the lock could definitely do with updating. Just give me a few more minutes and I'll check the rest of the entry points.'

'Thanks, I'd really appreciate that,' Rose said.

'What's going on, Rose? Has something happened?' Jake asked. A dark shadow crossed his brow. Rose explained the police's suspicions about the Fallons and saw a look of fury pass across Jake's face.

'Surely you can arrest them?' Jake asked PC Palmer, his voice rising.

'I'm afraid not, Jake. They haven't actually done anything as yet. They haven't even made any threats. It's just a feeling I got when I spoke to Rick, and it's exactly the sort of thing he might try. I'm just asking Rose to be vigilant at this point and make sure all of her doors and windows are locked securely.'

'You can leave all of that with me,' Jake said at once. 'If you let me know what Rose needs, I'll head over to the DIY store and I can get all the locks fitted this afternoon.' Rose opened her mouth to protest but Jake looked at her and said, 'It's the least I can do and I won't take no for an answer.' Rose smiled. 'Do you think I'd honestly get any sleep tonight if I was worrying about the Fallons breaking in here?'

'No, I suppose not,' she said, suddenly struck by the difference between Jake and Ollie. Here was Jake, who was prepared to drop everything to come to her aid when he really didn't know her that well, and her own fiancé hadn't even taken the time to stay with her for the weekend or really listen to any of her news about life in Blossom Heath.

'Well, you'll have to let me cook you dinner then to say thank you. How does a Sunday roast with all the trimmings sound?' she asked him.

'That sounds like a fair deal to me, Jake. I'd shake on that before Rose changes her mind,' PC Palmer said with a chuckle. 'I've written down everything that Rose needs, and you'll be able to get all of that at the DIY superstore, no problem. If you have any questions or any worries at all, Rose, don't hesitate to give me a call. You can rest assured that I'll be keeping a close eye on the Fallons for the next few days.'

'Thank you, PC Palmer. I really do appreciate that, and thanks again for coming to talk to me in person.'

'Not a problem,' said PC Palmer, 'and, Rose, do call me Ben, won't you? I'm sure we'll be seeing each other around the village and PC Palmer sounds so formal.'

Rose nodded in reply and smiled gratefully.

'The Fallons couldn't have anything to do with those other dogs that have gone missing recently, could they?' Jake asked quickly. 'I've seen a couple of posters up in the village for lost dogs.'

'The cockapoo and the French bulldog?' replied PC Palmer. Jake nodded. 'Well, there's nothing to suggest that at this stage, but when it comes to the Fallons, who knows?' he said, draining the last of his tea.

'Thanks for coming to talk to me in person today, Ben, I really do appreciate it.'

After making a quick trip to the DIY store, Jake spent the rest of the afternoon fitting new locks to the doors and windows at Jasmine Cottage. He'd even purchased a small CCTV camera, which he installed at the front of the cottage, and he spent time explaining it to Rose and setting up an app on her phone so that she could view the footage remotely.

'It's only a basic system but hopefully it'll give you some peace of mind. I've got a more high-tech version up at the farm,' he explained as he walked into the kitchen, 'so I know how it works. If you get stuck with it, just give me a shout. I know it took time for me to get my head around it all when I first had it installed. Theft of farm machinery is a real risk nowadays, so most farmers have some kind of security system.'

'Thanks, Jake, this looks fantastic. It'll definitely help me sleep a bit easier tonight.'

'Wow, this smells amazing,' Jake said as he caught the aroma coming from the oven. 'What are we having?'

'I've got roast lamb with all the trimmings, and I managed to find an apple pie of Aunt Jean's lurking in the back of the freezer, so you're in for a treat,' Rose said playfully.

'I'm not much of a chef myself . . . I should make more of an effort really, but when it's just me and the dogs it all seems a bit too much trouble,' he sighed. Did Rose detect a note of regret in his voice?

'I know what you mean. I've been living off microwave meals for the last few weeks, with the odd visit to the fish and chip van thrown in,' she said as she opened the oven door to check on the meat, 'so this is a treat for me too.'

With dinner nearly ready, Jake set the table and let the dogs out into the garden to play and burn off some of their excess energy. Rose grabbed a bottle of wine from the fridge.

'Red okay?'

'Yes,' Jake nodded. 'I think we could both do with a glass considering how hard we've worked today. This looks delicious,' he said with a smile as he picked up his knife and fork and dug into his meal.

'It's the least I can do,' Rose replied, taking a large sip of wine. 'Honestly, Jake, I really appreciate your help, and so does Scout. I can't think of anything worse than her going back to the Fallons,' she shuddered. Jake put his hand over the top of hers and Rose felt a jolt of electricity.

'That's *not* going to happen. You heard what PC Palmer said. Scout's here to stay. Grace told me that you've officially adopted her now?' he asked with a grin.

'Yep, it's a done deal. She's stuck with me, I'm afraid.'

Jake laughed. 'Well, if she could talk, I'm sure she'd say that she was pretty pleased with that arrangement.' Jake looked thoughtful for a moment, as if unsure whether to speak or not. 'So, what does that mean for you going back to London? Are you taking Scout with you? Or are you thinking that you might stay in Blossom Heath for good? I'm not prying,' he added quickly, 'it's just that Grace mentioned your fiancé is in London, so I figured you must be planning on going back at some point?'

Rose realized that she'd never mentioned Ollie to Jake before. Why was that exactly? Had she left him out of their conversations on purpose because she secretly had feelings for him? Or was it just an oversight?

'Do you mind if we change the subject?' Rose said quickly.

'Things with Ollie are ... well, let's just say they're complicated right now, and that's a conversation I need to have with him first.'

'Of course. Sorry, it's none of my business. Just forget I said anything ...' He stuffed half a Yorkshire pudding into his mouth to silence himself.

'It's fine, honestly. It's just a bit of a sensitive subject right now,' Rose said quietly. 'Anyway, what about you? I'm sure you must have no end of admirers queuing up.' Rose cringed. Why had she asked him that? She felt her heartbeat quicken and her throat tighten at the prospect he might tell her he had a girlfriend hidden away at the farm. She suddenly realized that she'd be devastated if he did.

'Oh, well ...' Jake flushed and looked a little awkward.

'Sorry, I shouldn't have put you on the spot like that. Your private life is none of my business. I don't know what I was thinking,' she blustered, feeling foolish. She reached over to pour him more wine and knocked his glass over, spilling the contents all over the table. 'Oh God, sorry,' she said as she stood to grab a tea towel to mop up the deep red liquid. She felt her cheeks burn with embarrassment.

'It's fine, honestly. I'd like to tell you.' He placed his knife and fork down on the table and looked directly at her. 'I was engaged a couple of years back to a girl called Sarah but it ended ... badly. She cheated on me with some guy she worked with. I came home early from a rugby match and walked in on the pair of them together. It was a huge shock. We'd been together since college, you see, and if I'm honest, it messed me up a bit. I've not been with anyone I was really serious about since ...' His voice trailed off and his eyes locked with Rose's.

'Oh, Jake, I'm so sorry. That must have been awful,' she said, reaching across the table and taking his hand in hers.

The electricity between them was palpable. There was no doubt in Rose's mind that she felt a huge attraction to Jake, there was no point in trying to deny it anymore. But did he feel the same? What if he only thought of her as a friend? With every fibre of her being, Rose wanted to reach across the kitchen table and kiss him, but she knew she had to resist. Not only would she make an utter fool of herself if he didn't reciprocate, she was still an engaged woman. She may have still been furious with Ollie, but she knew she needed to speak to him first and try to sort things out.

'Right, who's ready for a slice of Aunt Jean's apple pie?' she asked quickly, keen to change the subject and break the tension between them.

'I'll cheers to that,' he said, picking up his glass and clinking it against hers.

'To Aunt Jean's apple pie. You know, this place really does hold so many memories for me,' Rose said fondly. 'I used to be *so* excited to stay here as a child. I could stay up as late as I liked and Aunt Jean would always wake me up for a midnight feast, just for the fun of it. We'd be sat in our pyjamas eating chocolate cake and ice cream at two in the morning and I'd be telling her all about the latest celebrity gossip. She had no idea who I was talking about most of the time, but she listened anyway . . .'

'It sounds as though the two of you are pretty close?'

'We are,' Rose nodded. 'She really stepped up for me after losing Mum. I don't think I'll ever be able to repay her.'

'I think seeing you grow up into a pretty amazing woman is probably more than repayment enough,' said Jake, not quite meeting her eye.

After dinner, Rose put in a call to the hospital to check on her aunt's progress, thankful to discover that she was recovering from her surgery and responding well to the antibiotics. She'd received a voicemail from her dad overnight and had specifically put off replying until she had a positive update for him. She quickly fired off a text – *Jean's making good progress, no need to worry. Enjoy your holiday. Speak soon xx* – and spent the rest of the evening chatting happily to Jake about everything and anything. He told her all about his plans for the farm and how he hoped to expand and diversify to move with the times. Rose talked about her teaching career and her friend Maya back in London, and she even suggested that she could speak to Mrs Connolly about organizing a school trip up to the farm for her class, which Jake thought was an excellent idea. All of Rose's worries earlier in the day about the Fallons seemed to disappear from her mind, and she felt truly relaxed and at ease.

As the evening progressed, Rose realized that was what she really liked about Jake. It wasn't just that she was physically attracted to him, it was the fact that he put her completely at ease and she could talk to him about anything. She felt as though she could truly be herself around him. She didn't have to leave things out or censor herself, which was something she found herself doing often with Ollie. She knew she couldn't put off talking things through with Ollie any longer. *Was he really the man she wanted to marry?* she wondered. Was her vision for the future the same as his? She didn't care about the big house in Surrey with the 4x4 parked on the driveway, the fancy Caribbean holidays or the posh dinners out. She paused and found her gaze drawn to the engagement ring on her left hand. When she thought about it honestly, she wasn't sure if she had *ever* really wanted the same kind of life as Ollie.

Since Sarah's visit to the farm, Jake had been unable to think of little else. Why hadn't he told Rose about Sarah's break-up with Miles at dinner? It has been the perfect opportunity. Perhaps he didn't want to complicate things in her mind. Part of him wanted her to know that he was single and available. When he thought about how her long dark hair cascaded around her shoulders and how her bright green eyes lit up when she laughed … He gripped the steering wheel more tightly. *No!* He had to stop thinking about her like that. Rose was engaged and that was all there was to it.

Jake arrived at his sister's house after leaving Rose at Jasmine Cottage, ready to talk things through. Kate lived on a small development of new-build houses on the outskirts of

Blossom Heath, and he trusted her opinion on most things. Since their parents had died, they had relied on one another for support. Kate had been particularly close to Sarah and Jake recalled how his sister had been so incredibly happy for them when they had announced their engagement.

'Hey, little brother,' Kate called from the doorway. 'I just need to wrangle these two monsters into bed and then I'm all yours. Ian won't be back from work until late, so I'm on bedtime duties.'

'Uncle Jake! Uncle Jake!' two small voices called from the landing. Jake looked up and spotted Lily and Hannah. 'Can Uncle Jake read our bedtime story, Mummy?' Lily asked.

'Not tonight, sweetheart. Uncle Jake has got a lot on his mind.' The girls frowned.

'Sorry, girls,' he said. 'Anyway, your mum tells much better stories than I do.'

'She does not,' replied Hannah, pouting.

Kate smiled. 'See, I told you they were monsters. Grab yourself a drink and I'll be down in a minute,' she said.

Jake nodded and, after saying goodnight to his nieces, went through to the kitchen, helped himself to a beer from the fridge and made himself comfortable in the living room. It wasn't long before his sister returned.

Always one to get straight to the point, she folded her arms, sank into the nearest chair and said, 'So what did she have to say for herself, then?'

Jake recounted his conversation with Sarah and Kate didn't interrupt. She just listened.

'And what do you make of it all?' she said, her eyes narrowing as she studied her brother's features closely.

'I only wish I knew,' he said with a deep sigh, picking at the label of his empty beer bottle with his fingers. 'She did *seem* genuinely sorry and it was hard for me to see her without feeling anything. Part of me *wants* to believe her.'

Kate tutted loudly.

'I can't just switch off my feelings for her, Kate. It's not that easy,' he said defensively.

'No one's saying that it is, but don't forget what she did. Her fling with Miles wasn't exactly a one-off, was it? It had been going on behind your back for months.' Jake noticed the colour rise in his sister's cheeks. 'That's more than just a spur-of-the-moment mistake – it's calculated deception. The lies she told, the way she hurt you …' She paused. 'I don't know how you can even *think* of letting her back into your life,' she said, shaking her head.

'But if she felt pressured about the wedding … confused, like she said … Maybe she just wasn't thinking clearly?'

'What, for *six* months?' said Kate, raising her hands towards the ceiling. Jake's shoulders slumped. 'Listen,' she said more quietly, 'I'm not telling you what to do. You have to make your own decision but you've asked for my opinion and I'm giving it. I don't see how you can ever trust her again. In my experience, when someone breaks the trust in a relationship, things can never go back to how they were before. You'll always be on guard, always wondering every time she's stuck late at work or on a night out: is she *really* where she says she is? Is she lying to you again? That's no way to start out building a future with someone.'

'I know you're only looking out for me. I'll think about what you've said, I promise. You're right, though – this has to be *my* decision, and it's going to take some time for me to make it.'

# Chapter 19

Rose was awoken by her alarm early the next morning. It was her first day back at Blossom Heath Primary School since the EpiPen incident with Hayden last Wednesday. She was excited to see her class again and, more importantly, find out how Hayden was doing. She leapt out of bed feeling refreshed and invigorated, keen to put all thoughts of the weekend's events with Ollie and the Fallons out of her mind.

As Rose was making her morning coffee, she heard a knock on the front door and, to her surprise, found a beautiful bouquet of white roses and pink peonies on the doorstep. As she bent down to pick them up, she shouted a thank you to the delivery driver as he hopped back into his van. *Who could be sending her flowers?* It wasn't a special occasion. *Perhaps someone wanted to send a bouquet to Jean and got it delivered to the cottage?* Intrigued, Rose set the bouquet down on the kitchen table and opened the card.

*I'm sorry our weekend together didn't quite go to plan, darling. I promise I'll make it up to you, love you, Ollie xx*

It was a thoughtful gesture, but did he *seriously* think a bunch of flowers would be enough to patch up the cracks in their relationship? Rose felt anger rise inside her and she screwed the card up and threw it in the bin. She flung the bouquet into the sink and filled it with water – she'd decide what to do with it later.

Rose dropped Scout off with the dog-sitter a little earlier than usual so that she could explain PC Palmer's concerns about the Fallons and ask Jane to be vigilant when she was out walking Scout. News of the incident had already reached Jane, however, and she promised that she'd be more cautions than ever and wouldn't let Scout out of her sight, even in the garden.

Reassured, Rose completed the short walk to the village primary school and headed straight in to see Mrs Connolly, who greeted her with a beaming smile.

'Rose, oh I'm so pleased to see you. Do come in and take a seat,' Mrs Connolly said, opening her office door and pulling up a chair for her. 'How are you after all the excitement of last week?'

'Oh, I'm fine. I actually wanted to ask you how Hayden and the rest of the class had been? It was quite an event for them all to witness,' Rose asked, tucking her hair behind her ears.

'Well, you'll be pleased to know that Hayden has made a full recovery, although I don't think he'll be accepting any snacks from his classmates quite as eagerly in future,' Mrs Connolly said, rolling her eyes. 'The children were all concerned about him, but they seem to have recovered from the shock without any ill effects. Although, I must say they'll be pleased to see you back in school. They all think you're a superhero now. They'll be disappointed that you're not wearing a cape and mask,' she chuckled.

'It's such a relief that Hayden's okay,' Rose said, exhaling deeply. 'He gave all of us quite the scare.'

'Indeed he did,' Mrs Connolly said, nodding. She looked solemn. 'One outcome we didn't expect was Mason's reaction. You're aware of the recent death of his father and his trouble settling in?' Rose nodded. 'Well, Cheryl said that he excelled himself in dealing with the situation with Hayden, that he helped to reassure the rest of the children?'

'He really did. It surprised me too as he's always so quiet in class. He told the others that I had everything under control and that Hayden was going to be fine. He really was a star.'

'That's exactly what Cheryl said. His confidence has come on in leaps and bounds since then, so I'll be interested to see how you think he's doing today. He's firm friends with Billy Jenkins now apparently and has been playing football with him and some of the older boys at lunchtime, which is a real step in the right direction for him.'

'I'm so pleased to hear that. I love it when something positive comes out of such an awful situation.'

'I must say, Rose, you really have been thrown in at the deep end, haven't you? You've only been with us for a few weeks and you've made huge strides with the class already . . . and you've certainly proved that you keep a clear head in a crisis. I'm only sorry I don't have a permanent job to offer you for September. You'd be a great asset to the school,' she continued with a sigh.

'It can't be helped, Mrs Connolly. If there's no job here, that's just how it is,' she shrugged. 'Thanks for the vote of confidence, though. It means a lot coming from you.'

'What *are* your plans for September, Rose? Will you go back to London?'

'I'm not exactly sure … I've got quite a lot to figure out personally,' she said. 'So let's just say that I'm keeping my options open right now.'

'Noted. If I do hear of any jobs locally, I'll let you know. I'm familiar with most of the local heads and I'll be writing you a sterling reference.'

'Thanks, I really appreciate that,' Rose said with a smile. As she stood up to leave Mrs Connolly's office, a sudden thought occurred to her. 'Actually, Mrs Connolly, there was something I wanted to ask if you don't mind?'

'Of course, Rose, go ahead.'

'I was wondering if it would be possible to arrange a trip for my class before the end of term? I was thinking of taking them to Harper Farm. We're studying living things and their habitats, you see, and a farm visit would be a great learning opportunity.'

'I don't see why not. As long as Mr Harper agrees and we can get the necessary risk assessments completed,' Mrs Connolly replied, taking her spectacles out of their case and placing them on the bridge of her nose. Rose beamed at her. 'You'll have to go up to the farm yourself though and get that completed in your own time.'

'Oh, yes, of course. That's not a problem. I could go up on Thursday when I'm not teaching and get that done straight away,' she said, struggling to hide the excitement in her voice.

'Excellent, I'll get all the paperwork printed and you can collect it at the end of the day.'

Rose left Mrs Connolly's office, clapped her hands together and walked towards her classroom with a fizz of excitement bubbling in her stomach. She'd only been back in school for five minutes and Mrs Connolly had commended her teaching skills and given her the go-ahead for a class trip to Jake's farm. She couldn't wait to tell Jake in person to see his reaction. She just knew he'd be ecstatic. If he was looking for ways to diversify the farm, the potential for setting up an education programme for local schools was certainly going to be a great start. Jake had done so much for her since she'd arrived in Blossom Heath, the chance to repay his kindness in some small way was the least she could do.

When Rose's Year 2 class arrived in school that morning there was a palpable buzz of excitement among them. They were all keen to be the first to ask their teacher about her heroic efforts with Hayden last week and their questions came thick and fast.

'Did you think he was going to die, Miss?' Billy Jenkins shouted, wide eyed with interest.

'Were you scared, Miss?' Poppy asked.

'What was it like in the ambulance?' Tiffany called out. 'Did they put the sirens on, Miss?'

'Alright, alright, Butterfly Class. I know you're all excited this morning and you've got a lot of questions, but how about we get our coats and bags hung up first and come and sit down on the carpet?' The class let out a murmur of agreement and followed their teacher's instructions.

Rose took the first ten minutes of the day to answer the children's questions in a calm and sensitive way before she set them up for their first learning activity, which happened to be a guided reading session. The rest of the morning whizzed by and before long the class had forgotten all about Rose's heroic exploits and she was back to being regular Miss Hargreaves, which was actually a relief.

Before she knew it, the bell had rung to signal the end of the school day and Rose could see the children's parents ready and waiting to collect them at the classroom door. Hayden's mum, Zoe, was first in the queue, and she was holding the largest bunch of flowers that Rose had ever seen.

'Rose, these are for you to say thank you,' Zoe said, smiling. 'Not that a bunch of flowers can even begin to express how grateful we are for what you did for Hayden, but we wanted to give you a token of our appreciation.' Rose smiled at her and accepted the flowers gratefully.

'There's honestly no need but they're absolutely beautiful and I know just the spot in the cottage to show them off perfectly,' she said graciously.

'Wow, Miss, they're the biggest bunch of flowers ever,' Tiffany said.

'I helped to choose them,' Hayden said, standing up tall and straight.

'Did you? Well, you did an excellent job, Hayden. They're beautiful.'

As Rose let the children out of the classroom door, one by one, matching each child to the parent that was collecting them, she noticed Mason's mum, Mrs Rowe, hanging back.

'I was wondering if I could come inside for a chat?' Mrs Rowe asked quietly.

'Of course,' Rose said, holding the classroom door open, 'come in and take a seat. Mason, why don't you go and look for some toys in the role play area while your mum and I talk?'

Mason nodded eagerly and ran off to explore.

'I don't want to take up too much of your time,' Mrs Rowe said anxiously as she sat down on one of the tiny classroom chairs, 'but I just wanted to check in with you and see how Mason is getting on? I've noticed a really positive change in him since the incident with Hayden and, well, I wanted to find out how you think he's doing?'

'I'm so glad he's more settled, Mrs Rowe. He really did surprise me last week. What happened with Hayden was frightening for the whole class and Mason was so grown up ... such a calming influence on the others.'

Mrs Rowe's face broke into a smile. 'I'm so pleased to hear that,' she said, looking visibly relieved. 'I thought with everything that had happened with his dad, an incident like that might have been a bit of a setback for him but, if any-thing, it seems to have had the opposite effect.'

'I agree,' Rose said, nodding. 'Given how quiet he's been since I started here, I could see that he was taking time to adjust. He completely took me by surprise when he started reassuring the others. He really stepped up and coped incredibly well. Mrs Connolly tells me that he's become friends with Billy and Hayden and the three of them are practically inseparable?'

'They really are. We had them both round for tea on Saturday and it's as if they've all been friends for years. It's been a tough few months for the pair of us, so I can't tell you what it means to see that Mason's starting to settle.' Rose could spot tears forming at the corners of Mrs Rowe's eyes and she passed her a tissue. 'Thanks.'

'You know, I lost my own mum when I was around Mason's age. Going through the loss of a parent is tough for any child, but Mason's got a great support network around him of family and friends. I know that's what helped me to cope,' Rose said. 'I'll make sure I keep an eye on how he's doing, but I'd say all the signs are positive that he's adjusting well to school life.'

'Thanks, Miss Hargreaves. I'd really appreciate you sharing that. Are you going to stay with the class in September? Mason keeps asking if you're still going to be his teacher next year.'

'I'm afraid not. I'm sure Mrs Jackson will be well on the road to recovery by then and I'll have moved on to pastures new.'

'Oh, that is a shame,' Mrs Rowe replied, her face falling.

'I know all the children in Butterfly Class love having you as their teacher.'

'Thank you. That means a lot,' Rose replied, a lump forming in her throat. 'I've really enjoyed being their teacher too.'

# Chapter 20

As Rose left school for the day, she made a quick detour on the way home to collect Scout from the dog-sitter, rushed back to Jasmine Cottage to grab the car and set off for Harper Farm. She couldn't wait to tell Jake her news. It was only yesterday she'd come up with the idea of running educational visits up at the farm as a way to diversify the business, and here she was with the go-ahead for the first school trip already.

As Rose glanced in her rear-view mirror, she spotted a black jeep in the distance. Hadn't she seen that same car parked up outside the cottage when she got home? She looked up again. It was still there. She was just being paranoid after yesterday's warning from PC Palmer, surely? There were thousands of black jeeps in Sussex after all. *Get a grip, Rose*, she told herself, her hands tightening on the steering wheel. As she made the left turn into the single-lane track that led up to Jake's farm, she was relieved to see that the jeep didn't follow. *See? I'm being paranoid.* She shook her head and dismissed her concerns.

As Rose let Scout out of the car, Tagg and Finn were

quick to greet her. Scout yipped in delight at being reunited with her canine companions. At the sound of Scout's bark, Jake emerged from the workshop next to the farmhouse and Rose gave him a wave.

'Rose! What are you doing here? Is everything okay? You've not had any trouble with the Fallons, have you?' he said, striding towards her.

'No, it's nothing like that. I bring good news for once,' she laughed. 'Remember our conversation yesterday about ways to diversify the farm's income?'

'Yes . . .'

'Well, I spoke to Mrs Connolly this morning about organizing a trip to the farm for my class and she's given me the go-ahead!'

'Seriously?' Jake said, his face breaking into a grin. 'Wow, you are a fast worker, Miss Hargreaves! That's amazing news.' He put his arms around her waist, scooped her up into a hug and spun her around. Rose felt goosebumps erupt all over her skin. She threw her head back and laughed.

'Ah, when I come up with a plan I don't mess around,' she replied, beaming, as Jake placed her back down. He caught her gaze with his bright blue eyes and they stood completely still, just looking at each other. Rose didn't want to look away. Something about Jake's expression kept her attention solely fixed on him.

'And when will this field trip be taking place?' he said, clearing his throat and averting his gaze. And just like that, the moment was gone.

'Er, I haven't quite got that far as yet, but there's only a few weeks left of term, so soon, hopefully. There's quite a lot of paperwork to get done first though. We'll have to think about how to structure the visit and what will be important for the kids to see. There's also the risk assessments to be done ...' Rose's voice trailed off. She could see Jake was shaking his head and laughing.

'Risk assessments? Wow, how things have changed since I was at school.'

'It's nothing too onerous,' Rose promised. 'And anyway, I'm used to doing them, so it won't take me long. I was thinking I could pop over on Thursday and we could go for a walk around the farm looking for potential hazards? Keep an eye out for child-eating cows and abandoned well shafts? You know, that sort of thing.'

'Well, I'm not sure about abandoned well shafts but we definitely have a few child-eating cows roaming around,' he snorted. 'Seeing as you're here, how about we take the dogs for a walk before you head off? It looks like Scout has some energy to burn off.' He pointed towards Scout who was play-bowing and trying to engage Finn in a game of chase.

'Perfect,' Rose agreed, and the pair set off with the dogs trotting eagerly at their heels.

If he was being honest with himself, Jake knew that a walk with Rose and the dogs would be just what he needed to keep his mind from the prospect of Sarah's impending visit, so he was thrilled that she'd agree to stay.

Julie Haworth

As Jake waited for his ex to arrive at the farmhouse later that evening, he couldn't stop his thoughts drifting back to Rose. There had been something between them after he'd hugged her in the yard earlier, he was *sure* of it. What was it exactly, though? A moment? A connection? A spark? Had she felt it too? He was sure that she had – there was something in the way that she had looked at him, held his gaze with her eyes, that made him think she felt the same.

Sarah arrived at the farmhouse at exactly eight o'clock. It was a warm summer's evening and she was dressed in a knee-length pink floral wrap dress that Jake knew she would have remembered was one of his favourites. Her fingers and toe-nails were painted the same shade as her pink kitten-heeled sandals and she clutched a bottle of Pinot Noir, one of his favourite wines, in each carefully manicured hand. She had clearly thought through her strategy for the evening in detail, he noted. Jake hadn't planned on drinking this evening – he wanted to keep a clear head, but it was always difficult for him to say no to a Pinot Noir.

'Something smells delicious,' she said, kissing him on the cheek and lingering for a second longer than she needed to. He could smell the familiar scent of her favourite perfume linger in the air. The dogs rushed to greet her and she bent down to give them a stroke before refocusing her attention on Jake. 'You didn't have to go to all this trouble for me,' she continued, indicating the pots that were bubbling away on the Aga.

'It's no trouble. I'd have been cooking for myself anyway,' he said dismissively.

220

'Why don't I pour us both a glass?' she said, nodding towards the bottles of wine she had placed on the table.

Jake hesitated for a moment before giving in. 'Sure, why not?' he shrugged. Sarah opened one of the bottles and poured him a large glass. She brought her own glass up to her nose and inhaled deeply. She closed her eyes and took a sip.

'Ah, delicious,' she said. 'You always did have great taste in wine. Just one of the many things that I love about you . . .'

'Will you stop saying that?'

'Saying what?'

'That you love me. It's not fair.' He turned to face her.

'But it's the truth—'

'Just because I've invited you here tonight, doesn't mean I've decided anything. It doesn't mean that we're . . . getting back together,' he said, his shoulders stiffening.

'But surely we have to try? You must be considering it, Jakey, or you wouldn't have invited me here?' Jake was silent, he turned towards the pans on the Aga and began stirring one of the pots furiously. Sarah moved in behind him, placing a hand on his right hip. 'I was hoping that you might even invite me to stay the night?' Jake turned to face her and Sarah pressed her body up against him, placing her arms around his neck. She moved her mouth slowly towards his left ear and whispered, 'I just want things to go back to how they used to be, Jakey. You and me,' she said slowly, 'together.'

Jake's face felt hot, and his breathing quickened. Sarah placed a hand on the nape of his neck and he felt his skin tingle at her touch. Her head moved slowly towards his as she pulled him in even closer to her. He felt powerless at her touch. She pressed her lips lightly against his at first and then drew him into a deeper, more passionate kiss. Jake's body responded as if on autopilot. It was easy, familiar, to let himself give into her. Their bodies knew each other so well – they had done this a thousand times before, after all. Sarah began unbuttoning his shirt and kissing his chest. He groaned in pleasure. He found himself kissing her again more deeply, pulling her in even closer to him. His breathing became faster and hotter. Before he had time to think, she had untied the bow at the waist of her dress and it fell open to reveal her pink satin underwear. She took a step towards him, pushed her breasts up against him and kissed him slowly and deeply.

'C'mon, Jakey, let's take this to the bedroom,' she said breathlessly as she took him by the hand and led him to the room they had once shared together. She pushed him down gently onto the bed, straddled him and kissed him again while her hands reached for his belt buckle. Jake knew he was thinking with his body and not his mind, but this felt good, *really* good. Without thinking, he reached up and unclasped her bra. 'Oh, Jake,' he heard her whisper as their lips parted, 'I knew you'd see sense ... I knew you couldn't resist me.' As she kissed him again, Jake heard her words echoing in his head as if on a loop. *See sense?* What did she mean by that? She'd almost made it sound like he was the one at fault. His shoulders stiffened. Suddenly everything about this felt wrong to him. He pulled his lips away from hers abruptly. Sarah giggled.

'What's wrong, Jakey, why are we stopping? We're only just starting to make up.' She leaned in to kiss him again, but he turned his head away. 'Jake?' she said, looking confused.

'I'm sorry but I can't do this,' he said, sliding his body out from under her.

'But, Jakey?' She grabbed his hand and entwined her fingers with his. 'Don't be like that ... C'mon, making up's supposed to be the fun part,' she said, running her fingers through his hair. Jake pulled away from her and sat up on the bed.

'I'm sorry. I shouldn't have kissed you. That was a mistake. In fact, this whole thing is a mistake.'

'Well, technically I kissed you, but you certainly seemed to be pretty keen on the idea,' she said, laughing. 'Don't be silly, Jakey, you know you still want me. If you didn't, you wouldn't have kissed me like that, would you?' She twirled her long blonde hair around her fingers and tilted her head to one side. He didn't reply. 'You're just in a bit of shock, that's all. There's been a lot for you to take in the last few days. It's my fault. I'm trying to take things too ... quickly. I'm sorry, Jakey,' she said, reaching for his hand again. 'Let's slow things down a bit and you can come around to the idea at your own pace. I just know that, eventually, you're going to end up seeing things my way.'

Jake felt himself bristle again at her words. She was talking as though he had no choice in the matter. He gripped the edge of the mattress tightly. Sarah always managed to manip-ulate him into following her agenda and tonight was no different. She'd decided that she wanted to get back together, she'd decided to kiss him, and he'd almost fallen straight into bed with her again. He took a deep, steadying breath.

'That's the thing though, Sarah. I don't need time. If anything, what's just happened between us has helped me see things more clearly. We're over. There's no going back for us.'

'Don't be silly, Jakey, we've got too much history together to just throw things away. We're *meant* to be together,' she said soothingly, rubbing his back. 'You just need time to see it, that's all. I can wait. I'll give you all the time you need to come around.'

'You're wasting your time. I'm not going to change my mind. I've . . . moved on.' Sarah eyed him suspiciously, studying his face intently.

'What do you mean you've moved on? Is there someone else?' she asked sharply.

Jake hesitated, his thoughts turning to Rose.

'It doesn't matter if there is. It's nothing to do with you anymore—'

'There *is* someone, isn't there?' she said, pulling her dress around her and tying it at the front.

'Like I said, it's nothing to do with you—'

'Who is she?' Sarah demanded, her face tightening. Once again, Jake couldn't help his thoughts turning straight to Rose. He was starting to feel something for her, it was true, but that wasn't something he wanted to share with Sarah.

'All you need to know is that we're over, Sarah. I've really got nothing more to say to you. I'm sorry if you feel like I've led you on tonight, that wasn't my intention, but we really are done.' Sarah forced her features into a thin-lipped smile.

'I can see that I'm not going to be able to get through to you tonight, Jakey, but let's talk again ... I don't want to argue with you. Once you've slept on it, you'll see things more clearly. Take my word for it.' She stood up and slipped her feet back into her sandals. Jake shook his head. Sarah walked towards him and placed a gentle kiss on his cheek. 'I'm not giving up this easily, Jake Harper. You know I always get what I want, and what I want is ... *you*.'

As he watched Sarah's car pull out of the driveway, Jake wasn't sure if he truly believed what he'd told her this evening. *Were they really over? Had he really ended it for good?* All it had taken tonight was for Sarah to kiss him and he'd practically jumped straight back into bed with her. She seemed determined to test his resolve and, if there was one thing that he could say for certain about Sarah, it was that she almost always got what she wanted when she put her mind to it.

# Chapter 21

After another busy day at school the following day, Rose decided to pop into the village gift shop, the Pink Ribbon, before she set off for the hospital. She wanted to get something to lift her aunt's spirits, as she knew she'd be feeling low after the setback in her recovery. The shop was run by Simon and Anya, a couple in their mid-forties who had moved to Blossom Heath to take over the shop's lease when the previous tenant retired. Even though they'd been in the village for nearly a decade, that still made the couple relative newcomers to village life. Rose was a big fan of the little shop and made sure she stopped by whenever she visited Blossom Heath to pick up a new scented candle or two.

'Rose!' Anya cried when she spotted Rose enter the store. 'How lovely to have you back!' she continued, putting the greetings cards she was busy sorting down on the counter.

'Hiya, how's things?' asked Rose with a wave.

'Oh, we're both good. How's Jean? We heard about what happened.'

'Oh, you know, she's on the mend but it's been a tough few weeks for her.'

'I bet. Hang on, let me give Simon a shout. He won't forgive me if he misses you.' She opened the door at the bottom of the flight of stairs to the flat above the shop and shouted, 'Simon! Rose has just popped in. Come down and say hello, will you?'

'I just wanted to grab a get-well card, if you have any?' Rose asked.

'Do you know what, I've got just the thing in this box I'm unpacking.' Anya shuffled through the pile of cards that was on the counter in front of her and produced a cute little card with a basket of Border Collie puppies on the front and the letters 'Get Well Soon' emblazoned across it.

'Ah, that's perfect. Thanks, Anya,' said Rose, reaching for her purse.

'Well, I know Jean loves her collies. She bought a key ring with a similar dog on the front recently.'

'Yep, I know the one. It reminds her of Jack.'

'Oh, of course, I'd forgotten he was a collie too,' said Anya with a nod.

'Oooooh,' said Rose, turning quickly as something shiny caught her eye. 'I'm looking for something to put a smile on her face and these rainbow plaques are *gorgeous*.'

'I know, right? They only came in yesterday but they're selling really well. Jean could hang one next to her bed – I'm sure it would brighten things up for her.'

Rose picked the hanging plaque up to examine it more closely and she could see it had some engraving on it: '*The greater the storm, the brighter the rainbow.*'

'Perfect,' she agreed. 'I'll take it.'

Anya smiled and began expertly wrapping the plaque in some pale pink tissue paper. 'Just let me add a finishing touch,' she said as she tied the gift up beautifully with some silver ribbon and handed it to Rose.

'Thanks, Anya. Oh, I see you've got the posters up for the missing dogs?' said Rose, indicating towards the back wall of the shop. 'I'd heard a couple had gone missing locally.'

'I know, it's terrible, isn't it? Apparently another one went missing a few days ago from a village outside Hastings. A dachshund I think it was.'

'Really? That's awful.'

At that moment, Simon emerged from the door at the bottom of the stairs. 'Oh, Rose, great to see you. How's it going at the school? We'd heard you'd been helping out while they're a teacher short.'

'All good, thanks. Very different from teaching in London though,' she replied.

'I bet! I can't think of anywhere more different to Blossom Heath,' he agreed.

'They're worlds apart, but let's just say I'm enjoying my time here,' she said with a smile.

'Pleased to hear it,' said Simon.

'Listen, Rose, don't ever feel like you're stuck on your own up at Jasmine Cottage. Simon and I are usually around in the evenings, so if you feel like a bit of company or a trip out to the pub, just let us know,' said Anya.

'That's really kind,' said Rose with genuine gratitude.

'I might just take you up on that. Usually I'm hanging out with Aunt Jean when I visit, so it's strange not to have her around . . .' Rose felt her voice catch a little.

'That's understandable,' Simon agreed. 'She'll be home before you know it though and, remember, we're only a call away if you need anything.'

As Rose left the gift shop, popping her newly purchased items into her handbag, she couldn't help but smile when she thought of the way everyone looked out for each other in Blossom Heath. She really did feel *part* of something here and that's something she hadn't felt in London for a long time.

It was a warm June evening, and Rose enjoyed the gentle ripple of the breeze on her face through the open car window on the drive to the hospital. As she arrived on the ward, Rose made her way straight over to the nurses' station to speak to the sister.

'Ah, Miss Hargreaves, lovely to see you again. You'll be pleased to hear that your aunt is doing well. She's responding to the antibiotics nicely.'

'That's a relief,' said Rose, her shoulders relaxing.

'Her consultant is pleased with how she's doing but a second surgery does mean her recovery has been put back. She's going to have to stay with us a few weeks longer.'

'Ah, and I'm guessing she isn't too pleased about that?'

'Well, no. That would be putting it mildly, I'm afraid. I know she can't wait to get home but that's just not realistic at the moment.'

'Point taken. I'll do my best to try and rally her spirits but I can't blame her for feeling a little down. Luckily, I come bearing gifts,' she said, tapping her handbag. As she walked through the ward, her aunt spotted her from a distance.

'Rose, how lovely to see you, dear,' said Jean, folding up her knitting and stuffing it under her pillow. 'I wasn't expecting to see you today?'

'I thought I'd come and check up on you and see what trouble you've been causing,' she said, bending down to kiss her aunt on the cheek.

'Me? Causing trouble? I'd never dream of it,' Aunt Jean replied with mock indignation. 'I suppose Nurse Ratchett over there has told you all about them wanting to keep me in for a few more weeks?' she said, nodding her head towards the nurses' station.

'Afraid so. I'm just pleased that you're on the road to recovery. You gave me quite the scare over the weekend.'

'Oh, I am sorry, dear. I wasn't best pleased about having another op, I can tell you. But the doctors here seem to know what they're doing,' she admitted reluctantly.

'I brought you this to cheer you up,' said Rose, passing her aunt the gift and card.

'Oh, Rose, you shouldn't have,' said Aunt Jean as she pulled the wrapping paper away gently to reveal the rainbow plaque beneath. 'Oh, this is beautiful.' Her eyes paused for a moment to linger over the message engraved on the rainbow. 'Rose, I *love* it. Those are wise words, my dear – thanks for the reminder,' she said, taking Rose's hand.

'There *are* brighter days ahead, Auntie, don't you worry about that.'

'Whenever I'm feeling sorry for myself, I'll look at this to remind me.' Rose took the plaque from her aunt and carefully hung it next to her bed.

'I hope it helps,' said Rose, squeezing her aunt's hand.

'It already has. So, how are things with you and Jake?' Aunt Jean asked, changing the subject.

'There *is* no me and Jake. Honestly, Auntie, you really do need to stop trying to play matchmaker—'

'I'm doing no such thing.'

'Erm, I seem to remember that the last time I was here you ripped the phone out of my hand and told Jake to come and pick me up,' Rose reminded her.

'Well, it's hardly my fault if you don't know a good thing when you see it, Rose Hargreaves,' Aunt Jean replied, crossing her arms in front of her. She suddenly frowned. 'What's wrong, dear? You know I can always tell when something's bothering you.'

Rose's shoulders slumped. She hadn't planned on mentioning anything about Ollie this evening, but she realized that she should have known better than to try to get anything past Aunt Jean.

'Well, Ollie visited at the weekend, and let's just say things didn't go to plan.'

'Oh no, what happened?'

'I was so excited to show him the village and for him to meet Scout. I wanted him to see how happy I am since I've been in Blossom Heath and that there could be other possibilities for our future together, but . . .'

'But what, dear?'

'Well, he'd arranged a work dinner with his colleagues and he just turns into such a different person when he's around them. It's hard to explain unless you see it but it's almost like he's showing off in front of them, trying to prove something. He's so concerned with having the right car, the perfect house, and I just don't care about any of that stuff. I'm just not sure that it feels *right* between us anymore.'

Aunt Jean took Rose by the hand and looked her in the eyes.

'If it's not right, my dear, it's far better that you talk things through with Ollie now rather than just putting your head in the sand. Whatever you decide, you know that I'll support you. It's your life, my dear, and it's your call.' Rose reached across to hug her. Her aunt's support meant everything, and she should have known that she would react to her doubts about Ollie with kindness.

'Thanks, Auntie,' Rose said quietly.

'The only piece of advice I'll give you,' Aunt Jean continued, 'is that if you truly know that the boy isn't for you, make sure you face up to things and tell him straight away, won't you? Don't put it off any longer than you have to. And if you decide not to go back to London . . . you know there's always room for you at Jasmine Cottage for however long you'd like to stay.'

'Really? Are you sure you wouldn't mind if I stayed on?'

'Mind?' Aunt Jean replied with a chuckle. 'Rose, I'd be delighted. I'd love the company for one thing. It's no fun rattling around in that place on my own.'

'But what about Scout?'

'What about Scout? When have you ever known me not to want a dog around the place?' she continued with a smile. 'I'll have the best of both worlds – you can do all the walking and I can have all the cuddles.'

'Thanks, Auntie. You've definitely given me a lot to think about.'

'Do you remember that time I took you to the Rye Raft Race?' Aunt Jean asked out of nowhere.

'How could I forget! Most of us ended up in the water down at Rye Harbour!'

Jean threw her head back and laughed. 'That's right! Pete and Ted had built a raft out of barrels from the pub and the idiots hadn't considered whether the damn thing would actually float.'

'Well, it sort of did, for about thirty seconds,' Rose added with a smirk.

'Didn't Beth clout Pete with an oar? She'd had her hair done specially and she ended up looking like a drowned rat!'

'That's right! Wasn't there a free bar at the pub afterwards to make up for the soaking we all got?'

'Well, Pete had to make it up to us all somehow,' she laughed. 'Oh, Rose, I do miss those days. We had fun, didn't we? Even after your mum had passed?'

Rose took her aunt's hand. 'We did. Those were tough

days, and being with you in Blossom Heath put some sunshine into them. I think that's partly why I *love* this place so much. Oh, and you of course,' Rose giggled.

'Of course, my dear. I love you too,' she whispered as she squeezed Rose's hand tightly.

'I know, Auntie, I know.'

As Rose drove back to Jasmine Cottage, she received a call from her dad, which she quickly switched to hands free. 'Dad, hi! Thanks for calling, I'm just driving back from the hospital.'

'How's your aunt? Is everything okay?'

'She's good but—'

'What is it, Rose? Has something happened?'

'Look, it's nothing for you to worry about but, well ... Jean did run into some complications—'

'What kind of complications?'

'Erm, she had an infection—'

'An infection?'

'Yes, but she's fine now I promise,' said Rose.

'That's it, I'm booking a flight and heading back—'

'Dad, no! This is exactly why I didn't want to tell you! Jean's fine, honestly ... She's had another surgery and she's doing well. She's just going to have to stay in hospital for a few weeks longer, that's all.'

'I'm really not happy leaving you to deal with all this on your own, sweetheart. I should be there.' Rose could hear a catch in her dad's voice.

'But there's nothing you could do differently, Dad. I'm coping just fine and Jean's in good spirits. She'd be heartbroken if she thought she was the reason for you cutting your trip short ...' There was a long pause at the other end of the line.

'Well, if you *promise* to keep me up to speed on things and swear that you'll call me if anything changes ...'

'You've been saving for this trip for years, Dad. You never take time for yourself and I've got things covered. If anything changes, I *promise* I'll let you know straight away.' There was another long pause, and Rose could sense that her dad was considering what she'd said carefully.

'Okay, okay. I'll stay put for now, sweetheart, but let me know if you need me and I'll be there.'

'I've known that my whole life, Dad,' Rose said quietly. 'I love you.'

'I love you too, sweetheart,' he replied.

# Chapter 22

It didn't take long for Thursday to come around and Rose found herself back up at Harper Farm bright and early with the paperwork from school in hand. Jake greeted her at the front door of the farmhouse with a cup of tea.

'Fancy a brew?' he asked, as Rose let Scout out of the car.

'I wouldn't say no,' she replied, feeling as though she hadn't quite woken up yet. It was the first time in all the visits that she had made to Harper Farm that she had been inside the farmhouse. The back door opened straight from the yard into the kitchen, which was cosy and inviting. Tagg and Finn shared a large, chequered dog bed next to the fireplace and they greeted Scout with friendly wags as she settled down beside them.

There was a sizeable oak dining table and chairs in the centre of the kitchen, and Jake stood in front of a dark green Aga, warming the kettle.

'Milk and sugar?'

'Just milk, thanks.' Rose could see that the kitchen was the hub of the farmhouse, and she found herself imagining how cosy it must be on a winter's evening with the fireplace lit and a hearty pie cooking in the oven. 'This is such a lovely country kitchen, Jake. It's exactly what I'd imagine a farm kitchen to be. I bet it was lovely growing up here.'

'It was. Mum loved baking, so we'd always come home from school to find something delicious sitting on the cooling rack.' His smile broadened. 'I don't think I appreciated the peace and quiet as a kid though. You know what it's like when you're a teenager – living in the country seems like *miles* away from all the action. I used to pester Mum and Dad about getting my driver's licence as soon as I turned seventeen. All I wanted to do was head into Hastings and party.'

'Ah well, that's teenagers for you. They're all too quick to want to grow up and leave home.'

'Listen to us,' Jake laughed, 'we sound like a right pair of old codgers.'

'Oi! Speak for yourself,' Rose said, punching him playfully on the arm. 'Mind you, I am coming up for thirty in a couple of years,' she continued with a sigh.

'I didn't realize you were practically a pensioner!' he teased.

'As if! Come to think of it, I'm more than happy with a takeaway and a movie on a Saturday night, and if that makes me a pensioner, so be it! My clubbing days are long behind me.'

'Just give me a prawn biriyani and an episode of *Strictly* on a Saturday night and I'm all set,' he snorted.

'Seriously?' she said, almost splurting out her tea. 'Somehow I didn't have you pegged as a *Strictly* fan.'

'Hey!' Jake said with mock indignation. 'It's got music, sequins and a bit of fake tan. What's not to like?'

'Well, I'm certainly seeing you in a new light, Jake Harper!'

'C'mon,' Jake said after they'd finished their tea, 'we'd better make a start with this risk assessment or we'll be sat here all day talking about the Cha Cha Cha.'

The walk around the farm was a huge success, and Rose was able to come up with so many points of interest for the children. She decided that they would initially meet the animals, which included pigs, sheep, chickens and geese, and Jake would then talk them through their habitats, cover some animal care skills and let them help with feeding the pigs. There was also farm machinery to investigate and, as harvest time was coming up, there was lots that Rose could link back to the harvest festival learning earlier in the school year. They would have a picnic lunch in one of the fields and then Jake was going to show the children Tagg and Finn's herding skills, using the geese and then the sheep, which Rose knew they'd find thrilling.

'Honestly, Jake, this is going to be great. The children are going to love it here.'

'I hope you're right. If I'm being honest, doing something like this had never really occurred to me before.'

'Ah well, that's because you didn't have a highly skilled educational adviser like me in the mix before,' she chuckled. 'If this goes well, I wouldn't be surprised if Mrs Connolly makes it a regular thing, and I'm sure you'd get other local schools wanting to sign up too. They won't have huge budgets for things like trips, but if we can design something that links to the curriculum for certain year groups, I'm sure we could come up with something that would be financially viable for them *and* help you make some money.'

'Seriously? That would be amazing, and just what this place needs. Farming has changed so much recently. Relying on wool and produce sales isn't enough to make ends meet anymore,' he said with a sigh.

'I'll do whatever I can to help make it a success. I know you've got a lot riding on this.'

'I really am very lucky that you turned up in Blossom Heath,' he said, his eyes holding Rose's gaze. She felt her mouth go dry and her hands become clammy. As she said her goodbyes and drove home from the farm, she couldn't help thinking of Jake's parting words to her. *What exactly did he mean by lucky?* Was he talking about the help she was giving him on the farm, or did he mean something else? Maybe, she thought, it wasn't so ridiculous to think that he could have feelings for her after all.

As Jake walked back to the farmhouse after Rose had left, he thought back to how things had turned out with Sarah last week. He was going to have to see her again to straighten things out. He knew that he'd given her the wrong impression by kissing her when she'd visited, and no matter how badly she'd behaved towards him in the past, he didn't want to lead her on, to give her hope where there really wasn't any. He took his phone out of his pocket and sent her a text:

*Let's meet on Friday and clear the air. 8pm? The Apple Tree?*

Meeting in public would be the best option. That way there'd be no chance of him nearly falling into bed with her again. Before he had even put his phone back in his pocket, it beeped with a message from Sarah:

*I'll be there xx*

Jake's heart sank. What was it going to take for her to realize that they really were over?

# Chapter 23

When Rose woke up the next morning, she decided to take her Aunt Jean's advice and get in touch with Ollie. She would have to see him face to face and talk things through. There was too much at stake for them to have a conversation about their future together over the phone. Turning on her phone, she sent him a text.

*Are you free on Sunday? I'm coming back to London for the day. We need to talk about our relationship.*

Ollie replied quickly.

*I know I messed up last weekend, Rose. I hope you got the flowers? Let's talk on Sunday. Love you xx*

Rose gulped and felt the anxiety bubble up in her stomach. She knew this wasn't going to be an easy discussion to have, and the last thing she wanted to do was hurt Ollie, but the simple fact was that she just wasn't sure if they were right for each other anymore. He may have admitted that he had behaved badly last weekend, but an apology and a bunch of flowers wasn't enough. They were different people from when they had first got together, Rose could see that now, and she wasn't sure that she wanted the same things as him.

It may be painful to admit, but she knew she had to face up to the doubts that she was having about their relationship. Could it still be salvaged? She tapped out her reply.

*Yes, I got the flowers. I'll be back at the flat around midday.*

There. It was done.

Rose had arranged to meet Grace for a drink at the Apple Tree on Friday evening. As she came out of the house with Scout, she noticed the same dark jeep parked outside Jasmine Cottage that she thought had been following her earlier in the week. She looked at the car from a distance and could see that it was empty. It was probably just someone visiting one of the other cottages; 4x4s were very common in the country – practically everyone had one. *Come on, Rose*, she told herself. *Pull yourself together.* As Rose got nearer to the pub, she could hear footsteps in the distance behind her.

'Excuse me, love. You got a light?' a man's voice called from behind her.

'Sorry, I don't smoke,' Rose said, turning around. The man was tall and slender, with light blonde hair, and was dressed in jeans, a white T-shirt and dark, muddy trainers. Rose hadn't seen him in the village before.

'That's a lovely dog you've got there,' he said with a crooked smile that unnerved Rose slightly. 'What's her name?'

'Erm … it's Scout,' Rose said. The man bent down to fuss Scout and Rose heard the dog emit a very low growl that was barely audible. Rose tugged at the lead and walked on quickly.

'She's a Border Collie, right?' the man asked, seeming undeterred. 'Have you 'ad her long?'

'Not long, no,' Rose answered, looking at her watch. 'Look, I've got to rush – I'm meeting a friend.'

'No bother,' the man replied. Rose couldn't quite place his accent, but he sounded as though he was from the north of England. As she got closer to the pub, Rose was aware that he was still walking behind her. He entered the pub a few seconds after her and headed straight to the bar.

Rose spotted Grace and made her way over to her without stopping to order a drink.

'Grace, do you know that guy at the bar?' Rose said, nodding in the stranger's direction.

'What the tallish, blonde one?' Grace replied, raising an eyebrow. 'Can't say I've ever seen him before.'

'He was walking behind me all the way from the cottage and asked me for a light. He asked about Scout too. What sort of dog was she, how long had I had her, that sort of thing. You don't think he could be something to do with the Fallons, do you?' she asked in a whisper.

'I wouldn't have thought so. I've never seen him around and I know most of the Fallons by sight. He's probably just a tourist,' Grace said with a shrug, 'we get them here all the time in the summer.'

'Hm, maybe,' Rose said, relaxing a little and settling Scout underneath the table. 'Scout definitely thought there was something off about him though. She growled when he bent down to stroke her.'

'Did she?' said Grace, raising her eyebrows. 'Well, dogs can get spooked if they see someone that reminds them of a bad experience. I'm sure that's all it is.'

'You're probably right,' Rose agreed, grabbing her purse. 'Okay, I'll get the drinks in, shall I? What are you having?'

Rose spent most of the evening explaining her dilemma with Ollie. Grace listened without judgement and, when Rose had finished going over the events of the previous weekend, she said, 'For what it's worth, I've always felt as though you were having doubts whenever you've talked about Ollie. People change as they get older. I know I'm certainly nothing like I was when I was at uni. I just want different things out of life now – it's only natural really. It doesn't make you a bad person – your priorities have just changed.'

'I know it's going to be a difficult conversation, but I need to face up to it. It's no good just burying my head in the sand and hoping things will work themselves out. Coming to Blossom Heath has made me look at my life differently. I don't think I've really been that happy in London for a long time. It's just easier not to deal with these things sometimes though, isn't it?'

'You know, it's a pretty *brave* thing you're doing, Rose – facing up to things, I mean. Some people spend their whole lives stuck in a rut just because it's the easy option. Whatever happens on Sunday, I'll be here for you to vent at when you get back. Make sure you call me the minute you're home.'

'Don't worry, you'll be the first person I call,' Rose

promised, 'and thanks, Grace. You've been a really good friend to me since I've been in Blossom Heath.'

'Likewise,' Grace said with a smile. 'You know, you're the first *proper* friend I've made in the village. I'm usually so busy with work that there's never time for much else.'

'I know, I can't believe we've only known each other a few weeks . . . We just *clicked*, didn't we? You probably know more about me than half my friends in London. Between teaching and Ollie there's not much time for a social life. My teacher friend Maya is pretty much the only person I've been in touch with since I've been here. How crazy is that?'

Grace laughed. 'Sounds familiar. Sometimes life just kinda gets in the way, doesn't it? Do you think you'll go back to London when school breaks up for the summer? I have a vested interest of course . . . I'd love it if you and Scout were here to stay.'

'I'm honestly not sure. I guess a lot depends on how things go with Ollie. Aunt Jean has said I can stay at the cottage for as long as I like, which has given me a bit of breathing space.' She paused and took a sip of her drink. 'If I can find a teaching job locally, Ollie could still come and visit at weekends and I can go back to London in the holidays.'

'Well, fingers crossed. I'm sure all the local schools have heard about your heroics with Hayden by now, so there'll be a queue of headteachers waiting to sign you up,' Grace laughed. 'Honestly, though, if you're thinking about staying permanently, I'll chat to my dad and see if any of his contacts might know of a vacancy.'

'Would you?'

'I'll call him first thing and put some feelers out. Fingers crossed something turns up.'

'Fingers crossed.'

At that moment, Rose saw Jake walk into the pub and scan the room. Clearly he was looking for someone. She gave him a wave, but he looked straight through her. Within seconds, he had made his way towards a booth and sat down next to a stunning blonde, who kissed him on the cheek. For some reason the gesture startled Rose, and she turned her head away, knocking her wine glass slightly in the process and spilling some of the contents over Grace.

Grace hadn't seen Jake come in and began grabbing some tissues from her handbag to wipe up the mess. 'You really are a clutz,' she said in mock exasperation. 'What's got you so distracted anyway?'

'Who's that over there with Jake?' Rose asked quietly, nodding towards him.

'Crikey that is a surprise,' she said once she'd looked up.

'What is?'

'That's Sarah, Jake's ex. What on earth are they are doing out together—'

'*That's* Sarah?' Rose asked, feeling her chest tighten. 'Do you think they're back together then?'

'I wouldn't have thought so,' Grace said, shaking her head. 'Not after the way she treated him.'

'Well, they look pretty cosy to me,' Rose said, pulling apart one of the paper napkins on the table with her fingers. 'Not that it's any of my business of course,' she added quickly.

'I suppose they were together for a long time and Sarah always was one for getting her own way ... stranger things *have* happened,' Grace conceded.

Rose noticed that Sarah had placed a hand on Jake's knee and was sliding over to sit even closer to him. Jake looked up towards Rose and she turned her head away quickly, aware that she had been staring at the couple.

'Grace, did you see what happened to that guy who followed me in?' she asked, keen to change the subject. 'Is he still here?'

'Um, I don't know,' Grace replied, glancing around the pub. 'I can't see him anywhere, can you?'

'No, I guess he must have left. Maybe he was just a tourist stopping in for a pint like you said?'

'Honestly, you're worrying too much. I can't see the Fallons sending someone to follow you around. If they really were going to try and take Scout back – and I personally don't think they will – they'd do it themselves. They wouldn't get someone else involved.'

'I guess you know them better than I do,' Rose said with a sigh.

'Listen, if you're feeling that nervous, how about I walk back to the cottage with you and I'll call a cab from there?'

'If you really don't mind?' Rose said, her shoulders relaxing a little.

'Of course I don't,' Grace said with a smile, finishing off

the last of her gin and tonic in one gulp. 'C'mon, let's hit the road,' she said, linking her arm through Rose's.

Jake scanned the packed bar at the Apple Tree and was able to spot Sarah in one of the corner booths. He took a deep breath in and walked towards her, taking a seat on the bench next to her.

'Hiya, I got you a drink in,' she said, nodding towards a pint of Guinness on the table. 'I take it Guinness is still your favourite?'

He nodded and took a swig. 'Thanks.'

'Listen, thanks for suggesting we meet up. I know we left things a little awkwardly the other night,' she said, running her red manicured fingernail around the rim of her wine glass.

Jake took a deep breath in. This was going to be difficult. As he looked up from his drink, he spotted Rose sitting at the opposite end of the pub. She looked away quickly when she saw him. He felt his heartbeat quicken in his chest at the sight of her. The last thing he wanted was for Rose to spot him out with another woman. He didn't want her getting the wrong idea.

'Jake?' Sarah asked. 'Have you heard a word I've been saying?' He realized that he hadn't a clue what she had been telling him. 'Who are you looking at anyway?' Jake snapped his eyes straight back to her.

'No one,' he said, trying to sound innocent and taking a swig of his pint.

'Yes, you were. It's that girl over there, isn't it? I saw her staring at us earlier. Who is she?'

'Er, I thought we came here to talk about us?' he said, trying to change the subject. Sarah put her hand on his leg and slid her body closer towards him.

'You're right. I know I tried to move things along too quickly the other night, but I hope you've had time to see things more clearly now, Jakey?' she said, moving her hand further up his leg. Jake put his hand over hers firmly and moved it away. Sarah took the opportunity to weave her fingers through his and she gripped his hand tightly.

'I haven't changed my mind, Sarah. I'm not here to get back together – I shouldn't have let things go as far as they did between us the other night. That was wrong of me. I wanted to meet up today to explain. I don't want to lead you on. We really are . . . over.'

'You're not leading me on, Jakey,' she said, twirling her long blonde hair with her left hand. 'I may have made the first move the other night, but you kissed me right back. I could *feel* that you still wanted me – it was written all over your face. You just need a bit more time to realize it, that's all.' Jake swallowed hard.

'Look, I'm not saying there's no chemistry between us – there probably always will be. If I'm being honest, it threw me when you told me what happened with Miles and said you wanted me back. It messed with my head and I wasn't sure what I wanted. Then, when you kissed me, I just responded . . .'

249

'Exactly. You responded because you know that we're *right* together. C'mon, Jakey.' Sarah slid her hand back on to his knee. This time, Jake didn't move it away.

'I don't know what I want right now. I never expected you to turn up again like this. It's messing with my head.'

'You just need more time, Jakey, that's all. I know seeing me again was a shock for you . . . it's a lot to take in. It's going to take time for you to work through your feelings, but I'm patient. I can wait.' She leaned in towards him and planted a gentle kiss on his cheek, her hand moving slowly up his leg. 'How about we finish up and you walk me to my car?' she whispered. Jake nodded and took a final swig of his pint.

As he followed Sarah out to the car park, she slowed her pace, taking his hand in hers and, once again, Jake didn't pull away. As they reached her car, a green Mini Cooper, and she fumbled in her handbag for her keys, Jake couldn't help noticing how beautiful she was. This was the woman he had planned to marry. Could he really dismiss the possibility of a reconciliation so easily? Was Sarah right? Did he just need more time to come around to the idea? As though sensing his moment of weakness, Sarah made her move. She stepped in towards him, placed her hands on his hips and kissed him. Jake responded and kissed her back deeply. He ran his hands through her long blonde hair and the kiss intensified. It felt hot and urgent. It was as though logic and reason had been abandoned and all he could think of right now was the physical connection between them. Sarah pulled away first and giggled breathlessly.

'How about I give you a lift back to the farm for a nightcap and . . . we see where the evening takes us?' she said, running a finger down his chest. Jake hesitated. This was just like the other night. One kiss and he was about to forget everything he had told her this evening and jump into bed with her. Sensing his reluctance, Sarah grabbed his belt buckle and pulled him in towards her for a second kiss.

'Okay,' Jake whispered in her ear as they pulled apart.

Sarah flashed a smile at him and clapped her hands together. 'Perfect.'

As Jake got into the car and strapped himself into the passenger's seat, Sarah hit the accelerator and pulled out of the Apple Tree's car park, heading straight for Harper Farm.

# Chapter 24

Rose spent the day on Saturday trying to find anything to do that would distract her from the impending trip to London to see Ollie. Rose didn't think it was sensible for her to take Scout with her. The conversation was going to be difficult enough without Ollie freaking out about dog hairs on the sofa, so she'd already arranged for Grace to have Scout for the day.

She took some time to scour the *Times Educational Supplement* for teaching jobs in Sussex but, so far, she couldn't see anything suitable, which was somewhat disheartening. There were only a few weeks left of the summer term and she knew that any vacancies that were available would start becoming scarce as the holidays drew near.

Rose's phone rang and she saw it was Camille. *Camille? What on earth was that woman ringing her about?* She'd never got in touch with Rose before. In fact, she couldn't even remember ever adding Camille's details to her contact list. Rose hit the decline button. There was no way she wanted to ruin her day even further by hearing anything Camille had to say.

Rose spent the rest of the day trying, and failing, to keep

her mind off Ollie. If she did manage to forget about him, she found her thoughts turning to Jake. *What had he been doing in the pub with his ex last night? Could they be back together?* Sarah was absolutely stunning, and if she was back in Jake's life then she didn't stand a chance with him. Desperately trying to find a way to quash her thoughts, she cleaned the cottage from top to bottom, took Scout out for the longest walk ever and even decided to make a lemon drizzle cake from scratch. Rose was no baker – a fact that she reminded herself of while trying to prise the burnt sponge mix out of the cake tin. Before she knew it, evening was starting to draw in and she heard an unexpected knock at the front door. She opened it to find Ollie standing there.

'Ollie? What are you doing here?' Rose asked, taking a step backwards. 'I'm coming to London tomorrow, remember?' Ollie looked pale and extremely sleep-deprived. His eyes were bloodshot, and his clothing was crumpled and dishevelled. His grey BMW was parked in the driveway of Jasmine Cottage. He'd clearly driven down from London. 'What's wrong? Has something happened?' Rose asked, taking him by the arm and ushering him inside.

'Can we talk?'

'Yes, of course. What on earth's wrong?'

'Have you spoken to Camille today?'

'She rang earlier but I didn't pick up. I'm not exactly her number-one fan—'

'Oh, thank God, Rose. Let's just sit down and I can explain everything,' Ollie said, his face relaxing a little.

'Okay, but you need to tell me what's going on. You're scaring me,' she said as Ollie slumped onto the sofa. She sat down next to him.

'It's just, well, if you've not spoken to Camille, that's good. It means there's still time for me to explain things, to tell you . . . my side.'

'Your side of what? Ollie, what the *hell* is going on?'

'Er, the thing is, Rose . . . I'm not sure where to start but, well . . .'

'The thing is what?'

'Well, the thing is, there's a new girl at the office . . . Emily,' he started hesitantly.

'Yes . . .' Rose said, feeling herself stiffen slightly at the mention of the name. 'Go on.'

'I'm not quite sure how to say this exactly, but she made a beeline for me . . . made it clear that she was interested in me from day one. She knew I was engaged but it didn't put her off, you see. We might have had a bit of a, well . . . I guess you'd call it a . . . fling.' Ollie's eyes darted between Rose and the door.

'What do you mean, "a fling"? Do you mean that you've *slept* with her?' Rose gripped her knees until she saw her knuckles turn white.

'Well, erm, yes, I suppose so.' Rose noticed that he couldn't look her in the eye.

'You suppose so?' she said, her jaw clenching tightly.

'Well, technically yes, I guess you could say it was a one-night stand, but I was so drunk, Rose,' he added hurriedly,

254

'it was just a one-time thing, a stupid mistake, but Camille found out, she was going to tell you.' Ollie stared at the floor.

Rose sat, dumbfounded, unable to react. *Wow.* She really hadn't expected this. Even with all the issues that she and Ollie had been having, she had always trusted him. Strangely, however, once the initial shock had passed, she found that she didn't feel upset or angry, just relieved. As though a weight had been lifted from her shoulders. Ollie's revelation had somehow helped her to see things more clearly, to realize that breaking off their engagement was what she really wanted, that it was the right decision.

'Rose, I don't love her,' Ollie continued, taking her hand. 'It didn't *mean* anything. It's you I love. We can work through this, can't we?' Rose was silent. 'It was just a minor slip and we're not *actually* married yet, are we? Think of it as a moment of madness before the wedding. This kind of thing happens to lots of couples and they manage to work things out.'

'Perhaps the difference between us and other couples, Ollie, is that I don't want to work things out,' she said quietly, her arms folded. 'I was coming to London tomorrow because I wasn't sure if we should be together. What you've said tonight just confirms things for me. I think we should end things, Ollie.'

'What? But we're getting married. You're just saying this because you're in shock – it doesn't make any sense. You're just *angry* with me right now,' he insisted, 'but that will pass, Rose.'

'It makes *perfect* sense to me.' She took his hand and looked him directly in the eye. 'You know deep down that things haven't been right between us for a while. Last weekend showed me what different people we've become. We don't want the same things anymore. The fact that you've been with another woman just shows me you're not happy either, not deep down,' she said calmly.

'You've got it wrong, Rose. The thing with Emily was just a silly drunken mistake. It won't happen again.'

'I want to end things, and the fact that you've slept with another woman doesn't matter.' She looked at him and repeated, 'I don't want to marry you, Ollie.'

The little colour that Ollie had left drained from his face. He opened and closed his mouth several times, trying to formulate a response. In the end, he simply hung his head and placed his hands on his knees.

'I know,' he whispered. 'I know things haven't been right between us, have they?' he said, looking up at her.

'They really haven't,' Rose replied, taking his hand.

'I'm sorry, I know I've been behaving like an absolute idiot recently. I could see that you were pulling away from me, from us ... and I didn't want to admit that things weren't working, that we were drifting apart. It just seemed ... *easier* somehow not to face up to it.'

'We just want different things out of life. We've got different priorities,' she said gently.

'We've had some good times though, haven't we?'

'Of course. Do you think I'd have stayed with you if we hadn't?'

'I guess not,' he said, shrugging.

'Do you remember the night when we got the keys to the London flat?' she asked.

Ollie smiled and looked up at her. 'We spent our last twenty quid on takeaway pizza and a bottle of wine—'

'And we sat on packing boxes in the dark as we had no furniture or electricity,' she laughed.

'Yes! And no money left over to even go and buy candles.'

'Well, pizza and wine were the priorities.'

'Obviously,' he nodded and took Rose's hand.

'God, that wine was disgusting,' she laughed. 'It tasted like a cross between washing up liquid and vinegar.'

'I remember.' Ollie looked at her quietly for a moment and sighed. 'I am truly sorry about how things have turned out, you know. I never meant to hurt you with this thing with Emily.'

'I know.' The pair sat in silence for a few moments. 'Our lives are just taking different paths and, you know what? That's okay. It doesn't mean we didn't have something special. This is just, well . . . the end.'

Ollie nodded, stood up and pulled her into a hug. 'If there's anything you ever need, Rose . . .'

'I know,' she replied quietly before slipping the engagement ring off her left hand. She placed it in his and closed his fist tightly over it. She could see a single tear on his cheek. Ollie leant forward, kissed her on the top of the head, turned towards the door and left Jasmine Cottage forever.

# Chapter 25

Rose called Grace first thing in the morning to let her know that her dog-sitting services were no longer required, what with her trip to London being cancelled. Grace had been gobsmacked at her friend's news about Ollie's infidelity.

'It sounds like you're well shot of him if you ask me,' she said. 'You must be fuming?'

'That's the strange thing. It's all come as a bit of a relief really. It's just proved that we weren't right together. I know I won't ever look back and wonder "what if?"'

'Sure, I can understand that. It can't have been a very pleasant scene to deal with though?'

'Well, no, but at least it's over and done with and we've parted on good terms. How about we go for lunch or something to take my mind off things?

'That would be lovely, but I've agreed to stop off at Jake's to look at one of his sheep. Hey, why don't you come along and we can take Scout for a walk around the farm?'

'Are you sure Jake won't mind?' Rose said tentatively. 'I don't want to crash your plans . . .'

'As if! I'm sure he'll be over the moon to see you,' Grace said, laughing.

'What's that supposed to mean?'

'Just that it's pretty obvious you've both got a huge crush on one another—'

'What?'

'Look, I would never have said anything when you were still with Ollie, but you'd have to be blind not to notice the way you two look at each other. I did wonder if Jake was one of the reasons that you decided to end things with Ollie in the first place ...' Rose was silent at the other end of the line. 'Shall I take that as a yes?'

Rose hesitated. She wasn't sure she wanted to share her feelings about Jake. 'Well, no, not really. If I didn't know Jake, I'd still have ended things with Ollie, but I'd be lying if I said I don't have feelings for him. Oh, Grace, you must think I'm a terrible person. I mean, I've been engaged the whole time I've known Jake,' she said, slumping down onto the sofa.

'Of course not! But let me give you some advice ... Jake's been burned before by Sarah. He doesn't trust easily. You need to be honest with him about what's happened with Ollie, tell him everything. If you really do have feelings for him, be truthful and let him know. He'll never make the first move, take my word for it,' Grace said seriously.

'You don't ask for much, do you? What if you've got the wrong end of the stick and he's not interested? Don't forget we saw him out with his ex the other night. What if they're back together?'

'Honestly? I've known Jake long enough to know the way he looks as you is *definitely* not as just a friend. You need to trust me.'

'I'll do my best,' Rose said, tucking her hair behind her ears.

Did Rose really have the guts to tell Jake to his face that she had feelings for him? Less than twenty-four hours ago she was still an engaged woman and the last thing she wanted to do was make Jake think that she was on the rebound. No, perhaps it was better to wait and let fate take a hand. After all, if she and Jake were meant to be, *surely* things would take their course naturally?

When Rose arrived at Harper Farm, she could see that Grace's Land Rover was already parked in the yard. Rose hopped out of her car and was greeted eagerly by Tagg and Finn, but there were no humans to be seen.

'Jake? Grace?' Rose shouted as she let Scout out of the backseat. 'Is anyone here?' she called. There was no response. 'Well, it looks like it's just us then,' she said to the dogs with a smile. 'Are you sure you don't know where Jake is hiding?' she asked Tagg and Finn, squatting down to pet them both.

'Rose, have you gone completely mad or are you expecting one of them to answer?' a voice whispered from behind her. It was Jake. She spun around on the spot, laughing.

'Didn't anyone ever tell you that you shouldn't go creeping up on people like that?' she said, punching him playfully on the arm. 'You scared the life out of me.'

Jake laughed. 'Grace is down in the barn taking a look at one of the ewes. She'll be back in a bit. I thought I'd get the kettle on,' he said. 'Let's grab a cuppa and then we can all take the dogs for a walk.'

'Perfect,' said Rose. 'I could do with walking off some calories.

'Slap-up dinner last night, was it?'

'Well, not exactly,' Rose hesitated. Would this be a good moment to tell Jake about Ollie's visit? She noticed him shift his feet uncomfortably on the spot.

'Grace mentioned that Ollie was down so I thought you might have gone out?'

'Oh, did she?' *There's no time like the present*. Fate had provided her with the perfect opportunity to tell Jake about the break-up. 'Well, he did visit last night, but ... er ... we kind of broke up.'

Jake stopped what he was doing and looked up. It was as if he was frozen in time for a moment and Rose could see his brain whirring as it processed her news.

'Rose, I'm ... well, I'm so sorry. Are you okay? What happened? Sorry, you don't have to answer that, of course you don't, I shouldn't have asked,' he continued, reddening in the face and shaking his head.

'No, it's fine, Jake. I want to tell you. It's all come as a bit of a relief really. It turns out that Ollie had been seeing someone else, a girl from work. But the thing is, I'd actually decided that I wanted to break things off before that. I'd just been steeling myself to try and find the right way to tell him.'

'Even so, Rose, that must have been one hell of a shock. I know what it's like to be cheated on ... It's not a nice feeling, even if you had decided that you wanted to end things.' Jake looked deep in thought, and Rose supposed he must have been thinking about his own experience with Sarah. She toyed with the idea of asking him more about her, telling him that she'd seen him in the pub with her on Friday night. Her grip tightened around her mug.

'Well, yes, I suppose it was. I never thought Ollie would be capable of something like that. But it's just made me see even more clearly that I'd made the right decision. Things with Ollie and I hadn't been going well for a while ... I just didn't want to face up to it.'

'I can understand that, but don't be too hard on yourself, will you? It's much easier to look back on things and think about how we could have done things differently, but we can only act on how we feel at the time.'

'Thanks, Jake. It's good to know that I've got friends like you and Grace here in Blossom Heath.'

'Friends ... yep,' Jake said, his face falling slightly.

This was it. It was the perfect opportunity to tell Jake how she felt about him. As scary as it was, she knew that if she ever wanted to find out if he felt the same way, she'd have to make the first move. Before she had the chance to decide, the kitchen door banged open, Grace burst into the room and the moment was lost.

'That ewe's all sorted now, Jake,' Grace said with a smile on her face, oblivious to her dreadful sense of timing. 'Looks like it was an abscess in the foot causing the lameness. I've lanced it, drained the pus and applied some antibiotic spray.'

'Eurgh, Grace, that's enough talk about lancing pus while I'm trying to drink my tea, thanks,' Rose said, wrinkling her nose in disgust.

'Wow, you'll never make it as a country girl if a bit of talk about hoof pus turns your stomach,' Grace replied, throwing her head back with laughter.

'Yep, we can definitely tell that you're a city girl at heart,' Jake added.

'Well, that has its advantages. I bet neither of you can navigate your way around the London underground system?'

'While that *may* be true,' Grace said in mock indignation, 'you're forgetting one thing. I have no desire to!'

'Yep, give me a tractor over a Tube train any day,' Jake said in agreement. 'I never know how Londoners stand it. All crammed in like a tin of sardines with your nose stuck in some stranger's armpit. Gross,' he said, shaking his head in disgust.

'Well, I can't disagree there,' Rose said. 'It's definitely not the most pleasant of experiences. Anyway, don't we have dogs to walk?' she asked. At the mention of the work 'walk', all three of the Border Collies, who had been curled up by the back door, leapt into action, with Scout letting out a short, sharp yip.

'That's telling us,' Grace said laughing. 'Looks like these guys have been waiting long enough.'

The three of them spent the rest of Sunday afternoon

walking the dogs around the farm. Rose couldn't wait to show Grace and Jake all of the work she'd been putting into Scout's training. Scout was able to recall beautifully on command, and Rose was even able to demonstrate the 'wait' and 'down' commands, which she'd been practising at home.

'Wow, Rose, you really have done a fantastic job with her. She's come a long way since you brought her into the surgery for the first time,' Grace said, beaming.

'I know, that really does feel like a lifetime ago, doesn't it?' Rose said, linking arms with her friend. 'Where has the time gone? There's only three weeks of term left before the summer holidays and I need to think about finding myself a job for September.'

'Does that mean you're looking to stay in Blossom Heath?' Jake asked. Was Rose mistaken, or did she detect a hint of hopefulness in his voice?

'Aunt Jean has said that I can stay as long as I like and there's not much point in going back to London now that Ollie and I are over. I feel really settled here, so as long as I can find some teaching work, I'm hoping to stay on.' Jake's face broke into a wide grin, which Rose couldn't help but notice. Her heart leapt.

'Think positive, Rose,' Jake said. 'I'm sure your perfect job is just around the corner.'

'I hope so, Jake, I really do,' she said with a sigh.

Rose realized that, whatever may or may not happen with Jake, she loved living in Blossom Heath and she was desperate to stay in the village and take Aunt Jean up on her kind offer. In fact, she didn't know what she'd do if she couldn't find a teaching role locally. All she could do was cross her fingers and wait.

# Chapter 26

The following week in school passed quickly. There were now only two weeks left of term and Rose didn't know where the time was going. The village was in the middle of a heatwave, with temperatures soaring to over thirty degrees in the last few days. Her classroom at school was like a hothouse, and trying to get the children to focus on their learning had been a real challenge in the high temperatures.

As Rose was leaving school on Wednesday afternoon, she was called back by Mrs Connolly.

'Rose, can I grab you for a moment before you leave?' the headteacher said, beckoning Rose into her office. 'Have a seat,' she offered, indicating the set of sofas that were usually reserved for meetings with parents.

Bertie, Mrs Connolly's elderly chocolate Labrador, the school dog, got up slowly from his bed, tail wagging, and made his way over to greet Rose.

'Hello, Bertie,' said Rose, tickling the dog behind the ears, 'how are you doing in this heat, old boy? It's a bit too hot, isn't it?'

'He's definitely struggling,' Mrs Connolly agreed. 'It's too hot for all of us, isn't it, Bertie? He's starting to feel his age,' Mrs Connolly continued thoughtfully. 'I've been thinking it might be time for him to retire from his school work and enjoy more time at home.'

'Really? But the kids adore him, and he's *so* good with them. He's done wonders for Mason's confidence and he's great with the reluctant readers . . . They can't wait for their reading slots with Bertie.'

'You're right, the children will miss him, but he can still come in for the occasional visit. Nothing's decided yet . . . it's just something I'm considering. He's booked in with Grace for a full health check in the holidays, then I'll decide what's best. Anyway, Rose, I just wanted to catch up with you, as I've been asking around about vacancies for September—'

'Yes . . .'

'I'm so sorry but I've not come across anyone with a vacancy. Everyone appears to be fully staffed for September.'

'Oh well, it can't be helped, I suppose,' Rose replied, mustering a weak smile. 'I appreciate you trying. It's pretty late in the term, so I guess it makes sense that most heads have sorted out their plans for September.'

'Oh, Rose, I am sorry. I wish I had better news. What will you do if you can't find anything locally? Will you go back to London?'

'I genuinely don't know. I guess there's always supply? I could register with a few local agencies?'

'That could be a good starting point . . . but I have to warn you that most of the schools in this area are small village schools like us, and they won't have the budget to pay out for supply teachers very often. I'm honestly not sure how much regular work you'd get. It wouldn't be anything like working on supply back in London.'

'Ah, yes . . . I guess so. I hadn't thought of it like that.'

'Well, you never know, you've still got a fortnight with us at the very least, so let's just focus our minds on the end of term. You've got the visit to Harper Farm coming up next week, haven't you?'

'Yes, that's right,' Rose said, her smile returning. 'The children can't wait and Jake's really looking forward to it. If it goes well, he's hoping he might be able to start an education project and make visits from local schools a regular thing.'

'Now, that does sound like a good idea. What an enterprising young man. I know lots of local headteachers would jump at the chance to have a resource like that locally.'

'That's what I thought,' Rose said. 'It would be a great way for him to diversify the farm's income and provide valuable learning opportunities for the children.'

'Honestly, Rose, whatever school you end up at next year is going to be very lucky to have you. You've certainly made a *huge* impact in the time that you've been with us. If things were different and I had a vacancy for September, I'd be offering you a job on the spot.'

'Thanks, Mrs Connolly – as long as you remember to write that on my reference,' she said with a smile as she picked up her handbag and left the headteacher's office.

When Rose arrived at Jane's to collect Scout and take her

home, Scout was flaked out on the cool stone floor of the dog-sitter's kitchen, along with a much smaller, younger dog that must have been one of Jane's new canine clients. At the sight of Rose, Scout leapt up and ran over to greet her, and the smaller dog followed suit.

'Hello, you,' Rose said, kneeling down and giving Scout a tummy tickle. 'And who do we have here?' Rose asked Jane as the younger dog wiggled its whole body in excitement while trying to jump up at Rose and lick her on the face.

'Buttercup. She's only about six months old – still an excitable puppy,' Jane said, laughing.

'Oh, so *you're* Buttercup,' Rose said, smiling, and she scooped the little dog up into her arms for a cuddle. 'I've heard lots about what a cutie you are,' she said, turning towards Jane. 'I think Buttercup belongs to Tiffany, one of the girls in my class?'

'Oh yes, of course. I forgot that you'd know Tiffany. This one is a little trouble maker, aren't you?' she said to the dog, 'but when you're that cute nobody really minds,' she laughed.

'I can imagine you get away with murder, Buttercup,' Rose agreed, placing the puppy back down on the floor.

'I've not been able to give Scout her walk today,' Jane said, 'it's far too hot. It was thirty-five degrees at lunchtime and I didn't want to risk her overheating. She's spent most of the day flaked out in here with Buttercup and they've been playing together – well, before the heat got too much for them both.'

'No problem, I didn't think you'd have been able to take

her out. We'll go this evening when it's a bit cooler, won't we, Scout?'

When Rose and Scout arrived back at Jasmine Cottage, Rose noticed that the grey 4x4 was parked in the lane again, just in front of the metal gate where the lane ended and farmland began. *How odd.* She had no immediate neighbours, so it was hard to imagine that the driver was visiting someone. There were lots of footpaths running across the farmland that bordered Jasmine Cottage, though, so perhaps the car belonged to ramblers looking for a quiet spot to walk their dog? Yes, that made sense.

As she opened the door of Jasmine Cottage, Rose was hit by the stifling heat. Even after opening all the windows and the back door to try to create a breeze, all she could feel was hot, muggy air.

Rose opened the freezer door and the cold air hit her with a welcome blast. She rummaged around until she found the box of ice pops.

'What do you fancy? Strawberry or lime?' Scout raised her left paw and scratched at Rose's leg. 'Lime it is then.' She unwrapped the lolly, placed the strawberry one in her mouth and gave the lime one to Scout. The dog rushed off to lay down with her lolly in the kitchen doorway and began breaking it up with her teeth and eating it eagerly.

Rose sat down at the kitchen table to enjoy the coolness of the ice lolly, and found her mind wandering back to the conversation with Mrs Connolly. She couldn't deny it, it was a huge blow that the headteacher hadn't come across any possible job vacancies. Rose knew that Mrs Connolly would have connections with pretty much every primary school headteacher in Sussex, and if she didn't know about a vacancy, then it probably didn't exist. *What was she going to do if she couldn't turn up a job by September? Could she really stay in Blossom Heath permanently, or would she need to return to London? Would Aunt Jean even be able to manage alone back at the cottage without Rose's help?* With so many questions to answer, Rose found her brain whirring.

She decided that it was time to get in touch with her dad. Perhaps talking it through with him would help her to reach a decision about which path to take? And she hadn't told him yet about the break-up with Ollie, or the incident with the Fallons.

After a couple of attempts, she finally got through.

'Hello?'

'Dad, it's Rose. How are you?'

'Rose! Hello, sweetheart. I'm so glad you called. I've tried to catch you a few times but the signal on this damn cruise ship's been awful. I can only get any kind of reception when we're in port, and even that's patchy.'

'Don't worry, I know what it's like when you're cruising. I just wanted to call you with an update.'

Rose went on to explain everything that had happened with Ollie, her job, Scout, the Fallons and Aunt Jean. Her dad listened patiently and didn't interrupt. When he did speak, his tone was serious.

'In all honestly, love, I've noticed that you and Ollie have been on different paths for a while. I can't say I'm surprised that you've ended things.'

'But, Dad, I'm not sure *I* even really knew things had changed until recently. Why didn't you ever say anything?'

'I suppose I didn't want to interfere in things. I wanted you to make your own decisions. I noticed a change in Ollie over the last year or so, especially since he's been in that new job. I just wasn't sure how well suited you were anymore.'

'I wish you'd said something, Dad,' Rose said, as she processed this new information.

'I'd never have said anything, Rose. Your life is just that – *your* life. It's not my place to meddle in things. As long as you were happy with your choice and you loved Ollie, that's all that mattered to me.'

Rose could feel a lump forming in her throat.

'I guess I'd not been happy for a while, but you weren't to know that. I should have spoken to you before now and told you how I was feeling.'

'The past is the past, Rose. Let's not go worrying about that. But perhaps we've learned a lesson for the future. To *talk* to each other when things are bothering us?'

'You're right. I promise I'll try and be more open about things.'

'And as for all the job stuff – things will sort themselves out. You know I'm a firm believer that what's meant for you won't pass you by,' he continued, 'and don't worry about the financial side of things – I can help out and I'm sure the perfect job will come through for you soon enough.'

'Thanks, Dad. You don't have to do that though. I've got some savings in the bank – enough to get me through the next few months at least.'

'Well, the offer's there, sweetheart, if you need it. I'll be back in England in three weeks, so we can have a long chat about things once I'm home, and by then things might be looking a lot clearer.'

Rose spent the rest of the evening scouring teaching job websites searching for vacancies in Sussex, to no avail. *It was so frustrating that it was much harder to find a job here than in London.* Just as Rose was about to shut down her laptop for the evening and head out for a walk with Scout now that the temperature had cooled off, she noticed that she had a missed call from Maya, her teacher friend from Trinity Grove. *How odd.* She hadn't even heard her phone ring, but then again the signal in the village did leave a lot to be desired. There was a text from her too:

*Rose, call me asap, I have big news!!!!*

Intrigued, Rose settled herself back down on the sofa to return Maya's call. She picked up on the first ring.

'Rose, *finally*! I've been trying to get you all evening, but your phone just kept going straight to voicemail.'

'Ah, the reception in the cottage is a bit patchy. Sorry I've not been in touch for a while – there's been a lot going on,' Rose explained.

She brought Maya up to speed with everything that had transpired with Ollie and the break-up, as well as her temporary job at the school.

'Wow, you have been busy,' Maya said, sounding genuinely surprised. 'I can't *believe* Ollie cheated on you. What an absolute shit!'

Rose laughed. 'I guess it just took me a while to wake up to how much we'd both changed and *finally* realize that we weren't right together. To be honest, I was thinking of breaking things off before I found out about the cheating.'

'Really? Perhaps some time apart gave you time to reflect?' Maya suggested. 'It's still a shock though.'

'At least we ended things on relatively good terms. I've still got to get my stuff out of the flat at some point, but that can wait until the holidays.'

'Ah, speaking of London, I've got some news ...' Maya said, and Rose could detect the excitement in her voice. 'Dawson's got the sack!'

'What?' said Rose in shock, 'but he's only been there since Christmas—'

'I know! That's what makes it so exciting! We thought we'd be stuck with him for years.'

'But what happened?'

'Well, you know we've got Ofsted coming up next year?'

'Yeah ...'

'So, the local authority ran a mock inspection, and let's just say they were pretty horrified at what they found. Big gaps in the data ... flimsy policies ... unhappy staff ... Once they decided to dig a bit deeper, the whole thing came tumbling down around him like a pack of cards.'

'Wow! Well, it couldn't have happened to a more deserving man.'

'Exactly,' Maya agreed. 'He was told to pack up his office the very next day and the governors asked Mrs Barton to come back from retirement as a temporary fix. Apparently, they already have someone lined up to take over as head in September.'

'Wow, Maya, that's such amazing news! How have the staff reacted?'

'Everyone is overjoyed, naturally,' Maya laughed.

'I wouldn't expect anything less,' Rose said, chuckling.

'Hold on, I've not even got to the *really* exciting part yet,' Maya said, sounding as though she was about to burst.

'Well, go on then . . .'

'Mrs Barton recommended you to the new head and he wants you to come in for an interview for a vacancy that we've got for September!'

'What? You mean go back to Trinity Grove?'

'Yes, that's exactly what I mean! I don't think they're even going to interview anyone else, so the job is basically yours. It's a done deal! The new head is going to call you tomorrow but I begged Mrs Barton to let me break the news to you first.'

Rose was silent. *Go back to Trinity Grove?* Was that really an option? At Easter she would have jumped at the chance to stay on permanently at her old school, but *now*? Well, things were different. She loved living in Blossom Heath, and there was her Aunt Jean to think about, and Jake . . .

'Rose? Are you still there?'

'Oh yes, sorry, I was just thinking.'

'Thinking about what? I thought you'd *jump* at the chance to come back . . . We'd be working together again for one thing and you've always loved the school – well, before Dawson came along anyway . . .'

'I did. I mean, I *do*,' Rose corrected herself. 'Where would I even live though? I don't have a flat in London anymore.'

'I think the fates have aligned in your favour,' Maya said with delight. 'Do you remember Amber? The art student who was renting a room in my house?'

'Yes . . .'

'Well, she's moving out in a couple of weeks to live with her boyfriend and we were going to advertise her room, but you could move in here. It would be *perfect*!'

'Oh wow. Yes, that does seem like perfect timing,' Rose said rather unenthusiastically. 'What about Scout though? Does your landlord allow pets?'

'Not only does he allow pets, but our other housemate, Sian, works from home, so Scout will have company all day too!'

'Wow, that sounds ideal.'

'Sometimes things just have a way of working out, don't they? Honestly, Rose, this is going to be great! Listen, I've got to go as I'm meeting Steve for a drink, but text me tomorrow and let me know when your interview is.'

'Will do. Thanks for ringing, Maya.'

*A permanent job at Trinity Grove. A job back in London. A room available in Maya's houseshare.* Three months ago, it would have been everything she'd ever dreamed of, but *now* . . . what did she want now? It was true that she did love it in here in Blossom Heath, and ten minutes ago, before the phone call with Maya, she was seriously considering moving here permanently. But when she thought about things logically, there really wasn't anything to keep her here. She had no job, it was looking increasingly likely that Aunt Jean should be able to manage on her own at the cottage after a few adaptions were put in place, and as for her and Jake . . . well, there wasn't really a 'her and Jake'. It wasn't as though anything had happened between the two of them. She didn't know if Jake had feelings for her, or even whether his ex was still in the picture. If she *was* going to return to London, perhaps it would be best for both of them if she never found out?

# Chapter 27

Rose spent the next day pottering around the cottage and trying to keep her mind occupied so that she didn't dwell on the looming decision she was now faced with. She'd spoken to Mr Pearson, Trinity Grove's new headteacher, that morning and he had confirmed what Maya had already told her – the job was hers if she wanted it. She'd have to really mess up at the interview to do anything to scupper her chances by the sounds of things. She knew she should be feeling relieved she had a permanent job lined up for September. *Wasn't that exactly what she'd been waiting for?* So why did she feel so depressed about the whole thing? Was it just that she wanted to stay in Blossom Heath? Or did things run deeper than that? Was it her feelings for Jake that were causing her to feel so conflicted about leaving the village?

*Don't even go there, Rose Hargreaves*, she said to herself sternly. *This thing with Jake's in your head. There's no point trying to start something if you're leaving . . . forget him and move on.*

That evening, Rose had arranged to meet Grace at the Apple Tree for a drink. It had been another long, hot summer's day and the opportunity to sit outside in the cool evening air was one not to be missed. As Rose left the cottage, she noticed the grey 4x4 was back, parked in the same spot as before at the end of the lane. It must belong to ramblers, she thought again. It was a lovely evening for a dog walk after all.

Rose strolled slowly through the village, stopping every few yards to allow Scout to explore the grass verges. This was Scout's first walk of the day due to the heat, so taking things at a nice leisurely pace was fine by Rose. Every now and again Rose thought she could hear footsteps behind her, but whenever she turned around there was no one there. Scout seemed not to notice anything, though, so she told herself she was just being paranoid.

When they arrived at the pub, Rose walked straight around the back to the beer garden, which was full of apple trees heavy with fruit, providing just the right amount of shade for a hot summer's day. The pub's outside space was packed, which didn't surprise Rose given the good weather. She spotted Grace at one of the picnic tables, and it looked as though she had already got the drinks in.

'This is just what I need,' Rose said with a smile, pointing towards the large glass of gin and tonic on the table. 'You know me *too* well.'

'Well, there's nothing quite like a cold G&T on a hot summer's evening,' Grace replied, bending down to make a fuss of Scout, who settled herself in the shade under the table. 'So, how's things? Any news on the job front?'

'Funny you should ask,' Rose said with a deep intake of

breath. 'There is actually. My old school in London called this morning. They've sacked the headteacher and the new head has asked me to go in for an interview. He's basically said the job is mine if I want it.'

'Wow, that *is* big news! You must be over the moon ...' she continued, her voice faltering slightly. 'Although judging from the look on your face, I'm guessing that you're not?'

'Oh, I don't know,' Rose said, bending down to secure Scout's lead to the table leg, 'I'm just being silly really. It's a great school to work at and the staff are fantastic. But—'

'But what?'

'I just feel so settled here in Blossom Heath, and I'd finally decided that I was going to stay ... Let's just say this whole London thing has put a bit of a spanner in the works.'

'So, turn it down?' Grace suggested. 'I mean it's not like you have to take it. You could stay here if that's what you really want?'

'I'd be mad to turn it down though. It's a great school and a *permanent* job offer. It's everything I've ever dreamed of really,' Rose said, taking a large sip of her G&T. 'My friend Maya even has a room going in her houseshare, which would be perfect. I could just move everything out of Ollie's and I'd be good to go.'

'That does sound too good to turn down,' Grace said, wrinking her nose. 'Would I be right in thinking it's not just Blossom Heath you'll be missing? Maybe a certain farmer called—'

'Don't,' Rose cut in sharply. 'Sorry, Grace, I didn't mean

to snap. It's just that I'd be crazy to say no to the perfect job because of feelings I have for a man I've not even had the guts to tell about them,' she continued, staring intently into her G&T. 'No, it's better if I never mention anything to Jake. If we never get started, there'll be nothing to end. It'll just be easier that way.'

'Hey, it's not *me* you have to convince,' said Grace, holding her hands up. 'It's up to you, and that does *sound* like the logical option but ... well ... hearts aren't always logical, are they? You can't just shut your feelings down ...'

'I know,' Rose said with determination, 'but I can certainly try.'

As Rose walked home from her evening out with Grace, the village was already in darkness. It was a clear night and Rose stopped to look at the stars, which looked like tiny diamonds embedded in a piece of black velvet.

'Isn't that beautiful?' Rose said to Scout. 'Look, you can even see Orion from here. See? If you look at tha—'

Scout let out a short sharp bark and Rose felt a muscular hand grabbing her arm, trying to wrench Scout's lead away from her. She saw the flash of a heart tattoo on the man's forearm as he grappled for the lead.

'Hey! What are you doing?' Rose could make out the shadows of two men in the darkness. One of them was running away from her and trying to bundle Scout into the back of a van. The dog was wriggling valiantly, trying to break free from her captor's grasp. Rose ran towards the van.

Julie Haworth

'Scout! Scout! Give her back!' she shouted frantically. She stumbled in the darkness, losing her footing and, as she crashed to the ground, she felt something cold and hard strike her on the side of the head before darkness enveloped her.

Rose came to on the roadside, unsure of how much time had passed. Shocked and disorientated, she tried to stand, staggered and fell to the ground again. After two further attempts, she finally managed to clamber back to her feet.

'Scout, Scout!' she whispered hoarsely, but there was no sign of the van, or Scout, anywhere.

# Chapter 28

Rose groaned in pain. She was aware of a shooting sensation pulsing through her head and she could feel something wet, sticky and warm, most likely blood, running from the side of her head and down her cheek. *Scout.* Where was Scout? Rose scrambled to her knees as best she could and looked around her. There was no sign of the dog. She needed to raise the alarm. The nearest cottage was half a mile away on foot and Rose wasn't sure if she could walk. She fumbled in her pocket for her mobile phone and instinctively called Jake. He answered on the first ring.

'Rose, it's a bit late for a social call, isn't it? It's nearly midnight—'

Before he could finish his sentence, Rose cut in. 'Jake, I don't know what's happened. They've taken Scout and I'm bleeding ...'

Jake's tone changed. 'Rose, are you hurt? Where are you?'

'There were men ... I think I've hit my head ... Scout's ... gone,' she said, her voice breaking.

'Where are you, Rose?' Jake asked urgently.

'In the lane by the cottage, but Scout isn't here—' Rose said through tears.

'I'm getting in the car now and I'm calling the police. I'll be there soon. Don't move, Rose. *Don't* go looking for Scout – leave that to me.'

'But, Jake—'

'Don't argue, Rose. Stay put and wait for me. I'm on my way.'

Rose soon realized that she was unable to stay on her feet. She could feel the blood pouring from her head more thickly now and she lurched to her knees again. Her vision was blurry and pain was searing through her left temple. She took some tissues from her bag and tried to stem the bleeding.

After a few minutes had passed, Rose was blinded by headlights coming straight towards her and she waved her arms furiously. She saw Jake throw open the driver's door of his truck and he was at her side in seconds.

'Rose, what's happened? Who did this?' he said, taking her by the arm to steady her. 'Don't try and get up. Let's just get you out of the road.' He sat her down on the grass verge and tried to take a closer look at her injuries.

'I don't know . . . there were two of them, I think . . . Scout was barking . . . Oh God, Jake, I think they've taken her. I fell and hit my head and when I came to, she was . . . gone,' Rose said, cradling her head in her hands.

Rose wasn't sure how much time had passed before she saw a blue light in the distance getting closer, then PC Palmer was next to her and she was vaguely aware of someone shining a light into her eyes. She could hear Jake explaining things to the police and the next thing she knew she was being bundled into an ambulance.

'No, no, I *can't* leave. I *can't* go to hospital. I need to find Scout!' she shouted.

Jake placed his arm around her shoulders. It was warm and strong and comforting.

'Rose, you're in no condition to go anywhere. You've hit your head and you need to get checked out. You might even need stitches. PC Palmer has his team out looking for Scout. I've called Grace and she's organizing a team of volunteers. They're going to find her, I *promise*.'

'That's right, Rose. Can you remember anything about the men who took Scout? Anything at all?' PC Palmer asked.

'Not really, it was dark ... There is one thing though. One of them had a name tattooed on their forearm. I saw it when he grabbed Scout's lead from me ... What was it?' Rose screwed her face up tightly. 'Tina! That's it: Tina. It was inscribed inside a heart. On his left arm I think.'

'That's Rick Fallon's wife's name,' said PC Palmer. 'My first stop is going to be their place. You stop worrying, Rose, we'll have Scout back with you in no time,' PC Palmer said kindly, placing his hand on her shoulder. Rose just nodded.

'I'm coming with you,' Jake told her. 'And don't even bother arguing,' he said as he saw Rose open her mouth to tell him not to. She smiled weakly as PC Palmer got out of the ambulance.

As the ambulance crew closed the doors to their vehicle, Rose realized it was the same team that had come to Hayden's aid at the school.

'This is getting to be a habit, Rose,' one of them said with a smile. 'If I didn't know better, I'd think you just liked riding with us for the blue lights.'

'You've had a lucky escape there,' the A&E doctor told her after giving her a thorough examination. 'You've got a slight concussion, but there doesn't seem to be any lasting damage. We'll pop a few stitches in that head wound and you'll need to stay in overnight just to be on the safe side.'

Rose sat bolt upright.

'No! I can't! I've got to get out looking for my dog!' She swung her legs around the side of the bed and reached for her bag.

'I really wouldn't advise going anywhere. We need to be sure there aren't any complications,' said the doctor.

'But my dog, she's been stolen and I really need to . . .' she said quickly, pulling on her shoes.

'I heard,' the doctor said, placing a hand on Rose's shoulder. 'Listen, I've got a dog myself and I can only imagine how you're feeling right now. How about I agree to discharge you in a couple of hours but you *must* stay with someone tonight, just in case of any lasting dizziness or signs of concussion?'

Rose opened her mouth to speak but the doctor raised his hand.

'That part is absolutely non-negotiable, I'm afraid. I'm

guessing your husband here can keep an eye on you?' he asked, nodding towards Jake, who Rose now realized was holding her hand.

'Oh no, this isn't my husband. We're, erm, well ... we're friends,' Rose said, hurriedly pulling her hand away from Jake's.

'Rose can stay with me tonight, Doctor,' Jake said. 'There's no way I'm leaving you on your own,' he said, turning to face her, 'and before you even think about saying anything, you won't change my mind.'

'Well, there we are then, that's all sorted,' said the doctor, oblivious to any tension between them. 'I'll pop back in a few minutes to get your stitches done. There's a police officer waiting for you in reception, so I'll send him through. Oh, and I do hope you find your dog.'

'Thank you. And yes, please send him through,' Rose said, grabbing Jake's hand again.

'You do realize you've only been in the village a few weeks and already you've had more visits to this hospital than I have in my *entire* life,' said Jake, squeezing her hand. Rose offered him a weak smile.

'Well, at least this is the first time I've actually been the patient,' she replied.

A few moments later the curtain around the cubicle slid back and PC Palmer popped his head around the corner.

'Rose? Ah yes, there you are. How are you?' PC Palmer asked, looking concerned.

'Oh, I'm fine. What about Scout? Is there any news?'

'Well, we've arrested Rick Fallon based on the ID you gave us of the tattoo. We've done a full search of the Fallons' place and we had a shock when we got to their outbuildings. They were packed full of makeshift cages and we found around twenty dogs. Packed in tight they were, poor little mites.'

'Oh God,' said Rose, grabbing Jake's hand. 'And Scout? Was she there too?' She looked up at PC Palmer, her eyes wide, her grip on Jake's hand tightening.

'I'm afraid not. There was no sign of her at the property.' Rose put her head in her hands. 'The RSPCA are there now, and Grace has gone over to help. Some of the dogs are quite traumatized. All shapes and sizes they were, and not being kept in the best of conditions.'

'But ... why?' Rose asked, wringing her hands. 'What would the Fallons *want* with all those dogs?'

'We think it's some kind of dog theft ring – stealing dogs to order most likely. Some of these dogs can sell for thousands, especially the pedigrees and "designer" breeds. You know the sort I mean – maltipoos, puggles.' Rose nodded. 'It's easy money for criminals. A few of the dogs were microchipped and when the RSPCA inspectors checked their details, well, they'd *all* been reported stolen. The cockapoo and French bulldog that went missing locally were found there too.'

'But you're *sure* that there was no sign of Scout?'

'No sign at all, I'm afraid.'

'We're going to find her, Rose,' Jake said, looking her

288

directly in the eyes. 'Scout's a smart cookie. She's been out on her own before and she found her way to you, remember? She's going to find her way back again, I *promise*.' Rose forced a weak smile.

'That's right,' PC Palmer agreed. 'She's only been missing a few hours and Grace has practically the whole village out looking for her. We'll find her.'

'But what if she's hurt? What if she's lying in a ditch somewhere injured?'

'We'll find her, Rose,' Jake repeated, placing his arm around her shoulders.

'I noticed you have a CCTV camera up outside the cottage,' said PC Palmer. 'I was hoping we might get a look and see if we can place Fallon at the scene?'

'Oh, yes. Jake sorted all that out. I've got an app on my phone but I've no idea how to use it, I'm afraid,' Rose said, reaching for her bag.

'Let me,' Jake said, gently passing her the bag.

'Do you mind if I . . .?' PC Palmer said, nodding towards the phone.

'Be my guest,' Rose replied. 'Like I said, I've no idea how to use it.'

'What time did you leave the pub this evening, Rose?'

'Well, Grace and I were there until last orders, so around 11?' said Rose.

'And how long does it take you to walk back to the cottage?' PC Palmer asked.

'Less than 10 minutes. It's not far. I'm not sure if it's

important, but I have noticed a grey 4x4 parked at the end of the lane a few times recently, and it was there before I went out tonight. I've no idea who it belongs to, though,' Rose explained.

'Rick certainly owns a number of 4x4s, so we'll look into that. I don't suppose you got a reg number?' PC Palmer asked.

'Afraid not,' Rose replied. 'But I think it started with an E, if that's any use?'

'Well, it's a start. Now, let's have a look at this CCTV,' said PC Palmer, and after some assistance from Jake, he was soon scrolling through the footage from earlier that evening on Rose's phone.

'That's it. *Gotcha!*' he said, beaming. 'There he is. That's Rick Fallon, clear as day, looking through the window of Jasmine Cottage, time-stamped at 10.55pm. You can see the tattoo on his arm, just as you described, Rose. Tina, surrounded in a heart. There's no footage of him actually grabbing Scout, but this is certainly enough to place him at the scene. Oh, we've got you this time,' PC Palmer said, barely able to contain the glee in his voice. 'Look at him, he looks right up at the camera. Idiot.'

'If I get my hands on him . . .' Jake said, menacingly.

'You'd best leave that to us, Jake. We've got more than enough to charge him now. I'll have to run it past the CPS of course, but what with the stolen dogs up at his place, the CCTV footage and Rose's ID of his tattoo, they should be satisfied that there's a case to answer. There's another man in the footage that I don't recognize, but he's definitely not one of the Fallon clan. Rose, have you seen this man before?' PC Palmer passed the phone back to Rose and she recognized the second man instantly.

'Yes, I have!' she replied. 'Well, I don't know his name, but I've seen him before. He followed me to the pub the other week and asked me for a light. I thought there was something off about him. Grace saw him too and she didn't recognize him either. She thought he might be a tourist but obviously not.'

'Okay, well, I'll show this to Grace too, and then hopefully we can put a name to the face. He must be one of the Fallons' associates.'

At that moment, the curtain around the cubicle was whipped back and the doctor reappeared.

'Sorry, Officer, it's time to get Rose stitched up. You'll have to come back later if you want to ask her anything else. She's going to be here for another couple of hours so I can keep an eye on her.'

'I think that's enough questions for one night, eh, Rose?' PC Palmer said kindly. 'You just get some rest.'

'Rose is staying with me tonight. Doctor's orders,' Jake explained. 'I'll take you back to the farm,' he said, turning to face Rose. 'I've got a spare room and that way I can keep an eye on you.' He hesitated, waiting for Rose to protest. 'What, no arguments?' he said, raising his eyebrows.

'Who said I was going to argue? Thanks, Jake.'

'Right, I'll be off then,' PC Palmer said. 'I want to make sure that I'm there in person when we charge Rick Fallon.

He's gone too far this time. I'll drop by the farm in the morning to take your official statement, Rose.'

'Thanks,' Rose replied. 'I appreciate everything you've done tonight, Ben. I honestly can't thank you enough.'

'Don't you worry about thanking me. I should be thanking *you*. We've got Rick Fallon bang to rights this time.'

'I really must insist that everyone apart from the patient waits outside,' the doctor said impatiently. 'I need to get these stitches done.'

PC Palmer nodded and Jake bent down and gave Rose a kiss on the cheek.

'I'll be back with a cup of coffee for you before you know it,' he promised.

# Chapter 29

Rose must have fallen asleep during the car journey back to Blossom Heath as she only realized that they'd arrived back at Harper Farm when Jake nudged her gently awake. Tagg and Finn were delighted to see her and, after saying hello, they snuggled up together and fell fast asleep next to the Aga within minutes. Jake showed Rose to the guest bedroom and dug out one of his oversized shirts for her to sleep in.

'Why don't you settle in, get changed and I'll heat up some warm milk?' Jake suggested.

'Are you going to tuck me in and tell me a bedtime story too?' Rose asked, mustering a weak smile.

'Well, my nieces will tell you that I'm an expert in bed-time stories.'

'I'll definitely need to put that to the test one day then,' she said. 'I don't know how I'm going to manage to sleep tonight. I just can't bear the thought of Scout being out there all alone.'

Jake stepped towards Rose and engulfed her in a hug.

'I know it's tough, but there's nothing you can do tonight.' He lifted her head up towards him to look her directly in the eyes. 'The best thing you can do for Scout is get a good night's rest, so you can help with the search in the morning. My phone's on and I'll wake you if there's the slightest bit of news.'

'But there must be something we can do tonight? What about your laptop? We could check the lost dog websites to make sure her details have been posted?'

Rose sat down at the kitchen table, opening up the laptop that was sat on top of a pile of newspapers.

'Rose,' said Jake, taking a seat next to her and closing the laptop lid again, 'I can do all that once you're in bed. You've been through a trauma. You need *sleep*.'

'No!' She grabbed the laptop back. 'I read an article about dog theft and it said if you don't find them in the first twenty-four hours, the chances go way down. I'm *not* letting that happen to Scout. Am I clear?' She was looking Jake right in the eyes, challenging him to argue back. 'I mean it. I'll get a cab back to Jasmine Cottage right now if you try to argue with me.'

'Okay, fine,' he said, exhaling, 'but just for the record, if your head feels worse in the morning, you've only got yourself to blame.'

'I take full responsibility,' she said, relief washing over her. 'Now, what was the name of that website ... Lost Dogs? No ... DogLost. That's it! Yes, this is it. Look,' she said, pointing at the screen, 'it's the largest lost-and-found service for dogs. Now, just let me do a search to find Scout's details ...' She gazed intently at the laptop screen, her eyes moving up and down as she scrolled through the hundreds of dogs listed on the site. 'What? She's not here! I thought you said Grace had posted her details everywhere?'

'She has.'

'Well, clearly not. I can't find a dog even remotely matching Scout's description.'

'Maybe she's busy organizing the search?'

'Look, I need to stay up and get Scout's details listed. I can't go to bed knowing I could be doing something.'

'Have I got *any* chance of convincing you that I can do all this?' said Jake, placing his hand over hers. She pulled her hand away from him sharply.

'Absolutely zero.'

'Well, let me make us both that hot milk and you do what you need to do.' Rose nodded without even looking up from the screen. 'Why don't you take the laptop to the spare bedroom and get settled? You'll be more comfortable there, and then if you get sleepy—'

'For the last time, I am NOT going to bed.'

'I'm not the enemy here, Rose. You do realize that, don't you? I'm only trying to look out for you.'

'Okay, fine. I'll take the laptop to bed with me if it makes you happy,' she said, getting up and padding out of the kitchen without a backwards glance.

By the time Jake returned to the bedroom, Rose was already fast asleep on top of the duvet with the laptop balanced on her chest. He carefully placed the mug down on the bedside table, picked up the laptop and pulled the covers over her.

'Goodnight, Rose Hargreaves. Sleep tight,' he whispered, before turning off the bedside lamp and shutting the door behind him.

Rose was awoken the next morning by the smell of bacon wafting into the bedroom. She turned over slowly and reached for her mobile phone. It was already 8.30am. She never slept in this late. As she tentatively sat herself up in bed, she became aware of a pounding sensation in her head. The events of the previous evening slowly came back to her and she checked her phone for messages to see if there was any news of Scout. Nothing. She placed her hand on the back of her head and gingerly felt where her stitches were located.

'Oww,' she groaned as she pulled the duvet back. She saw she was wearing one of Jake's shirts. It was a red and black plaid design and was far too big for her, but it was warm, cosy, and she could detect Jake's scent woven delicately into the fabric. She pulled the shirt up towards her nose and inhaled deeply. Jake . . . *Oh no!*

Rose cast her mind back to last night and, despite the traumatic events of the evening, she remembered how ungratefully she had acted when Jake had brought her back to the farmhouse. She had been downright rude to him. She had been frantic about finding Scout but, even so, that was no excuse. At that moment Rose heard some scuffling and a knock at the door.

'Come in,' she called. The door opened slowly and Tagg

and Finn came running into the room and jumped eagerly up onto the bed to greet her.

'Morning,' said Jake, standing at the door, 'I thought I heard you moving around and the dogs have been desperate to get in here to see you. I didn't want them waking you up though – I thought it best to let you sleep. You clearly needed it after last night.'

'Thanks,' she said as she gave Tagg and Finn cuddles. 'I can't remember the last time I slept in so late. But what about Scout? Is there any news?'

'Nothing yet,' he replied, his face falling. 'Grace already has a search party out this morning. And before you ask,' he said, holding up his hand, 'I've registered Scout's details with DogLost and printed out posters to plaster up all over the village. We're *going* to find her,' he said, placing his hand on top of hers. Rose smiled. She wanted desperately to believe that was true.

'Jake, listen. I'm so sorry about the way I acted when we got back here last night,' she said, looking down at her hands, unable to meet his gaze. 'I was so rude to you and there's no excuse. I shouldn't have taken my frustration out on you.'

'I haven't given it a second's thought.' He placed his hand on her cheek. 'Let's just chalk it up to a nasty bang on the head and say no more about it.'

Rose smiled at him. 'Come on, you two, off the bed. I'm sure Jake doesn't want you messing up the guest bedroom.'

'Oh, it's fine,' he replied, 'don't worry about it. We have a house rule that dogs are most definitely allowed on the bed.'

Rose laughed. 'Did you hear that? Jake said it's fine.' Tagg rolled onto his back, waiting for a belly rub. 'Honestly, my ex would have a fit if he could see me now—' She looked away, realizing how that sounded. 'I mean, the idea of having a dog on the bed would be unimaginable to him. He wasn't the greatest animal lover, you see.'

'Well, you don't have to worry about that here,' Jake said with a smile. 'Animals kinda go with the territory on a farm.'

Once Rose had got dressed, she followed the dogs down into the kitchen. Jake was busy at the Aga and Rose noticed that there was a freshly poured cup of coffee waiting for her on the table.

'I'm just cooking up some breakfast. I've gone for a full English, hope that's okay? I figured you could do with a decent breakfast after last night.'

'I thought I could smell bacon, but we just don't have time, Jake. We need to get on the road *now*.'

'You *need* to eat,' Jake said, placing his hands on her shoulders and meeting her gaze. 'The food is practically ready and you're going to need a full stomach. We could be out searching for who knows how long.'

'But—'

Jake placed a finger to Rose's lips. Her head fell forwards and she dissolved into deep, long sobs, her shoulders shaking.

'What am I going to do without her, Jake? What if she's gone forever?' she said in between gasps.

'Listen, that's not going to happen,' he said, pulling her in towards him. 'Just eat breakfast and I *promise* I won't make any more demands on you today. Once you've got a stomach full of food, you can call the shots all day if you like.'

'Okay,' she said, raising her head to look at him. She could see a wet patch on his shirt where her tears had left their mark. 'I'll have breakfast, but then we need to leave.'

# Chapter 30

'Wow, you certainly were hungry,' Jake said as Rose made quick work of her bacon, eggs, sausages, mushrooms and toast.

'Oh God, sorry! Have I just embarrassed myself by eating like a pig?'

'Not at all,' said Jake. 'It's actually nice to see a girl enjoying her food and not calorie counting or trying to turn me into a vegan.' Rose stood up and began clearing away the breakfast things. Jake gave her a stern look.

'Will you sit down, rest and let me clear up? You're *supposed* to be recuperating.'

Rose put her hands up in surrender and retook her seat at the breakfast table.

'I don't think I'd survive long as a vegan,' she said, taking a sip of her orange juice. 'I like bacon too much. Oh, and don't forget ribs, sausages, steak . . . I could go on?'

'You're a girl after my own heart,' he said. 'Sarah is always talking about my carb intake and telling me I should go "plant-based", whatever that means,' he continued. 'Sorry . . . I don't know why I told you that.' Rose was slightly rattled that he was referring to Sarah in the present tense. *Could that mean they were back together?*

'Don't apologise. Sarah's part of your history. She's bound to come up in conversation. It's the same for me and Ollie, I guess.' Jake's eyes darted away from hers and she noticed that he couldn't quite meet her gaze.

'How are things with you and Ollie? I mean, you've only split up quite recently. Do you think you'll get back together?'

'God no, it's definitely over. I do still need to get in touch with him and sort out getting my stuff out of his flat though,' Rose groaned, rolling her eyes. 'I'm not looking forward to it if I'm honest, but it has to be done.'

'If you need a hand with anything, Rose, you know you only have to ask. I've got the jeep to help get things moved if you want.'

'Thanks, Jake. That's really kind.'

'How are you feeling this morning, anyway?'

'Oh, I'm fine, just a bit of a headache. Speaking of which, have you got any painkillers around?'

Jake opened one of the kitchen cupboards and pulled out a small red packet. He popped two tablets out of the foil packaging and into the palm of his hand. Rose was surprised at how comfortable she felt over breakfast with Jake. It was almost as if sharing a meal at the farmhouse was a regular occurrence for the pair of them.

'Perfect,' said Rose, standing up to take them from him. She felt a jolt of anticipation course through her as their hands touched. They maintained the contact longer than was necessary, and their eyes locked. Rose felt that familiar butterfly sensation again. In that moment, she couldn't deny the effect that Jake had on her. All she wanted to do was to kiss him, or for him to kiss her. She could sense his head moving slowly towards hers and she responded, inclining hers towards him, bringing her lips closer to his.

Just as their lips were about to touch, there was a sudden knock on the door and the dogs leapt up barking. And just like that, the moment between them was broken, the possibility of a kiss lost.

When Jake opened the door, she saw it was PC Palmer.

'Hello, Jake. How are you feeling this morning, Rose?'

'A bit like I've gone five rounds with Anthony Joshua, but I'll survive. Is there news on Scout? What happened with the Fallons last night? Did you charge Rick?' she asked quickly.

'We certainly did,' PC Palmer replied with relish, pulling up a chair. 'After we raided Rick's house, we managed to track down his accomplice. It turns out Scout has done quite the number on his leg. He had a nasty bite wound which we had to get cleaned up by the medic.'

'Well done, Scout,' Jake said encouragingly.

'She's certainly a brave little dog,' PC Palmer agreed. 'It turns out that the Fallons' accomplice was a man called Jason Owens. Fallon did time with him a few years back and it looks like they've struck up quite the friendship since. Owens has a history of being involved with a dog theft ring and it looks like he's brought the Fallons in on the act. He also owns a grey 4x4 exactly like the one you described, Rose. I'll wager it was him that's been keeping an eye on your comings and goings for Fallon.'

'What about Scout? Did they mention *anything* about what they've done with her? Where she might be?' she asked, reaching out to take Jake's hand.

'According to Rick, she wriggled free of them and ran off into woodland before they could get her back to their place.'

'But you have them both in custody now, don't you?' Rose asked anxiously.

'Don't you worry about that, Rose, they've both been charged with theft. They won't have a leg to stand on in court. What with the dogs the RSPCA have seized, your CCTV footage and the ID of Fallon's tattoo, we've got more than enough to prosecute.'

'Thank God. The thought of them being able to wander around the village is just too horrible,' Rose said with a shudder. 'One thing I don't understand, though, is if they've stolen so many dogs, why would they risk a tussle with me just to get Scout back? I mean, she's just one dog?'

'Ah well, you don't know Rick Fallon like I do, Rose. He'll not have taken kindly to Scout finding her way to you. He'll have seen it as you getting one over on him, slighting him, and he won't have liked that one bit. He'll have wanted to even the score.'

'Well, that seems pretty petty if you ask me. If he hadn't come after Scout, he might not have been caught.'

'He's a petty man, Rose, that's for certain. Doesn't always think things through, does Rick – lets his temper get the better of him.'

'At least he's locked up, and that's the best result for all of us,' said Rose. 'We need to get on and join the search. If Scout escaped before the Fallons took her home, she should still be in the village somewhere.'

'I've spoken to Grace this morning and arranged to meet her at the practice. She's organizing the search from there. As for the Fallons, let's hope the judge throws the book at them,' Jake said, gritting his teeth.

'I'll leave you both to get on, then,' said PC Palmer. 'I'll need you to come into the station at some point to give a formal statement, but that can wait for now.'

'Thanks for everything, Ben. I'll come in and go through my statement as soon as we've found Scout,' Rose assured him.

'Much appreciated,' PC Palmer said, draining the last of his tea. 'I'd best be off. Take care of yourself, Rose. If I have any news on Scout, you'll be the first to hear it.'

'Bye,' Jake said, closing the door behind him.

'At least they've got the Fallons,' said Rose. 'I don't know how I would have coped if they'd got away with it. If it wasn't for that CCTV camera you insisted I install—'

'Don't even go there with the what ifs. Let's get over to Grace's. I think we should take these two with us,' said Jake, indicating Tagg and Finn. 'They might be able to track Scout more easily than us. They're not trained for search and rescue, obviously, but they're pretty smart dogs.'

'Great idea,' Rose agreed.

As Rose and Jake pulled up at Brook House vets, they could see that the practice's car park was much fuller than usual. Jake had been right when he said that the whole village was involved in the search. Before Jake had even put the jeep's handbrake on, Rose was out of the car and rushing in to see her friend.

'Grace?' Rose called as she entered the building.

'Rose? In here.'

Rose found Grace in her consulting room. She had covered the examination table in a large map marked with Post-it notes, indicating areas that had been searched. Grace ran straight towards her friend and hugged her. 'How are you? I can't believe those Fallons—'

Rose cut her off. 'Is there any news?'

Grace shook her head as Jake and the dogs entered the consulting room.

'Nothing concrete,' she said. 'Maggie thinks she may have seen a flash of her in the woodland behind the school, just here.' Grace pointed to a large area on the map. 'But she can't be sure. We're centring our search there.'

'That sounds sensible,' Jake agreed, nodding.

'Hello? Is anyone here?' Mrs Connolly called from reception.

'Mrs Connolly? We're in here,' Rose shouted, and

after a moment the headteacher's smiling face appeared around the door.

'Oh, Rose dear, thank goodness you're okay.' Mrs Connolly pulled Rose into a hug. 'Naturally, the entire village has heard about what happened last night and we're all eager to help with the search. We won't rest until Scout is found safe and well. I know how I'd feel if it was my Bertie.'

'Thank you, Mrs Connolly, that's really kind of you—'

'I hope you won't mind, dear, but I activated the village phone tree and everyone was eager to help out.'

'You activated the village what?'

'The phone tree, dear. It's a list of phone numbers for everyone in the village. If there's ever an emergency – a snowstorm or flood, say – everyone takes it in turns to call the next person on the list and we all pitch in to help out.'

'Oh, I see, well—' But before Rose could finish she heard Jane the dog-sitter's voice in the doorway, followed by her teaching assistant Cheryl's and then Tara, the receptionist at Brook House vets.

'Tara, Cheryl, Jane . . .' Rose said in surprise.

'Oh, it's not just us,' Cheryl explained, 'there are more volunteers on their way back from the early morning search.' And, as if on cue, in walked Maggie, Ted and Jess from Harrisons, Zoe Mackenzie, Beth and Pete, the landlords from the Apple Tree, Heather Phillips from school, Simon and Anya from the Pink Ribbon and Joyce from the Cosy Cup, along with some other faces that Rose didn't even recognize.

'As soon as we heard about what happened, Rose, we all wanted to help. We've been out searching for Scout since dawn, but we thought it was time we regrouped here,' Zoe explained.

'Is there any news on the Fallons?' Jane asked. Jake explained what PC Palmer had relayed to them about the Fallons being involved in a possible dog theft ring and what they had seen on the CCTV from Jasmine Cottage. Jane looked stricken.

'We all know the Fallons are a nasty bunch, but I'd *never* have thought they'd have done anything this dreadful. All those poor dogs ... it's just too awful.'

'You know,' Jess said, 'I've got some biker mates who I'm sure would happily have a *word* with Rick Fallon for you, Rose. If you get my meaning ...' She threw a wink in Rose's direction.

'I don't think that will be necessary, Jessica,' replied Mrs Connolly with the kind of steely look that she usually reserved for pupils in detention. 'You've done a lot for this village since you've been here, Rose,' she continued, 'and everyone wants to show their appreciation.'

'I don't know what to say,' Rose said through misty eyes. 'I can't thank you all enough, and I know this would mean a lot to my aunt too.'

'You're part of this community, and we all help each other out in times of need,' Joyce said with a smile, 'and if this isn't a time of need then I don't know what is.'

'I've brought supplies,' said Maggie, pulling out a box

laden with cups, tea bags, sugar, long-life milk and more packets of biscuits than Rose could count.

'And Sean is making up platters of sandwiches at the pub to bring over later, so no one will be going hungry,' Beth added.

'Well, it looks like we've thought of everything,' Joyce said with a flourish.

'Anything else we need we can pop back to Harrisons for,' said Ted. 'On the house, of course.'

'Thanks, Ted, I really appreciate that,' Rose said with a smile. 'Mags, was it you who thought you might have spotted Scout in the woods earlier?'

'Well, I can't be sure, Rose. I don't want to go getting your hopes up, but I thought I did see a flash of something black and white in the shrubland at the back of the school early this morning,' said Maggie. 'It's so dense up there, I just couldn't get a good look and, if it was Scout, she was gone in a flash.'

'Can you show me exactly where this was on the map, Mags?' asked Jake.

'Around here,' said Maggie, circling a small area with one of the highlighters laying on Grace's consulting table.

'And when was this?' Rose asked quickly.

'Around 6am, at first light,' Maggie replied.

'That was hours ago,' said Rose checking her watch. 'She could be anywhere by now.'

'Let's make a start there,' Jake said to Rose. 'It's as good a place as any to start, and Finn and Tagg will be able to search any areas of the woodland that are too dense for us to reach.'

'Good idea. Let's get cracking,' said Rose, turning to leave.

'Simon and Anya, why don't you head up to the farmland at the back of Jasmine Cottage, in case Scout's decided to head for home?' said Grace. The couple nodded.

'We'll take the area on the way up to Harper Farm,' said Pete, pointing to the map. 'You never know, she might be trying to get to Jake's if it's closer than Jasmine Cottage?'

'Great idea,' said Mrs Connolly. 'Joyce and I will take the road out towards that new estate.'

'And we'll circle back around the Fallons' place, in case she's hiding out up there,' said Jess, nodding towards her parents.

'I'll stay here and co-ordinate things,' Grace said. 'If we get any sightings of her at all, I'll keep you all in the loop.' The villagers nodded and began making their way outside. 'Rose, before you go, can I have a quiet word?' asked Grace, taking her friend to one side. 'There's something you need to be aware of. The thing is ... well, what with it looking as though Scout is a stolen dog ...'

'Stolen by the Fallons, you mean?' said Rose.

'Yes, exactly. Well, it means that Scout might have an owner out there. An owner that might be looking for her.' Rose opened her mouth to speak, but no words came out.

'An owner?'

'Yes, I'm afraid so,' said Grace. 'This case is going to generate a lot of publicity. It's possible that Scout's original owner might come forward.'

Rose was silent.

'Look, let's not think about that now,' said Jake, taking her hand. 'Let's just focus on finding her and then we can worry about everything else.'

'Jake's right,' Grace agreed. 'I just wanted to warn you, so you're prepared for what might happen.'

'I understand,' Rose replied, nodding.

Rose was exceptionally quiet as Jake drove the short distance from Brook House vets to the school. Could what Grace had just told her be true? Could Scout's original owners be out there, ready to claim her back? She'd just got used to the idea that she was adopting Scout forever. The thought of finding her today only to lose her again tomorrow was too painful to contemplate. As Jake pulled up in the school's car park and cut the jeep's engine, his mobile phone began to ring. As he reached down to grab it from one of the car's cup holders, Rose couldn't help but notice the name 'Sarah'.

Jake declined the call. 'Just another farm supplier,' he said, looking up at her, 'they can wait.' He placed a hand on her shoulder. 'Look, I know what Grace said has thrown you, but don't think about that. All we need to focus on right now is finding Scout. Put everything else out of your head.'

Rose nodded. As she got out of the jeep, Jake let the dogs out of the boot and they headed straight into the woodland. Rose noticed a feeling of nausea sweep over her and, this time, it wasn't just about Scout. *Why had Jake lied about it being Sarah on the phone?* She shook her head. She couldn't think about that now. Jake was right – she had to focus on finding Scout.

'Go find,' Jake said to Finn and Tagg. 'Go find Scout.' The pair set off in hot pursuit.

'Scout! Scout!' Rose called with all the breath she could muster. 'It's safe now, Scout, it's all over!'

They walked through the trees for what seemed like hours, but when Rose glanced at her watch it wasn't even midday. Her mouth was dry and her voice hoarse from calling Scout's name. With each step she took, her hopes of finding Scout faded a little.

'This is hopeless,' she said, sinking to sit down on a tree stump and rest her legs for a minute. 'There's no sign of her anywhere.' Jake pulled a bottle of water out of his rucksack.

'Here, take this. Let's rest for five minutes and give the dogs a drink.'

'What if we don't find her? What if something terrible has happened?' Rose tightened her grip on the water bottle and hung her head. She could feel the sharp sting of tears building in her eyes. Jake dropped his rucksack and put his arm around her. Rose let her head rest on his shoulder.

'We *are* going to find her. Don't give up at the first hurdle. She's a tough little dog and there's no way she's going to let the Fallons get the better of her. Okay?'

'Okay,' said Rose, nodding and wiping her tears firmly away. 'You're right, she's out there somewhere.'

'That's more like it. I know it's hard, but you have to stay positive.' Jake stood up, extended his hand out to Rose and pulled her to her feet. 'Ready to crack on?'

'Yep, let's keep going.'

Rose walked through the woods with renewed vigour and purpose. Jake was right, Scout was a tough cookie. They just had to keep going. She felt her phone vibrate in her pocket and she reached for it frantically. Grace was calling.

'Grace! What is it? Has someone found her?' Rose asked quickly, switching the phone to speaker so that Jake could hear the conversation too.

'Nothing yet, I'm afraid. I just wanted to check in and see how things were going at your end?' said Grace. 'I'm assuming no luck?'

'None,' Rose replied, feeling tears starting to burn at the back of her eyes. Jake squeezed her hand.

'Well, don't give up hope yet. Mrs Connolly and Joyce are driving out to all the farms that border the village, just so we've got the local farmers aware too.'

'That's a great idea,' said Jake. 'Believe me, when any of the sheep escape, all the local farmers come out to help. It's a real team effort. They know this area better than anyone, Rose.' Rose mustered a weak smile.

'Let us know as soon as you've got any news, Grace, won't you?' said Rose.

'I promise, you'll be the first call I make,' Grace replied.

'Speak soon,' said Rose, ending the call. She sighed deeply. 'I can't believe there's still no news.'

'I've not seen the dogs for a while. Tagg! Finn! Come!' Jake called. It was hard to keep track of them both in the dense undergrowth of the woodland and they hadn't checked in with Jake for a while. Finn came running back towards them at the sound of Jake's voice, but there was no sign of Tagg. Jake poured some water into a collapsible dog bowl and Finn drank eagerly. 'Tagg? Here, boy!' There was no sign of the dog.

'Listen,' whispered Rose, grabbing Jake's forearm. 'Did you hear that?'

'What?'

'Just listen—' Rose and Jake sat in silence. 'That! Did you hear it?' said Rose, standing upright.

'That's Tagg barking,' he said. 'Listen, there he is again!'

'Come on, he might have found something,' Rose said, starting to run towards the sound of the barking. 'Tagg? Tagg? Where are you?'

'This way,' said Jake, taking Rose's hand and pulling her to the left. In the distance, Rose could see Tagg barking frantically, and there was something else obscured from view. *Was it? Could it be? Scout?*

'There he is! And I think he's found her!' Rose began running even faster. She scratched her legs on the brambles in the dense undergrowth but she didn't care. 'Scout? Scout?' She could clearly see a black and white tail wagging frantically. Rose fell to her knees as she reached the dogs. Scout was lying on the floor, yipping quietly with Tagg standing over her, licking her face. Rose dropped to her knees. She threw her arms around the little dog's neck and sobbed into her fur. 'Oh, Scout. I'm pleased to see you too, sweetheart. I thought I'd lost you. What a brave girl.'

'You found her, Tagg, what a clever boy,' said Jake, bending down and fussing the dog proudly. 'How is she?'

'I don't think she's hurt. Just exhausted, maybe? Pass me that water bowl, will you?' Rose filled the bowl with water and Scout got to her feet and drank eagerly.

'That's it, girl, have a good drink,' Jake said. 'I've got some treats too,' he passed the bag to Rose.

'Here you go. I bet you're starving, little one.' Scout took the treats gratefully and, not wanting to miss out, Tagg and Finn were quick to stick their noses into the bag too. Rose laughed. 'Well, I guess you two deserve some – you did find her.' She kissed Tagg on the head.

'I can't believe it,' she said, taking Jake's hand. 'We've done it. We've found her. I don't know how I can even begin to say thank you, Jake,' she said, her tears flowing freely now. 'If anything had happened to Scout, I don't know what I would have done.'

'Well, thankfully, that's not something you have to think about now,' he replied, squeezing her hand tightly.

As they walked back to the jeep, Rose found that she was unable to let go of Jake's hand, despite how uneasy she felt about Sarah's call earlier. She let him call Grace to tell her the good news so that she could call off the search, and she smiled when she heard her friend's squeals of delight down the phone. Although she was now reunited with Scout, Rose couldn't help but feel a rising sense of foreboding. If Scout really was a stolen dog, how much longer would they have together before she lost her all over again?

# Chapter 31

'Can we head back to the cottage now? I'd like to get Scout settled in,' said Rose.

'Of course. I'll get the dogs into the truck and grab my keys.'

'Thanks, Jake. Oh God, Aunt Jean! I haven't even thought about telling her what's happened! I was at the hospital last night – I should have gone to the ward and explained everything. I don't want her to hear about it from anyone else.'

'Rose, there's no way they'd have let you on the ward at gone midnight. Jean would have been fast asleep. What were you planning on doing? Waking her up in the middle of the night to tell her that Scout had been stolen?'

'You're right. I hadn't thought about it like that.'

'How about we take a trip to the hospital once we've been to the cottage? You can explain everything to her then.'

'Okay, great. Thanks, Jake. Are you *sure* you don't mind though? You've done nothing but run around after me for the last twenty-four hours.'

'It's not a problem. That's what friends are for. Michael's got everything under control back at the farm.'

*Friends?* Was that how he thought of her – just as a friend? She cast her mind back to their near kiss in the kitchen before PC Palmer had arrived and the way that they had held hands on the walk back through the forest. Had she misread the situation? She was sure Jake had been about to kiss her earlier. *Had she got things wrong?* Maybe she still had a touch of concussion after all and was imagining things?

Jake and Rose loaded the dogs into the truck and made the short drive down to Jasmine Cottage. When they arrived, Rose let the three Border Collies out into the garden, where they started playing a game of chase together. Rose heard Grace's voice behind her from the open front door.

'Oh, Rose, I'm so relieved you've found her,' she said, walking through to the kitchen.

'Grace,' Rose said, turning to face her friend and pulling her in for a tight hug. 'I'm so grateful for everything you've done to help find Scout.'

'Don't be daft, I'm just pleased that you're *both* okay. I feel partly responsible,' Grace said, her head hung low.

'Why on earth would you?'

'Well, that guy who was Fallon's accomplice, the one who followed you to the pub that night. I told you he was just a tourist and not to worry. I've been up all night thinking about it. I got it so wrong,' she said, pulling a tissue out of her pocket and blowing her nose.

'Hey, there's no way you could have known. None of us could have. I won't have you blaming yourself for this.'

'Rose is right, Grace,' Jake added. 'You had no reason to

think that he was anything other than a tourist. Don't go blaming yourself.'

'Thanks, guys,' Grace said, wiping a tear from her cheek.

'Fancy a cuppa?' Rose said with a smile. 'Scout's in the garden if you want to go and see her?'

'Yes, please. It wouldn't hurt for me to give her a quick check-over to make sure she's okay.'

'Thanks,' said Rose. There was a knock on the door, which Jake ran to answer. He reappeared in the kitchen with Mrs Connolly and Joyce at his side.

'Rose, we've just heard the good news,' said Mrs Connolly, clapping her hands in delight.

'We thought we'd pop in and give you a hand, Rose. You must be exhausted!' said Joyce.

'Oh, I'm fine honestly, there's no need ...'

'I'll not have you wearing yourself out while you're still recovering, Rose,' Mrs Connolly insisted. 'Let us make you some tea at least and we can entertain the dogs if you need to rest?'

Before Rose could open her mouth to protest, Jake suggested that this gave them the perfect opportunity to go back to the hospital to visit Jean.

'That sounds like a great idea,' Joyce said, 'and why don't you two stop in at the pub on the way home for a Sunday roast? Beth said she'd put something by for you both.'

'And don't worry about the dogs,' Grace chipped in, poking her head in from the garden, 'they'll be fine here with us.' Rose wasn't sure she wanted to leave Scout so soon but knowing she'd be in safe hands with Grace, she allowed Mrs Connolly and Joyce to practically bundle her into Jake's jeep and, before she knew it, they were on their way back to the hospital.

'Wow, they really don't take no for an answer, do they?' said Rose as they pulled away from the cottage.

'That's all part of living in Blossom Heath, I guess,' Jake replied. 'Everyone pulls together in a crisis. It was the same after my parents died – the whole village rallied around to help us get back on our feet. It's one of the reasons I love living here, I suppose.'

'Me too. And a visit to Aunt Jean and Sunday lunch at the pub does sound like just what the doctor ordered.'

'Exactly,' said Jake. 'You're meant to be taking it easy today. Just sit back, relax, close your eyes and we'll be at the hospital in no time.'

Jake wasn't wrong. Within what felt like seconds, he was tapping Rose on the shoulder as he parked the car at the hospital.

'Why don't you go and see your aunt first and I'll grab us some coffees and bring them up to the ward?'

'Excellent idea,' Rose said, and the pair parted company in the foyer as Rose made her way up to Nightingale Ward. Her aunt spotted her as soon as she walked onto the ward.

'Rose! How lovely to see you, my dear! But what's happened to your face?' Rose brought her hand up to her left cheek. *Ouch!* she thought as she ran her hand across it. The bruising must be more visible now than she'd thought.

318

'Well, I guess that's why I'm here. It's been an eventful twenty-four hours, and I wanted to fill you in.'

She went on to tell her aunt all about the events of the previous evening with the Fallons, the search for Scout, her break-up with Ollie and her job offer in London.

'I'll *murder* that Rick Fallon if he ever crosses my path again,' Aunt Jean said, and Rose had no doubt that her aunt would be quite the match for him if the situation arose. 'I remember when he was a boy, *always* causing trouble that one, and he was never sorry about it either,' she added quickly. 'It makes my blood boil to think of what he's done.'

'Don't worry, Auntie, I'm fine and Scout's back where she belongs, so there's no real damage done.'

'Well, that bruise on your face tells a different story,' she continued, her face softening.

'Oh, don't worry about me.' Rose reached out to take her aunt's hand.

'Honestly, all those years living in London and something like this happens right here in Blossom Heath! It's unbelievable.' Rose heard footsteps coming up behind her and she saw her aunt's face beaming. 'Hello, Jake, love. I hear you were quite the hero last night.'

'I only did what anyone else would have,' he replied, reddening. 'I've brought you both some coffee. I'm betting the stuff on the ward is undrinkable.'

'Jake, you really are a saint,' said Aunt Jean as he bent down to give her a kiss on the cheek and pass her a takeaway coffee cup. 'Cappuccino?'

'Naturally.'

'Well remembered,' said Aunt Jean with a twinkle in her eye. 'Honestly, Rose, you could do a lot worse than a man who remembers how you like your coffee.'

Rose, choosing to ignore her aunt, said, 'We'd better be getting back to the cottage, Auntie. I want to get back to Scout.'

'Of course, my dear. Before you go, though, I have some good news to share. They're letting me go home on the twenty-first of July!'

'Oh wow! That *is* good news.'

'They're going to send someone to the cottage to see what adaptations it might need, but the consultant thinks that, once everything's in place, I should be mobile enough to manage on my own.'

Rose bent down to give her aunt a hug. 'We'll have everything ready for you well before then. I bet you can't wait!'

'I'm counting the days.'

When Rose and Jake arrived back at Jasmine Cottage, Rose was amazed to see that Mrs Connolly and Joyce had been busy baking and the kitchen was full of delectable treats. There were sausage rolls and cheese straws, cupcakes and scones all cooling on wire racks on the table. All three Border Collies were sitting obediently at Mrs Connolly's feet, obviously hoping there was a treat in the offing. As soon as they realized this wasn't going to happen, they headed out to the garden to continue their games.

'Wow! Mrs Connolly, Joyce, I don't know what to say,' Rose said in shock, 'this is amazing. I'm *so* grateful. You've made enough food to feed an army and it smells delicious.'

'It's like the old saying goes,' Mrs Connolly explained, 'many hands make light work.'

'They certainly do,' Rose agreed.

'We both love baking,' said Joyce, 'so Eileen and I thought we may as well put our talents to good use.'

'We'll make ourselves scarce now and give you a bit of time to yourself,' said Mrs Connolly. 'Jake, I suggest you do the same. I'm sure Rose could do with some time alone to process the events of the last twenty-four hours,' she added, slipping into headteacher mode.

'Oh ... yes ... of course ... Tagg! Finn! Come on, boys, it's time to go,' he called to the dogs in the garden who came running in obediently, with Scout right behind them. 'Are you sure you're okay on your own, Rose?' Jake whispered, out of Mrs Connolly's earshot. 'I can stay longer if you need me to.'

'I'll be fine. I think Mrs Connolly's right, some time alone is just what I need to process everything. But here, take some sausages rolls for the road – I'm never going to eat all of this,' she said, passing him a plate full.

'Thanks, and if you change your mind, you know where I am.'

'Thanks, Jake. You've been an absolute star these past twenty-four hours,' Rose said as she hugged him. 'I honestly don't know how I would have got through this without you.'

'I'll see you on Tuesday at the farm for the school trip?' said Jake.

'Oh, of course, yes. That had completely slipped my mind.'

'That's not surprising given the circumstances,' added Mrs Connolly. 'The children are really looking forward it, Jake. I'm sure it will be a roaring success.'

As Jake, Joyce and Mrs Connolly said their goodbyes and left the cottage, Rose shut the door and said, 'Well, Scout, it looks like it's just me and you.' The prospect of some time alone to process the day's events filled her with dread ... All she could think about was Jake and the reason he'd lied to her about Sarah's call.

# Chapter 32

Jake awoke early the following morning. Before he'd even had the chance to finish his breakfast, he heard a car pull up outside the farmhouse. He looked out of the window and saw that it was Sarah. His heart sank. *What was she doing here?* He knew he'd made a mistake in bringing her back to the farmhouse after they'd met at the pub last week. That's why he'd asked her to leave before things went any further. *At least I didn't sleep with her,* he thought. *That really would have made things even worse.* She was calling him several times a day now and he had decided that the best way forward was to just ignore her calls. Clearly, however, she hadn't got the message and had decided to turn up at the farm unannounced.

Jake took a deep breath and opened the farmhouse door. He'd be civil, but he needed to make it clear that they were over.

'What are you doing here?' he asked as he opened the farmhouse door.

'I wanted to see if you'd had a chance to think things over,' she blurted out before Jake had a chance to speak. 'I shouldn't have tried to push things along so quickly. I can see now that it was too much, too soon.' Jake waved her into the kitchen, she took a seat at the kitchen table and he placed a coffee in front of her. She took a sip.

'It's not that. I know you'd hoped that I might see things differently in time but . . . I don't. It really is over, Sarah. Like I said, if anything, I'm glad we kissed. It showed me that I don't have those kinds of feelings for you.'

'But—' Sarah tried to interrupt, but Jake pressed on.

'And I'm glad we talked things through. I don't hate you, Sarah – for what you did with Miles, I mean. I appreciate you explaining things and I can forgive the betrayal, but there's just no *future* for us.'

Sarah hung her head. 'And there's *nothing* I can do or say to change your mind?' she said. Jake shook his head. As Sarah stood up abruptly to leave, she knocked her coffee cup into her lap and yelped in pain. 'Damn!' Jake could see her bare legs were rapidly turning red and her dress was soaked through. 'You don't mind if I get some cold water on this? It stings like hell.'

'No, of course, do what you need to,' said Jake, rising from his chair. Sarah returned a few minutes later and Jake was surprised to see that she was wrapped in a towel.

'I thought it would be quicker to jump in the shower,' she said, patting her legs dry.

'Do you want to borrow some clothes to wear home?' Jake asked, averting his eyes. The sooner he could get her out of the farmhouse, he thought, the better.

'No, it's fine. I'll just pop my dress in the wash if that's okay? It'll be ruined otherwise and it's one of my favourites. I'll shove it in the drier afterwards.' Jake shifted uncomfortably in his seat. The towel Sarah was wearing didn't leave much to the imagination. As he was about to answer her, a sudden thought crossed his mind. Could she have done this deliberately? Thrown coffee over herself to give her a reason to stay longer and take her clothes off? Surely not. It was a ridiculous thought. He knew Sarah liked to get her own way, but even she wouldn't go that far.

'Erm, sure. You're welcome to wait, but I have to go out. I've got a supplier meeting and I'm already running late,' he lied.

'Do you *really* have to go, Jakey? Can't you give them a call and say something's come up?' she said, starting to roll her towel down provocatively. He hated it when she called him 'Jakey'. Jake stood up and grabbed his car keys. He was suddenly desperate to escape the farmhouse.

'Afraid not. I'll have to leave you to it. You know how the drier works – just let yourself out once you're done,' he said hurriedly, closing the front door behind him.

As Rose pulled into the yard of Harper Farm, she wondered if it was too early to be calling on Jake. She shook her head. Farmers are up at the crack of dawn, she told herself, especially on a Monday morning. She wanted to thank him in person for everything that he'd done for her over the weekend. As she pulled into the yard, however, she realized that she couldn't see Jake's truck. In the space where it should be was a Mini Cooper in racing green. How odd. Perhaps Jake had a visitor? She left Scout in the car and knocked on the farmhouse door. It was opened by a stunningly beautiful blonde woman that Rose instantly recognized as Sarah, wearing nothing but a towel.

'Hello? Can I help you?'

'Oh, er . . . hi,' Rose said awkwardly. 'Is Jake around?'

'I'm afraid not,' Sarah answered, smiling sweetly at her. 'Can I help at all?'

'Oh, don't worry, I was just dropping by on the off chance he might want to walk the dogs together.'

'And *you* are?'

'Sorry, I should have introduced myself. I'm Rose, Rose Hargreaves. I'm a friend of Jake's.'

Sarah's eyes narrowed. 'Oh yes, I think I saw you in the pub the other night. Well, you've just missed him I'm afraid. He's popped out to grab us some breakfast. He's so *thoughtful* like that, isn't he?'

Rose felt a wave of nausea wash over her. *Sarah must have spent the night . . .*

'Oh well, not to worry. If you could just let him know I called, that would be great.'

'Of course. Rachel, is it? I'll do that.' Rose didn't correct her. 'Oh, I don't think I introduced myself. I'm Sarah,' she said, holding out her hand to shake Rose's.

Rose felt her hand go clammy as she took Sarah's. Jake and Sarah must be back together. That explained why she had been calling him yesterday and why he'd lied to Rose about it. She felt sick.

'Great to meet you, Sarah,' she said, plastering a smile onto her face to try and hide what she was really feeling. As Rose walked slowly back to her car, she could feel her pulse quickening and her hands trembling. All hopes of romance with Jake were extinguished from her mind.

When Rose arrived at school that morning, she was still reeling from her encounter with Sarah at Harper Farm. *If Jake was back with his ex, why hadn't he mentioned anything to her?* It was only twenty-four hours ago that she'd stayed the night at the farm herself and she'd been with him for most of the weekend. They'd nearly kissed in his kitchen and held hands on their walk back through the woods yesterday. He'd said nothing to her about reconciling with Sarah. *Maybe he thought it was none of her business? Perhaps he was just another player and not the man she'd thought he was?* If he did see her as 'just a friend', he probably thought it wasn't important. As she absent mindedly walked towards the school, she was greeted by a host of well-wishers among the parents at the gates. The whole village had heard about the incident with Rick Fallon and everyone had been shocked and horrified that something so dreadful could happen in the village. The children in Butterfly Class, however, were more concerned with their impending visit to Harper Farm the following day.

Rose had sent them home on Monday afternoon with

strict instructions about how they were to behave and what they needed to bring along with them – wellies and water-proof jackets, even though the weather forecast promised sunshine, as well as a packed lunch, plenty of water, hats and sun cream. Rose wanted to ensure that they were prepared for every eventuality. This was England after all.

If Rose had thought her day couldn't get any worse after her encounter with Sarah at Harper Farm this morning, she was sorely mistaken. As she walked home from school that afternoon, her phone buzzed in her bag. She had a message from Grace asking her to go straight to the surgery after school. Rose felt her stomach knot and her chest tightened. What had happened? Was it Scout? Perhaps she hadn't come away from her encounter with the Fallons as unscathed as they'd all thought? Grace's surgery wasn't far from the school and Rose picked up her walking pace so that she was there in mere minutes.

'Is it Scout?' she said to Tara the receptionist as she burst into the waiting room.

'Scout's fine,' Tara said, 'no need to panic. Grace just needs a quick word, but I'll let her explain. You can go straight through,' she said, waving towards the consulting room door. Rose knocked and went in.

'Rose . . .' said Grace, looking up from the notes she was making.

'What's wrong?' she asked sharply.

'Now, don't freak out when you hear this – nothing's certain—'

'What's not certain? What are you talking about?'

'That conversation we had yesterday about Scout being a stolen dog?'

'What about it?'

'It's just, the story got some publicity on local news and someone has come forward today claiming to be Scout's original owner.'

'What?' Rose gasped, grabbing the corner of the consulting room table to steady herself. The news felt like a physical blow. She felt winded.

'Nothing's certain yet. The RSPCA put the owner in touch with me and they've sent over a picture of their dog, Tess.'

'And?'

'It's hard to say for sure, but it does look like she *could* be Scout.'

Rose's shoulders slumped. 'So, what does this mean? Could they take her back?'

'I've arranged for them to come to the surgery in the morning to meet Scout. As she wasn't microchipped when we found her, there's no official record of ownership. They didn't realize it was something they legally had to do, but it definitely makes things harder. It's going to be a case of seeing if Scout recognizes them and vice versa. We won't know one way or another until then.'

'And they could just ... take her back? Tomorrow?' Rose swallowed hard.

'I need to get some advice on the legal side of things, since

Scout has done her seven days as a stray. But if she *was* stolen, I'm afraid that might change things.'

Rose was silent. She didn't know what to say, how to react.

'I'm so sorry, Rose. None of us could have predicted this.'

Rose straightened up. She had to try and steady herself. Be practical. If Scout really was in fact Tess, then her owners must have been missing her a great deal.

'What time tomorrow do you need her here?'

'Not until eleven. If you're teaching, I can collect her from Jane's,' Grace suggested.

'Thanks.'

'If it helps, they do sound like lovely people, and they've been looking for her everywhere. They really have missed her.'

'It helps a little,' said Rose weakly. 'If she is their dog, will you promise me one thing?'

'Name it.'

'That you won't let them take her until I've had a chance to say goodbye.'

# Chapter 33

Rose spent a difficult evening alone with Scout at Jasmine Cottage. She was constantly close to tears and couldn't shake the thought that this could be their last evening together. She instinctively wanted to call Jake and her fingers hovered over the buttons on her phone to do just that on more than one occasion. *But how could she call him after what had happened this morning?* He was probably having a romantic evening in with Sarah. *Sarah.* Could she have looked any more stunning, with her long blonde hair and ridiculously long legs, wrapped in that towel this morning. Legs that had probably been wrapped around Jake the night before ... *No*, she thought, shaking her head, *don't go there*. But it was too late, that thought caused her almost as much pain as the thought of losing Scout. It seemed madness that only last night she was overflowing with happiness at finding Scout and a future for her and Jake was starting to look like a real possibility. The job offer in London was now looking more attractive than it ever had before. If a future with Scout and with Jake really was off the table, she couldn't wait to leave Blossom Heath as soon as Jean was home and settled.

Rose took herself off to bed early that night but she tossed and turned for hours, finally dozing off as the sun was starting to rise. During the little sleep that she did have, her dreams turned to Scout. The dog was being ripped away from her by Sarah, who laughed as Rose screamed, 'No, come back! Scout, come back!' She woke with a start to find Scout sat looking at her quizzically from the end of the bed. Rose reached out and ruffled her fur.

'What am I going to do without you?' she sighed as Scout rolled onto her back for a belly rub. 'Is it wrong that I hope you don't recognize those people coming to see you today? Can you at least just *pretend* to hate them? For me?'

When Rose arrived at Jane's, she was pleased that Grace had called ahead to fill her in on all the details about Scout's possible previous owners.

'Oh, Rose, I can't tell you how sorry I am,' said Jane as soon as she opened the front door. 'After everything that you two have been through, it just doesn't seem right for you to be separated now.'

'Thanks. I guess there's still a chance that Scout isn't their dog. I'm just trying to hang onto that right now.'

'That's the spirit. Keep thinking positive. I'm sure it'll all work out for the best.' Rose bent down to give Scout a kiss on the top of her head and then turned and began the short walk to school.

When she arrived, Rose made sure that she had ticked off all the parental permission slips in readiness for the trip and had time to go through the risk assessment one last time. It was just her and Cheryl accompanying the children to the farm, as well as a parent helper in the form of Zoe Mackenzie, Hayden's mum.

By the time the children arrived at school at 8.55am, the rental coach was already parked up in the school playground and Butterfly Class were giddy with excitement. Rose could hear the children arguing with each other about who was going to sit at a window seat on the coach and who had brought along the best treats for their lunch. She sat the class down calmly and quietly and ran through the rules for the trip one last time.

'Now remember, Butterfly Class, we are representing Blossom Heath Primary School today and we want to make a good impression on Mr Harper or he won't be inviting us back.'

The class were unable to contain their excitement on the coach journey up to Jake's farm and, as the coach driver reversed the vehicle into the yard, Rose could see that Jake was waiting to greet them with a wave and a smile. She felt sick at the thought of seeing him. She'd been such a fool for thinking that he could be interested in her when he was clearly back together with his ex. She decided the best way forward was to say nothing about her encounter with Sarah yesterday morning, unless Jake brought it up. She wasn't going to mention anything about Scout either. She didn't think she could handle his sympathy right now.

Julie Haworth

'Is that him?' Poppy asked, wide-eyed. 'Is that the farmer – Mr Harper?'

'Yes, Poppy.' Rose stood up on the coach and addressed the entire class. 'Now remember, Butterfly Class, best behaviour today, please. Make sure you stay with your partner while we're walking around the farm and keep Mrs Morse and me in sight at all times,' she explained, pointing towards Cheryl. 'No wandering off.'

The children unbuckled their seatbelts and disembarked the coach amid murmurs of excitement. They gathered around Jake eagerly as Rose introduced him and he explained to them a bit about the farm and the kinds of animals that were kept there.

'Do you have any bulls?' Billy Jenkins called out.

'Billy, remember to put your hand up if you have a question. Don't shout out, please.'

'Sorry, Miss.'

'We don't have any bulls I'm afraid, Billy. Just sheep and goats, chickens and pigs,' Jake answered. He let out a whistle and Tagg and Finn came running out of the farmhouse obediently and sat at Jake's side.

'Wow,' Tiffany exclaimed, 'I wish Buttercup could do that, Miss,' she said, looking at Tagg and Finn in awe.

'Well, these aren't just any dogs,' Jake explained to the children. 'These are trained sheepdogs. They work here on the farm by helping me herd the sheep. They're very clever and you'll see them in action later.'

The children gathered around the two dogs and made a

great fuss of them. Tagg and Finn lapped up all the attention, rolling over for belly rubs, much to the excitement and delight of the class.

Jake spent the morning giving the children a tour around the farm, introducing them to the various animals that lived there and talking to them about how they needed to be cared for. Although some of the children were familiar with farm life already, the rest of the class had a multitude of questions to ask him, and, although Rose was impressed with how much patience and humour he displayed, she found she couldn't quite meet his eye whenever he smiled at her.

By the time they stopped for a picnic lunch in one of the fields, most of Butterfly Class were declaring that they either wanted to be a farmer when they grew up or were going to ask their parents if they could start keeping chickens and have their own eggs.

'I think you might have a few converts there,' Rose said to Jake without making eye contact.

'I know,' Cheryl agreed, 'the village is going to be full of chicken coups by the end of the week, if the children have their way.'

Just as the class were clearing up from lunch, placing all their rubbish into two black bin bags that Cheryl had brought for the occasion, Rose spotted Mrs Connolly's car pull up in the yard.

'Mrs Connolly?'

'Hello, Butterfly Class,' the headteacher waved as she made her way down to join them. 'Rose told me all about the sheepdog display you've got planned for this afternoon, Jake, and I was dying to come along and see it.'

'Great, the more the merrier,' Jake replied, beaming. 'We're just about to head over to the sheep field to get started.'

'Perfect,' Mrs Connolly said, clapping her hands together.

'Give me a five-minute head start and I'll get everything set up,' said Jake.

Rose nodded at him curtly without saying anything, but she did as instructed and waited for a few minutes before heading down to see the sheep, giving Jake a chance to prepare. When the class arrived, Rose could see that Jake had set the field up with around twelve sheep and an empty pen, the gate of which was open. Tagg and Finn were sat by his feet, raring to go. The children stood wide-eyed behind the fencing of the paddock and they watched in awe as Jake set the Border Collies to work rounding up the sheep.

The dogs worked as a team, responding to Jake's every whistle and command. As he called 'come by', they changed direction at breakneck speed, gradually pushing the flock in the direction of the pen.

'Wow!' exclaimed Billy Jenkins. 'How is he getting the dogs to do that, Miss?'

'It's magic,' Hayden added. 'They must be magic dogs.'

Rose chuckled. 'No, Hayden, they're not magic, they're just really well trained. Mr Harper has worked really hard to get his dogs to listen to his commands.'

As the dogs successfully herded the flock of sheep into the

pen and Jake closed the gate behind them, Butterfly Class erupted into applause and cheers. Jake took a bow and walked back towards the class, a grin splitting across his face, which quickly faded when he noticed that Rose wasn't smiling back at him.

'Well, Mr Harper, that really was quite the display,' Mrs Connolly said, clapping appreciatively. 'Would you mind answering some questions from the children? I'm sure they've got lots they'd like to ask you.' Jake nodded and the children's hands shot up into the air like rockets.

'Shall we hear from Poppy first?' Rose suggested. 'She looks as though she's fit to burst.'

'Thanks, Miss,' said Poppy, relaxing her arm down by her side and taking a deep breath. 'How long did it take to get your dogs to be so clever?'

'Well, I started introducing them to the sheep when they were puppies and we did lots of exercises out here in the field to start their training. By the time they were two years old they could herd the sheep into the pen, just like you saw today.'

'Two years?' Poppy replied, looking horrified. 'I wanted to teach Tiffany's puppy, Buttercup, to do that,' she said, pointing down at the sheep in the pen, 'but I don't think I could wait *two years*.' She looked genuinely crestfallen, and Mrs Connolly and Rose both stifled a giggle.

'Good dog training isn't a quick process I'm afraid, Poppy. When I started bringing Bertie into school, he tried to eat the chair in my office during the first week,' Mrs Connolly explained. The children broke out into hysterical laughter at the thought of Bertie the school dog being so naughty.

Jake continued to answer all the children's questions. He was a natural with the kids and the afternoon couldn't have gone better. Rose was sure that Mrs Connolly would be giving him a resounding endorsement to other schools in the area, which would be just what Jake and the farm needed.

'Right, children, I think we've taken up enough of Mr Harper's time today, don't you?' Rose said to the class. 'We'd better be getting back on the coach if we're going to get back to school ready for home time.'

'Oh, Miss,' the children murmured in unison, looking disappointed at the thought of returning to school so soon.

'Let's say thank you to Mr Harper for making us so welcome today,' said Rose.

'Thank you, Mr Harper,' the children parroted in unison.

'You're welcome, Butterfly Class. It was great to have you all here. Tagg and Finn have enjoyed themselves too.'

Cheryl led the children back to the coach and began loading them on in pairs. Jake hung back to say goodbye to Rose and Mrs Connolly.

'That really was an excellent display, Mr Harper. The children have had such a great day,' Rose said quickly.

'Since when do you call me Mr Harper?' Jake asked, looking confused. Rose turned quickly towards Mrs Connolly.

'Fantastic work, Jake. I'll be recommending you to all the local headteachers, so I'm sure you'll be inundated with bookings for next year,' Mrs Connolly assured him.

'Thanks,' Jake replied, beaming at Rose. She shifted her feet awkwardly.

'Of course, we'll all be missing Rose next year when she returns to London,' said Mrs Connolly.

Jake's face fell and he looked at Rose. 'What? You're . . . going back to London?'

'Your interview's Thursday, isn't it, Rose?' Mrs Connolly went on before Rose could reply. 'Of course, it sounds like a done deal to me, just a formality really. Jake, are you quite alright? You look white as a sheet.'

'I'm fine,' Jake replied. Rose could tell he was looking at her for an explanation. She didn't see why he was reacting like this given that he'd failed to even mention to her that he was back with his fiancée.

'I meant to explain about the job at the weekend, but with everything that happened, there just wasn't the right moment,' Rose said, looking down at her handbag and twisting the tassel on its clasp.

'Miss Hargreaves, we're ready to leave now,' Cheryl called down from the coach.

'Right, that's me off too then,' said Mrs Connolly as she waved a goodbye to the children and walked back to her car.

'I have to go, but I'll talk to you later?' she said, placing a hand on his arm. Jake pulled it away.

'You don't owe me any explanations, Rose.' His shoulders slumped and the hurt was evident on his face. He turned away from her, waved goodbye to the children and made his way back to the farmhouse. Rose had no choice but to get on the coach herself and, as they drove away from Harper Farm, she felt a single tear roll slowly down her cheek. *If Jake was reconciled with Sarah and had spent the night with her, why was he reacting to the news of her leaving so badly?*

Wiping the tear away, she reminded herself that she had bigger problems to deal with right now than Jake Harper's love life. She needed to get straight to Grace's after school to find out what had happened with Scout.

# Chapter 34

Rose practically ran towards Brook House vets after school. She didn't think she'd ever felt so nervous in her life. She crashed through the surgery's entrance doors with a bang and the whole waiting room turned to look at her. She felt her cheeks burn hot. Grace was behind the reception desk, talking to a client. Rose wanted to butt in, to interrupt the conversation. She *had* to know, to find out what had happened. Scout jumped up from behind the reception desk, placing her front paws on the counter. Her whole body wiggled when she spotted Rose.

'Scout!' she said. She looked desperately at Grace, who stopped talking as soon as she spotted her.

'Rose! It's good news! Scout isn't Tess after all.' The entire waiting room broke into applause. It seemed, once again, that everyone in Blossom Heath had already heard about the drama of Scout's potential previous owners showing up. 'Head into the consulting room and I'll explain,' she gestured towards the door. 'You don't mind if I pop Rose in before you, Mrs Andersen?'

'Not at all,' Mrs Andersen replied. 'I think the poor girl has been kept in suspense long enough.'

Grace followed Rose into the consulting room with Scout and shut the door.

'You're sure? This other couple, they're certain?'

'One hundred per cent. As soon as they met her, they knew she wasn't Tess. I knew too. Don't get me wrong, Scout clearly liked them – she likes everyone – but she didn't react to them in the way she just did when *you* walked into the surgery.'

'I can't believe it,' Rose said, tears glistening in her eyes. 'I've spent the whole day convincing myself that I had to get ready to say goodbye.'

'I really felt for them. They were so excited at the prospect of finding Tess and their faces fell as soon as they saw Scout. Dog theft really is such an awful thing to go through.'

'I can't imagine. Scout was only missing overnight and I was devastated. I don't know how I'd cope if she'd been gone for weeks, months even.'

'It's just dreadful, it really is,' said Grace, shaking her head. 'I do have more good news though . . .'

'What?'

'Well, PC Palmer called just before you arrived and Rick Fallon has finally come clean about Scout's background.'

'And?'

'Apparently he bought her from a guy in a pub in Hastings for fifty quid a few months back. Fallon reckons the bloke said his kids had got bored of her and his wife couldn't cope. Rick probably thought he could make a quick buck by selling her on or trying to breed from her.'

'But what does that mean? Scout won't have to go back to him, will she?' Rose bent down and pulled Scout in close to her.

'Nope, Fallon's not going to contest ownership, so Scout is well and truly yours.'

'Do you hear that, Scout? It's all official now,' said Rose, kissing the dog on the top of the head and wiping a tear from the corner of her eye.

'I'm more than a little relieved that Scout's staying put,' said Grace. Rose beamed and hugged her friend.

'This calls for a celebration! Extra doggie treats tonight,' she said, nodding at Scout, 'and a large glass of wine for me. Although not too much – I'm trying to keep a clear head before my interview.'

'The interview?' asked Grace. Rose nodded. 'I'd forgotten all about that with everything going on. Are you *sure* that going back to London is what you really want? Things with Ollie are over and you know Scout would prefer to be a country dog.' Rose was silent. 'Plus, there's Jake to consider. I saw how you two were looking at each other at the weekend. I think you'd be perfect together—'

'He's back with Sarah.'

'What, *Jake*?'

'Yep.'

'*Sarah*? That can't be right, not after what she did. He'd never get back with her. Did Jake tell you that?'

'No, he hasn't said a thing. That's what makes it even worse. I was starting to think there could be a future for us and then I turned up at the farmhouse yesterday morning and met Sarah. Wrapped in a towel. It was pretty clear what her and Jake had been up to the previous evening.'

'Wow,' said Grace, inhaling deeply. 'I can't say I'm not shocked. I honestly never thought Jake would go there again. I can't believe he's not said anything.'

'I don't know,' Rose replied with a shrug. 'I've given up trying to figure men out. She even rang him yesterday when we were out looking for Scout and he *lied* about it. I thought Jake was different to Ollie . . . but maybe he isn't?'

'I'm sorry,' Grace said, placing her hand on her friend's shoulder. 'I know you've got feelings for him and it must have been rough finding out about Sarah like that. I'm disappointed in him. Sarah was always a manipulative cowbag and it looks like she's managed to work her magic on him again.'

'I guess it's none of my business. I suppose it has made the decision to take the job in London a little easier.'

'Have you thought about telling him how you feel? Even with Sarah back in the picture, I'm still convinced he has feelings for you. If he knew you felt the same, it might be enough?'

'No way! I'm not getting involved when his ex is still on the scene. I've been through enough with Ollie.'

'That's understandable. Well, good luck for the interview. I'll be rooting for you.'

That evening Rose tried to call Jake hoping that they could talk things through. She didn't want to go off to London with any bad feelings or misunderstandings lingering between them. He didn't pick up. After her third attempt, Rose decided to leave him a voicemail message to explain. It wasn't ideal – she'd wanted to speak to him in person before she left for London, but she had to try and give him some kind of explanation.

'Hi Jake, it's Rose. I'm sorry about Mrs Connolly springing the news about my interview like that. I wanted to explain things in person, but the weekend was … well, you know how it went. Anyway, a job's come up at my old school and they're interviewing me on Thursday. It's a great opportunity … I'd be *mad* to turn it down. And, after all, there's no reason for me to stay on in Blossom Heath, as long as my aunt's recovery stays on track and she can cope alone.'

Rose cursed under her breath. *Why had she said there was nothing to keep her in Blossom Heath?* Jake was a pretty good reason to stay, but what could she do? He was back with his ex and she couldn't come clean about her feelings for him in a voicemail. That was it. She'd missed her chance. It clearly wasn't meant to be. Perhaps if she'd said something sooner, he wouldn't have reconciled with Sarah, but it was too late to think about that now. Rose took a deep breath and steeled herself. She needed to keep her mind focused on her interview tomorrow. London was clearly where her future lay and the sooner she accepted that, the better.

# Chapter 35

Thursday morning came around all too quickly and Rose woke before 6am, nerves about her interview bubbling in her stomach. Ollie had rung before she went to bed and she'd arranged to meet him for a coffee that afternoon before going to the flat to collect her things. After she'd hung up, she fleetingly wondered if she had missed him? Had she been wrong to break off their engagement so quickly? She shook her head. She knew she'd made the right choice, and she couldn't think about Ollie right now, she needed to focus on the day ahead.

She gave Scout her breakfast and hopped into the shower. Rose was planning to drive back to London so that she had the car to load up all her possessions from Ollie's flat, and Maya was going to go with her so that she could keep everything at her houseshare before Rose moved in officially in September.

Scout seemed to notice Rose's nerves that morning, as the little dog didn't leave her side. When Rose sat down at her dressing table to put her make-up on, Scout placed her head in Rose's lap and whimpered quietly.

'I know, Scout, it's a nerve-racking day for all of us, isn't it? If things work out, you're going to be moving to London too.' Scout let out an audible sigh. 'Don't sound so upset. You'll love London. Maya's housemate, Sian, works from home, so you'll have company all day. There'll be no need for doggie day care and just think of all the parks you'll be able to explore.'

Rose got herself ready and packed her interview outfit. She'd decided to wear a navy suit dress that she'd bought in Whistles for her last job interview. She didn't want to crease the dress by travelling in it and she planned to stop at a coffee shop near to the school when she arrived and change in the toilets. It was going to be another warm July day and it was likely to be even warmer in London. Rose didn't think she'd need the matching suit jacket, but she packed it just in case. After dropping Scout off with Jane for the day, Rose's phone buzzed with a message from Grace.

*Good luck today, you'll do great. xx*

Rose smiled. She had made a good friend in Grace, and she'd certainly miss her if she did get the job in London:

*Thanks! I'm meeting Ollie for coffee afterwards. Will let you know how I get on. xx*

As she drove down the winding lane leading towards the village green, the sun shone brightly and Rose smiled as she spotted a few members of Butterfly Class making their way to school. As she passed the village green, she could see that it was busy with early morning dog walkers and people making their way to work. She spotted Maggie outside Harrisons, stocking the fruit and vegetable displays with apples from the local orchard. Joyce was outside the Cosy Cup, setting up tables and chairs for the diners who wanted to take advantage of the summer sunshine and the view over the village green. Rose gave her a wave as she passed the tearoom and she felt a lump form in her throat. She really was going to miss this place. Rose reached the main road by 8am and she tried, and failed, to take her mind off everything that she was going to miss about life in Blossom Heath by listening to her favourite compilation CD.

The journey was long and tedious and, as Rose got nearer to the city, she was stuck in what seemed to be an endless queue of traffic on the M25. She looked up at the illuminated signs above.

'Uh, roadworks. Typical,' she said to herself, and put her handbrake on as the traffic in front of her ground to a halt. Just then, her phone cut in through the radio and she answered via hands-free.

'Hello?'

'Hello, Rose?' a voice with a familiar drawl answered, 'it's Camille, have you got time to talk?'

'Camille?'

'I saw Ollie last night, darling. He mentioned that you were driving up today to meet him.'

'Okay . . .' said Rose, wondering why Camille was calling her. 'That's not strictly true; I am grabbing coffee with him later but I'm heading back for a job interview at my old school.'

'Ah well, he left that part out.' Camille paused. 'Listen, darling, the reason I'm ringing is that I've got a juicy bit of info that I just *had* to share you with you.'

Rose could hear the delight in Camille's voice. She could tell that Camille was just *dying* to tell her something that was going to be unbelievably awful. She took a deep breath.

'And what's that exactly?' Rose asked, biting her lower lip.

'I'm sorry to have to be the one to break it to you, Rose, darling, but I thought you had a *right* to know,' Camille said, with a half-laugh.

'Break what to me?' Rose's patience was wearing thin. The temptation to hang up on this awful woman was almost overwhelming.

'Well, it's just that . . . well, the green dress that you wore to Le Maison du Blanc . . .'

'Yes . . .'

'Well, Ollie bought the exact same one for Emily the week before.'

'What? Camille, are you sure?'

'One hundred per cent, darling. She wore it to some client drinks and made a point of telling me how Ollie had chosen it especially for her, from Selfridges.'

And there it was. The real reason Camille was calling her.

'Wow.' Rose's mouth went dry and she tightened her grip on the steering wheel. She had been touched by the care she *thought* Ollie had put into choosing that dress for her. It had fitted her beautifully and complemented her colouring perfectly. As it turned out, it looked more likely that it was part of a 2 for 1 offer for her and the 'other woman'. Even though she knew things with Ollie were over, this information still hurt. Despite this, she leapt to Ollie's defence.

'To be fair to Ollie, I do think the thing with Emily was just a drunken mistake. He really regrets it.'

'Look, Rose, I wanted to give you a heads up,' Camille said, her tone softening. 'If you're coming back to London for Ollie's sake, make sure you're not too quick to forgive him. Once a cheat, always a cheat in my book, and that's certainly true if Marcus is anything to go by.' Camille gave a bitter laugh.

'If truth be told, I'd been planning on ending things *before* I found out about Emily.'

'Really, darling? Now that is a surprise. You know, Emily's got the personality of an ironing board. She's not a patch on you,' Camille said. 'Why are you coming back to London anyway – I thought you were so happy in Sussex, darling. What's changed?'

Rose struggled to find the right words. 'Well, nothing really, I still love it there . . .' Her mind automatically turned to Jake. 'I just don't think there's anything there for me right now,' she felt her voice catch.

'Don't tell me, has this got something to do with that *delicious* farmer you've met?' said Camille, and Rose could almost hear her licking her lips in anticipation. Rose was silent, thinking about what to say next. She wasn't sure that her thoughts about Jake were something that she wanted to share with Camille of all people, but she found herself saying, 'I don't suppose it matters now but there *was* someone . . . well, there could have been. He's back with his ex, so I've missed my chance,' she said, emotion catching in her voice. 'Like I said, I'm interviewing for a job in London, so I guess I'll never really know what could have happened.'

'Listen, Rose,' Camille's tone became suddenly serious. 'You may not realize this but I've always admired you. You're different to the other vacuous wives and girlfriends that Marcus' colleagues parade around, me included. You've had a career of your own and done your own thing, I respect that.'

'Camille, you honestly don't have to explain yourself to me.'

'You need to hear this, Rose. Do you think I enjoy being the trophy wife with the new boob job that Marcus flaunts around whilst he has his affairs? No, I don't. But it's the life I've chosen and I play my part. I want the money, the lifestyle and the status, but those things come at a cost. Don't get me wrong, I have my fun too with my personal trainers and fitness coaches and Marcus chooses to look the other way. That's the deal. I have my little dalliances, he has his and we never mention it to each other.'

'Camille, I . . . I had no idea,' Rose stuttered.

'If I could do things differently, have my time over, then I would. You've got this far, Rose, you're free of being trapped in a loveless marriage with Ollie. But if there's someone ... if you've met someone that you *truly* have feelings for, don't throw it all away to come back to London for a job. Even if he is back with his ex, you should at least let him know how you feel. Who knows what his reaction might be?'

'Wow! I'm not sure what to say. I had no idea you felt like that with Marcus.'

'Of course, if you repeat what I've told you to anyone, I'll obviously deny it,' Camille said, the familiar guarded tone back in her voice, 'I can't have Marcus' London cronies thinking I have *actual* feelings,' she said with a hollow laugh.

'Don't worry, Camille, your secret is safe with me.'

'Right, well I must be off, darling, I have an afternoon appointment for some personal training, and I do intend on putting my instructor through his paces afterwards. There's a waxing appointment to get to first, a girl needs to make sure her bikini line is in order before any bedroom athletics,' Camille continued with a husky laugh, clearly intent on trying to shock Rose with her bad behaviour.

'Well, what can I say. I appreciate your honesty. I don't imagine that our paths will cross again. Enjoy your "training" session,' she said with a nervous laugh.

'Oh, I intend to, darling, I intend to,' Camille replied and then rung off.

Well, that was a surprise. She never expected to be taking relationship advice from Camille of all people. She switched her phone to silent and slung it into her bag; she didn't need any more distractions today. As the traffic started to speed up and move more quickly through the roadworks, Rose struggled to clear her mind of anything other than thoughts of Jake for the remainder of the journey to London. *Should she listen to Camille's advice?*

# Chapter 36

Jake had been out on the farm with the dogs all morning. One of the sheep had managed to escape from the top field and ended up out on the road. It had taken him most of the morning to find and repair the gap in the fence.

'There,' he said with relief. 'That should stop any more escapees. Come on you two,' he said, looking down at Tagg and Finn, 'I think we've earned ourselves a cuppa.' As he walked back towards the farmhouse, he heard his phone buzzing in his pocket. He pulled it out and could see from the caller ID that it was Grace.

'Grace, how's things?' he asked brightly.

'Jake! About time you picked up. I've been trying to call you all morning.' Her voice was shrill.

'My phone's been playing up. What's wrong?' he asked quickly.

'I've had a call from Mrs Connolly. You don't have any contact details for Rose's teacher friend, Maya, do you?'

'No, why would I?'

'Rose isn't picking up and we need to get in touch with her before she goes into that damn interview.'

'Why, what's happened?'

'Well, it's good news really. A permanent job's come up at Blossom Heath Primary. Carol Jackson's decided she's retiring.'

'So Rose doesn't need to go back to London! Well, that's great news.' He felt his face break into a smile.

'Not if we can't get hold of her before the interview it isn't. Mrs Connolly's just explained to me that teaching interviews aren't really like regular interviews. You're usually offered the job on the same day and if Rose verbally accepts, that's it. We've got to stop Rose before she says yes to the job. Otherwise, it'll all be too late.'

'Seriously? So, what are we going to do about it?'

'We *need* to get hold of her. I've tried ringing the school and leaving a message but whether they'll pass it on, who knows? If we could get a message to Maya . . .' Grace's voice faltered. 'Mind you, I'm not even sure how keen she'll be to stay now she knows you and Sarah are back together.'

'Me and Sarah? *Back together*? Where has she got that idea from?'

'She stopped off at the farmhouse Monday morning. Apparently, Sarah opened the door. In a towel. Rose thought that the two of you had made things up.'

'*What*?' said Jake. He could feel the heat rising in his face. 'We most definitely are *not* back together. Why would Rose assume that? Sarah spilt coffee on her dress and I let her stay to get cleaned up. Why didn't Sarah put her straight? I don't understand—'

'Well, Sarah always liked to get her own way. Maybe she sees Rose as competition and wanted to scare her off?'

'That woman!' said Jake through gritted teeth. 'Hasn't she done me enough damage? I *thought* Rose seemed off with me when she came up for the school trip.'

'So, you're *not* back with Sarah?'

Jake took a deep breath.

'I thought about it, at first. Sarah came to see me, told me she'd made a mistake with Miles, that she wanted me back. She said she still loved me and, I don't know, Grace, maybe she does? We did kiss, that much is true, but that just made me realize that I don't have feelings for her. Turns out I think I'm love with—'

'Rose!' Grace yelped in excitement. 'I *knew* it!' Jake could almost hear her punching the air.

'Alright, alright,' Jake said, laughing. 'You don't *always* have to be right about everything, you know.'

'No, but it feels good when I am. Listen, there's something else you need to know too.'

'What?'

'Rose is meeting Ollie for a coffee this afternoon.'

'She's not thinking about going back to him, is she?'

'Well,' Grace paused. 'Twenty-four hours ago I would have said no, but now Rose thinks you're back with Sarah, who knows?'

'Arrgh,' Jake groaned, 'Sarah really has got no idea the damage she's caused.'

'I know. What are you going to do?'

'Well, I'd better stop talking to you and get myself in the car,' he replied, quickening his pace towards the house. 'Looks like I'm heading to London.'

'Good luck,' said Grace as she hung up.

# Chapter 37

Rose walked into Trinity Grove Primary School just before 1pm and Sandra was there to greet her at reception.

'Oh, Rose, it's so good to see you,' she said warmly.

'Hi, Sandra, it's lovely to be back,' Rose replied with a smile.

'Can I get you to sign in the visitors' book before I buzz you through?'

'Of course.'

As she bent down to sign in, Rose heard Maya call her name through the door.

'Rose!' Maya cried at the sight of her old friend. Sandra buzzed the entrance doors open and Rose stepped through and gave Maya a hug. 'I can't stay long as I'm teaching but I just wanted to wish you luck before you go in.'

'Thanks, it's lovely to see you. It feels weird being back here.'

'Good weird though?' Maya asked. 'I bet you can't wait to get back to London. It's going to be soooo exciting being housemates.'

'Yes, of course,' Rose replied with a weak smile. Although

it felt comforting and familiar being back at Trinity Grove – Rose had so many lovely memories of the place after all – something about being back in her old teaching haunt wasn't sitting right with her. *Why was that?* She had a sinking, uneasy feeling in the pit of her stomach and found herself wondering how Scout was doing without her today. She'd never left her this long with Jane before . . .

'Well, good luck, not that you need it of course – you're an absolute shoo-in,' Maya said, flashing Rose a smile as she picked up her afternoon register and waved her goodbye. 'I'll meet you in the staffroom after?'

Rose nodded.

'Rose, if you take a seat in the staffroom, Mr Pearson will call you in when he's ready for you,' Sandra explained.

'Thanks, Sandra.'

'Can I get you a drink? Tea? Coffee?'

'Actually, a glass of water would be great. My mouth has gone really dry.'

'That'll be the nerves. You've got nothing to worry about though, Rose. You'll be fantastic,' Sandra assured her, passing her a glass of water and leaving her alone in the staffroom.

Rose took a seat and tapped her fingers nervously on the table. She felt as though she might be sick. But it wasn't because of the interview. Rose couldn't get what Camille had said out of her head. That she shouldn't just give up on someone she cared about without putting up a fight. She hadn't put up a fight though, had she? She hadn't even had the guts to tell Jake how she really felt about him, let alone confront him about Sarah.

'Ahem ... Miss Hargreaves? Miss Hargreaves?' the sound of a male voice brought Rose's attention back to the present.

'Oh, uh ... I'm sorry. You must be Mr Pearson?' Rose replied, standing up and shaking the headteacher by the hand.

'Yes, but please call me Rory,' Mr Pearson insisted. 'I've heard lots about you, Rose, and only good things I might add. Thank you for attending today, and you're still available for a September start?' Rose nodded. 'Excellent. Please come through,' said Mr Pearson, opening his office door for her. 'Take a seat. Make yourself comfortable.'

Rose sat down and took a large gulp of her glass of water before placing it on Mr Pearson's desk.

'So, tell me about yourself, Rose. What attracted you to a career in teaching?'

Rose explained a little about her background and her early career, her desire to make a difference to the lives of children in the local area. Mr Pearson progressed the interview by asking Rose all the standard questions that she had come to expect. What age group did she have most experience with? How did she make use of data to inform her lesson planning? What were her views on the new curriculum? As Mr Pearson began explaining more about his vision for improving Trinity Grove and his perspective on the school's strengths and areas for improvement, Rose found her attention waning.

Was coming back to London *really* the right thing to do?

Even if Jake was with Sarah and she had no job to go back to, did she really *want* to move back to London? What about Aunt Jean? And Scout? She really had been so in love with her country life, she wished things could have ended differently ... And if Rose was honest with herself, *really* honest, she knew what she felt for Jake was more than just a crush or a fling. She had real feelings for him. She could even see herself falling in love with him ...

'Sorry, Mr Pearson. Would you remind repeating that please?' Rose asked Trinity Grove's new headteacher, when she realized that he had stopped speaking.

'I said, it gives me great pleasure to offer you a permanent teaching position with us in September. Do you accept?' Mr Pearson repeated, looking just a little irked at Rose's lack of attention. 'Rose? I said do you accept our offer of employment?'

# Chapter 38

Jake had never experienced such a difficult journey to London. Every traffic light he hit on the way seemed to be red, every roundabout and junction had a longer queue than was usual. He tried ringing the school again but all he got was an answerphone message. Would Rose think he was crazy for driving all the way to London to tell her about the job at Blossom Heath Primary? He didn't have a choice; he didn't know what else to do. He felt sick when he thought that he might lose her for good. Rose had been in Blossom Heath for months; why had it taken the prospect of her leaving for him to be able to tell her how he really felt about her?

Jake couldn't believe that Rose had happened to turn up at the farmhouse at the exact moment Sarah had been there alone. He'd always known that she could be devious and he could guess at her motives for not telling Rose the whole truth. *What must Rose have thought of him? That he'd nearly kissed her on Sunday morning and then gone to bed with Sarah that evening?* She had seemed off with him during the school trip on Monday. Now he knew why. His hands clenched the steering wheel more tightly. If he didn't arrive at Trinity

362

Grove in time to catch her before she went into her interview ... he couldn't bear the thought.

Eventually, he turned into the north London cul-de-sac where the school was located. The area couldn't have been more different to Blossom Heath. There were high-rise housing blocks for as far as the eye could see, concrete, tarmac and pavement everywhere. He soon spotted the school next to the local newsagents. A few teenagers wearing hoodies were hanging around outside the shop smoking and performing tricks on their skateboards. The school itself was surrounded by high metal gates and security fencing, a world away from the village school he had left behind in Blossom Heath, with its well-tended gardens and the word 'Welcome' embossed in mosaics over the entrance. Here there was barely a tree or patch of grass to be seen. Jake parked up and raced towards the school's main entrance. He checked his watch. It was already 1.10pm. *Was he too late?* Surely he couldn't have come all this way just to miss Rose by ten minutes?

Out of breath and with a bang of the entrance doors, Jake burst into the school's foyer. Sandra greeted him from behind the Perspex panel to the office.

'Can I help you?'

'Hello ... yes, I hope so ... I'm here to see Rose Hargreaves.'

'Rose? I'm afraid she's in with the headteacher right now. But if you'd like to wait—'

'I don't mean to be rude, but is it possible to interrupt her? Only, I've got a rather important message for her.'

'I'm afraid not. She's in an interview and I really can't disturb her.'

'I know … the thing is … well … the thing is …' Jake spluttered, 'the thing is I think I might be … in love with her and I need to tell her that before she accepts the job.' That was it. He'd said it. He was in love with Rose. There really was no going back now.

'I'm sorry but there's nothing I can do,' Sandra said, looking shocked. 'If you leave a name, I can tell Rose that you came by as soon as she's free.'

'If you can tell her that Jake is here and I'll be parked up outside. Maybe don't mention the bit about me being in love with her though?' he said, hanging his head as he walked out of the school.

He was too late. By the time he saw Rose again she'd have already accepted the job and Mrs Connolly wouldn't be able to offer her the position in Blossom Heath. Rose would be ready to start her new life in London. He climbed back into his jeep. *What was his next move? Should he tell Rose about his feelings or remain silent? After all, if she was moving to London, what good would it do?*

# Chapter 39

A silence hung in the air as Mr Pearson waited slightly impatiently now for Rose's response to his offer of employment. Rose took a deep breath.

'I'm sorry, Mr Pearson, but I'm afraid I can't.'

'You can't? I don't understand?'

'I'm sorry to have wasted your time, but I can't come back to Trinity Grove after all.'

'Why ever not?'

'Well, it turns out that I've only just realized that I belong in Sussex . . . in Blossom Heath to be exact. I'm not moving back to London, I'm afraid. I'm so sorry to have wasted your time, Mr Pearson, and thank you for the opportunity, but I'm afraid I have to go,' she explained, standing up and picking up her handbag.

That was it. She'd made up her mind. Whatever happened or didn't happen between her and Jake, Rose knew that Blossom Heath was where she belonged. The sense of community and friendship she'd found since she'd arrived back in the village had made her happier than she'd been in years, happier than she'd ever been in London if she was being honest with herself, and she wasn't ready to give that up. Not for anything.

Rose raced out of the school's main entrance, waving goodbye to Sandra with one hand and checking her mobile with the other. She was vaguely aware of Sandra shouting out something about a visitor and a message, but she carried on regardless. She noticed that she had missed calls from Grace and Mrs Connolly. What could that possibly be about?

'Rose!' she heard a familiar voice call out from behind her.

'Jake? What ... what are you doing here?'

'Rose, I'm so sorry I didn't get here in time. I was trying to stop you before you went in for your interview.'

'Stop me? Why?'

'Well, the thing is ...' Jake started, 'a vacancy has come up at Blossom Heath Primary. Mrs Connolly's been trying to get hold of you. She wanted to offer it to *you*, Rose,' he said, looking crestfallen.

Rose broke into a broad grin. She grabbed Jake and pulled him in towards her, embracing him. Jake pulled back to look at her.

'But, Rose, I was too late. You've already had your interview. I didn't get here in time to stop you,' he continued.

'It doesn't matter,' said Rose. 'You can tell Mrs Connolly that I accept.'

'What? But haven't you just accepted a job here?'

'As in turns out, no, I haven't.'

'You *haven't*?'

She knew then that she had to be brave. She had to tell

Jake how she felt about him. Even if he didn't feel the same way, she had to let him know, had to take the risk. Camille was right. She might not get another chance.

'When I said there was no reason for me to stay in Blossom Heath, I was wrong, *very* wrong.'

'Okay . . .'

'In fact, there's a *very* good reason for me to stay in Blossom Heath . . . and he's just driven nearly seventy miles to try and stop me from taking a job.' She took a deep breath. 'I know this might be out of line, seeing that you're back with Sarah, but the truth is I've got feelings for you, Jake, and I need to be honest about them.'

Jake took a step towards her and took her hand in his. 'I'm not.'

'You're not what?'

'Back with Sarah.'

'But I went to the farmhouse . . . I saw her—'

'I know, Grace told me. You've got it wrong though.'

'Wrong?' Rose asked.

'Me and Sarah. We're *not* back together. She didn't spend the night. She visited that morning and deliberately spilt coffee on her dress. I said she could stay and clean up while I was out. I think she was hoping she could tempt me into getting back with her somehow, but I've set her straight, Rose. It's *over* between me and her.'

'So, you're . . . *not* back together?' Rose repeated slowly, trying to process the information.

'But what about you and Ollie?'

'What about me and Ollie?'

'Grace told me that you're meeting him today, and I was worried that you might be having second thoughts about breaking things off, especially after you thought I was back with Sarah ...' Rose shook her head and bit her lower lip.

'We had arranged to meet and it's not easy, you know, ending things with someone who's been such a big part of your life. But it really is over with him, I promise.'

'Good,' said Jake, grinning. He pulled her in close to him and whispered into her ear, 'Because the thing is, Miss Hargreaves, it turns out that I might be a little bit in love with you, and I'm *kicking* myself that I've waited so long to tell you.'

Rose looked up at Jake and their eyes locked. She placed a hand on his chest and could feel his heart beating.

She reached up and stroked his hair. 'Well, that is very fortunate indeed, Mr Harper, as I'm a little bit in love with you too.'

Jake's head moved slowly towards hers and their lips met at last in a long, deep kiss. After what seemed like an age, the couple parted.

'Well, that was definitely long overdue,' said Jake, his voice cracking. 'So, are you going to call Mrs Connolly back and accept this job, or shall I?'

'Mrs Connolly can wait. It's taken me weeks to finally kiss you and I hadn't planned on stopping just yet,' Rose said breathlessly as she pulled him in towards her to kiss him for a second time.

As they broke apart, Jake smiled and said, 'You know, I don't think I'm the only one who is going to be pretty pleased that you're becoming a permanent fixture in Blossom Heath.'

'Oh, really?' said Rose, taking his hand in hers.

'Well, there's Scout for one thing. You know she's a country dog at heart. She'd have been devasted to leave the village. Just think how much she'd have missed Tagg and Finn.'

'True,' Rose laughed, 'the three of them really do make the perfect pack.'

'And then there's Jean of course . . .'

'Aunt Jean!' said Rose, her grin spreading even more widely across her face. 'I can't wait to tell her I'm staying. She'll be over the moon. Of course we'll have to get the cottage ready for her to come home to as soon as we can and—'

Before she could finish her sentence, Jake pulled Rose in towards him to kiss her again. And with that third kiss, the world around them melted away. This was it. With Blossom Heath and with Jake she had finally found what she'd been looking for. She was home.

# Acknowledgements

Where do I start? Publishing my debut novel is something that's been on my list of life ambitions for a while, but it's not something I thought I'd ever *actually* achieve. There's still a fair chance that I'm going to wake up from this dream any second now and realize that none of it was real. I'm still pinching myself.

There are so many people to thank, people who have helped to get me to this point and make my dream a reality. I have to start by thanking my wonderful mum, Glynis. How many years is it you've been telling me I should write a novel? Three? Four? Six? I've lost count. As it turns out, you were right. There's a lesson to be learnt here, Reader: always listen to your mum, she has the best advice.

I owe a huge debt of thanks to the fabulous organization that is the Romantic Novelists' Association (RNA). I was accepted onto the RNA's New Writers' Scheme in January 2021 and it's thanks to them that I had the opportunity to submit to Books and the City the very same year. I'm honoured to be part of such an amazing community of romance writers and the support and guidance that the NWS has given me has been invaluable.

To the entire team at Books and the City, thank you! I honestly can't imagine working with a more supportive and encouraging group of people. Sara-Jade Virtue, thank you doesn't seem enough to express how grateful I am that you decided to take a chance on me! Thank you for believing in me and for loving Blossom Heath and Rose and Jake's story just as much as I do. I will be forever grateful for this opportunity. Louise Davies, thank you for guiding a newbie author through the editing process with so much support and good humour. It can be a daunting process for a new writer and you've made it an absolute pleasure. Thank you!

Thank you to my partner, Chris, for believing I could do this (even when I doubted it myself). Thanks for answering my endless questions about Rye and life in the countryside and being my sounding board whenever I needed to untangle the story in my head. Thanks for cooking all the dinners and giving me some much-needed perspective when I was glued to my laptop. I am truly grateful to have you in my life.

To my awesome friend Shelley Bosworth, thank you for always encouraging me to follow my dreams. I remember you telling me over pizza that even if I only wrote a chapter a week, I'd have written an entire novel in less than a year! Thank you for giving me that push when I needed it. To fellow Essex author and RNA member, Lizzie Chantree, thank you for introducing me to the RNA and being a constant source of inspiration with all that you achieve.

Finally, there is one incredibly special person that I wanted to save until last: Great Aunt Jean, who we lost on New Year's Day 2022 at the impressive age of 94. It breaks my heart that you didn't get to see this book in print, I know how much you wanted to. Thank you for being such an inspiration to me throughout my life. You've always been there to encourage and support me in everything that I've done and this book is no exception.

Read on for an exclusive extract from
*New Beginnings at the Cosy Cat Café*, the wonderful
new book from Julie Haworth, coming soon.

The drive from the airport whizzed by. Tori had so much to tell her mum about, she hadn't seen her for just over a year and the pair of them had always been close. Tori's dad had left when she was fifteen and he hadn't kept in touch much since. She got the obligatory Christmas and birthday card and the odd phone call, but they hadn't seen much of each other over the past few years. Tori had found it hard to forgive him after he left Joyce for another woman, and her dad had made little effort to stay in contact with her since. The way she saw it, if he couldn't be bothered to make the effort then neither could she. Perhaps he was embarrassed about the way he'd treated her mum and was too ashamed to show his face? Either way, they were better off without him, things were easier, just the two of them against the world.

As they pulled up outside the Cosy Cup, Tori smiled. It felt good to be back with her mum again, to be back in Blossom Heath, even if it wasn't in the circumstances she'd hoped for.

'I'm so happy to be back, everything looks exactly the same,' said Tori as she walked into the tearoom and eyed the cakes behind the counter. 'How come you're closed this afternoon? I thought Cathy would be holding the fort?'

'Oh, I thought I'd told you, love; it must have slipped my mind. Cathy left a couple of weeks ago, met a new man and moved to Northampton, I've been on my own since. As it's Sunday, I thought I'd close early.'

'On your own? But, Mum, that's way too much for one person, you can't possibly manage to bake, serve and keep up with all the orders at the same time,' said Tori, her brow furrowed.

'I manage. I've reduced the opening hours and I've scaled the menu back a bit. Anyway, I only needed to get through until you were home and I knew I'd have reinforcements.'

'Oh, I see,' said Tori, exhaling. She wasn't sure that working at the Cosy Cup was exactly what she had planned for her future. *What exactly was her plan?* She felt her heart beat slightly faster when she realized that she didn't know. She hadn't thought that far ahead.

'Now you're back for good, there's no need to worry about hiring someone new. It's all worked out perfectly,' Joyce said with a smile.

'Perfectly, yes.' Tori nodded, feeling a queasy sensation in her stomach. 'Ooooh, you've got coffee and walnut cake,' she said, keen to change the subject.

'You could give me a chance to get my coat off,' Joyce laughed. 'You know where everything is, grab yourself a slice and I'll get to work on the hot chocolates.'

Tori threw her handbag down on her favourite chair by the window, picked up a plate and cut a huge slice of cake. She was ravenous. She picked up a fork and made a beeline for the window table. It had always been her favourite spot in the tearoom as she could see all the comings and goings on the village green. She'd lost count of the hours she must have sat here watching the world go by over the years. She was just getting comfy, when she saw a large ginger cat, around the size of a small dog, appear at the café door, meowing frantically, hoping to be let in.

'Ernie!' cried Tori, jumping up from her seat.

'You know the rules, he's not allowed in here,' Joyce called out. Tori and Joyce lived in the house next to the Cosy Cup and one of the rules was that Ernie was never allowed in the tearoom.

'Oh, come on, Mum, it won't hurt just once. He hasn't seen me for a year!'

'Go on then,' Joyce said relenting. 'As long as it's just this once.'

Tori opened the front door and scooped Ernie up in her arms; the cat immediately began purring contentedly.

'Oh, I missed you, Ernie, I'd forgotten just how *adorable* you are,' she said as she popped him down on the floor so he could begin exploring. Tori looked around the little tearoom fondly, she loved how warm and inviting the place had always been. Tori took a huge bite of her cake. 'Mmmmm, I can't tell you how much I've missed your baking, Mum,' she said, closing her eyes as she savoured the rich frosting. Joyce laughed.

'Well, now you're back home you can eat all the cake you want, love. You can stand to gain a few pounds, you know.'

'Honestly, Mum. My jeans are finally feeling roomy and I'm planning on keeping it that way. Turns out, after all those fad diets I've tried, all I needed was to live off rice and beans for six months.'

'Well, no fear of that here,' Joyce said with a smile as she placed two mugfuls of hot chocolate and whipped cream on the table and pulled up a chair opposite Tori. 'I've made your favourite for tea later . . . lasagne.'

'Aw, thanks, Mum.'

'So, tell me. Now you've explored Asia, what was the highlight . . . the number one thing that you loved more than anything else?'

'That's tough, I mean the whole thing was just, well … amazing. I *loved* Tokyo, it's so bright and vibrant, there are quirky coffee shops everywhere, you'd love them!'

'It certainly sounds as though it was a wonderful experience,' said Joyce.

'You know what you'd *really* love about the café culture in Tokyo though, Mum?' Tori said, leaning in towards Joyce. 'The cat cafés!'

'The what?'

'Cat cafés. They have loads of them in Tokyo, lots of people can't have their own pets, they all live in small apartments you see, so it's a way for them to spend time with cats if they can't have one of their own. It's a *genius* idea.'